SOME
KIND
OF
ANIMAL

SOME KIND OF ANIMAL

MARIA ROMASCO-MOORE

DELACORTE PRESS

Text copyright © 2020 by Maria Romasco-Moore
Jacket art copyright © 2020 by Nona Limmen
Jacket design by Jennifer Heuer

GetUnderlined.com

Educators and librarians, for a variety of teaching tools, visit us at RHTeachersLibrarians.com

Library of Congress Cataloging-in-Publication Data is available upon request.
ISBN 978-1-9848-9354-3 (hc) — ISBN 978-1-9848-9355-0 (lib. bdg.)
ISBN 978-1-9848-9356-7 (ebook)

The text of this book is set in 12-point Arno Pro.
Interior design by Ken Crossland

Printed in the United States of America
10 9 8 7 6 5 4 3 2 1
First Edition

For Magnolia

CHAPTER ONE

My sister and I sit side by side in the dark. She is pulling little bones out of her heart-shaped plastic purse and tossing them down the hillside onto the empty road below.

The bones are from a rabbit she caught earlier in the night. She ran out ahead of me, and by the time I reached her, she'd already stripped away most of the skin with her knife. Was gnawing on the raw flesh.

"You need a new dress," I tell her.

"No," she says, wriggling her bare feet in the dirt.

The truth is I've given her many new dresses, but she never wears them. She prefers to wear the lace-trimmed blue party dress I gave her when we were ten. It's five years old now, full of rips and much too short. It only barely reaches her thighs.

"You look like a slut," I tell her.

"No," she says. She sticks her tongue out at me, throws another bone down the hill.

I shouldn't have said that, but she probably doesn't even know what the word means. I really should be home by now. The sun will be up soon.

Normally, I would be home by now, but tonight I am stalling, avoiding what I have to say.

My sister, Lee, and I don't live in the same house. My sister doesn't live in a house at all. She lives in the forest. She sleeps during the day and runs at night.

I snuck out this morning around three, an hour after the bar downstairs closed, half an hour after Aunt Aggie went to sleep. Aggie has raised me since I was a baby, since Mama went missing, but she doesn't know about my sister. No one does.

No one but me.

Even I didn't know I had a sister, until I was five. Until she appeared one night, coming out of the woods like a dream. I see her only in the small dark hours, when I can slip out my window, run with her through the trees, and slip back before anyone knows I've been gone.

I used to only manage it once or twice a week. This past summer, though, Aunt Aggie was busy with her new boyfriend, and my best friend, Savannah, was busy with an endless string of them and so I went to see my sister every night. No one was paying attention to me. No one cared. I could sleep all day.

But it's October now.

My sister has run out of rabbit bones, so she picks up a big rock and throws that at the road instead. It bounces down the hill, hits the asphalt, and cracks in two.

"I can't run with you tomorrow night, Lee," I say.

"No," she says.

"Yes," I say, I'm not thrilled about it either—I love running at night—but I've got no choice. "I can't run tomorrow night, or the night after that, or the night after that. I need more sleep. They sent a letter home from school."

It's true. I'm failing everything but chorus. If I don't get my shit together I might have to repeat the whole ninth grade. Aunt Aggie was livid when she found out. She wanted to know what the hell was wrong with me, whether it was drugs or boys or just a relentless desire to piss her off at every opportunity. But I couldn't tell her the real reason I've been sleeping through all the classes I don't cut. The real reason I'm bone-tired constantly these days.

"You can run away," my sister says.

Lee and I are twins. We've got the same build, straight up and down, though she's far skinnier than me, skinny enough that people would probably whisper behind her back if they ever saw her, say she was anorexic or something. We've got the same plain face, though hers is smeared with dirt. Same mud-colored hair, except mine is chin length and hers hangs most of the way down her back in a snarled mat.

"I'll come run with you once a week," I say. "Okay? Saturday nights. Like I used to."

"Run away," she says again, insistent.

And sure, it would be nice if it were that easy. If I could just let everything go, stop trying to be everything everyone says I'm supposed to be—a good girl, a normal girl, a pretty girl, a cool girl, a smart girl, a girl who gives even half a shit about school.

My sister's never gone to school and so to be perfectly honest she's kind of dumb. I mean, she's smart in some ways, knows more about the woods than anybody, but she can only read books that don't have too many words. I used to bring her stuff from the library, comic books and picture books, but I'm banned now, after returning too many books with leaves pressed between the pages, dirt caked into the spines, spots of blood on the covers.

"You know I can't run away," I tell her, as I've told her a thousand times. "I have a life."

Lee bares her teeth as she scowls, then reaches out to grab my arm, but I twist away and jump to my feet. I'm cutting it way too close.

"I'll see you Saturday night," I say, "I'll bring you some chocolate or something."

I try to run down the hill but end up mostly sliding. When I reach the bottom, my jeans are streaked with dirt. I turn and wave at my sister. She throws a pebble that hits me right in the shoulder and then she darts back into the trees.

I usually go the long way home, circling through the national forest, which surrounds my hometown of Lester, Ohio, on three sides. But the sky is growing more gray by the second, the morning light erasing the stars. So I head down the road, running on the shoulder, past the old abandoned high school with the blown-out windows and the outline of a girl spray-painted halfway up an inside wall. I wave at the painted girl. She just floats there, a ghostly silhouette, someone's misplaced shadow half.

I cut through the No. 5 Mine disaster Memorial Park and the empty Dollar General parking lot and then I run alongside the railroad tracks, that long string on which Lester is threaded like a small, dull bead.

In the old days, the hills around here were studded with mines, and freight trains carried away tons of coal every day. People called Lester "the magic city" because of how it sprang up almost overnight and grew like crazy. Half the people in Lester worked in the mines, but now, as Aunt Aggie likes to say, half the people in Lester work nowhere.

The sky is getting brighter. I push myself to run faster, heart racing. It must be nearly six. If Aggie catches me out she will lose her mind. It's bad enough that she knows I'm failing. She isn't strict, exactly, but she worries her head off if I give her half a reason. I am usually more careful than this.

When I finally reach Joe's Bar and Grill, I sprint around the side and scramble up the crumbling wall. The bricks jut out unevenly here, and half the mortar has crumbled to dust. Little puffs of it fall away like cigarette ash as I climb.

I pull myself onto the rusty fire escape and force myself to go slow, easing my bedroom window open gently, wiggling it in its socket like a loose tooth.

When it's open just far enough, I tumble inside, yank off my muddy clothes, shove them under the bed. I shut the window, jump into bed, pull the covers up to my chin. There's no time for sleep and anyway I'm too keyed up from how close I cut things. Aunt Aggie will be knocking on my door any minute now, telling me to get up for school.

Sometimes I feel like two different people, loosely attached by the dawn. A girl with a secret shadow half.

When I'm with my sister I don't have to think about school. I don't have to think about anything. I can just exist. Breathe in and out. Move through the world. Run until all the stress and worry I've built up over the course of the day streams out of me. Sometimes I envy my sister, getting to live that freely all the time.

Usually I have more time to adjust, to move from one world to the other. From the person I am at night to the person I have to pretend to be in the day.

Now all I can do is stare up at the plastic stars on my ceiling, glowing their faint and sickly green, and wait.

Pastor Jones is sitting at the card table in the kitchen when I come out of my room. He's wearing a faux silk bomber jacket with embroidered tigers and a black T-shirt with a white cross on it. He shoots me an idiotic grin.

"Will you get that toast for me, honey," says Aunt Aggie, bustling around the tiny kitchen in her plaid robe. She's making eggs. She only does that when the pastor is over. When it's just us we have Cheerios.

"Good morning, Jolene," says the pastor.

"Morning," I say, which is my way of saying *I hate you*. I grab the toast right out of the toaster and it burns my fingers.

The pastor never used to stick around for breakfast. When he started staying nights, back at the beginning of summer, he would sneak out before the sun was up. I almost ran into him once in the alley behind the bar. He had that dumb jacket draped over one shoulder and his boots were untied. It was kind of funny: him sneaking out, me sneaking in. Toward the middle of summer, he'd creep down the stairs, wait a while, then make a big show of knocking on the front door. Aggie would greet him, pretend to be surprised, invite him in for eggs. I never commented on it and after a while they gave up pretending.

Aggie spoons a poached egg onto each of our plates. The pastor closes his eyes and holds his hands out over the table.

"Lord," he says, "you are more precious than silver, more costly than gold, more beautiful than diamonds. Lord, you are darker than coal, you are slicker than oil, you are faster than a Ford Thunderbird. Nothing I desire compares with you. Amen."

"Amen," says Aggie.

My poached egg looks like a big lidless eye. I pretend it is the eye of God, watching over me. I poke it in the pupil with my fork and let the yolk ooze out.

The pastor thinks he's so damn clever. When he first came to Lester two years ago, hardly anybody showed up to his church on Sundays, so he started coming around the bar and preaching to the drunks. Aunt Aggie used to laugh at him, call him a joke, but the drunks loved him, and after a while I guess she did too.

The pastor is shoveling sugar into his coffee. Aggie is lighting her cigarette on the stove burner. I want nothing more than to crawl back under the covers. I've started going to bed earlier on weeknights. I tuck myself in by ten some nights, but that's still only five hours at best before I'm up again and running. Aggie can't understand why I'm always so tired. She keeps threatening to take me to a sleep specialist, but I know she won't. The nearest hospital is twenty miles away, in Delphi, and Aggie never goes more than ten minutes outside of Lester.

It's a superstition she inherited from Grandpa Joe, who she loved more than anyone. He was the kind one, to hear her tell it, the one who protected Aggie and Mama, loved them, encouraged them. He was everything that Grandma Margaret wasn't. But he drank too much and died of liver failure when Aggie was thirteen and Mama was ten. I don't think Aggie ever really got over that. Maybe Mama didn't either.

"I'll be late for school if I don't leave soon," I say, which is a lie.

"Eat your breakfast, Jo," says Aggie. "The pastor can ride you over."

"Have you ever seen those pictures of Jesus where he's carrying a lamb over his shoulders?" the pastor asks me in the car.

"No." I lean my head against the car door, close my eyes, hope he takes the hint to shut the hell up. The pastor, unsurprisingly, loves to talk about Jesus. I've tried silence, sarcasm, eye rolling, but nothing can dissuade him.

"It's a common picture," the pastor goes on. "Do you know why Jesus is carrying the lamb?"

Because he's really into CrossFit? No, the pastor would only take that as encouragement, an opportunity to make some awful joke of his own. I try silence.

"Back in Jesus's day," the pastor says, undeterred, "if a shepherd had a lamb that wouldn't stop wandering off from the flock, what the shepherd would do is break the lamb's legs."

I make an involuntary sound of disgust and regret it immediately. It betrays that I was listening.

"The lamb would need to be carried until the legs healed, of course," says the pastor, cheerily, "but afterward, you can be sure, that lamb would never wander again."

"Whatever," I say, to show the story had no effect on me, though the truth is I feel a bit ill. I'm doing my best to commit every word to memory so I can tell Savannah about it later. She already thinks the pastor is a creep, so she'll eat this up.

We're only about two blocks from school, but the light up ahead turns red. I silently curse it. The pastor's shitty old car (vintage, he calls it) squeals to a stop.

"Look," says the pastor. "I don't know where it is you go when you sneak out at night. I don't know what you do. I'm not sure I want to know."

Well, shit. I stare out the window as hard as I can, but in my head I'm screaming. The goddamn pastor. Aggie's such a heavy sleeper. Grandma Margaret was, too, when we lived with her. I thought I was being careful, thought I was getting away with it, but I should have realized not everyone sleeps as soundly as them.

"I know you went out last night," the pastor says. "And twice last week."

He's wrong about that part, at least. I went out every night last week. And every night but one the week before. To see my sister, to run with her. I've been going out too often. I know that already.

"I can't make you see things the way I do, Jolene," says the pastor, "but whatever it is you're doing, I want you to think real hard about whether it's worth it."

He must think I sneak off to party, to drink, to kiss boys. Normal stuff.

The light changes, thank the Lord.

"I just don't want to see you end up like your mother," says the pastor. "You're nearly the age she was when she went bad."

The car is starting to lurch forward, but before it can pick up speed I slam the door open and jump out. The pastor shouts, but I'm already on the sidewalk, already running as fast as I can, as fast as I run at night.

He doesn't know Mama, never met her, doesn't know a thing beyond what everyone knows: that she was fifteen when she had me, that she disappeared right after, that she was almost definitely murdered, and how dare he even mention her, how dare he say she *went bad* as if she was a piece of fruit left to rot, how dare he act as if he knows a thing about her, as if he knows a thing about me.

My legs ache, but I don't stop until the front doors of the school are shut behind me and I am slumped, back against the lockers, breathing hard, full of hate.

CHAPTER TWO

The high school I go to is bigger than the old abandoned one I run past, with the spray-painted shadow girl. It serves not just Lester but also Needle, the next town over, because Lester is too small to have a whole high school itself. I'm only two months or so into my freshman year but I already hate it.

I barely stay awake in first period. Mr. Blackburn is droning on about World War I, but all I can think about is what the pastor said in the car.

Has he told Aggie that I'm sneaking out? She didn't seem angry at breakfast, which gives me hope. She'd be angry if she found out, but more than that, I know she'd be hurt. Devastated, even, that I'd been lying to her, and I feel like shit about that. I know she does her best. I know how badly she wants a better life for me. Better than Mama's, though she would never say that out loud. When we moved out of Grandma Margaret's house, Aggie claimed it was for her, so she could be closer to the bar, so she could finally get out of her childhood home. But I know that's only half true. It was also for me, to get me away from Margaret.

To keep me from being raised the same way Aggie and Mama were.

I was going to stop sneaking out so much anyway. Yesterday, I'd fallen asleep in the middle of chorus, which is usually the only class I actually enjoy. After Savannah poked me awake, I'd made a vow: I will stop going out to run at night, except on Saturdays. I will stop cutting class. I will sleep through the night, like a normal girl.

Maybe it's unfair, to leave my sister alone for so long during the week, but she managed all right before this summer. I've told her she just needs to wait. In three years, I'll be eighteen. I won't need to go to school or sneak out anymore.

I've been helping out at the bar after school and over the last few summers, but Aggie doesn't pay me. She considers it chores. I get an allowance of a dollar a week because that's what Aggie got from Grandpa Joe back in the day and she refuses to adjust for inflation. I know that some months we're only just scraping by, so I shouldn't complain. But once I'm out of high school, Aggie will have to pay me for real and I'll save up for a car so I can get a job in Delphi, where they have more than one bar that hasn't gone out of business, and then I can buy a house far out in the forest, like Grandma Margaret's, though smaller probably. Maybe just a trailer. Or a tent even, while I save up, but a fancy one, the kind with multiple rooms. My sister and I can live there, the two of us, and no one will be able to tell me what to do.

But that's a long way off. Right now all I have is fifty dollars (saved up from my meagre allowance and a few small tips from friendly regulars) in an envelope under my mattress, so I've got to compromise. I've got to play by the rules for a while to survive.

Of course, if I stop sneaking out now, the stupid pastor is going to think it's because of him. He's going to think he won. The thought of giving him that satisfaction makes me almost as miserable as the prospect of having to repeat ninth grade.

Mr. Blackburn has found a way to segue from trench warfare to his most recent weekend fishing trip. Henry, who sits two desks up and one to the right of me, turns around and draws a finger across his throat, sticks his tongue out, rolls his eyes back until there's nothing but white. I grin. Maisie, who sits at the desk next to me, notices and scowls. She and I used to be friends, but we drifted apart around the end of eighth grade when she started hanging out with a different group of girls. Cooler ones. She and Henry dated for most of last year, then broke up this summer.

Henry turns around and I stare at the back of his neck. It's got this dusting of pale hairs like the secret fur of a leaf. When the sunlight hits them, they glow.

He died once when he was younger. His mother found him flat on his back on the front porch with his heart stopped. The EMTs shocked him back to life. Afterward everybody wanted to know what it was like, if he'd seen God. Henry said he didn't remember, but people kept asking, so eventually he said he had seen a brilliant blue light in the shape of a lion. He said the lion padded toward him and opened its mouth wide and fitted its jaws around his head. It held him there, teeth pressing against his skin, until he woke.

He made that up, though. I know because he told me so himself. Told me he didn't see a thing. Just darkness.

Henry and I used to be friends, too. When we were all younger, he'd hang out with me and Savannah. I mean, basically every kid hung out with every other kid back then. Lester is small. I liked Henry particularly, though. He was quiet and good at playing along with games. Didn't try to ruin things the way some of the other boys did.

It's all different now. Has been since some invisible line got crossed back at the start of seventh grade and suddenly nobody wanted to play games anymore because it didn't look cool and boys couldn't hang out with girls anymore or else they were dating.

So I don't really talk to Henry anymore except in school. Savannah says she thinks he has a crush on me, but I'm not sure.

Sometimes when I'm sitting in history class I will take whatever Mr. Blackburn is going on about and put Henry and me in it. Henry marching off to war, and me, hair shorn and disguised in men's clothing, marching off beside him. Henry mustard-gassed and shrapnelled, and me nursing him slowly back to health, cradling his bandaged head in my lap, gently sponging his wounds. It's always very tragic, whatever I imagine. I don't know if that's the fault of history, or if there's something wrong with me, that I like to imagine Henry broken and bleeding, helpless, in need of rescue. Henry and I shot at, captured, tortured. Henry and I fugitives, persecuted, living in the woods, sleeping under the stars. Henry warming his frostbitten fingers by the fire, and me catching rabbits for us to eat, breaking their necks swift as my sister does. But cooking them because I am not like my sister, not really.

In math class I actually do fall asleep, with my head leaning against the wall. When the bell jolts me awake, the teacher glares but doesn't say anything. For the first month of school he'd come over and wake me up when I fell asleep in class but by now he's obviously decided that I'm not worth the effort.

When I get to chorus, I take my seat in the back row next to Savannah, who's got her phone hidden behind her music folder. I lean over and whisper, "Let's leave after this."

Savannah snorts. "That was quick."

I'd told her yesterday about my vow. Or part of it anyway. Told her I was going to stop cutting class, start actually trying in school.

"This will be the last time," I say.

"Right," says Savannah, and then Mrs. Carol calls us to attention and starts hammering out scales for us to yowl along to.

When the bell rings, Savannah and I duck out and hide behind the gym supply shed until the second bell. The high school is nestled at the foot of a hill, with hardly fifty feet between it and the start of the national forest, so it's easy for us to book it to the trees. We go the long way to Queen of Heaven Cemetery, winding through the woods by our usual route.

When we get there, Savannah goes to visit the grave of her uncle Tad, who was her all-time favorite uncle before he wrecked his motorcycle. He was only eighteen when it happened, three years older than we are now, which makes his death seem more real, somehow.

Mama was only fifteen, the same age as I am now, when she disappeared, but the police never found her body. She doesn't have a proper grave, so I walk around the edges of the cemetery and collect all the silk flowers that blew away in the wind and I lay them at the base of a tree and I pretend that's where she is.

Aggie and Grandma Margaret don't like talking to me about Mama. They always tell me not to bring it up, to let the pain of the past stay in the past, so most of what I know I've learned from the drunks in Joe's Bar. They aren't the most reliable source, perhaps, but I take what I can get. Every scrap of Mama I can gather is precious. I would give anything to see her, to talk to her, even just to touch her hand. To have one single memory of her that was my own.

As it is, all I have are other people's memories. Details change depending on who I ask or how drunk they are at the time, but there are a few things I'm certain about. Mama was fifteen when she got pregnant. Grandma Margaret kicked her out of the house when she found out about it. Mama bounced from couch to couch for a while, ended up living with the Cantrell boys, Logan and Brandon, in their double-wide trailer out on the ridge. Logan Cantrell is probably my daddy, though nobody's sure. Logan was a drug dealer and a thief. People say he was violent. People say they're pretty sure he hit her. Say they saw the bruises.

People also say Logan wasn't the only guy Mama hung around with. They say she was wild. Say she was *friendly,* a little too friendly, and I know what they really mean by that.

Officially, Mama is still missing. Officially, no one knows what happened to her. Not a soul laid eyes on her after she gave birth. But you ask practically anyone in Lester and they will tell you that they *do* know what happened. Logan Cantrell killed her, they'll tell you, and buried her body in the woods.

When we're done at the cemetery, we climb the hill behind it and pass through a band of trees into an overgrown yard with a sagging two-story house in the center of it. Technically, the house belongs to Myron, Savannah's oldest uncle, but it's been empty since he got put away for dealing a few years back. No one ever comes here except the two of us, so in a way the house is ours.

The porch has collapsed and the back door is nailed shut, so I give Savannah, who is a good half a foot shorter than me, a boost through the kitchen window, and then I clamber through myself.

We hold our breath and creep through the hallway, past the Hornet Room (where Savannah once got stung four times) and the Pit-of-Hell Room (where the floor has given way to the basement) until we reach our favorite: the Naked Lady Room, where the walls are papered with pages from old nudie magazines. It used to be Myron's bedroom. There's a bare mattress on the floor and a dresser with two out of three drawers.

Savannah pulls out the bottom drawer and extracts her Tupperware of assorted cigarettes, begged and stolen from various sources and carefully hoarded here.

"Can I have the blanket?" I ask. "I was up all night."

Savannah pouts, but she pulls the folded quilt from the drawer and hands it over. I spread it across the mattress, run my hands over the faded squares, each one a slightly different shade of blue, like little windows into a hundred summer days.

This is our secret hideout. We used to come here and play games. We'd pretend the house was haunted by Victorian-era ghosts or that we were archaeologists exploring an ancient and musty ruin. We'd make up elaborate backstories for the ladies on the walls. We'd carve pictures into the rotting floorboards with nails. I'd be Myron sometimes. She'd be Myron's pretend girlfriend. We'd fool around.

Now, though, Savannah settles down cross-legged in the corner, cigarette in one hand, phone in the other. It's a hand-me-down from her sister Dakota, its screen spiderwebbed with cracks, but it's still way better than my phone, which is no phone at all. Aggie refuses to buy me one and I can't afford it on my own. I don't need to ask Savannah who she's texting. I know who it is: a boy. She's been obsessed with the damn things since she first kissed one last year. She's kissed at least eight more since then. Done more than that, even, with a few of them, though she's never gone all the way.

The sorry truth is I've never kissed any boys at all. The only person I've ever kissed is Savannah, right here in this very room. But that was just a game, I guess.

I curl up on the quilt. My eyelids are already heavy. I let them close.

"Jo?"

I startle. "What?"

"Were you asleep?" asks Savannah.

"No. Almost."

"Well, do you think you'll sleep for long?" Savannah sounds petulant. Maybe she wants me to stay awake and talk. I would if I could, I guess, though she rarely wants to talk about anything in- teresting these days. It's all boring real things with her these days instead of stories. She wants to talk about the other kids at school. About boys.

"I don't know," I say. I was out way later than usual last night, and I can barely keep my head up.

Savannah huffs. "You're going to trip and break your leg some night and then get eaten by wild deer and it will serve you right."

"Uh-huh," I say, settling my head back down on the quilt. Savannah knows I run at night, but she thinks I do it alone. She thinks I'm an insomniac. I've told her that I am, told her I run to relax. Which isn't entirely a lie. Sometimes I get so angry that I am certain I will burn up from the inside out. If I run long enough, hard enough, push myself past pain and aching muscles, I can break through, into a state of absolute calm.

In middle school Savannah and I both did track and field, both loved to run (she did sprints, I did long distance), but Savannah quit at the end of last year and I wasn't about to keep doing it without her. So now I only run with my sister.

When Savannah and I were little, I would talk about Lee sometimes. The first time Savannah stayed for a sleepover at Grandma Margaret's house, I made her climb out the window of my first-floor bedroom with me at midnight. Margaret's house is way out on one of the ridges, built by *her* granddaddy nearly a hundred years ago. It's surrounded by forest and accessible only by a narrow dirt road. Savannah and I stood in the backyard for hours, staring at the dark wall of trees, waiting. But my sister didn't show up that night, or any of the other nights that I forced Savannah to wait with me. Lee is scared of people, so I should have known that she would never come out of the woods if there was anyone other than me in the yard. After a while I stopped trying to convince Savannah that my sister existed.

In fact, I stopped mentioning my sister at all, to anyone. It was safer that way. If people found out about her, about the way she lived, they would take her away from me. When I was younger I thought that someday she could come live with me and Aggie and Margaret and go to school and be a normal person, but I understand now that could never happen, even if my sister weren't afraid, because there's this thing called the state and the state takes children.

When Savannah told me in second grade that the state took her cousins, I imagined a monster, something with claws and teeth, dragging them out of their beds while they screamed. Her aunt hadn't been doing a good enough job raising her kids, I guess. Someone called the state and said her kids were too skinny and had bruises and were left alone in the house overnight while their mother went out to score drugs. If that's all it took for the state to step in, what the hell would they make of Lee? Left alone for years. Skinnier than any kid in town. Matted hair and yellowed teeth. Fleas in the summer. Tick bites. Scars from head to toe. Two of her toes permanently numb from frostbite she got before she met me.

Someone would have to answer for that. Grandma Margaret still has custody of me, even though she lets Aggie do all the work, the same way she owns Joe's Bar and Grill but does nothing except collect a check every month. Margaret owns me and Aggie both, in a way. And Lee should be her responsibility by law, I guess. Maybe they'd charge her for neglect. After all, I did try to tell Margaret. When I was very little, I told her about my sister, but she didn't believe me and so nobody but me has taken care of Lee all these years.

I've done my best, but the state wouldn't care about that, wouldn't care that being forced into a foster home with strangers would send Lee wild with fear, that being locked up in a hospital or a psych ward (and I'm sure they'd think she was crazy, mentally challenged, stunted, backward, strange) would probably kill her. I think of her locked up, strapped to a bed, and my chest seizes as if her terror were my terror. She would be an animal caught in a trap, gnawing off her own leg to get free. I don't know if she could survive it. I don't know if I could, either.

Because I hide myself as much as I hide my sister. I hide the person I am when I'm with her. When I was a kid it was easier. How I acted in the day wasn't much different from how I acted at night. Outside of school at least, the kids of Lester roved about, playing in the woods behind someone's house or alongside the train tracks, fighting with sticks, running races, trying to catch fish in Monday Creek, acting out plays with dead bugs as the actors. But as I got older, there were more and more things that weren't acceptable or cool, especially for a girl.

I added them all to the secret half of me.

Sometimes I wish I could put the two halves back together. I wish my sister could come and live here, with me and Savannah, in Myron's house, which the forest is taking back anyway.

I blink sleepily at Savannah, who is smiling down at something on her phone, the screen's glow reflecting onto her cheeks.

There is nothing more peaceful than this. Smoke fluttering from her fingertips toward the ceiling. The naked ladies on the wall behind her gazing down protectively, big-breasted angels with '80s hair.

I feel myself drifting. The ladies blur into a landscape. Bosomy clouds, blond waterfalls. Savannah a distant mountain.

I think of my sister, sleeping somewhere in the woods even now. I close my eyes.

I wake to the sound of banging on the wall. I roll over to ask Savannah what's going on, but she's gone.

I jump up, heart pounding.

It must be the pastor. He must have followed us here somehow. Must have been watching me. Waiting to break my legs. I run down the hallway, kicking up clouds of plaster dust in my wake. The banging continues.

Then suddenly: silence.

I skid into the kitchen, and there's Savannah. She's leaning out the window, elbows on the paint-flaked sill, talking to somebody.

She's swaying her hips a little side to side. She's giggling. She's shed her oversized hoodie, has it wrapped around her waist. Her pink bra straps clash with her olive-green tank.

I come up behind her. Standing outside is Tanner Burch, one of several boys she currently has a crush on. Just last week, he took her for a ride on his friend's four-wheeler and they kissed in the fog. He's got on a too-big camo jacket, ripped jeans, orange trucker cap. How the hell did he find us?

"You going to let us in or what?" says Tanner.

"What'll you give me if I do?" asks Savannah.

But of course he didn't find us. Savannah must have told him where we were. She must have texted him to come here. To our house. Our secret.

"I'll shoot you if you come any nearer!" I shout at Tanner, doing my pretend Uncle Myron voice. I used to crack Savannah up doing that voice, drawling, *Hey there, hunny pie, you bring that sweet ass over here, give your favorite uncle some sugar.*

"Who's that?" says Tanner. He moves closer to the window, trying to peer in past Savannah. I see then that there's someone else with him, someone standing a little ways back, toeing the dirt with his boot. Someone with pale skin and freckles and a shock of dandelion fluff hair.

Henry.

"It's Jo," I say in my normal voice, my anger tempered now with some other feeling, a sort of fluttering nervousness. I see

Henry all the time in history, sure, but it's different seeing him outside of school. "Wait there. We'll come out in a second."

I grab the back of Savannah's tank top, haul her away from the window, over toward the rusted stove, the warped cabinets, the sink clogged with dead bluebottles.

"Dammit, Van," I say. "Why are they here? What are you doing?"

We'd agreed, when we first started coming to Myron's house, never to bring anyone else here. Especially guys. Savannah had promised. We both had.

She shrugs. She must have put on more mascara while I was sleeping, because her lashes are all sticking together now. "You said this was the last time you'd cut class with me. Figured I better make the most of it."

I want to haul back and slap her across the face. My hand practically itches for it. But last time I did that she didn't talk to me for weeks (she'd had a fight with her mother and said without thinking, *I wish she was dead*), so I settle for giving her a playful punch in the arm, but a little too hard.

"Come on," she says. "You were over there snoring anyway. You're no fun lately. All you do is sleep."

"I get tired."

"Well, I get lonely."

"Fine," I say.

"You ought to thank me," Savannah says, "Henry's here too."

"Oh, shut up."

Savannah's grinning now. She loves to tease me about Henry, always saying I should make a move. Sometimes it seems like she wants me and him to get together more than I do. Maybe she thinks if I start kissing boys I'll turn into her. A perfect partner in crime.

I go back over to the window. Tanner and Henry are leaning against the side of the house, passing a cigarette back and forth.

"Hey, let me help you," says Tanner when he sees me, but I jump down on my own.

When Savannah climbs out after me she does it clumsy on purpose so that Tanner will put his hands on her hips to steady her. She plonks down to the ground and his hands slide up to her waist, her tank top bunching far enough that we can see the tiny tattoo on her hip that she got from her uncle Tad before he died. It's supposed to be a bumblebee but the stripes kind of blurred together, so it looks more like a fly.

"Is school over already?" I ask. Henry won't meet my eyes, like maybe he, too, feels how different it is to see each other outside of school.

Or maybe he's embarrassed of me? Doesn't want Tanner to know we're sort of friends? He mostly hangs out with an older crowd these days. His brother's friends. And Tanner, I guess, who is a grade above us.

"We skipped last period," says Tanner. "This is a cool house. Never even knew it was here."

"It's full of wasps," I tell him. "They're used to us, but if you try to go in they'll sting you in the face until you die."

Tanner laughs. Savannah is scowling at me. I'm not acting how I'm supposed to, not flirting, not helping her out.

"What do we do now?" she asks, eyeing Myron's house ruefully. Palace of lost make-out opportunities.

Henry pipes up for the first time. "Got some beers round my place."

———

Henry's mom is working a double shift at a restaurant in Needle, and his dad is out, probably drinking or something. Their house is at the edge of town, up an old brick road.

In Lester, everything gets shittier-looking the farther you go from Main Street. Out here, the stop signs are faded nearly to white, the letters outlined faintly in rust. The trees lean over the roads, over the houses, threatening to take back what is theirs. Vines strangle the mailboxes. Weeds and wildflowers burst through every crack in the pavement. Given half a chance, I'm sure, the forest would swallow Lester whole.

We wait on the porch while Henry goes inside. When he comes back out he has a six-pack (minus one can) of Schlitz and his guitar. He sits next to me on the beat-up floral couch.

I've seen him play guitar a few times before, back in the middle school talent shows, and even I have to admit that he's terrible. But I like watching his hands go up and down the strings. I like the way his knuckles are always kind of swollen, pink and wrinkled as roses.

We drink the beers, which are warm and flat. I'm used to that, since most of the beer I've had so far is the dregs left at the bottom of other's people bottles, which I drink when no one's looking. A whole can to myself, flat or not, is a luxury. Tanner tries to chug his beer to show off and nearly chokes. Henry plays a few bars of "Smells like Teen Spirit." Savannah tells us about her sister's friend's baby's problem, which is that it was born addicted to painkillers.

"Baby's more hardcore than any of us," she says.

"Babies are weird," says Tanner.

I should go home soon. It's Friday, one of the busiest nights at the bar, and Aggie will want me to help. She started helping

Grandpa Joe around the bar from basically the moment she could walk, to hear her tell it. I don't mind helping. I even enjoy it sometimes and Aggie says if I do a good job she'll hire me for real someday, but I know the pastor will be there. Just thinking about what he said in the car makes my skin crawl. He thinks he knows me. Thinks he's got power over me now. I've got to show him he doesn't.

And what better chance than this? It's the first time I've been to Henry's house since sixth grade, when he made every kid in the neighborhood come see the half-decayed deer at the end of the road. It was mostly bones, with a few scraps of rotting fur still clinging to it. I wanted to show that I wasn't afraid, so I walked right up and stuck my hand inside the rib cage, where the heart would have been. Afterward Henry and Savannah and Maisie and me and one or two other kids hung out in Henry's backyard and played at hunter (we took turns being the deer) until his dad came home.

Now, I announce that I've got to go to the bathroom and I grab Savannah's arm and drag her with me.

"Girls are weird," I hear Tanner say as the screen door bangs shut behind us.

When we get to the bathroom, I make Savannah call the bar and ask Aggie if I can stay over for dinner. Aggie says fine, as long I'm home by nine. I offer to call Savannah's mom, but Savannah says her mom won't even notice she's gone. Savannah's one of seven kids, so she's probably right.

When we get back to the porch, Tanner's gone. Henry says he got a text and ran off. Savannah shoots me a dirty look, as if it's my fault somehow. Henry offers her the last beer as a consolation.

Henry is about halfway through the slowest version of

"Wonderwall" in the history of the world, when his brother Jack comes out of the house. He's got no shirt on, just jeans. I can see his hip bones, the waistband of his underwear, the trail of hair that disappears beneath it. Henry is sixteen, a year older than Savannah and me (he got held back when he was a kid on account of his heart problems). Jack is eighteen, a senior.

Jack slouches down next to Savannah, with a nonchalance that must be practiced. Either that or he's already stoned stupid. He moves slow and liquid. Doesn't say anything, just pulls a joint out of his pocket, lights it up. I can't help but look at the muscles shifting under his skin. Savannah's looking too. Danger. He takes a hit and then passes the joint.

Normally I don't smoke, cigarettes or anything else, a holdover from my middle school track days when our coach told us that he didn't give a shit if we all wanted to die of cancer, but he could guarantee that smoking would cut our running times in half. Tonight, though, when Henry holds out the joint, I take it, letting our fingers brush on purpose. I feel silly immediately for that. It's the sort of move Savannah would pull. The smoke catches in my throat and I feel a cough coming. I hold my breath, force it down.

Pastor Jones, I think, eat your heart out. I picture a whole herd of little broken-legged lambs, limping along on their own.

After the joint goes around a few times, Jack and Savannah start doing that thing where they blow smoke into each other's mouths. The sun drips down toward the trees.

Henry puts his hand on my knee. We both just sit there for a while, staring straight ahead, and then he takes his hand back.

But I can still feel a pressure there, like the ghost of a hand, like the way I feel my sister, even when she isn't with me.

"What was that?" asks Savannah, sitting up abruptly.

"What was what?" says Jack, sounding unconcerned, his voice as languid as his movements.

"I saw something move, there." She points toward the woods that back up to Henry's house. The trees are dark and thick and I know from experience that they keep on going for a long, long way. The national forest covers more than three thousand square miles and even with all the time I've spent out there, I'm sure I've seen only a fraction of it.

"Probably a squirrel," says Henry.

"No, it was bigger than that." Savannah sounds genuinely frightened. I wonder if she's putting it on. She's started doing that kind of thing more and more lately. Acting sillier than she really is, stupider, more fragile. I hate it. I wish she'd act like Savannah. The real one. The one I've always known.

"Deer, then," says Henry.

"It looked like a person," says Savannah.

My heart twists and I strain my eyes, focusing on the tree line. It couldn't be her, right? She'd never come this close to town, to people. All I see is dark.

"Bet it's a ghost," says Jack.

"Nah," says Henry, uncertainly. "Probably just a deer."

"You don't know shit, little brother," says Jack. "A lot of people died around here. Hell, right there in our yard a guy shot himself in the head once."

"Really?" asks Savannah, eyes wide.

"Sure," says Jack, grinning at her, leaning forward. "They were picking brains out of the bushes for days."

I snort. "Yeah, right."

"It's true," says Jack, though he doesn't look at me. He's focused on Savannah. "You probably haven't heard about it because it was a long time ago, before any of us were born. This guy Richard Hornbeam shot himself in the head with a .357 pistol. And the worst part is he didn't die right away. You'd think you couldn't mess that up, shooting yourself in the head. But this poor bastard did. He died in the hospital later, but he was alive for hours first."

Jack is making this up, I'm pretty sure, to scare us little freshmen, because I've never heard about it and we get every story down at the bar, no matter how old. But I've got to admit he's a good liar. Even I kind of want to believe him. Savannah has scooted closer to Jack, her eyes wide with exaggerated fright.

Jack takes a long hit off the joint, lets the smoke out slow.

"Some nights," he says, "real late, when nobody in their right mind would be hunting, we hear gunshots. Out behind the house. It's that same poor bastard and he's shooting himself in the head, over and over, trying to get it right."

"We do hear gunshots," admits Henry. If someone is actually shooting guns in their backyard late at night, I bet it's their dad. I'll need to warn my sister to stay far, far away.

She probably already knows.

"Sure do," says Jack. He's having too much fun with this, grinning wildly. He puts his arm around Savannah, pulls her against his side. I feel a pang of something. Concern, maybe. Jealousy. "And that's not even the worst thing we hear."

CHAPTER THREE

About twenty minutes later we're all in Jack's car, on our way to Crybaby Bridge. Jack told us the story, back on the porch. Years ago a young woman came at midnight and threw her baby off the bridge into the water and then threw herself off too and if you stand in the right place you can hear the baby crying to this day. Jack said he and Henry have both heard it.

I know Jack didn't make this story up, because I've actually heard it before, from an out-of-towner who came to the bar once. He was traveling across Ohio, hitting up every haunted place in the state. Lester made his list because of the No. 5 Mine disaster site, where a tunnel collapsed and crushed fifty men. The out-of-towner said there are half a dozen Crybaby Bridges in Ohio. He'd been to four of them so far and hadn't heard a thing.

Henry's driving, though he only has a learner's permit. We're going down a winding gravel road, which makes the car bump and rattle and sends bits of rock shooting up from under the tires. There are no houses out this way, no people, just trees.

Henry is biting his bottom lip, squinting at the road, clutching the wheel hard enough that his fingers are white. The beer and the joint are giving me this dreamy feeling, like we've crossed over into a different reality. The normal rules don't apply here. Tonight is magic. Tonight doesn't really count.

In the backseat, Savannah has the straps of her tank top down around her shoulders and Jack's nuzzling against her chest like a cat. He's got a Mountain Dew bottle, which he takes sips from and sometimes hands to Savannah. I watch them in the side mirror until Henry pulls the car up short along the side of the road.

"Here we are," he says, and Savannah pulls her straps up and she and Jack tumble out the side door.

There are no streetlights here. But the moon is out. It would be a good night for running. The upturned faces of the leaves catch the moonlight like mirrors and everything is bathed in shades of silver. If only we had names for all those shades, maybe more people would notice them, would appreciate how bright and alive they can be. I want to point this out to Henry or Savannah, but they'd only laugh at me.

Henry digs a flashlight out of the trunk and leads us down an old dirt road, if it can even be called a road anymore. It's overrun with weeds and lined with sticker bushes that snatch at my sleeves like little hands as I pass.

The flashlight makes the forest seem strange, washing out the trees, casting jumpy shadows that move along with us. I'd be happier in the dark, honestly. The light just means our eyes have no chance to adjust. Jack hands me the Mountain Dew bottle.

"What was your name again?" he asks. I tell him and take a sip of whatever is in the bottle. It burns, but I swallow it, writing a smug little speech in my mind about how this is all the pastor's fault, how he drove me to it by expecting the worst of me, how I would probably be home safe in bed if it weren't for him. Oh ye of little faith heed not the call of the something or other lest you face my eternal judgment. Prince of peace! I take another sip of the foul, numbing stuff in the bottle and hand it back.

The bridge, when we finally reach it, is tiny, barely wide enough for a car, with rusted metal guardrails and moss dappling the pavement. It arches over Monday Creek, the orange-brown rivulet of spit and mine runoff that winds through Lester. Savannah is giggling. She runs out onto the bridge and Jack runs after her. He's at least a foot taller than her, so he has to bend down pretty far to whisper something into her ear. He takes her hand and they run the rest of the way across the bridge. I feel a pang as the two of them disappear into the trees. I start out onto the bridge, but stop halfway, uncertain.

"I wouldn't believe it," Henry says behind me, "if I hadn't heard it my own self."

I turn.

"The crying, I mean," he says.

"It was probably the wind," I say.

"No way. I know the wind."

I've been here before, actually, with my sister, though not recently. The bridge is somewhere roughly north of Lester, I'm pretty sure. My sister is a far better navigator than me, so I always let her lead the way. We never heard anything strange when we came. Just owls and insects. The normal cries of the forest at night.

"Has anybody seen them?" I ask Henry. "The ghosts?"

"I don't know. Probably." He's got the flashlight pointing down at his side. I snatch it away from him and point it at the creek, sweep it back and forth like a searchlight.

"Just imagine," I say, as serious as I can manage, "if we were looking down and all of a sudden we saw a pair of eyes looking back up at us."

"Shut up," says Henry. He tries to grab the flashlight, but I jerk it out of his reach.

"Or a tiny baby hand," I say, "reaching out of the water." I flick the flashlight off and on, off and on. The beam catches on a branch sticking out of the mud by the bank and Henry gasps. I laugh. The night is making us young again. I can almost forget that we aren't kids anymore, that we aren't friends. That we are teenagers, a boy and a girl alone and there are rules about that.

"Quit it, Jo," Henry says.

I swing the flashlight beam toward the woods on the far side of the bridge, where Savannah went, but I can't see anything except trees. Maybe I should have gone after her. I don't really know Jack; don't know what kind of guy he is. He was too old to hang out with us when we were kids. He'd be playing video games with his friends, telling us to fuck off. And he's eighteen now. I know what they say about older guys. The kind of things they expect from girls.

Henry takes advantage of my distraction to grab for the flashlight again. His hand closes over mine. I swing the flashlight beam so it shines in his eyes. He squeezes them shut but doesn't let go. His eyelids glow red in the light.

Tonight is magic. Tonight doesn't count. This is my chance. Savannah will never forgive me if I don't take it. Henry and I are almost exactly the same height, so all I have to do is lean forward a little and then my lips are grazing his. I close my eyes, too.

There's a moment of perfect stillness and then Henry presses his mouth against mine. I press back. He lets go of the flashlight, moves his hands to grasp my shoulders. I grab the fabric of his

T-shirt in my fists, pull him toward me. It's like kissing Savannah, only better, maybe, because I think he actually means it. I get this feeling in my chest like when I'm running, like when I'm racing my sister, moving so fast my feet barely touch the ground. Nearly flying, every nerve in my body alive. I feel Henry's tongue pushing at my lips like a little animal trying to crawl into the earth, and that's when I hear it.

An unearthly wail. High and pained. So loud and so close.

Not like a baby. Not like an animal either. Henry and I pull away from each other at the same time. His face looks how I'm sure mine does. Eyes wide and startled.

"There it is," he whispers.

"Shit," I say, and I am, for a moment, genuinely afraid.

Just as suddenly as the wail started, it stops. I reach out to take Henry's hand again, but before I can, something comes barreling out of nowhere and knocks him to the ground. Knocks him right over and it's her. It's my sister. She's here, on the bridge with us. Here in her blue dress.

I don't understand. Can't believe it. Can't breathe.

Henry is on his back and she is pinning him down, straddling him, her dress bunching up around her hips. For a second I think she's going to kiss him, think that she saw me kiss him and was jealous, wanting him too, but then her hands are around his neck and I think of my sister, my sister who I know so well, think of her snatching up rabbits, squirrels, mourning doves, how I've seen her a thousand times, her hands so quick, her thin hands snapping their necks like dry spaghetti.

I think of that and I scream.

CHAPTER FOUR

The last time anyone in town saw my mother alive was at the Country Lanes bowling alley in Needle. She sat in a booth eating onion rings, silent, her belly huge, while Logan Cantrell and his younger brother, Brandon, bowled frame after frame. About a week later, Brandon showed up before the sun and banged on Grandma Margaret's front door. When she answered he shoved a bundle wrapped in a hunting jacket into her arms and ran off.

That bundle was me.

Lee and I are twins. We look enough alike that when I peered out my window one night ten years ago and saw her standing at the edge of Grandma Margaret's yard, wearing an oversized T-shirt as a dress, legs all mud to the knees, I knew right away that she was my sister.

I was five. I'd believed up until that moment that I was an only child, but at five the world was endlessly surprising, my picture of reality pliable as Play-Doh. In a way I'd already been expecting something like this to happen—for someone to show up out of the blue and change everything. Except I thought it would be my mother, coming back to get me.

Sure, Grandma Margaret told me that Mama had gone to Jesus (or, if she'd been drinking, gone to hell), but I believed back then that if I just wanted it hard enough, she might come back for me anyway.

When I first saw my sister, I thought about running to the bottom of the staircase, calling for Aggie or Grandma Margaret, but I was afraid that if I took my eyes off her she would disappear.

So, instead, I stood on the bed, unlatched the window, and climbed out. It was summer, and the ground felt cool beneath my feet. Crickets thrummed. Fireflies floated up from the grass like shooting stars in reverse.

My sister stood very still, watching me, as I walked toward her. She didn't smile, didn't respond to my "Hi." When I reached out to touch her she flinched.

I asked her a thousand questions, that first night. Where did she come from? What was her name? Was her favorite color the same as mine? She didn't answer, just stared at me, and I worried that maybe she couldn't talk, but when I asked if she was hungry, she said yes, and when I asked if she wanted to come inside, she said no, and when I asked if I should go get Aggie to make us some food, her eyes went very wide and she turned around and ran back into the woods.

The next night, I climbed out my window again and I waited at the edge of the yard and sure enough, she came back. I gave her half a bag of Skittles I had saved for her and she took my hand and led me into the trees.

I didn't think it was so strange at first, to have a secret sister. I'd sneak out at night, spend a few hours with her, sneak back in.

Sometimes I'd bring toys out to the forest, sometimes we'd just chase each other or play hide-and-seek. When Aggie and Margaret noticed the scratches on my legs, the mud between my toes, they thought I was sleepwalking. They bolted guardrails to my bed, fed me hot milk with whiskey. When I said I had a sister, they told me not to be silly.

When I said, *No, really I do, she comes to see me at night,* Aggie told me not to talk about sisters to her, that I didn't know what it felt like to have your heart ripped in two and I was lucky I never would.

Grandma Margaret told me lying was a sin and did I know what happens to sinners? I did, of course, because she told me every chance she got. God struck them down in their tracks and sent them straight to hell.

Do you know how hot it gets in hell? she asked me once. When I shrugged she took me by the wrist and dragged me to the kitchen. She switched on one of the stovetop gas burners and pulled my hand closer and closer, until I felt the heat, until the edges of the flames licked my fingers and I shrieked and Aggie came running from the other room. The two of them shouted at each other and I slunk away to my bedroom and pressed my throbbing fingers to the cold glass of the window by my bed, wishing my sister would come and take me away.

Eventually I realized.

It *is* strange. *She* is strange.

Nearly everyone in town knows the story of Brandon bringing me to Grandma Margaret. They differ on the specifics. Dawn. Midnight. His coat covered in blood or not a drop of blood on him. A wicked smile on his face or a look of terror.

But nobody has ever said a thing about another baby. On this detail, everyone agrees. Brandon brought one bundle that day. One baby.

The police could never get much out of him. He changed his story each time they asked him. Sometimes he said strange things, about devils or aliens. No one could agree on whether he was crazy or just a liar, but as far as I know he never mentioned another baby.

The best I can figure it is that the Cantrells kept my sister, hid her from the police somehow during the investigation into Mama's disappearance. I've asked Lee about it many times, but she won't tell me. *Did Logan and Brandon raise you?* I'll say, and she'll shake her head or shrug or ignore me. *Who raised you?* I'll say, and she'll point to a tree or a rock or a dead squirrel caught in one of her wire traps, just to fuck with me. If I keep asking, she'll clam up for the rest of the night. I tried to trick her once, told her I'd heard Logan was out of jail and on his way home, just to see if she'd react. But it was no use. She could tell I was lying. She's pretty much the only person in my whole life who I can't lie to. I half believe she can smell it.

I suspect her early years were rough. Maybe really rough, and that's why she won't talk about them. All I know is this: by five, my sister was already terrified of people. She was terrified of being seen, of being caught. She told me that people were bad, that they wanted to hurt her. She made me promise not to tell anyone about her. I tried to convince her that some people were okay. I told her about Savannah, about Aggie. I'd point at characters in the picture books I brought her, say, *They don't seem so bad, right?* Sometimes, I tried to make her come inside with me. I thought if she could just once sleep in a bed, take a bath, eat a bowl of mac 'n' cheese, then maybe she would transform into a normal girl. We could be normal sisters.

But it made no difference. If I pushed her too hard, she'd stop coming around for a week or two. I would cry every night, sure I'd lost her for good. Eventually I stopped trying. To this day, my sister believes that everyone other than the two of us is evil. She has made me promise over and over that I will never let them see her, never let them get her.

Which is why I don't understand.

On the bridge.

My sister. Henry.

He saw her. She let herself be seen.

Her hands are on his neck. He must have hit his head when he fell. He's not moving. She is leaning her face down to his neck.

I think again that she is going to kiss him. I don't understand.

I step forward and throw myself against my sister. Just fall on her, really. Knock her sideways. We tumble, roll. She tries to hit me. I get my arms around her, hold tight. We could just be wrestling. Playing like we did as kids. Lee kicks wildly. Her foot clangs off the bridge railing. Her elbow stabs into my ribs.

I hear Savannah's voice in the distance, shouting my name.

Lee jerks her head forward and pain explodes through my left wrist.

I cry out, let go.

In an instant, she is up and running. I point the flashlight in time to see her disappear into the trees, a tail of torn lace trailing in the dirt.

I swing the flashlight down. Lee's teeth left two arcs of indents on my wrist, some of them already filling with blood.

And Henry. There's blood on his neck. I drop to my knees beside him.

"Jo?" Savannah says again, much closer this time.

Henry isn't moving. His eyes are closed. I touch his neck. Try to wipe the blood away. I can feel a pulse hammering under my fingers, as fast as mine. His neck isn't broken. Maybe she was trying to tear out his windpipe with her teeth. I've seen her do that with rabbits. But humans have bigger necks than rabbits. She's not that strong, is she? And I got there in time. Her teeth only broke the skin a little. She didn't hit an artery.

"What the fuck happened?" Jack's voice is very close. In another moment he is pushing me aside, dropping to his knees. Did he see her? Did either of them see her? I fumble at the sleeve of my black hoodie, pull it clumsily over my bleeding wrist.

"Call 911," Jack snaps at Savannah. He presses one ear against his brother's chest, listening to his heart.

His heart.

I hadn't even thought about his heart. Savannah has on Jack's jacket. It goes down to her knees. She's fumbling in the pockets.

"What the hell did you do?" Jack is shouting at me. I scoot back against the railing of the bridge, hide my wrist behind myself.

"An animal," I say. My voice doesn't sound like my own. "It was an animal."

I shine the flashlight on Henry's face. His hair glows white. I can see small veins on the pale hills of his eyelids. Henry. His heart. He died once when he was younger. He told me he didn't see anything. Just darkness.

"I don't know," I hear Savannah say. "He's bleeding."

He's fine. He's got to be. We kissed. Jack is back on his feet, yanking the phone out of Savannah's hand. She hugs herself. The ends of the jacket sleeves hang loose, as if she has no hands.

"He's got a weak heart," I hear Jack say into the phone. "Congenital."

My own heart is pounding so loud it nearly drowns out everything else.

"A wolf," I say. Did they see her? I don't think they saw her. They can't have seen her.

"Off County Road 407," I hear Jack say. "You'll see a car parked. Gray Nissan."

"It was a wolf," I say.

Jack is beside me again. Kneeling, he scoops his brother up in his arms. I am jealous for a second. It should be me. I should be carrying Henry in my arms, struggling through no-man's-land toward our foxhole as mortars hit the dirt and explode behind us. Like I imagined in history class. I should press my lips to his. He should open his eyes, wrap his arms around me. Poor Henry. I'll save you.

My hands are shaking, though it isn't cold. I push the sleeve farther over my wrist, press my other wrist against it, though it hurts so bad I gasp. I try to apply pressure, try to stop the blood leaking out. I want to hide too. I want to run. The stars are so bright out here, with no light from the town to compete. They stare down at us. A thousand angry eyes.

A wolf, streaking through the night. Silver fur and yellow teeth. Are there wolves in Ohio? My sister and I thought we saw one once, in the distance, but it was dark and so maybe it was only a dog.

I've asked her before, is she ever afraid? Of animals in the woods? She says no. She's only afraid of people. She keeps a small folding knife in her plastic purse. Thank God she didn't use it tonight.

What the hell was she thinking?

Did she think he was hurting me? Was she protecting me?

Jack is carrying his brother across the bridge, down the path through the woods. Savannah is trailing behind him, the empty ends of the jacket sleeves flapping at her sides.

I run after them, shine the flashlight beam on the path so Jack won't stumble. I scan the dark forest around us, try to catch a glimpse of blue.

The cry. I remember the cry. We heard it on the bridge and I thought it was a ghost. For a moment, I had believed in ghosts.

But it wasn't a ghost. Of course it wasn't. It was her. My sister.

Maybe she didn't misunderstand.

Maybe she wasn't trying to save me.

Maybe she was angry. I told her I wasn't going to come out to the forest at night anymore, but here I was. In our forest. At night. With strangers. I was worse than Savannah bringing boys to Myron's. Maybe she meant to punish me. I knew she'd be mad at me, when I said I couldn't run every night, but I'd never thought—

I hadn't thought—

"Oh man," says Savannah beside me. She turns big eyes on me, the mascara streaked beneath them, so it looks like she has two black eyes. "We are so fucked."

The walk feels longer on the way back, though we hurry. I make Savannah take the flashlight. Under the cover of dark, I clamp a hand over my wrist, squeezing tight, gritting my teeth. The bleeding stops, but the pain does not. It feels far off, though, almost like it doesn't belong to me—the numbing effect of whatever was in the Mountain Dew bottle. We reach the road, stand on the shoulder long enough for Savannah to say how fucked we are a few more times, and then the ambulance is there, a storm of flashing lights.

I feel as though I'm watching all this on TV: the EMTs placing Henry onto a stretcher, sliding him into the back of the ambulance like a tray into the oven; one of the EMTS lowering an oxygen mask onto Henry's face, the other pushing a needle into the crook of his elbow; Henry's eyes fluttering open; Savannah trying to cling to Jack's arm, Jack pushing her away.

A cop car goes whooping past. It brakes hard and swerves over to park just in front of Jack's car. Two cops get out. This isn't a dream. Isn't magic. This counts.

"What do we tell them?" asks Savannah. Her eyes meet mine for a moment. She looks scared. My gaze drifts down to my left sleeve. The blood that soaked through is dried now, barely visible against the black fabric.

"Tell 'em the truth," says Jack.

I run and leap up into the back of the ambulance. Before anyone can stop me, I crouch beside Henry. He looks up at me, eyes wide and wet as egg yolks. I'm happy to see him awake. He's fine. He'll be fine.

"It was a wolf," I tell him. He saw her. He must have. For an instant, before she knocked him over. I don't know if he'll remember, don't know if anyone would believe him. "Or a dog. A big dog. It attacked you. I tried to stop it."

"Get her out of there!" shouts one of the EMTs. The next moment I'm being pulled backward, an EMT gripping one of my

43

arms, Jack the other. The doors of the ambulance are being pulled shut. Jack is climbing into the passenger seat.

I can see through the little window in the back door like a TV screen. Henry glows in the middle of it all. The ambulance screams away.

Then it's just me and Savannah and the two cops, one old, one young. I recognize the older one. He's come into the bar a few times, gotten raging drunk and ranted at length to anyone who will listen about how Lester cops are only paid eight bucks an hour and there aren't enough of them and yet everyone acts like it's their fault that there are still meth houses sprouting around town like dandelions on untended lawns, and heroin trickling down from the cities to fill the gaps left by prescription painkillers that got too pricey. How would you feel, he'd like to know, if everyone treated you like scum until suddenly they needed you?

I clasp my hands behind my back, to hide my wrist. Savannah reaches for my right arm and I let her grab it, let her squeeze it too hard. I know how she feels about the police. Her family is huge (Aggie likes to say that half the town is related to Savannah), so even though her mom stays resolutely on the right side of the law, they still have to deal with cops pounding on their door at all hours, looking for uncles or cousins who don't.

"Okay," says the older cop. "Names?" He pulls a notepad out of his pocket. The younger cop is squinting at Savannah.

"You used to date my sister," Savannah blurts out.

"What?" says the older cop.

"She means me," says the younger cop.

"That true, Jake?"

"Yeah."

"Well, it's a small world."

"There was a wolf," I say quickly, "or maybe a dog. Maybe a German shepherd or something. Or one of those half-wolves that people have, you know? Maybe it was somebody's guard dog or something and it got loose. It came out of nowhere and it knocked him down and there was nothing I could do."

"Now, just slow down there, darling," says the older cop. "I haven't even got your name yet."

"Jolene" I say. "Jolene Richards."

He makes a show of writing it on his pad.

"Are we under arrest?" asks Savannah.

"Jolene Richards," says the cop. "That's ringing a real bell. I book you before?"

"No."

"Well, there's a first time for—" he stops, looking past me, into the woods. I feel a wave of dread.

No. She wouldn't.

I whip around, follow the cop's gaze into the dark, but there's nothing there.

"Oh," says the cop. "Right."

"What?" asks Jake.

"It's nothing," says the older cop. "I'll tell you later."

I realize then. It wasn't nothing.

He recognized my name because it's the same as my mother's.

Our family was never very creative when it came to naming kids, so my grandparents Margaret and Joe named one daughter Margaret (Aggie for short) and the other Jolene. When I showed up, everyone just called me "Jolene's baby" until the second part was no longer true.

When we were little, my sister had trouble saying my name. The closest she would come to Jolene was "Leelee," which was close enough. And I'd call her Lee. Like an echo of me.

As far as I know, that's the only name my sister has.

This cop is more than old enough to remember Mama's case, to have worked on it. Her disappearance was a big deal. Her murder. People still talk about how the cops should have tried harder, how it was a crying shame that they were never able to pin it on the Cantrell boys in a way that would stick. In the beginning, some people thought Mama might have just run away. But as time wore on with no sign of her and, to hear them tell it, all kinds of strange things going on up at the Cantrells' trailer, they made up their minds. A few people think Brandon might have been the one who killed Mama, rather than his brother. He's the one who brought me into town, after all, and his story kept changing. Most people think that, at the very least, he helped.

Logan Cantrell got put away anyway, four years later, for possession, trafficking, and "engaging in a pattern of corrupt activity," as part of a big drug bust in the area. He's been locked up nearly my whole life, so I've never met him. Never wanted to, either, knowing what he did to Mama. As far as I'm concerned, I don't have a father, not really. Just Mama and Aggie. That's enough.

From what I've heard, Brandon skipped town not long after Logan's arrest, abandoned their double-wide trailer at the top of the ridge. Ran off to who knows where.

There's a rustling in the underbrush nearby and the older cop flinches. He's thinking of glowing eyes maybe, teeth red with blood.

"I think it's still out there," I say, trying to sound scared, Savannah's trick. The noise was probably just a possum or something, but the cop seems rattled.

"Maybe you better get on the horn," he says to Jake. "Call in animal services." He turns back to us, looking embarrassed. "All right, why don't we all just go sit in the car and you can tell us what happened and then we'll get you gals home."

When Savannah tells her part of the story she leaves out the joint, of course, leaves out the Mountain Dew bottle. I'm sure the cops can tell we've been drinking, but if they tried to crack down on underage drinking around here my guess is they'd run out of room in the cells after half a day. Savannah claims that she and Jack were "looking for ghosts" on the other side of the creek. She says she heard me scream and came running. Says she doesn't know what happened. The cop writes it all down.

"You girls ought to be more careful," he says finally. "You shouldn't be wandering around at night. It isn't safe." He gives us a patronizing smile and then he turns around and starts the car while I fume, silently.

People always think teenage girls are stupid, or naive. Like we are fawns wandering out onto the highway, like we don't know about the things people out there want to do to us, like we aren't steeped in that shit from the moment we hit adolescence. Before that, even. We know. I know. Aggie and Margaret made sure of it. Your body is a bomb, a trap, a constant danger to yourself and others.

But what am I supposed to do? Walk around thinking about it every moment? Never leave the house? Wrap my whole body up in caution tape, in chains?

People would say Mama was evidence enough that you should. But that's bullshit. What happened to her wasn't her fault.

And if she was as wild as people say, then she wouldn't want me to hide. She'd want me to enjoy myself, wouldn't she? She probably had nights like this all the time. Well, the first part anyway.

As futile as it is, as dumb and sentimental, the truth is that I want more than anything in this world to make Mama proud.

Savannah and I don't speak during the ride. She won't even look at me, just stares out the window. I stare out my window, too, clutch my aching wrist to my side. When we reach Savannah's house, the older cop gets out of the car to knock on her front door. Jake twists around to check on us.

"Aren't you going to go say hi to Dakota?" asks Savannah. "She's single again, you know."

Jake twists back around quick. Savannah sneers at the back of his head. The older cop is walking across the lawn. He's almost at the car, when Savannah suddenly leans across the seat and whispers in my ear.

"You're lying," she says. "I know you are."

And then the older cop is opening the door and grabbing Savannah's arm. He's leading her away and there's nothing I can do.

Aggie comes running out of Joe's Bar the moment we pull up, tipped off by Savannah's mother no doubt. Savannah's mom has probably told half the town by now, honestly, knowing her. Aggie must have been waiting by the window, peering out through the neon signs. *Blue Moon. Bud Light. On Tap. All Night.*

A small crowd of drinkers pours out of the bar after her, craning their necks to see what the fuss is about. The pastor is one of them. He's standing behind Aggie, his arm outstretched, touching her shoulder in a way that could pass, I guess, as simply comforting.

The older cop gets out and talks to Aggie, but her eyes remain fixed on the car where I'm sitting. I try to sink down into the seat, below her line of sight. Eventually the cop comes over and opens the door and I have no choice but to get out. I only make it a few steps before Aggie's got her arms around me, squeezing too hard.

"Don't you ever lie to me like that again," she says into my hair.

"Sorry," I mumble.

She lets go of me then, hauls back, and slaps me across the face. The pain is sharp, shocking. Almost as bad as the bite. I put my hand to my cheek, tears springing to my eyes, too surprised to do more than stare at her.

A funny look crosses her face. She's never hit me like that before, like her mother does, and she's sorry. I can tell. The look is only there for a second and then she's grabbing my hand, the right one luckily, leading me into the bar like I'm a baby. Jessi the bartender looks up as we pass, starts to say something, but Aggie marches right past her and into the narrow kitchen. She pushes me into the folding chair next to the sink.

"I've got to square things out there," she says, voice tight. "Don't you move."

She goes back into the bar. I stare at the speckled black floor tiles and test out different answers to the questions she hasn't asked yet. When she comes back, I don't give her a chance. I just launch right into it.

"Savannah was feeling sick," I say, "so we walked over to the gas station to get her some ginger ale and Jack Bickle was there and he said he'd give us a ride home but he took us to his house instead and he said beer was better than ginger ale for an upset stomach and I wanted to come home but I couldn't just leave Savannah, you know? I had to watch out for her."

Aggie frowns, but she wants to believe me, I can tell. She grabs my wrist, the left one this time—the bite marks are hidden by my sleeve—and I yelp in pain, but she doesn't let go. She jerks me off the chair and up the back stairs.

In the old days, when Grandpa Joe was alive, the first floor of the bar was for sitting or playing pool, and the second was for dancing. The town had more people back then, but the population has been declining steadily for years, according to Aggie, so while we do enough business to get by, there's no need for so much space. When we moved out of Margaret's house, the year I turned nine, Aggie converted the second floor of the bar into an apartment. We keep our sofa and TV on the little wooden stage where bands once played. Our bathroom still has a urinal on the wall. Aggie keeps a plastic plant in it so guests won't be tempted.

She steers me toward the bathroom now.

"Can I call—" I start, thinking maybe I can check in with Savannah, find out how her mother reacted, see if she's heard anything about Henry yet.

Ask what the hell she meant by *You're lying, I know you are.*

"No." Aggie cuts me off, her tone leaving no room for argument. "Shower. Don't dawdle."

When I take my shirt off in the bathroom, the left sleeve sticks to the drying blood on my wrist. I yank it free and the bite starts bleeding again. I rinse the sleeve and the wound in the shower, swallow my pain. It hurts worse now than it did in the woods. I try to think about track, about running, those moments when all your muscles are screaming at you to stop, to rest, but you push through it. This is just a different kind of pain. I can push through it.

When I come out of the bathroom wrapped in a towel, hiding my wrist under my bundled clothes, Aggie shoves my pajamas at me and pushes me to my bedroom. It's a room that didn't use to exist. The walls are thin, put up quick by the guys Aggie hired to renovate. We moved in earlier than Aggie had planned, before construction on the rooms was done. We had to camp downstairs in sleeping bags for weeks.

Aggie and Grandma Margaret had always argued, but in the months leading up to the move, it got worse and worse, until one morning Aggie woke me up at dawn and said, *We're leaving, Jo. Come on, pack quick.* The night before, they'd had one of their big screaming, throwing-things fights. The fight was about God. I could hear it all from my bedroom, even with a pillow over my head, Aggie shouting, *How can you stand there and tell me to just have faith after what happened? No, go on, you tell me where the hell your goddamn guardian angels were for my baby sister? You go on and tell me where the hell was your God?* And then Grandma Margaret saying, *She turned her back on him. She turned her back.* And then a glass breaking and a door slamming so hard it shook the whole house.

"Go to sleep," says Aggie, before she closes my door. "I'll deal with you tomorrow."

I lie awake listening to the murmur of the drinkers downstairs, feeling sick. I'm used to sneaking dregs of beer in the bar, but whatever was in that Mountain Dew bottle was strong. I can feel it sloshing around in my stomach even now. All the pleasant, numbing effects are wearing off, leaving only the poison.

All I can think about is what I left out of the story I told Aggie. Who I left out.

Henry.

Henry Henry Henry.

He's fine, right? He opened his eyes. His heart was still going.

He's probably already sitting up in a hospital bed, smiling, brushing off jokes from Jack about what a baby he is, what an absolute girl. He's probably laughing, probably saying—

Saying what? That a girl in a dirty blue dress came out of the woods and attacked him? A girl who looks a lot like me? Almost exactly like me.

It's too much to expect that he told my lie. He was barely conscious. Will he even remember what I said? If he does, what will he think of me?

Even if Henry does lie, a doctor can probably tell the difference between a wolf bite and a human bite. Our teeth are different shapes. What the hell was I thinking?

I'm out of bed almost before I realize what I'm doing. I'm pulling on jeans and a hoodie, wincing as the fabric brushes my left wrist. I'm easing the window open. I left my sister out of the story, too, but I always leave her out.

I don't know where I'm going. The hospital is twenty miles away, in Delphi. Even if I knew how to get there, it would take me hours on foot. I don't have a plan. It's all too much, the weight of what happened pressing down on me, and I need to get out. Need to run. Run until I no longer feel anything.

I'm swinging my leg over the sill, when the clouds part and sunlight strikes me.

Except that makes no sense.

It's the middle of the night. The sky in the distance is pitch black.

I look up, and there, bolted to the side of the building where before there was nothing, is one of those motion sensor lamps people put over their garages.

I freeze, half in, half out, straddling the windowsill, and blink away the ghosts.

CHAPTER FIVE

The summer after Aggie and I moved into the bar, my sister would sneak into town some nights. She was reluctant at first, but I convinced her slowly, meeting her in the deep woods by Margaret's house and leading her a little farther each time, keeping to the dark streets around the edges of town. After a few weeks, she grew confident enough to come into town on her own. When I snuck out, I'd meet up with her in the abandoned building three doors over. We would play a game of staying in the shadows, skirting the edges of the streetlights.

I had a plan, that summer. I'd given up on the idea that Lee could ever live with me and be a normal girl. But maybe there was a way to compromise. I'd started stashing supplies, bought with my allowance, on the second floor of the abandoned building. I thought I could make a secret home for her there. The upstairs windows were bricked up, so no one would see her. She could sleep during the day still, but with a roof over her head instead of leaves. We'd set trip wires around the perimeter to guard against junkies (there were some needles on the first floor, but they looked old, half-buried in the dirt and weeds). She'd be close to me. I could protect her.

Maybe eventually, when she got comfortable, I could bring Savannah to see her. Maybe even Aggie, if I could get her to swear on the memory of Grandpa Joe that she'd keep my secret safe.

The plan didn't work out, of course, and the freedom of that summer didn't last. Still, it was thrilling while it did. Sometimes, when my sister and I crept down an alleyway, a light on someone's garage would snap on suddenly and then we'd run like hell and hide, as if the light were chasing us. Crouched under a bush, I would laugh and my sister's eyes would shine.

But in the window I'm caught. Usually I wait until the bar is closed before I sneak out. Our street is mostly empty storefronts, so it's pretty dead after two a.m. Tonight, though, I didn't wait. I can still hear, faintly, the music from downstairs.

And there's a spotlight shining right on me.

I hold my breath, as if that will make me invisible. The motion sensor's timer runs out and the light clicks off. I feel a rush of relief, but really I'm no better off than I was before.

I take a deep breath, swing my leg over the sill and hop onto the slats of the fire escape. The light snaps back on.

"Jolene," says the pastor.

He's in my room, by the door, barely a shadow. I didn't even hear him come in. I take a step back, away from the window.

The pastor crosses the room in a few quick strides, holds out his hand. "Come back inside," he says.

I don't move. His fingers are in the open window. I could slam the frame down and run.

"If you don't," he says, "I will have to go get Aggie."

I stare at his hand. If I were my sister, I would pull out my folding knife and stab him right in the life line. Although who knows, maybe he'd love that. His own personal stigmata. He'd probably go around making people touch the wound. Stick their fingers down inside. Feel the Holy Spirit move.

"And," says the pastor, voice calm and even, "I will call the police. I doubt they'll be pleased, having to come back here so soon."

Defeated, I climb through the window, ignoring his hand. He shuts the window behind me, latches it.

"I need to find out if Henry is okay," I say. I don't know how much the pastor knows already. "He got hurt. They took him to the hospital."

"And what," says the pastor, "you were going to *run* there?"

I shrug.

"Jolene," he says, and I hate the sound of that name in his mouth. Jolene is Mama. I'm just Jo. "You are running headlong down the wrong path right now."

"Fuck you," I say. It tumbles out before I can stop it, but the pastor just frowns. I stomp over to where I left my pajamas in a heap on the floor.

"I want to help you," says the pastor. He's still standing by the window, leaning against the sill, blocking it, as if he thinks I'll make another run for it. "Your mother didn't have anyone to help her," he says.

"Stop it," I say. "Stop talking about her. You didn't even know her. You weren't even—"

"I did," he says, cutting me off. "I knew her."

"No you didn't." How can he even say that? Is he trying to make me mad? "You only came to town like two years ago."

"I came *back* to town. I'm from here, Jo. You really didn't know that?"

I didn't.

But why should I? I hate the guy.

Grandma Margaret hates him too. Says he's all show. Says his idea of preaching in bars to reach the sinners on their own turf is just an excuse to drink on the job. If she knew about the pastor and Aggie she'd probably drop dead on the spot.

Maybe that's why Aggie is dating him. Maybe she didn't get a chance to rebel properly when she was my age—Mama was rebellious enough for both of them—so she's doing it now. It makes no sense otherwise. Aggie and the pastor are opposites in every way.

"Fine, whatever. I'm going to bed," I say, shaking my pajamas out.

"I saw what happened to her," the pastor says. "What her choices led to. It would break Aggie's heart if she thought you were headed the same way."

Can he really have known Mama? I look at him, really look at him. He's got this doughy kind of face, boyish. Always clean-shaven. I know he's a few years younger than Aggie, which I guess puts him around the same age as Mama.

"It would break Aggie's heart," he goes on, "if she knew you were trying to climb out your bedroom window on the very same night the cops brought you home."

He's made his point already. He's just rubbing it in, the righteous asshole.

"Don't tell her, then," I snap.

"I won't," he says.

"You won't?" I wasn't expecting that.

"If you agree to my conditions."

Ah, right. I feel another *fuck you* hovering on the tip of my tongue, but I bite it back.

"If you tell on me I'll just tell everyone in town about you," I say. "You and Aggie."

Maybe if I do, I'll get lucky and Grandma Margaret will come by with her shotgun.

He shrugs. "Go ahead. I don't care who knows."

Bullshit. "Why are you always sneaking around then?"

"It's for Aggie." He pushes himself up from the window. "She doesn't want people to talk."

Is he bluffing? I honestly can't tell. Aggie has always been really private about her personal life. It's funny, because she's a terrible gossip when it comes to other people's business. Maybe that's why she keeps secrets herself.

Or maybe it's because of Mama.

Everyone in town knows about Mama. Knows what happened. Whispers about it. When they look at me sometimes I can see their thoughts as clearly as if they were written on their foreheads. *Isn't it just too tragic, what happened to her mother? But then again, that girl always was a wild one. We all saw it coming. Oh yes, she had it coming. Better hope this little apple fell a long way from that tree.*

Well, whatever. They can all go to hell. None of them really knew Mama. And none of them know me.

The pastor strides toward me. I back up. My hands grope at my bedside table, close over a hairbrush, but the pastor stops a few feet away, with the bed between us.

"I am going to help you, Jo," he says. "I am on your side."

"You are definitely not."

"I am," he says. "I swear. I'll see what I can find out about your friend, let you know as soon as I hear anything. But that's exactly what I'm talking about. The kind of reckless behavior you are engaging in isn't safe. I'm trying to help you."

I open my mouth to tell him where he can shove his so-called help, but then I stop.

This is exactly what he wants, isn't it? The little lost lamb running straight into the jaws of the wolf, so intent on doing wrong that the shepherd has no choice but to break its legs. It's the story he's trying to write me into. His story. And I'm playing the role he's written for me to perfection.

"Fine," I say, "I don't care. I'm going to sleep." I swallow my hate and lie down on the bed, still in my jeans and hoodie. I cross my arms, close my eyes, pretend the pastor isn't there. I'll wait. I'll write my own damn story, one without him in it at all.

"May the angels watch over you always," he says, before he leaves. "May they never let you out of their sight."

I wake to a pounding headache and Aggie banging on my bedroom door.

"I'm up!" I shout. "I'm up."

I ooze my way slowly out of bed. If I turn my head too fast I swear I can feel my brain slamming against my skull. Flashes of last night, each one worse than the last, come back to me.

Lee. Running, trailing her ripped lace. Does she have any idea how close she came to being caught?

I inspect my left wrist in the morning light. It's red and so swollen that I can no longer make out the bite marks. The skin, when I gently prod it with my finger, is hot as a summer sidewalk. I pull on my baggiest top: a gray 3XL Lester Middle School Track and Field hoodie that my coach ordered by accident. The sleeves are long enough that only the tips of my fingers are visible.

Out in the kitchen, Aggie's making pancakes. I don't remember her ever making pancakes before. She's even humming. The smell of burnt oil fills the whole second floor. Smoke sizzles up from the cast iron pan.

It reminds me of when we first moved here and she'd cook for us downstairs in the bar kitchen. It was just me and her, back then. I thought of her as old, the way kids think of all grown-ups, but she was only in her twenties. She'd never lived on her own before, never had the money to afford it, so those first weeks were thrilling for both of us, like an endless sleepover, free of Margaret's supervision. Aggie would fry mozzarella sticks and onion rings for dinner. She let me eat maraschino cherries straight out of the jar. She was more like a big sister than a parent. We would stay up all night. Watch late-night reruns, gossip about the patrons of the bar.

Aggie would tell me about her childhood, about Grandpa Joe taking her out to hunt deer. How much she loved it. She told me how she'd been called a tomboy all her life, how nobody thought she was pretty, unlike her sister (and her voice got tight when she said that word and she looked away and I thought she'd cry), but *Let me tell you, Jo,* she'd said, *being pretty is overrated. You know what happened to all the pretty girls in my school? They had babies and got married and they spend their days running around cleaning up after their kids and husbands and nobody cares if they were pretty once. Don't try to be pretty, Jo. Better to be tough. Better to be hard and smart. Better to be free.*

I miss it, miss how Aggie used to be, before the pastor came along. She's been different since they started seeing each other.

She's distracted. She doesn't have time for me, and even when she does, she acts less like a sister and more like a mom.

I know exactly whose fault that is.

The pastor's sitting in his now-usual spot at the card table. There's a fleck of shaving cream on his neck, which means he must have shaved this morning in *our* bathroom. I bet there'll be tiny dark hairs all over the sink, clinging to the faucet, stuck in the grouting.

I sit. Aggie slides a plate with two lopsided pancakes on it in front of me, and as she leans down I notice a reddish blotch on her neck. The same kind Savannah is always so proud of, making a point to swish her hair, tug at the neck of her shirt, show it off.

Aggie has a hickey.

"I feel sick," I say. The pancakes are slightly burnt. They've got chocolate chips in them, but those are even more burnt, lodged like little black coal deposits in the lumpy pancake hills.

"I'm sure you do," says Aggie. She plunks a mug of black coffee on the table in front of me so forcefully that some of it sloshes onto my plate and soaks into the pancakes. "That's what they call a hangover. Serves you right."

I guess the cops told on us for drinking. Or else she could smell it on me when I came home.

"Have you heard anything about Henry?" I ask. "Is he okay?"

Aggie exchanges a glance with the pastor and my stomach drops. Surely he can't be . . .

"I made some calls," the pastor says. "Sounds like the kid'll be just fine."

He shoves a whole pancake into his mouth, smiles at me, cheeks puffed out. Aggie has turned back to the stove. She slops more batter into the pan. I push my plate away.

"Can I call Savannah now?" I ask.

"Go get dressed," Aggie says, without turning around. "The pastor is going to take you to Saturday-morning Bible study."

"Bible study?" No way I just heard those words come out of Aggie's mouth.

When Aggie and I still lived with Grandma Margaret, God was always this tug-of-war between them: Margaret trying to get me to say *thank you, Jesus* before each meal, Aggie cutting in loudly to say, *Thank you, cow who died to make this burger, thank you, Fred who works the meat counter at the Kroger, don't fill her head with nonsense, Ma, that's what you did with the two of us and see how that turned out.*

"Yes," says Aggie, "and don't even try to wriggle out of it. You earned this." So it's a punishment. In the old days she never punished me.

The pastor grins at me. This was his idea, obviously He must have talked Aggie into it. Go die in a fire, I think. I picture it, the flames licking up the sides of his face, fake silk jacket dripping off his back, skin bubbling.

"You going to eat those?" he asks. I shake my head, too full of hate to speak, and he reaches over with his fork, steals a soggy bite.

I reluctantly follow the pastor, dragging my feet and kicking at stones on the pavement, over to Minnie's Home Cooking, which is just two blocks from the bar, down Main Street. It's a short building, sandwiched between the old Elks Club and a pile of rubble that used to be a lawyer's office. Inside, the ceiling sags and the floor bulges in the middle, the gray-blue carpet rumpled up like waves. The walls are lined with old photos of Lester from when the mines were still open.

Savannah and I used to come here after school sometimes. It costs a dollar seventy-five for a grilled cheese sandwich, crisp and buttery. Seventy-five cents for a side of fries.

I wish Savannah were here with me now, instead of the pastor. Last night was stupid, yes, reckless. But this is too cruel a punishment.

Minnie's is packed. People turn to look at me as I pass. Do I look that bad? Or have they heard about last night? I hope not. I keep my head down, pretend I don't notice them. The pastor and I sit at a table beneath a photo of Lester during the 1907 flood.

"We're a little early," he says. "You want some pie?"

The day's flavors are on a whiteboard by the counter: key lime, chocolate cream, peanut butter, peach. I wish I could say yes, but I know he's just trying to bribe me.

"I don't like pie," I say, which is perhaps the biggest lie I've ever told.

"Suit yourself." The pastor waves the waitress—Lacey, one of Minnie's daughters—over and orders a slice of key lime.

"You getting anything?" Lacey asks me. She's friends with Savannah's older sister, so she knows me.

"I'll have a root beer," I say.

"Sure thing, wolf girl," says Lacey, with an exaggerated smile, before she swishes away.

I dig my fingernails into my palms, force my expression to stay neutral. So she's heard about last night. Heard the details, even. The bite on Henry's neck. My lie about the wolf.

Everybody's probably heard. The whole damn town.

Who told them? Jack? Savannah? What about Henry? Did he say what I told him to? Does he remember seeing Lee? Did he tell anyone about her? I don't know what I'd do, if my secret got out. The pastor clears his throat.

I close my eyes. I want to open them and be back in the woods two nights ago, running through the forest with my sister, letting all the pointless daytime things go streaming out of my head like so much smoke. Out there, at night, it all seems like nothing. Electric lights, math books, judgmental people, closed doors. There's no use for any of them. The trees are spreading their arms wide. The sky is limitless, dark and full of stars.

I open my eyes. The pastor has pulled a thick gold book from his bag.

"You ever read any of this?" he asks.

"Of course," I snap. He probably thinks I'm some ignorant little heathen who just needs to be shown the light. But I've had plenty of exposure to religion in my life.

"Apologies," he says. "I wasn't sure." Grandma Margaret bought me an illustrated Bible for my fifth birthday. I can still remember the watercolor painting of Noah's ark. Cheery little blob animals lined up on the deck. The broad blue-green swoop of the waves. And in the foreground, sticking up from the water, so small that anybody who wasn't looking real close would probably miss it: a hand.

Grandma Margaret's version of religion was like that picture. Sunlight and happiness and God's love if you followed all the rules, if you were the right kind of person. But the ones who didn't make it on that boat? They didn't matter. They deserved what was coming to them.

I understand why Aggie wants no part of it. She raised me

to be skeptical, tried to provide a counterbalance to Margaret's dogma. It was hard to have much of an opinion on my own, caught between the two of them.

"Aggie says it's all lies," I tell the pastor. Her atheism's got to be a sore spot, right? Maybe if I press it hard enough I can make him suffer as much as I'm suffering. "She says a bunch of dumb old men wrote it."

The pastor flinches a little. I silently congratulate myself.

Aggie dating the pastor is the height of hypocrisy. She hates religion, hates women who throw away everything in the pursuit of romance, who change themselves for a man. I desperately hope she hasn't started to believe any of the things the pastor preaches about, hope he doesn't have that kind of power over her, hope that it's just a fling and it will burn itself out.

I've been hoping that since the beginning of summer, though.

"If you think you're going to convert her or something you're crazy," I tell the pastor. "Aggie wouldn't believe in God if he showed up in the bar and ordered a double scotch on the rocks."

The pastor is flipping through the pages of the gold Bible. His face has gone a little red. I am running imaginary victory laps around the smug bastard.

"You know," he says, not looking up, "your Mama and me used to go to Bible study together."

"Yeah, right," I say. I know what he's up to. He's just trying to get a rise out of me, the same way I was doing to him.

"It's true. With Pastor Nelson. In his living room. We all had to kneel on the floor for ten minutes at the end while he led prayer. He had hardwood floors. Not even an area rug. Thought pain was good for the soul or something. Jolene, though, she would wait until he closed his eyes, then she'd pull off her cardigan and use it as a cushion. When the prayer was almost done, she'd sneak it back on before the pastor noticed."

I can't help myself, I'm imagining it. Mama kneeling there on her sweater, smiling beatifically while the other kids stare.

"She was really quite devout," the pastor goes on. "Came every week. She knew this book backward and forward." He shakes the Bible in front of him.

"That doesn't sound like her," I say, which is stupid, I know. I never met her, not really. But everybody says she was wild. Grandma Margaret calls her a sinner, says she had the devil in her. "She drank and smoked and hung out with a bad crowd. Everybody says so."

"People can be more than one thing," says the pastor.

If I'd been drinking something, I might have spit it out. I blink at him, uncomfortable with how close that is to how I feel about myself. A girl with a shadow side.

"Yeah," I say cautiously. "They can."

"She had this little silver cross necklace," he goes on. "She told me once that she never took that necklace off, even at night. Even in the shower."

He stares down at the open Bible in his hands. I realize I am leaning forward in my chair and I force myself to sit back, hating myself for my own eagerness, for how much I want to believe him.

I'm trying to remember if Mama had on a cross necklace in the pictures I've seen. I haven't seen many. Grandma Margaret ripped all the photos of Mama out of the family albums. But once I snuck down into the basement and rooted around in the dusty cardboard boxes until I found an envelope with a newspaper clipping and a few snapshots. I wanted to keep them all, but I was worried that Grandma Margaret would find out and punish me, so I only kept one, Mama's sophomore photo, the same one they reproduced in the papers when she went missing. I hid it behind some peeling wallpaper in my room. I used to look at it every night before I went to sleep. Used to talk to it.

"The last time I saw her," the pastor says, "she was wearing it then, too."

I guess he figured out that this is the way to get to me. Not threats, not pie.

"When was the last time you saw her?" I ask. I'm giving in, I know, taking the bait, but I have to know. If there's even a chance that he's telling the truth, I want every last scrap. I'd give in to the devil himself for that kind of knowledge.

"It was outside Pastor Nelson's house," he says. "About two weeks before . . . well, before what happened. We hadn't seen her for months, not since it came out that she was pregnant, but she showed up to study and she wanted us to pray for her."

"Did you?" I'm so far forward on my chair I'm in danger of falling.

"No," says the pastor, quietly. "He turned her away. That motherfucker wouldn't even let her in the house." In all the months he's been coming to the bar, skulking around our apartment before dawn, I don't think I've ever heard the pastor curse. For a second, it's like all his artifice falls away—his stupid shiny jacket, his vintage car, his fire and brimstone—and he's just a person.

A person who knew Mama. Who knelt with her, once a week. There was real emotion in his voice when he spoke about her just now, and I believe him. Lacey comes over, plunks a root beer in a tall red glass in front of me, slides a slice of pie to the pastor. I avoid her eyes.

I don't know what to say now, what to think. I lift my root beer glass, sip it slow. The light through the red plastic makes the ice at the bottom of the cup look like rubies. The pastor digs his fork into the pie, takes a bite.

I think maybe I hate him even more now.

He knew Mama. I never will.

"Hey, Butch," says the pastor to an old man with wispy hair and blotchy skin who has shuffled over to our table. "Take a seat. This is Jolene."

"Jo," I say, correcting him.

Butch takes the chair next to me. He and the pastor chat about the halfway house over in Needle where Butch is staying. The rest of the Bible study group shows up shortly after. One of them, Sheila, is a regular at the bar. She's always deeply tan, and she dyes her hair icy blond, which gives her a sort of reverse-negative look. Aggie doesn't like her much; says she dresses like a teenager. Though you can't really win with Aggie. She hates the women who wear girlie clothes, fitted baby doll tees, too much makeup, but she's just as angry at the women who she thinks have given up, whose oversized T-shirts have holes in the pits, who let their stomachs loll over the bands of their sweatpants. It's hypocritical, since Aggie thinks women shouldn't be judged by their looks. But Aggie *is* a hypocrite. Shacking up with the pastor proves that. Aggie herself dresses a lot like Grandpa Joe in the pictures I've seen of him. Worn jeans and work shirts. That's one thing that hasn't changed since she started seeing the pastor, at least.

The pastor opens the gold Bible to a page with a blue Post-it note and reads us a passage about the devil trying to tempt Jesus in the desert. Jesus refuses the devil's temptations and then some angels show up and then the pastor turns to us and says, "So what can this story teach us?"

Sheila is chewing on her fake nails. Butch pokes at his pie crumbs with a fork.

"Just say no," I suggest.

"You bring up a great point there, Jo," says the pastor.

"I do?" I can't tell if he's calling me out on my sarcasm or if he's oblivious.

"Brother and sisters," says the pastor. He's really pouring it on, holding his hands out to the sides, palms up, like he's testing for rain. "The devil is not some ancient figure, not some myth, some symbol. The devil is alive in these hills. Alive and well. The devil lives in glass pipes. The devil lives in ground-up pills. Some of us at this very table have fought the devil. Some of us are fighting him still."

"Amen," says Butch, his voice like a cough.

"Jo?" says Savannah.

I whip around in my seat, and there she is. Standing a few feet from our table. She looks like hell, face puffy, eyes bleary and red, eyeliner applied so heavily that she might as well be in disguise as a raccoon.

I've never been so happy to see anyone in my life.

"I went by the bar," she says, "but Aggie said you were here."

"Savannah—" I say, but before I can get another word out, the pastor cuts me off.

"Excuse me, young lady," he says. "We're in the middle of something important here."

"Oh," says Savannah. She looks around the table, skeptical.

"You will have to wait." The pastor stares her down.

Savannah scowls, turns, trudges away. I face the pastor, eyes pleading.

"Can I just talk to her? Please? For like a minute? We won't go anywhere. We'll just be out front. Please? She's probably really upset about last night. I've got to talk to her. Please?"

Behind me, I hear the bell over the front door ding.

"Please," I say one last time, putting every ounce of desperation I can muster behind it.

"Fine," says the pastor. "Just for a few—"

But I'm already up and running.

I push through the front door and skid to a stop on the sidewalk. Savannah is leaning against the rough bricks of the Elks Club building next door with her phone out, texting.

"Who are you talking to?" I ask. She shoves her phone in her pocket.

"Jack." She's staring down at the ground.

"How is Henry? Have you heard anything?"

"He's okay."

"Okay?" That's good, I guess, but not enough. "Is he still in the hospital?"

Is he talking? I don't say, *Has he said anything? Said anything I wish he wouldn't?*

Savannah looks up at me, finally. Her eyes look even more bloodshot up close. She must be feeling pretty sick, too. She swigged way more Mountain Dew mystery drink than I did.

"What happened last night?" she asks. It sounds like an accusation.

I just stare. I'd been so excited to see her, I'd almost forgotten the last thing she said to me. *You're lying. I know you are.*

"Tell me what happened on the bridge," she says. "Tell me for real."

"I already told you." I pull the sleeve of my hoodie lower over my left wrist, force myself not to look away, though Savannah is glaring at me, nose wrinkled as though I am a smell that offends her.

"You're a liar," she says. "It wasn't a wolf."

"It might have been a dog," I say, desperate. "I don't know."

"No. It wasn't. I know it wasn't."

My heart sinks. A wolf is probably the stupidest lie I could have come up with, but I wasn't thinking straight last night. I remember Jack shouting, *What the hell did you do!* How did it look to the two of them, stumbling out of the woods on the other side of the bridge? Henry on his back, bloody. Me kneeling over him, touching his neck. My sister already gone. It must have looked bad. But Savannah should trust me, she should know I'd never do anything like that.

"Tell me what happened," she says. "Tell me the truth."

"I—" But what do I say?

Savannah turns away again, pulls out her phone, types furiously.

"Me and Henry kissed," I say.

"Really?" Savannah looks up, suddenly interested. I'm pulling the same trick as the pastor, offering her information I know she can't resist.

"Yeah. I made the first move, but he totally kissed me back. We almost French-kissed, even, but then we heard the ghost." My sister, actually. But that isn't the point. Savannah should be happy for me. She'd been rooting for this. If my sister hadn't ruined everything, we'd be celebrating right now.

"Yeah," says Savannah, wide-eyed, and I think it's working. She's back. My best friend. "We heard that too."

"And what were you two doing at the time?" I poke her in the arm, grinning.

"Doesn't matter." She looks away and just like that she's gone again. "Jack thinks you attacked Henry."

I let out an exasperated breath. Jack can shove a stick up his ass. "I didn't. You know I wouldn't."

"At the hospital they said the bite was from a person. Not an animal. Jack told me."

Well, shit.

"It wasn't me," I say, trying my hardest to sound like I'm telling the truth. Which I am, but I can hear how desperate I sound anyway. I should have come up with a different lie last night, but what could I have said? An escaped convict came running past? A crazed cannibal? "I swear."

"Then why won't you tell me what happened?"

I don't know how to answer that.

"I saw something," Savannah says flatly. "On the bridge."

I blink at her. I don't get it.

"There was someone else there," she says.

She tries to meet my eye, but this time I'm the one who looks away. I feel dizzy.

Savannah saw my sister.

"Who was it?" Savannah asks. She steps forward, puts a hand on my arm. She sounds less angry now, more pleading. "It can't have been a stranger or you wouldn't be lying about it. It's someone you know."

Someone I know. Yes. But how could I say, *Someone I've known nearly all my life.*

It was dark, right? So Savannah can't have seen her very well. And she just said she saw *some*one. Not a girl. Not a girl in a blue dress who looked like me. But still.

"Goddammit, Jo. Say something." Savannah's voice catches like she's going to cry.

I want to cry too. Or melt into a puddle. Or run and run and never stop. It was what I wanted to happen, all those years ago. But now I don't know what to think. I don't know what to say.

"I don't understand," she says. "Did you plan it? You and whoever that was? I thought you liked Henry."

"I do." My voice comes out very small.

"I thought you were my best friend." She actually is crying now, the tears mixing with her eyeliner, glistening like an oil spill.

"I am," I say. *Don't be stupid,* I want to say, but I'm on shaky ground here. I know I am. How do I make her understand, make her forgive me, without telling the truth?

Savannah shakes her head, wipes roughly at her eyes. She seems about to speak again, when her gaze shifts to something behind me. She waves.

I turn around.

Up the block, Jack is cutting across the street, heading right for us.

He must be the one Savannah was texting. She must have told him I was here.

I turn back to her. She's avoiding my eyes, dabbing at her makeup with her sleeve. She's trying to look casual, but I've known her for too long. She's got the same look in her eyes she had last night. She's scared.

"Hey!" shouts Jack from behind me.

I turn to face him.

"How is Henry?" I ask as he stomps over. He doesn't answer, just barrels forward so fast I'm sure he's going to hit me. I want to stand my ground, but I still remember how much it hurt when Aggie hit me last night. And that was Aggie, who loves me. I stumble backward, bump into the wall of the Elks Club, but Jack stops short, with barely a foot of air between us, his hands clenched into fists at his sides.

"Psycho bitch," he says, and I feel flecks of spit hitting my face. I need to remain calm. Be the bigger person. I am innocent. Falsely accused. A martyr. And Savannah needs to see who the real monster is. Him. Not me. "You stay away from my brother."

"I didn't hurt him," I say, more to her than to him. "I swear I didn't."

"Well, it weren't no fucking wolf," Jack says. He's not that much taller, but it still feels as though he's towering over me. He's so close I can smell his sweat, practically feel the heat off his body. My heart pounds, no matter how much I try to calm it through sheer force of will. I want to shrink away, to run, but my back is against the wall. Savannah's just standing there, looking down at her feet again.

"Henry knows it wasn't me," I say, though I don't know if that's true.

I try to step sideways, but Jack slams his right hand against the bricks by my shoulder. Hard. So hard I think it must have hurt him, but his expression remains the same.

"You're a fucking liar," he says, leaning in. His face is so close to mine I can't even focus on it. When I try, his eyes blur into one monstrous cyclops eye.

"Okay," I say, breathing through my mouth to avoid the sour smoke smell of his breath. I hold my left arm behind my back, to hide my wrist. "It wasn't a wolf. But it wasn't me."

"Well, who the fuck was it then?" Jack leans back a little, thank goodness, though he's still got one arm stretched out, half a cage.

"It was—" I start, but of course I still don't have a good answer to that question. "It was someone else," I finish lamely.

"This is a fucking joke to you?" Jack asks.

"Savannah," I say, twisting as much as I can to look at her, "tell him it wasn't me. You know it wasn't—"

Jack reaches out and jams a big sweaty hand over my mouth to shut me up.

Which is just too much.

Rage flares fast and hot through my body. I nearly bite his hand, but even in the moment I can see how bad that would look, so instead I grab his shirt and yank my knee up hard, slamming it right into the space between his legs. That soft, vulnerable place. Like a bundle of beanbags. A bag of rotten fruit.

Jack roars, doubling over, hands clutching at his groin.

I lunge away.

A booming voice shouts, "Stop!" and there, pushing through the front door of Minnie's, is the goddamn pastor. Great timing. Just perfect.

He marches over, Sheila tagging along behind him. Jack's still clutching himself and groaning. The pastor gets right up in his face, putting himself physically between Jack and me.

"What's going on here?" demands the pastor.

Jack mumbles something about how I'm a raging psychotic c-word. I look desperately at Savannah. Did she hear that? Surely she can't let that stand. She's shuffled back toward the sidewalk, both hands shoved deep in her pockets. She won't look at me.

"Do I need to call the police?" asks the pastor.

"Go ahead," says Jack. "Have them arrest her." He lifts one hand from his crotch and points at me. "She attacked my brother. And me. You saw it. That bitch is crazy."

"I saw you trying to fight a young girl half your size," says the pastor, "and I saw her defend herself. Now, Jack Bickle, given your illustrious record with local law enforcement, I think it might be best if you just walk away."

Jack calls him a dickless piece of kiddie-diddling shit, but then he glances over at the front window of Minnie's Home Cooking. There are at least a dozen faces pressed up against it, watching him.

Watching me, too.

I wonder if this was how Mama felt when she was pregnant. Everybody in town staring at her, judging her. Sheila sidles over to me and puts a hand on my arm. Her fingernails are long as claws and painted a pale pink.

"You okay, honey?" she whispers. I shrug.

I'm not.

"Come on, Savannah," Jack says. "Let's go." He spits on the ground by my feet and strides away, brushing past Savannah on the sidewalk.

Savannah finally looks up at me. Our eyes meet. Please, I want to say, don't do this. But I can't speak. Her eyes slide away from mine. She turns and runs down the sidewalk after Jack.

My heart breaks.

CHAPTER SIX

I lost the picture of Mama that I used to talk to. I took it to the woods one night to show my sister.

"I've got a surprise for you," I told her.

"Chocolate?" she asked. The dress she wore back then was pink.

"Nope." I pulled the picture out of my pocket, held it out so she could see.

Lee took one look at it and then she snatched it out of my hands and ran.

I chased her for ages, but it was no use. I lost sight of her eventually. Gave up, exhausted. Sat down on a rock and cried.

I didn't know how to get home and I thought I might be doomed to die out there, but she came back. I tackled her to the ground, pawed at the pockets of her pink dress. The picture was gone. She'd stashed it. Wouldn't tell me where.

I chased her to the edge of Grandma Margaret's backyard.

"If you don't give it back," I shouted as she disappeared into the trees, "I'll tell on you!"

And I did. I told Grandma Margaret.

"My sister stole from me," I said.

"What have I told you about lying?" Grandma Margaret said. I was seven, I think. It had been a long time since I'd mentioned my sister to Margaret or Aggie. It had been a long time since I'd mentioned her to anyone.

"It's a sin," I said. "I know, but I'm not lying, I swear. My sister is real and she lives in the woods and she stole from me. Isn't stealing a sin too?"

I knew it was risky, knew I might get slapped or spanked or worse, but I was too furious to care. I wanted to punish Lee, the worst way I knew how.

Grandma Margaret sipped her coffee. "Yes," she said after a moment. "Stealing is a sin all right, so how about this. You tell your little imaginary friend that if she comes near you again, I'll shoot her right in the heart."

"She's not imaginary," I said, frustrated that she wasn't taking me seriously.

Margaret pushed her chair back from the table and left the room. I was worried she'd gone off to get a belt, but when she returned a minute later, she was holding her hunting rifle. She didn't point it at me, to my great relief. Instead, she crossed to the window that faced the backyard. She knelt, pushed the window open, braced her rifle against the sill.

She took aim and fired into the forest, again and again. My relief evaporated, replaced with cold terror.

The sound was deafening in the small room. I couldn't think over that sound, could hardly breathe. The windows rattled with the force of it. Later I would find the bullets, count them. Seventeen, each of them lodged squarely in the bark of a different tree. I cried then, when no one could see. I was sorry for telling on my sister. I knew I was lucky Margaret hadn't believed me. Lucky it was still light out.

"There," Margaret had told me, when she finally stopped shooting. The sudden silence rang out almost as loud as the shots had. "Your imaginary friend is dead now. I've killed her and she'll never steal again."

"This is a pretty special weekend, you know," the pastor tells me on our way back to the bar after Bible study. I don't know what the hell he's talking about and I don't much care. Jack came this close to punching me in the face and Savannah just stood there. That's almost as bad as not talking to me for two weeks. Whose side is she on?

"Sheila is going to be baptized tomorrow," the pastor says. I glance at Sheila, who's walking with us. She's beaming.

"I thought that was for babies," I say, half-heartedly.

"In some churches," says the pastor. "But in mine, we believe people need to choose."

A group of kids is hanging out on the steps of the old town hall down the street from Joe's Bar: Tanner, a girl named Lisa from the tenth grade, her little sister Katie, and a few others. Tanner's messing with a skateboard. Katie's kicking a rock around.

I would not describe myself as particularly well liked among people my own age. The opposite, actually. It's funny, when I'm with my sister I'm the talkative one, but the kids at school consider me almost freakishly quiet. A daydreamer. Sometimes they think I'm being rude. They think me being quiet means I don't like them, means I think I'm better than them. That's what Savannah tells me, anyway. She thinks I should make more of an effort.

But I can't relate to most of them and I don't want to pretend to care about the stupid stuff they care about. Who's dating or flirting with or cheating on who else. What some celebrity just did. It's not that I'm smarter or anything. I'm not that smart. Savannah's the smart one. Or she used to be. Before she got dumb on purpose. Now she is always having to pretend to be interested in idiotic stuff to please boys.

Having to pretend like I'm not her best friend.

I hope she was only pretending.

I try to keep my head down, but the group on the steps notice me. The noise of the skateboard and the rock stop abruptly. Have they heard about last night? How much have they heard? Are they staring? I look anywhere but at them. At the lone pickup truck trundling past. At the faded mural on the side of a brick building half choked by ivy. At the distant ridges that rise like great green walls all around us.

That's the one thing we do all have in common. Pretty much every kid I know is looking forward to the day when they can escape this place. Savannah dreams about moving to a city. She's always going on about her second cousin in Cincinnati. Other kids talk about heading up to Columbus or down to Delphi.

Me, though, I already escape every single night.

I walk faster, pushing ahead, leaving the pastor and Sheila behind, going as quickly as I can without actually running. Aggie must have seen us out the window, because she's waiting in the doorway of the bar. I'm nearly there when I hear a weird flapping sound behind me. I turn, tensing, half expecting to see Jack again, but it's just little Katie, her too-big flip-flops slapping the pavement as she runs. She stops a few feet away from me and stares.

"What?" I say, hoping against hope that she's just going to ask me to hang out or start rambling about some dumb little-kid stuff.

She's got on a dirty white T-shirt with a glittery pink heart in the middle, but big patches of glitter have rubbed off, so the heart looks like it has mange. She keeps staring.

"What?" I say again, heart sinking.

"Lisa says you're a crazy slut!" she shouts, and then her eyes go huge as if she can't believe what she just said and she turns and runs back down the sidewalk, flip-flops beating like wings.

The group down the street is watching, waiting to see how I'll react. Does Lisa know that Henry and I kissed? Only Savannah could have told her that. Or Henry. I need to know who told them, what people are saying about me. How much they know.

This is a terrible idea. I know it's a terrible idea and some part of my brain is shouting at my feet to stop, but it's too late, I'm already walking over there, anger overruling reason. I walk with long strides, but not stomping, not with clenched fists. I try to appear cool and collected.

Katie hides behind Lisa as I approach.

"Fuck you," I say to Lisa, which is a great start. Really beginning from a position of power there, Jo. Fantastic job.

Lisa laughs. "You going to bite me?"

"You got the taste for blood?" asks another girl. Nicole. She's in my math class, but we never talk. She isn't rich. Nobody in Lester is or they would live somewhere else. But she must have more money than me or Savannah because she always has nice clothes (Savannah only ever gets hand-me-downs, the bane of her existence) and a nice manicure. If I tried to wear nail polish it wouldn't last more than a day, I imagine, between doing dishes at the bar and climbing trees at night. Being around Nicole always makes me feel dirty and poor.

"You're a bunch of petty, gossiping bitches," I say. I'm not proud of that, but I'm too angry to stop. "Where are you getting this shit?"

"Everybody knows it," says Nicole. "You went out with Henry Bickle and you attacked him."

"It could have been me," says Tanner seriously, putting a protective hand to his neck.

"Oh, fuck you too," I say. "Your face looks like a shovel." Accurate, though not helpful.

"I never knew you were into such kinky shit," says Lisa.

It's a new experience to be called a slut—historically I've only ever been labeled a frigid nun or a struck-up prude—but it doesn't feel any better. In eighth grade, someone started a rumor that Savannah and I were lesbians. She stopped hanging out with me for two whole weeks. I was devastated. She apologized, eventually. We never talk about that time, though I still think about it sometimes and get sad.

"Always knew you were a freak, though," Lisa adds. Nicole nods in agreement.

They all think I'm weird, but their definition of normal is too narrow. They have no idea what weird truly is.

I picture Lee stalking the halls of the high school, throwing her dress off in the middle of class. *Slut,* they'd all cry. My sister would bare her teeth. Stand on a desk and rip out the beating heart of some baby animal with her teeth. Spit the blood in Lisa's face.

It was a mistake coming over here. A big one. Lisa is looking so smug I can't stand it.

So I don't try to. I launch myself forward. Little Katie bolts, a few of the others jump clear. I barrel into Lisa, knock her backward against the steps, hit indiscriminately. Slapping, punching, wrestling like I do with my sister. Tanner whistles. Another boy says something idiotic about a cat fight. I am sick with regret, sicker with rage. Lisa's flailing hand hits my wrist and pain shoots up my arm. I manage to grab a handful of her hair and yank. She shrieks.

And then the pastor is there, right on fucking time, once again, to pull me away.

Aggie, newly furious about the spectacle I made of myself right down the street, forces me to clean the whole bar from top to bottom. Neon-filled windows, scratched wooden tables, rickety chairs, sticky black floor. Scrubbed and polished to a shine, she says. Everything takes me longer than usual because my left wrist throbs if I move it too much and I keep stopping to yank my sleeve back down over the wound. At least the pastor didn't tell Aggie about the fight with Jack, or I'd probably have to clean it all twice.

The bar is mostly empty. Just a few regulars. Old men who used to work in the mines. Gerald who is only sixty but looks eighty. Roscoe who carries an actual handkerchief in the pocket of his Carhartt jacket and coughs like a jackhammer. Carl who ran a secondhand shop down the street until it went out of business last year. My version of uncles. I suspect they must have been here last night when the police dropped me off, but they don't mention it, for which I am grateful.

The pastor and Sheila are playing pool over in the corner. I catch Aggie shooting glances at them while she polishes glasses. Maybe she's jealous. Good. Hopefully she and the pastor will fight and break up and everything can go back to normal.

I'm watching her watch them when the bell over the door chimes. Aggie looks to see who it is. The glass slips out of her hands. Clanks onto the counter. Rolls.

Only one person could make her react like that. I wonder if it's too late to duck under a table and hide.

"Little girl," says Grandma Margaret from behind me.

It's too late.

I turn, steeling myself. She's still in the doorway. The inside of the bar is dim even in the daytime, artificial evening, so she's backlit dramatically.

Everyone is staring at her. It's funny. She's almost like Lee, up to a point. They both dislike most people. Both keep to themselves, far away from people, deep in the woods.

When Grandma Margaret deigns to come to town, though, she doesn't mind attention. She demands it, in fact.

"I hear you been running wild." Margaret steps forward. The door bangs shut behind her. If it weren't for her wild gray hair, you could squint and mistake her for Aggie.

A hush has fallen over the bar. Roscoe coughs and I flinch at the sound.

Since moving out, we only go to Margaret's house three times a year. Christmas. Easter. Her birthday in June. Aggie fumes on the drive there, fumes on the way back. These visits are obligations, like paying tribute to a tyrant. If we are late, if we don't bring a gift, if she doesn't like the way we say hello, she'll punish us with icy looks, thinly veiled insults.

Margaret, meanwhile, stops by the bar once a month or so.

She never gives advance warning, just appears, always at a different time or a different day from her last visit, as if she wants to catch us off guard. She treats these visits like an inspection. Of both the property itself, and of her other property: us.

She'll criticize my posture, my clothes, threaten to take me back home with her and raise me right. It's an empty threat. At least I hope it is. I believe she was glad to be rid of me, glad she didn't have to look at my face every day, didn't have to be reminded of where I came from, *who* I came from. She usually has some complaint about how Aggie runs the bar, too. She'll threaten to start running the place herself, but that's equally unlikely. Margaret prefers to spend most of her time alone, up in her big house on the ridge, with nobody but the trees to know her business. She doesn't come into town more than once a week if she can help it. *Nothing but trash down there,* she always says.

"I come down for the milk this morning," Margaret says, talking loudly, as though she were on a stage, rather than in the doorway of a small bar, "not expecting no trouble and what do I find out nearly the minute I walk through the doors of the Kroger? My own granddaughter has been out there biting boys in the neck. Whole damn town is talking about it."

"Mother," says Aggie, icy. "Can we discuss this privately?"

"I'm thinking it's about time I stepped in," says Margaret, not lowering her voice.

The last time we saw her was nearly a month ago, when she stopped by the bar on a Saturday night to help herself to our priciest scotch and glare daggers at the pastor. I was wearing jean shorts that day and as soon as she saw me she looked me up and down and said I was showing too much skin. Said, *You don't want people getting the wrong idea about what kind of girl you are, now, do you?*

"I'm handling it," says Aggie. She grabs a bottle of scotch from the top shelf, pours some into a glass, sets it firmly onto the bar.

"Seems she needs a firmer hand," Margaret says, though she goes over to the bar, takes a seat and a long sip of the scotch.

Some low conversation has resumed between the other patrons and I miss the next thing Aggie says, but then to my dismay Margaret is waving me over.

"Go right upstairs and pack your things, Jo," she says when I approach. "You're coming home with me today."

My stomach drops. No. She wouldn't. Would she? She's threatened before, but always in a vague way. She's never gone this far.

I look desperately at Aggie. She's staring fixedly at her mother, hands clutching the edge of the bar.

"There'll be no more of this running off," Margaret says coolly. "I know how to deal with that kind of nonsense."

"Right," says Aggie. "Like you dealt with it before. Like you dealt with *her*. That worked out just great, didn't it?"

Margaret, usually implacable, bristles. "How dare you," she hisses, voice low for the first time since she walked in. "You have no idea what it was like, dealing with that girl."

"You gave up on her," says Aggie. She is angry, face going red, muscles straining, fingers gripping the edge of the bar harder and harder.

"So help me God," says Margaret. She's angry, too, but icy.

I glance around to see if everyone is staring. They are. The pastor is actually coming over. Great. Just what this situation needs. He stops beside me, puts a hand on my shoulder. I only flinch a little.

"What man," he intones, addressing Margaret, "having a hundred sheep, if he loses one of them, does not leave the ninety-nine in the wilderness, and go after the one that is lost, until he finds it? Luke fifteen, four."

"Mr. Jones," Margaret says. I note she does not call him pastor. "This is a family conversation."

"I believe, ma'am," he fires back, "that the whole bar can hear it."

Margaret huffs, taken aback. She's used to people being intimidated by her. If I didn't hate the pastor, I would almost have to admire him.

"Aggie here," the pastor continues, "has asked me to assist in the religious education of young Jolene."

"Jo," I say automatically, correcting him, but regret it immediately, since they all three look at me. I shrink under their gaze. If only I could run.

"What Jo needs," says the pastor, "is a close personal relationship with our savior Jesus."

I catch Aggie rolling her eyes, but the tension between mother and daughter has been broken.

"Charlatan," Margaret says, her ire redirected fully at the pastor. "I remember you. You were a good-for-nothing punk."

"Oh certainly," says the pastor. "I myself was, it could be said, *conflicted* when I was young Jo's age. But then, by the grace of the Lord, I saw the light."

"You saw the light at the end of a bottle," says Margaret.

Aggie, who has come out from behind the bar, takes me by the arm.

"Come on," she whispers.

"Let beer be for those who are perishing," I hear the pastor declare as Aggie drags me back to the kitchen, "wine for those who are in anguish."

Aggie directs me to the stovetop, shoves a grimy steel wool scrubber into my hands.

"Scour it," she says, "and when you're done find something else." She gestures around the kitchen, which admittedly is rife with grease-caked implements and surfaces.

"I don't want to go to Margaret's," I say, gripping the steel wool. The thought, now that it's had more time to sink in, is truly chilling. I'd be there alone, without even Aggie for company, isolated from the rest of town, totally reliant on Margaret. She'd be stricter than she'd ever been before. Meaner, I bet, now that I'm the same age Mama was when she died. A painful reminder every time she looks at me. "You won't let her take me, will you?"

Aggie hesitates. I can see her warring with herself, wanting to say she'd never let me go back to that woman, but still too mad at me to offer such easy reassurance.

"You just stay out of sight and out of trouble," she says finally, with a sigh, "and we'll see."

Margaret leaves, empty-handed, after about an hour of arguing with the pastor over scripture. I can hear snatches of it from the kitchen. I don't even try to stick my head out and nobody but Aggie, and Jessi when she arrives for her shift, comes back to the kitchen.

Business picks up around five and Aggie has me switch to bussing empties. People shoot me sidelong glances and some just full-on stare, but I make a point of never meeting anyone's eyes, never standing still long enough for them to speak to me. I catch snatches of whispers though. *Do you think she—what was she—*

I heard she—with her teeth!—the poor boy—Rob Bickle's son, no, not the bad one, the younger one—like her mother—must be crazy.

After about an hour of this, I start draining the dregs. Whenever somebody leaves a little bit of hard-to-get-to alcohol in the bottom of their bottle or glass, I hustle back to the kitchen and get shameless, hold the bottles upside down with my mouth open like a kid catching snowflakes, lick the shot glasses, suck on the ice from the bottom of mixed drinks.

I've done this a million times, and I know it's probably not worth the trouble. If I really wanted to get drunk I'd steal a bottle from behind the bar. But I'd be more likely to get caught that way. And besides, it's more the sport of the thing.

About an hour into my spree, I luck out. Somebody leaves half a beer sitting on a table. I watch the guy get up and walk outside. He probably just went out for a smoke or a phone call, but he left his beer and there's no one else at the table. It's fair game. I snatch it quick, slide it to the middle of the tray between the other glasses and bottles.

Back in the kitchen, I chug the beer. It's warm. Guy must have been nursing it.

It hits me quick. I'm not drunk like the other night. But I'm feeling good. My body feels kind of cottony, the throbbing in my left wrist muted.

When I head back out, I see that the pastor's sitting alone at a table, paging through the gold Bible again. His glass is nearly empty. Just a thin layer of whiskey at the bottom. It's risky, but he seems pretty absorbed.

I walk over, reach for the glass.

He looks up.

Shit.

The pastor's eyes go from me to the glass and then back to me.

"Bring me another," he says, looking back down at the Bible. "Wild Turkey."

I speed walk the glass back to the kitchen, slurp the burning brown liquid at the bottom, slot the glass into the industrial dishwasher. This night is going pretty well, I decide. I feel good. I feel fine.

I'm not allowed to pour drinks, but I relay the pastor's order to Jessi, who puts it on his tab. I carry the whiskey back to his table.

He gestures for me to sit, so I do. He puts the Bible down, leans forward across the table. The bar is crowded enough to be noisy now. Sheila laughs loudly over by the pool table. There's music on the jukebox. Some song about the Blue Ridge mountains, a place I've never been. I've never been anywhere but Ohio, though at least I've gone a little farther than Aggie ever has thanks to away track meets.

"I would have killed him if I'd gotten the chance," the pastor says.

I blink at him. "What?"

"Logan Cantrell," he says. "I could have killed him for what he did."

"Oh." I'd been expecting a lecture about Jesus and livestock management, was prepared to sit through it meekly in exchange for the whiskey, but now he knows how to get my attention. He's doing the same thing he was at Minnie's, pushing the one advantage he's got. I should resist, but curiosity gets the better of me again. "Why didn't you?"

The pastor shrugs. "A group of us went out there in the middle of the night once, but he must have seen us coming."

"You wouldn't actually have killed him," I say. He just wants to sound cool. Tough. "You're bluffing."

The pastor leans back in his chair. "Maybe you're right. I don't know. After he got busted, some of us went out there again. The little brother had skipped town, so we burnt their trailer down."

"No way." I vaguely remember hearing about this, actually. The trailer burning down. Suspected arson. Nothing proved. Not that the police would have tried too hard. But the *pastor*?

"Right hand to God. We'd all had too much to drink. I guess we were lucky the whole forest didn't catch."

I try to imagine him out there: young, drunk, splashing kerosene into the dark, lighting a match. For a second it almost makes me like him.

"We dug up the ground underneath it, too," he says. "Just in case."

I get a little shock when I realize what he means by that. *Just in case.* They were looking for her body.

"Did you find anything?"

"No." He takes a long sip of his whiskey. His cheeks are slightly red, and I wonder if he's drunk.

"So you knew him, too? Logan?" I'm hooked again. I can't help it. No use even pretending I'm not interested.

"No. I mean, I knew of him. Everybody did. He was a few years older than me, though."

"You think he did it?"

"Oh, absolutely. He put his own brother in the hospital twice. The man was a fucking monster."

I've heard this kind of thing before, but it's still a little hard to take. I try not to think of him as my father. I don't have a father. I've got Aggie.

Still.

If half of my DNA comes from a murderer, a monster, what does that make me?

The pastor must have seen something in my expression because he actually reaches across the table and puts one hand over mine.

"She wouldn't have gone down without a fight, you know," he says. "Jolene was tough."

He's got this funny look on his face, sad but hopeful, and I want so badly for him to say it. Say, *Just like you.*

"Jo," says Aggie, "get back to work."

I jump, nearly fall off my chair. Aggie's standing right behind me, arms crossed.

"Sorry, Aggie," says the pastor calmly. "We got chatting about Jesus's time in the wilderness."

"Did you now?" Aggie looks like she's never heard anything more ridiculous.

"Certainly. Jo here thinks Jesus was being, what was the word you used?" He turns to me. I just blink at him, my mind still full of fire in the night. Of Mama. "Oh right, a 'total pussy' for refusing the devil's trials."

Aggie snorts. The pastor is a pretty smooth liar, I've got to hand it to him.

"I was thinking," says the pastor, "maybe Jo could come with me to the service tomorrow. Sheila's getting baptized. Jo said she'd like to see it."

"Really?" asks Aggie, looking down at me. Out of the corner of my eye, I can see the pastor raising his eyebrows meaningfully and I think I understand. He's making a deal. He'll answer my questions about Mama, and he won't tell Aggie about the whiskey, but there's a cost.

"Yeah," I say. "I would. Sure."

Aggie shrugs.

"I need to go over to Savannah's house," I add, before she can turn away.

Aggie snorts again. "You think I'm stupid?"

"I really need to talk to her. I need to apologize."

"I'm not letting you out of my sight until you prove you can be trusted."

I want to ask how the hell I'm supposed to prove that if she never gives me the chance. But I'm not actually trying to convince her. I'm negotiating terms.

"Please, Aggie, please, just let me go talk to Savannah. Just for an hour. I'll come right back." I glance over at the pastor, just for a second. "Please, she's really upset. I need to talk to her."

"I could take her," says the pastor, and it takes great strength of will for me not to do a fist pump. "I can wait in the car."

"You don't need to do that," says Aggie.

"I don't mind," says the pastor. "Really, I'd be happy to."

He smiles at me and I give a small, hesitant smile back. Deal.

Savannah is not happy to see me.

"Why are you here?" she asks, her head poking around the door, the noise of the TV and the voices of her family mingling from within the house. I was hoping maybe she'd actually apologize to me as soon as she saw me. Say she didn't know what came over her earlier, but now she's seen the error of her ways. Jack is an ass. She'll never let anyone treat me that way again.

"Can I come in?" I ask.

"No." She's giving me a look like I'm scum. Like we haven't been friends nearly our whole lives. It hurts.

"I won't stay long," I say, desperate. "I can't stay long." I point toward the car, where the pastor is fiddling with the radio.

"Gross," says Savannah, and her mask of anger slips for a second. I see a glimmer of the old Savannah. My friend is still under there.

"Please, Savannah. I need to tell you what happened."

She frowns. I want to scream at her, but I take a deep breath, try to see things her way. She feels like I'm lying to her. And I am, kind of.

"I need to tell you what *really* happened," I say.

"Fine," she says, "but you got to be quiet, there's a couple of babies staying."

I wave at the pastor as I go inside, grinning with relief. He waves back.

There are three babies total at Savannah's house. One belongs to her aunt, one to her sister Dakota, and one to Dakota's friend Jaclyn. Two out of three babies are crying. A guy with a mustache is bouncing one of them on his knee. I've seen him around before, but I can't remember if he's an uncle or a cousin or somebody's husband. Savannah's got so much family I honestly have trouble keeping them all straight.

As we make our way through the living room, one of her little sisters goes racing across our path, pursued by a nephew holding a popgun and shouting, "'Sassination! 'Sassination!" which sets off the third baby crying, which sets off Savannah's mom, who is getting her hair colored in the kitchen by Jaclyn, to scream at them both to knock it off.

"Am I being quiet enough?" I ask Savannah when we are safely in her room with the door shut, hoping she'll laugh or take it as an opportunity to start complaining about her family instead of about me. But she just slumps onto the single bed in the corner and crosses her arms.

The room, which she shares with two of her sisters, is carpeted with stuffed animals and books. One of the walls is almost entirely covered with stickers, another with taped-up pictures Savannah has cut out of magazines. Like Myron's room, except the pictures are of celebrities and the inside of fancy houses—orderly, gleaming, full of bright white expanses and plenty of empty space.

"Have you heard anything more about Henry?" I ask.

She looks like she's debating whether to answer or not, but she relents. "Yeah. Jack says he's stable or whatever. They released him from the hospital."

"That's good." I feel a little guilty that part of me is honestly more worried about what Henry might be saying than how he's doing. But I'm glad he's okay.

"Jack also says I should stay away from you. He says you're dangerous and insane."

I lean back against the ladder of the bunk bed across from her bed. I know she's just trying to hurt me, to get to a rise out of me. "That's the stupidest thing I've ever heard."

"He says you're probably a compulsive liar."

"Jack can fuck off."

Savannah shrugs. "You do lie a lot."

I cross my arms, kick at a stuffed dog by my feet. She's got me there.

"Jack says—" she starts, but I don't let her finish.

"What's wrong with you?" I push myself away from the bunk

bed. "Why are you on his side all of a sudden? You hardly even know him."

Savannah flops sideways on the bed, shoves a pillow over her face, embarrassed. But I already know the answer, even though I wish I didn't. She's fallen for him. He's lit golden in her mind now. New and exciting. I've seen it before. Savannah's relationships always burn bright and hot. Flame out fast. I march over and yank the pillow away.

"Hey!" she yelps.

"Savannah," I say. "Jack doesn't know me. You do."

She tries to grab the pillow back, but I throw it on the floor.

"Do you really think I would attack Henry?" I ask, standing over her.

"No." She frowns up at me. "I don't know."

"You're my best friend." I want to scream at her, can feel the anger making my face go red. "You should be on my side."

"Well, you should tell me the truth."

"I am!" I shout, desperate. I didn't attack Henry. It's not fair.

Savannah sits up. "No, you're not. You said you'd tell me what really happened. Well, fucking tell me then. Who attacked Henry? I saw someone. When I came out of the woods. I saw someone running. Why are you protecting them? Who was it?"

"Savannah—" I start, but I don't know how to finish.

She scowls, scoots farther back on the bed, picks at a picture of a country bungalow decorated in nothing but shades of blue. She looks like she's holding back tears.

In first grade we only had a single basketball for the whole class, and one day this girl Jessa got to it first at recess, but instead of shooting hoops she stuffed it under her shirt and then pretended to give birth. She named the basketball Bobby Jr., after a boy in the class. The boys declared war.

For the price of one penny, I switched sides. Savannah did it for free.

She distracted the girls and I ran in and snatched Bobby Jr. right out of his crib of sticks. We were supposed to deliver him to the boys, but Savannah and I changed our minds, spent the rest of recess as renegades, keeping the ball away from the whole class, tossing it back and forth.

The two of us against everyone.

I take a deep breath. There's no good option here. I'm betraying someone either way and there's a good chance Savannah still won't believe me. But I've got to tell her something. Why not the truth? She's my best friend. She deserves that much.

"It was my sister," I say. It's such a simple word. *Sister.* But it feels strange on my tongue now. Feels like a swear word almost. "She's the one who attacked Henry."

"Goddammit," says Savannah. She sounds disappointed, not surprised. "Not this shit again."

"I don't know why my sister was at the bridge," I say, all the details tumbling out now that I've started, "but she was. She's the one who wailed. That was the cry we all heard. I think she must have followed us somehow. I think she was watching us at Henry's house."

"You don't have a sister," Savannah says flatly.

I knew this was the most likely outcome, but now that I've come out and said it, I feel like she *has* to believe me. It's a big deal. I haven't breathed a word about my sister for years. I've been holding it all in, keeping it a secret. It feels oddly good to let it out. "I do," I say. "She lives in the woods."

"Stop lying," says Savannah, her voice rising almost to a whine.

"I'm not lying. I have a sister. Lee. She attacked Henry."

"Stop it." Savannah sounds like she's going to cry again.

"Here," I say, "look." I sit on the bed beside her, push my sleeve up, show her the bite mark. I'm surprised myself to see how red and swollen it still is.

"What's that?" Savannah leans forward, frowns at my wrist. She can't deny this.

"She attacked me, too," I say. "She bit me."

"Why would she do that?"

"I don't know. I was trying to stop her and she freaked out. She was probably scared you'd see her."

"No," Savannah says quietly, leaning away again. "You're crazy."

"This is the truth, Savannah, I promise." I know it's probably hard for her to accept, but there's no taking it back now. She has to believe me. I've got to make her understand. "It's why I go running at night. I run with her. I was never lying, when I used to tell you about her. I wish you could have met her, but she wouldn't come to Margaret's yard because she was afraid."

"You're crazy," Savannah says again. "Jack was right."

I want to reach out and shake her. She's only sitting a few feet away from me on the bed, but she's looking at me like she really thinks I might be crazy, and the distance between us feels like miles.

"Did Henry say anything?" I try, a little desperately. "At the hospital? Did they ask him what happened?"

"I don't know."

"He saw her up close. Just ask him." He must have seen her. Before I hoped he didn't remember, but now I hope he does. Maybe we can call him up. I'd do anything at this point.

"No," she says. "This is insane. You don't have a sister. I know you don't."

"I'll prove it," I say. I need her to believe me. I need her back on my side. "Come with me right now and I'll show you."

I stand, cross to the window, push it open. I turn back to Savannah. She's squished into the corner, arms wrapped around herself.

"You're crazy," she says in a tiny voice. She sounds like a little kid, like she's trying to convince herself monsters don't exist. It isn't fair. "Jack says you're crazy."

"Oh, for fuck's sake." Something snaps inside me. Jack, Jack, Jack. I'm sick of hearing his name. She won't even give me a chance.

Savannah's phone is sitting on top of the blue plastic drawer unit that serves as her bedside table. I grab it.

"What are you doing?" she asks, straightening up.

"I'm just going to borrow it," I snap.

I shove the phone into my pocket and slide out the window, drop softly onto the grass below. Savannah jumps up from the bed.

"Give me my phone," she shouts, angry again. Her phone is her lifeline to Jack. Without it, how will he text her about what a crazy bitch I am?

"I'll bring it back," I say. "I'm going to take a picture of her. Then you'll see."

I take a step backward, stumble over a plastic dollhouse sitting in the dirt, its first floor flooded with dead leaves. The sun is going down already and Savannah's yard is dark, her bedroom window a buttery square of light.

"Come back," says Savannah, sounding desperate now instead of angry. "Please, Jo." She reaches a hand out the window toward me, into the dark.

I turn and run.

CHAPTER SEVEN

You're supposed to grow out of childhood fears, but my sister never did. If anything, she grew into them. I thought it was progress when she started coming into town, that summer after Aggie and I moved to the bar. But it didn't last.

Somebody saw us. It was bound to happen eventually I guess, no matter how careful we were. We were chasing each other through someone's backyard when the back porch light flicked on and a man came barreling out, shouting at us to stay away from his goddamn tomatoes. Lee ran so fast I couldn't keep up. I didn't see her again for a month.

I went out night after night, alone, to search for her. I was scared. She'd never stayed away from me for that long before, unless you count the first five years. Maybe it's because she came into my life so suddenly, but there was always this fear, at the back of my mind, that she might just as suddenly be gone forever.

I was sure that if people found out about her, I would lose her, but there were dangers to keeping her secret, too. What if she got hurt, out in the woods alone? Hurt worse than scrapes and scratches and bruises? What if a wild animal attacked her or a hunter mistook her, from a distance, for a doe? What if she got sick? I'd never seen her with worse than a cold (which she also faked having a few times, I'm pretty sure, just so I'd bring her cough drops, which she ate like candy), but that didn't mean it couldn't happen. I knew about Lyme disease, made a point to pull ticks off her when I spotted them, but I doubt I got them all. If anything happened, I'd have no way to find her in all those miles of forest.

She found me, finally. Dropped down out of a tree one night when I was searching, scared me half to death. I cried with relief and tried to hug her, but she just bit me, gently, on the shoulder and then ran off, slowing only long enough to let me catch up.

Since then, she won't step foot inside Lester.

Our current meeting spot is a big sycamore at the far edge of Queen of Heaven. The cemetery's not too far from Savannah's house, though Lester is only about a mile across, so nowhere is too far from anywhere, really. When I reach the tree, I climb up through the broad branches until leaves blot out the sky. Lee made a rough hammock up here a few years back by looping thick rope between two branches.

She's not here now. I knew it was unlikely.

I point Savannah's phone at a small hollow in the trunk, about squirrel-sized, right above one of the hammock branches. The weak light of the screen glints off a couple of nails, a brown knit cap, and a blue plastic horse with a chewed-off hoof.

My sister has stashes like this all over the national forest. Somewhere, I know, she's got a big winter coat stowed. It's a man's coat that she stole or found somewhere. She's got some tights, too, that I gave her, and some of my old shoes for when the temperature dips below freezing.

I could use one of the nails maybe, scratch a message in the trunk of the sycamore, but I don't know when I'll be able to sneak out again. This might be my last chance for a while.

So I do something I haven't done in ages. I take a deep breath, open my mouth wide as it will go, open my throat, and I howl.

Long and loud. A big round vowel sound that would make the chorus teacher proud. I tend to sing quiet in chorus. But out here I let loose. Put all my air behind it.

I think of Lee, of Henry, of Savannah, of Aggie and Jack and Margaret and the pastor, of Lisa and all the kids who hate me, of everything that's gone down in the last day and a half, and I put that behind it too.

When I run out of air, I breathe deep and I do it again.

AAAAAAOOOOOUUUUUUUU is how it sounds, more or less.

Free, is how it feels. Like my voice is running barefoot through the woods.

If my sister is near, she'll hear it. She'll know it's me. She's the one who taught me to do it, when we were kids. Who threw her head back and let out a sound so big it seemed like it couldn't have come from a girl so small.

When I'm out of breath, throat ragged, I scramble down from the tree and run toward the center of the cemetery. From there I can see the tree line all along the border of Queen of Heaven.

I don't know if she'll come. Even if she was close enough. Even if she heard me.

I wait, scan the trees, heart pounding.

In the beginning, my sister's appearances were always unpredictable. Some nights she would come, some nights she wouldn't. I would often wait like this, standing at the edge of Grandma Margaret's backyard.

I blink and then there she is, melting out of the trees.

She's at the opposite end of the cemetery, closer to the processing plant than to Myron's house, just a pale smudge against the dark of the forest.

I run toward her, weaving around gravestones. I look down once to keep from stumbling. When I look back up she's gone.

I push myself up to full speed, sprinting like hell. I skid to a stop at the edge of the trees, duck under a branch, crash into the underbrush. She's waiting for me just beyond the first layer, standing with her knees slightly bent, one hand resting on a thin tree.

"Lee," I say, fumbling to pull the phone out of my pocket. "I need to talk to—"

She's off again, running.

"Wait!" I shout, scrambling after her. The ground slopes swiftly upward, so I have to climb instead of run, grabbing rocks and roots and thin trees to haul myself up.

Up ahead, Lee stops and watches me. She doesn't usually show her feelings the way other people do. She smiles sometimes, sure, or snarls, but she tends to default to blank. I've got to look at her posture, how she's standing. Right now she's holding herself tense, ready to bolt again. She's jiggling her left leg. This is a game.

I scramble up the last few feet between us, lunge forward, but she's too fast for that, she's off again. Her legs flash in the dark, that piece of loose lace still trailing from her hem.

I run after her. At the bottom of the hill the ground is crowded with plants, but the higher we go up on the ridge, the more the forest floor clears out, like it's making way for something. Making way for us, maybe.

The dirt feels more real than pavement. My sister runs barefoot, with calluses hard as hooves, but even through my shoes I feel it. The give of the soil. The rise and fall of the hills. Slick fallen leaves. Little sticks cracking like bones.

I'm matching my sister's pace now, weaving through the trees at the top of the ridge. She's still ahead of me, but then she feints left. Acting on instinct, I veer right. Lee doesn't look back to see if she fooled me. Trusting that she did, she makes a hard right.

I throw myself at her, tackle her sideways to the ground. She yowls, trying to wrench herself free.

Her heart purse knocks against my leg. I brought that to her when we were seven. It's made of translucent, glittery plastic. She's replaced the strap, which broke off ages ago, with a length of rope so she can wear it strapped across her chest. "Hold still!" I shout at her.

I twist my fingers into the fabric of her dress. She jabs me with her elbow. Flashes of last night. Has she lost her mind? "Stop it," I say. My voice is hoarse, comes out half whine. "I just want to talk to you."

My sister twists herself around and closes her mouth, carefully, over my left wrist. She doesn't bite down. Just rests her teeth on the skin. My wound throbs from the pressure. I hold my arm as still as possible, but I don't let go of her dress.

"That boy," I say. "That was Henry. I've told you about him. He's my friend." My sister grunts. I feel the vibration, painfully, in my wrist. There a twig poking me in the hip but I don't move. This close, I can see how Lee's collarbones jut sharply from the ragged lace collar of her dress. I can see the scratches on her arms from branches and thorns. I don't think my sister even notices scratches like that anymore. She always has so many.

"You could have killed him," I say.

She doesn't answer. She's turned away from me, so I can't see her face, but she doesn't even flinch.

"Were you trying to kill him?" I demand. "Why?"

"He hurt you," she says.

"No," I say. I squint at her, trying to determine from her body language whether she's being honest. "No, you don't believe that. You're not that stupid, Lee. I know you."

No response. Savannah said Henry was stable, so I hope that means he's out of danger. Still, he's got a weak heart. He died once when he was younger. Didn't see anything.

Just darkness.

"People think it was me," I say. "If you'd killed him, they would have put me in jail." I don't know if that's true. It might be. "They would have locked me up and I would never be able to see you again."

That gets to her, finally. At least she still gives a shit about me. She releases my wrist, turns to look me in the eyes.

"Run away," she says.

"What the hell were you thinking, Lee?" I scoot backward, clutch my wrist protectively to my chest. "You really hurt me, you know. Why were you even there? Did you follow us?"

She stares at me so hard I swear I can feel it on my skin. The moon is bright. There's a fresh cut on her cheek. She must have nicked it on a rock when we were struggling. "Run away," she says again. "Run away Aggie."

I sigh and sit back, brush leaves and dirt from my jeans.

"The pastor's watching me now," I say. "Because of what you did. He put a light on my window."

"Run away light."

"From the light. Run away *from* the light. You sound like an idiot."

My sister can talk right, but only if I force her to. She's not stupid, not really. She can read. Only kid books, sure, and she prefers it when I read to her, but whatever. I used to make her play school with me. I'd teach her whatever I'd learned that day, give her quizzes, yell at her when she ran off in the middle of class. She was decent at memorizing things, repeating them back to me.

Still, left to her own devices she prefers to use as few words as possible. As if words were a precious resource, to be hoarded, treasured, doled out begrudgingly if at all.

"You sound like an idiot," she says. Like an echo of me.

"Well, you are acting like an idiot. What the hell is wrong with you? People *saw* you."

She flinches a little at that, but she must know. Must know, at the very least, that Henry saw her. Maybe she really did mean to kill him.

"Run away," she says. Her face twists up a little. If she were anyone else, I might think she was about to cry. But I've never seen my sister cry. Not once. "Please."

"I've told you. I just can't." It's no use having this argument again, but it's almost comforting, to fall back into our old patterns, as if last night hadn't changed everything. "I've got school and stuff. I've got to—"

"Run away *from* school," Lee cuts me off, urgent. "Run away from Aggie. Run away from bar. Run away from everybody. Just you and me."

That's practically a speech, by her standards.

"I can't leave," I say, sighing. "They'll send the police after me."

"Stop them," she says.

"I have a life, Lee. I have friends."

"Slut."

"What?"

"Slut," she repeats flatly.

"Do you even know what that means?" I ask. But I think she does.

And I think I must have been right, about what happened last night. She was jealous. Not of me kissing a boy. Of me being with *anyone*. She doesn't want me spending time with anyone else. *Just you and me.*

My sister doesn't show her emotions well, but that doesn't mean she doesn't have them. She must have been far more upset than I realized, when I said I was going to come see her less. More afraid, maybe, more lonely. I guess I can understand that, though it doesn't justify what she did.

"We're going to go back to how it was before," I say. "Okay? We managed before, didn't we? I'll still run with you on Saturday nights. And it's just until we turn eighteen. After that, things will be different. Things will be better."

"No."

"But you can't do anything like that again," I continue, ignoring her. "You can't hurt anyone."

"No."

"I mean it," I say. "You can't just attack people."

"No," my sister says again, as if that's the only damn word she knows. Maybe she's scared, maybe she's lonely, but she's acting selfish and stupid and insane and I don't know how to make her see.

"If you do something like that again," I say, "I'll have to tell everyone about you. Then they'll catch you. They'll lock *you* up."

She jolts away from me. She doesn't look angry, just terrified, and I immediately regret my words. Regret, too, what I'm about to do, even before I do it. She's scrabbling backward, pushing herself up, ready to run.

It's too late to take it back. I fumble the phone out of my pocket, hold it up, stab at the screen. My hands are shaking. The camera flashes once, twice.

Lee yowls, slaps the phone out of my hand, jumps at me, knocks me to the ground. She stands over me. Her eyes are wide, showing too much white. She is breathing too fast and too loud. She looks insane. Not like a girl at all, but like a wild animal.

I've been scared of my sister before. The first time I saw her kill something with her bare hands, for instance. It was a squirrel, I remember, caught in one of the traps she'd set up around the forest. They were simple things, made of sticks and string and a loop of wire. They were supposed to snap an animal's neck, but this squirrel had been caught by the leg instead. It was struggling, I remember, twisting around, trying to bite through its own leg to get free. Lee reached down with her small hands, her child's strength, and she took the squirrel's head in one hand and its body in the other and she gave a quick sharp jerk and the squirrel went still. I was only five and had never seen anything die before. Later, lying awake in my bed at home, I reassured myself that what my sister had done was, in its own way, a kindness.

Over the years, I've grown accustomed to her violence. We

fight sometimes, wrestle as a game or out of annoyance with each other. Skinny or not, she is stronger than me. She usually wins, pins me to the dirt. Still, I'd always believed that she would never truly hurt me. Not badly. Not on purpose.

After last night, I don't believe that anymore.

She stares down at me for another moment, then turns on her heel.

"Wait," I say, "I'm sorry." I swing myself forward, grab at her, manage to grasp the lace at the hem of her dress, but she lunges forward and it rips away in my hand.

I'm left sitting in the dark, alone, holding the tail of dirty lace.

CHAPTER EIGHT

I spend a while down on my knees, sifting through the dead leaves, until I find Savannah's phone. I brush the dirt from it. The screen lights up okay. I don't think it's any more cracked than it was to start with, though it's hard to say for certain.

In the first picture I took, you can clearly see my sister's face. She's washed out from the flash and her eyes are shut. But it's her. The second one is just her arm and shoulder, with some motion blur as she ducks out of the way.

I feel guilty for threatening to tell people about her, felt guilty the moment I saw how scared she was, but she's the one who should feel guilty. She's the one who revealed herself. She's the one who chose to attack Henry. She's fucking up my whole life and she doesn't even seem sorry.

It was an empty threat anyway. Savannah is proof that I can barely reveal my sister's secret even if I try. Maybe Savannah will believe me when I show her the pictures. I can hope.

I put the phone back into my pocket. Of course now my night vision is shot. I blink hard at the trees around me.

I'm definitely lost.

I've spent a lot of time in these woods. I know their night faces. Their smells and sounds. How they change from season to season. But I couldn't draw you a map. When I'm with my sister I never worry about where we're going. She always knows the way.

If we ran straight, and I know we didn't, but maybe the lefts and rights balanced out somehow, then Queen of Heaven should be to the east.

It's a clear night and the stars hang bright as berries from the tops of the trees. I don't see any constellations, so I jog until there's more sky showing. I locate the Big Dipper, the North Star.

I point myself in the right direction and run.

When I finally emerge from the forest, I'm a long way from the cemetery, at the crest of a hill past the meat processing plant. The lights of Lester are spread out below me. I scramble down the hill into a drainage ditch. The weeds are tall and thick and I have to wade through them as if they were water.

I could book it toward Savannah's house, sneak back in her window, but the chance that the pastor is still waiting patiently out front, unaware of my absence, seems slim. I've been gone too long. Maybe Savannah even ran right out and told him. I wouldn't put it past her. In any case, this might be my last chance for a while to move freely through the world, unwatched. I should take advantage of it.

Henry's house is bordered by forest, so it's easy to get to without being spotted. I stand at the edge of his backyard, just within the shadow of the trees. Now that I'm here I'm not sure what to do.

In the movies everyone is always throwing pebbles at windows.

But I don't know which bedroom is his. I throw a pebble and I'm probably twice as likely to get Jack's window.

I'm hatching a complicated plan that involves climbing onto the roof when I remember. Henry has a phone. I've seen him use it. And now, for once in my damn life, I have a phone too. I pull it out, scroll through the contacts. Savannah has Henry's number. I have a quick stab of suspicion.

I'm not proud of this, but I read their past texts. They're all from last year, just a back and forth about a chemistry group project. Feeling relieved, and a little guilty, I text Henry.

Hey, are you at home?

Something hoots in the dark behind me. Something chitters. Something shrieks. The phone lights up.

Yeah. They let me out of the hospital. Are you okay?

I'm in the middle of typing a reply when another text comes through.

Is Jo okay?

My heart fucking soars.

Can you come outside right now? To the backyard? Alone.

Why?

Please.

The screen times out. There's no reply. I'm thinking maybe I should tell him that it's me, not Savannah, but then I hear a door open and shut. I squint into the darkness. There's a figure padding around the side of the house. I tense myself, ready to run in case it's Jack.

But he steps forward, out of the shadow of the house, into the backyard, where the moon can touch him, and it's Henry. Alone. He's wearing camo-green pajama pants and an enormous gray cardigan.

I step out from where I'm hiding.

"Jo?" he asks, squinting into the dark. He's got a big bandage taped to the side of his neck, with bruises puddling out from beneath it. I wonder if it hurts as much as my wrist.

"Jack's wrong," I say, walking toward him. "I didn't attack you. I don't know what he's told you, but I swear I would never do something like that."

"I know," he says. "I told him that."

"You did?" I'm not sure if I should be relieved or terrified. He must have seen her. He must know.

"Of course," says Henry. "I told him it was the ghost."

"What?" I think he must be joking, but he looks dead serious.

"The ghost," he says, earnestly. "The river ghost."

"Oh." Should I tell him he's wrong? I'm still not one hundred percent certain he's not messing with me.

"We heard her right beforehand," he adds.

"Yeah," I say. I guess, when I heard the wailing, even *I* thought it was a ghost, for a moment. It makes as much sense as anything, I guess. My sister the shadow girl, the spirit.

"You saw her too, right?" He's frowning. He looks so worried, so sad, and I want to laugh, but I stifle it. "No one believes me. They think I have a concussion."

"*Do* you have a concussion?" I reach out and touch his forehead, gently. Graze my fingers along it. It's so soft. I brush his hair aside. The ground is uneven where we're standing, so I'm actually a little taller than him. Poor Henry. I know exactly how it feels to have no one believe you. We are in this together now.

"Just a mild one," he says, blinking. He looks tired, a bit dazed. "Did you see her? Am I crazy?"

"I saw her," I say slowly. No need to mention I mean a different *her.* He's wrong, but it's better than the truth. And why shouldn't he believe in ghosts? He died, once, and came back. It's kind of sweet. No crazier than the nonsense the pastor spouts.

"Oh thank God." Henry lets out this goofy sigh and smiles at me. That smile is like an island in a hundred square miles of empty ocean.

I've been drowning until now. Every single person in my life is against me. Even Aggie, even Savannah, even my sister, for God's sakes. Nobody has smiled at me. Nobody has been on my side.

Finally, though, here's Henry. He isn't accusing, isn't shouting, isn't demanding. He's the only one. We could run away. Just the two of us. Steal Jack's car. Leave all this behind. Like every daydream I had in history class made real.

"We should tell Jack," Henry says.

"What?" I take a step backward, daydream shattered.

"He doesn't believe me about the ghost, but you can tell him you saw her too."

"Jack hates me." Doesn't he realize that? First ghosts, now this. How bad is his concussion?

"Well, yeah." Henry's smile falters and his hand drifts up toward his neck. "But only because he thinks it was you. He's been trying to convince me."

"It wasn't me," I say, gripped with a sudden fear. Maybe this ghost thing is just because of the concussion. Maybe when his mind clears, Jack will talk him around. Then Henry will hate me just like everyone else.

"I know."

"But it wasn't a ghost," I say quickly, before I can change my mind. I need one person to believe me. One person to be on my side.

I hold up the phone, fumble with the touch screen a moment until I've got the picture of my sister. I turn it around so he can see. He takes the phone, studies it. I reach over and swipe to the second picture.

I'm nervous now, wishing I'd just let it go, been content with what I had: one person who didn't hate me. But maybe it will work this time. Maybe he likes me enough to believe me, or at least give me the benefit of the doubt. We kissed, after all. Maybe I'm lit up golden in his mind like Jack is for Savannah. Maybe he can be the only one.

"I don't understand," he says, still staring at the screen.

"That's who attacked you," I say. "Not a ghost. My sister."

He looks up at me, brow furrowed.

"You don't—" he starts, but before he can get the words out, I lean forward and I put my hands on his arms and I kiss him.

It's not like last time. Our lips smoosh together off-center and his are slightly open since he was talking. It's wet and weird and my thoughts are racing, full of what a stupid idea this was. Coming here. Telling him. Henry pulls away and I take my hands off his arms.

"You don't have a sister," he says, our faces still so close that his breath puffs against my cheek.

"Never mind," I tell him, deflated. I barely know him, really. He barely knows me. Why did I think there was any hope? I could show him my wrist, go through the whole story, but it would sound absurd. I know that. My sister is stranger than a ghost. I got caught up in romantic ideas, as bad as Savannah. Worse. I shouldn't have told him. I'd take it back if I could. "Don't mention this to Jack," I add.

Henry furrows his brow, but he looks confused, not angry.

"You're weird," he says.

"So are you," I say. But he's not. He's ordinary.

He shrugs. "I'm supposed to be resting. Jack's been checking on me every fifteen minutes." He tries to hand the phone back to me.

"Run away," I say.

"What?"

"You should just run away." I don't know if I really mean it, but I know I want him to say yes. I want him to want me, to be willing to do anything for me. I want that kind of power. Maybe that's how Savannah feels.

I put my hand on Henry's arm again. His cardigan is scratchy and thick. I squeeze until I can feel his bicep, squeeze hard enough that it probably hurts. Maybe it's not too late. He can still be the one on my side. I want to steal him. Hide him away in the woods. Nurse him back to health. Stroke his forehead while he gazes up at me as if I'm the only thing in the world.

"Jack says I could have died," he says.

"That's not true." I say this too quickly. Wishful thinking. "They didn't even keep you in the hospital a whole day."

"They did give me a lot of drugs."

"Great," I say, grinning, trying to keep things light. "We can sell them."

He laughs. I lean toward him, thinking maybe I can try again, but then a voice comes from inside the house, shouting. "Henry?" It's Jack. I freeze. He shouts again. "Henry!"

I put a finger to my lips. We need to be quiet.

But Henry shoots me an apologetic look and shouts back, "I'm out here!"

I let go of his arm, take a step backward. I feel like I've been slapped. Betrayed again.

"You better go," Henry says. He holds out the phone. "I'll see you in history, yeah?"

He smiles. Not an island, at all. Not even a rocky outcropping. I hear the front door open, close.

Henry is lovely in the moonlight. I know that sounds stupid, but it's true. His pale skin reflects the light like a still pond. He is shallow liquid. He is water all the way through. I could reach right into him. I could rip him apart.

I snatch the phone from his hand and run.

I tear through the woods, heart pounding, until I'm sure that no one is coming after me. Then I turn back toward town. According to Savannah's phone, it's nearly ten. I've been gone a long time. I figure I'll keep to backyards, stay low, sneak through the shadows like my sister and I used to do. Maybe, if I'm extraordinarily lucky, I can make it to the alley beside Joe's Bar without getting spotted, can climb through my window and jump into bed, pretend I've been there all along, somehow. Although there's that damn light.

I cross the first road I come to, scramble down a hill, up another hill. I'm crossing the next road, when a car accelerates behind me. I turn just as a beat-up car swerves onto the shoulder and brakes hard, spraying gravel. The driver's door swings open.

"Jolene," says the pastor. "Get in the car. Now."

The pastor reaches across me and locks the door as soon as I get in, then grabs his phone from the cupholder. I lean my head back, try to pretend I'm fine with this turn of events.

"Don't tell Aggie," I suggest. "She'll be mad at you, too."

The pastor ignores me, dials.

"She's fine," he says into the phone. "I found her." So it's too late, I guess. Aggie already knows. I put a hand to my cheek involuntarily. She'll be mad again. Out of her skin. "I'm heading to the bar now."

The pastor hangs up and jerks the car back onto the road.

"You made a fool out of me," he says.

I cross my arms, stare out the window. I don't ask him what happened, but he tells me anyway. It turns out Savannah didn't snitch on me after all, which is something, I guess. It wasn't until the pastor got impatient and barged in to check on me that Savannah admitted I had crawled out the window.

Apparently Aggie's driving around right now too, looking for me. Which honestly surprises me. She hates leaving Jessi in charge of the bar. Aggie always likes to say that Jessi is as dumb as she is pretty, and that girl sure is pretty.

But when we pull up I see that the bar is closed. Which is absolutely crazy. It's Friday night. It's not even that late. And yet all the neon signs are off. I knew she'd be mad, but as Savannah would say, I am fucked.

The pastor and I wait outside in stubborn silence until Aggie pulls up in the rusty pickup she inherited from Grandpa Joe. I'm thinking maybe she'll slap me again; I'm bracing myself for it, but she doesn't even look at us. She just goes straight for the front door, unlocks it, lets it swing shut behind her with a bang.

"You're grounded," she says. I'm sitting at one of the scratched wooden tables downstairs. The pastor's at another table nearby and Aggie's pacing in front of me. There are empty glasses and bottles on some of the tables. She must have closed up in a hurry. "Hell, you're on house arrest. You are locked up. Life sentence. No parole."

The bar is dark, except for the one Budweiser ceiling lamp with the little plastic horses caught inside like a snow globe. I stare at the long shadows they cast on the wood-paneled wall. Aggie never would have tried to ground me a year ago. A year ago, she didn't believe in stuff like that. This is all the pastor's fault. It was probably his idea, even.

Not that I don't deserve it, I guess.

"I *should* send you back to your grandmother," Aggie says, banging a hand on the table in front of me. "She'd whip you into shape."

I cringe, but she can't mean it. Right? Aggie would sooner bleed out than ask Grandma Margaret for a bandage. Stubbornness runs in the family. God knows I've got it, but so does Aggie. She took me away from Margaret for a reason.

I know that for all the punishments I endured from Grandma Margaret, Aggie and Mama had it far worse when they were kids. Aggie blames Margaret for what happened to Mama. If Margaret hadn't kicked her out of the house, she'd still be alive today. I know Aggie blames herself too, though.

"I expected better than this from you," says Aggie, turning to pace again.

"Sorry," I mumble. I'm tired and my wrist still hurts like hell and I don't feel up to this. I've had enough from Savannah, from my sister.

I slump in my chair. The floor is uneven here and the chair wobbles drunkenly. Aggie stomps to one end of the bar, wheels around, marches back.

"I hardly know who you are anymore," she says when she passes my table.

I could say the same of you, I want to point out, but I bite my tongue. Maybe I'm wrong. Things have changed. Maybe she really would send me back to Margaret. The thought is sobering.

Aggie marches over to the bar. Makes herself a drink. A long pour of Jack. Shorter shot of Coke from the nozzle. She takes a sip. Turns back to me.

"Everyone is saying you attacked this boy Henry."

"I didn't." I can tell I don't sound very convincing. My heart's not in it. I'm worn out, tired of trying to convince people I'm not a monster.

"Everybody's talking about it. You should have seen the looks I got when I was out there just now asking people if anyone had seen you. They all heard what you did." She waves an arm, spilling some of her drink.

"I didn't, though. I swear, Aggie." Does she truly not believe me? It hurts that she'd be so willing to think the worst of me. Surely she should know not to put too much stock in gossip.

"How am I supposed to believe a word out of your mouth?" She marches back toward me. "After you lie to me twice? After you lie to him?" She jabs a finger at the pastor, who is brooding silently over a beer. "After you run off to God knows where?" I fidget with my sleeve, try to avoid looking at her. This isn't how it used to be. We used to be like sisters, coconspirators. It was us against Margaret, and Aggie was always on my side.

I want to go back to that.

"Are you out of your mind?" Aggie leans on the table in front of me, eyes searching my face. "Is that it? Are you going crazy too?"

I'm not sure what she means by *too*. I shrug. I just want to go to bed.

"Is it drugs?" She grabs my chin, tilts my face up so she can scrutinize my pupils.

"No." I pull away, hunching lower in my seat. Aggie downs the rest of her drink.

"Where did you even go?" she demands.

"Savannah's," I answer.

"I know. After that."

"Henry," I say. It's not a lie, though I'm leaving out one stop. "I went to see Henry."

"Jesus Christ." Aggie straightens up from the table, eyes hard. "Did you do anything else to that kid?"

"No! I wouldn't. I didn't. Aggie, please." My voice catches. Does she really believe that I would do that? Is she thinking about my father now? How there's evil in my blood? I don't want to cry. "I just had to make sure he was okay."

"So you tricked us and ran off?"

"I'm really sorry, Aggie," I say. "I swear it won't happen again."

"You think I'm stupid? He told me how you've been going out your window for weeks." She points at the pastor, who doesn't meet my eyes. "Right under my nose."

"I—"

"Don't fuck with me, little girl," Aggie says, and in that moment she sounds just like her mother. She bangs a hand on the table again. "I don't want to hear any more excuses. You are going to tell me where it is you've been going all these nights and you are going to tell me the truth."

I slump down as far in my chair as I can. What can I say? *Yes, Aggie, I've been sneaking off to shoot up?* She'd ship me off to rehab, maybe. Make me piss in a cup every day. Staying clean would be easy. I have zero desire to go anywhere near hard drugs. I've seen what they can do. We've had enough overdoses at Joe's that Aggie keeps a supply of Narcan behind the bar.

I could tell her I'm a thief. Could tell her I've got a secret boy-friend. Could say it's Henry. Why not? I've been sneaking off to have sex. I could tell her that. She'd be disappointed, ashamed. Is this how I repay her? She'd yell at me, hate me maybe. Her failure of an almost-daughter.

But it isn't fair. I shouldn't have to confess to a sin I've never committed.

"I went to see my sister," I say.

"What?" She reels back. Her expression alone almost makes the confession worth it. She wasn't expecting that.

"I went to see my sister," I repeat, matter-of-fact.

"You don't have a goddamn sister," she says, still more stunned than angry.

"I do," I say. "I've always had one. She lives in the woods."

It really is satisfying to tell the truth, even though I know Aggie thinks I'm lying.

"You are testing my patience," Aggie says, rubbing her fore-head with both palms.

"No, I'm telling you the truth," I say calmly, because I am, for once. "Mama had twins."

Aggie hauls back and slaps me. It hurts, bad. Worse than last time. And I'm no more prepared for it, no less stunned. She doesn't even look sorry.

"Don't you dare bring her into this," she says, voice hard and burning with anger. "Don't you even talk about her."

I can't help it, then, I start crying. Not out loud or anything. Just hot tears drying on my cheeks, the salt stinging my skin. It's too much. When we were younger, I would make fun of Savannah if she cried. Crying is for babies and drunk old men who've pissed them-selves, I'd say. That's what Aggie always told me. Apparently when she and Mama would cry as children, Grandma Margaret would show them a picture of Jesus stuck to the cross, jab a finger at his face. *See any tears there, little girl? You telling me that you scraping your knee is worse than this man having nails pounded through his hands?*

Crying is a weakness. But I'm feeling pretty weak. My cheek rings with pain. It isn't fair. I'm telling the truth and it makes no difference. I didn't even expect Aggie to believe me, but it still hurts that not a single person in my life is willing to trust me.

I pull Savannah's phone out of my pocket.

"Where the hell did you get that?" demands Aggie. "Are you stealing now, too?"

"No, I borrowed it from Savannah." I pull up the pictures of Lee and hold the phone out. "Just look."

"What is this supposed to be?"

"My sister. I'm telling the truth, I swear." I sound desperate.

Aggie squints at the picture. "That looks like you."

"We're *twins*," I say, and realize, much too late, that I should have tried to get a picture of both of us. It seems obvious to me that Lee looks different, despite our similar features. Her face is thinner, eyebrows thicker, unplucked across the bridge of her nose. You can see her matted hair in the picture, and the cut on her cheek. There's no cut on my cheek.

But Aggie's eyes are tight with barely contained fury, her mouth pressed into a thin hard line. "I'm not falling for that old lie." She turns away, rubs her face with her hands. "You were right," she says to the pastor. "I've been an idiot."

"No," says the pastor gently. "She's out of control. But this stops now. All of it."

She strides over to the door that leads to the basement, stomps down the stairs. I can hear her banging around down there.

I rub my cheeks dry with my sleeve. "You told her I've been sneaking out the window." I scowl at the pastor. "I thought you said you were on my side."

"Now hold on," he says. "I'm still on your side, but you tricked me. You disappeared. What was I supposed to do?"

He looks sheepish. Extra young, slouching in his chair. As if he actually thinks I believed we were in this together. But I never did.

"I hate you," I say.

"Hey," he says, looking genuinely crestfallen, which makes me feel just the tiniest bit better.

Aggie stomps back up from the basement. She's got a couple of warped boards tucked under one arm, leftovers from the old renovation, and a toolbox swinging from the other arm. She marches right past us and into the kitchen. We hear her clomping up the stairs to the second floor.

By the time I catch up to her, Aggie's in my room, pressing one of the boards against my window.

"What are you doing?" I ask.

"Help me out here," she says. The pastor shoots me an apologetic look, then goes to hold the board still.

I stand in the doorway and watch as Aggie picks up the hammer and drives a nail into the board. Then another. And another.

She doesn't stop until my whole window is boarded shut. She won't say a word to me, even when I try to talk to her, to plead my case, to apologize.

After the pastor and Aggie leave, I check Savannah's phone. There are three messages from her sister Dakota's number, although it is clear they are actually from Savannah.

where are u

bring my fuckin phone back
u bitcch

I turn the phone off, hide it under the mattress, next to my envelope of money, and crawl into bed. I cry for real now, pulling the blanket over my head to muffle my sobs.

My wrist hurts, my cheek hurts, and no one is on my side.

Not Aggie. Not Savannah. Not Henry.

Not even my sister.

She ruined everything. My first kiss. My best friend. She doesn't even realize how badly she ruined everything. She was mad that I couldn't run every night, but now I probably can't run ever again. Now everyone thinks I'm a monster.

But it's her. Not me. I'm just a girl. I'm normal. I'm nothing.

I'm woken by a bang. I sit bolt upright in bed. It's dark and my mind is still stuck in the mud of sleep. Light pushes through a crack between the boards over the window, but it doesn't feel like morning. I check the clock: 4:00 a.m. A moment later, I hear scraping on the other side of the door and then it swings open. The pastor is silhouetted. He fumbles along the wall, flips the light switch on. I shield my eyes.

"Is she trying to get out?" Aggie's voice comes from behind him.

"No," he says. "She's still in bed."

Aggie pushes past him. Her eyes go from me to the window, where the boards are firmly in place. She crosses the room, tries to peer through the cracks between the boards.

"What the hell was that?" she demands.

"I don't know." I rub my eyes. My mouth feels stale and dry.

"Must have been something outside," says the pastor, who is still standing in the doorway. He's wearing boxers and that's it. There's a big tattoo of a cross on his bicep. His chest is surprisingly hairless. He's much doughier-looking than Jack. Kind of has the start of a beer belly going. Just a little swell, like he's a few months pregnant or something.

"Do you live here now?" I ask him.

"No," he says.

"Mind your own damn business," snaps Aggie. "Go back to sleep."

As if on cue, the motion sensor light outside the window clicks off and the boards go dark.

CHAPTER NINE

When I wake up again a few hours later, I feel sick. Really sick. Worse than I did yesterday morning. And my wrist aches terribly.

My room is dark. Just one thin sliver of sun forcing itself through the boards. I pad over to the door. It doesn't open. I jiggle the handle, jiggle it harder. What the hell? My door doesn't even have a lock. I bang on the door with my good hand.

A moment later, there's a scraping noise and the pastor opens the door. He's wearing his proper black pastoring clothes, complete with the stiff white collar. No goofy jacket. By his feet, I see the fifteen-gallon keg that had been blocking me in.

"This is bullshit," I tell him.

"It wasn't my idea," he whispers as I push past him.

In the bathroom, I study my wrist. It's still red and the swelling hasn't gone down even a little. The skin is glistening, wet, but not with blood. I poke around in the cupboard under the sink, find some self-sticking stretchy wrap left over from my track days. I wash my wrist, rub soap into the wound even though touching it makes the pain blaze. Then I wrap it as tight as I can stand with the stretchy wrap.

Aggie's in the kitchen when I come out, but she's not cooking anything. Just sitting at the card table in her robe, hunched over a bit, drinking her coffee mechanically. I pour myself some Cheerios, trace the little maze on the back of the box, find all the dead ends.

"You'd better get dressed," Aggie says, "you've got church."

I'd forgotten all about that. Sheila's baptism. The deal I made with the pastor. I start to say something about how I'm feeling sick, but Aggie turns and shoots me a look so cold that it shuts me right up.

"The police called," she says. "You're going to have to go down to the station later today to give another statement."

My appetite is gone. I drop my Cheerios bowl back down on the counter so hard it rings.

I guess I shouldn't be surprised. Henry's parents must be angry. I bet they think I'm the one who attacked him, just like everyone else does.

Even Aggie.

Will they press charges? Will I be arrested? Locked up for my sister's crimes? She has no idea what she's done. No idea how she's ruined everything.

Defeated, I slink away and get dressed for church. Choose my rattiest hoodie and jeans as a small rebellion. Before I leave my bedroom, I pull Savannah's phone from under the mattress and slip it into my pocket.

I follow the pastor outside. His car is parked in the alley behind the building. Before we reach it, though, he stops and stares up at my bedroom window.

It's smashed. There's a jagged hole in the middle and cracks shooting out in all directions. Slivers of broken glass glitter along the rungs of the fire escape. I remember the noise that woke me last night. I feel cold. Hot at the same time. Burning from the inside out. What if the boards hadn't been there?

"Who the hell did that?" asks the pastor.

"No idea," I say, honestly.

I think of Jack first. Maybe he was trying to scare me. Send me a message. Maybe he was coming to beat me up, to kill me.

"Aggie won't be happy," the pastor says.

Could it have been Savannah? She's mad as hell, for sure (*bitcch*). Maybe she'd come over to take her phone back. Or maybe it was just someone who'd heard what I did and thought I deserved to be punished.

I nudge a sliver of broken glass with the toe of my sneaker. It flashes in the sun. A warning.

"Might as well file a report," says the pastor. "We'll be going to the station when we get back anyway."

Of course, there is someone else I know who's also angry at me. Who might communicate that anger by throwing rocks. But it couldn't have been her. She would never come this far into town. Not for all the chocolate in the world.

A few blocks away, the pastor pulls up in front of a raggedy shotgun house. Sheila's sister's place. He honks once. I pick at some peeling plastic on the dashboard.

"She never mentioned twins," the pastor says into the silence.

"Nobody did."

It takes me a moment to understand. Twins. I said it last night. *Mama had twins.*

I don't know why he's bringing that up now, out of nowhere.

Does he want to lecture me more about lying? Recite the commandments at me?

Or is he giving me the benefit of the doubt?

"Maybe nobody knew," I say softly.

He *hmm*s, stares out the window. Doesn't tell me I'm wrong. Doesn't tell me not to lie.

I shouldn't take the bait. I know I shouldn't. He's a wolf, picking on the weakest lamb in the flock. I'm broken, alone. No one is on my side.

"Did she ever get one of those ultrasound things?" I ask, trying to use the opening to my advantage, dig for information. Did Mama know she was having twins? I've often wondered this, but Aggie refuses to talk about Mama and I don't dare ask Margaret.

When Savannah's sister Dakota was pregnant, they had a picture from the scan taped up on the fridge. It was the freakiest-looking thing, the baby just a vague white outline, like a chalked body at a crime scene.

"I don't know," the pastor says. "I know she didn't give birth in a hospital, though."

He glances over at me. I look away, disappointed.

"Yeah, everybody knows that."

"If she had twins," says the pastor, "what happened to the other baby?"

I turn back, look him in the eye. No grin, no glint, no smirk. He looks serious. He looks like he really wants to know.

There's no way he believes me. Savannah didn't even believe me and she's my best friend. There's no way the goddamn pastor is the only one who believes me. This must be some kind of trick.

Right?

"Well," I say slowly, watching his face, trying to gauge his sincerity by his reaction, "I always figured the Cantrells must have kept her."

"Wouldn't the police have found out?"

"Why would they?" I scoff. "They never even found Mama's body."

He frowns at me. I know what's coming next. Don't lie, Jolene. Don't make up stories.

"She did look pretty huge toward the end," he says instead, tilting his head, considering.

A picture pops into my mind of Mama as a giant, towering over the tiny town of Lester, stomping houses with her bare feet, uprooting trees and munching on the leaves.

But he means her belly of course. Full of the two of us.

"How did you find out about her?" he asks, drumming his fingers on the steering wheel. "Your sister."

This isn't how I expected this conversation to go. I gape at him for a moment. *Your sister.* Did I hear him right? He didn't say, *Your sister who doesn't exist?*

"She just showed up one day," I say. "When I was younger. She came out of the woods."

Again, I expect him to protest, same as everyone else. *Girls don't just come out of the woods. Stop being stupid, Jo.*

"How old were you?" he asks instead.

I let out a breath. "About five."

"Five," he repeats. "Logan and Brandon were both gone by then. Did she tell you she'd been living with them?"

"Well, no, but it makes sense." Someone obviously cared for Lee through infancy. Brandon Cantrell is the one who dropped me off at Grandma Margaret's house, so he must have been involved somehow.

I often wonder why he did it. Maybe Logan wanted to kill us, too, and Brandon saved me, and then Logan changed his mind and raised Lee. Maybe they tried to keep us both, but two babies were too much to handle, so they tossed a coin and only kept one. "How did she survive?" the pastor asks. "After they left?"

I know that Logan went to jail when Lee and I were four. From what I can gather, Brandon skipped town a few months after. So, yeah, there's a little bit of missing time there, before Lee showed up in my backyard. Maybe that's when she went feral. She certainly didn't look well cared for when we met.

But that's not the important thing right now.

How did *she survive?* the pastor said. Not, *How could anyone have possibly survived?* But *how did she.* There's no denying it now. The goddamn pastor believes me.

"She wasn't like other kids," I say. "She's not—"

And then Sheila's rapping on the back window. I jump at the sound. The pastor pops the lock for her, shoots me a quick smile.

"Look what my cousin did for me last night," Sheila says as she slides into the backseat.

She fans out her fingers. There are tiny crosses painted on each nail. For a second I think they are silver like Mama's necklace, but then she tilts them so they catch the light and I see that they are gold.

Sheila keeps up a running commentary the rest of the way to church, so I don't get to ask the pastor why he believes me. I don't know if I'm relieved about that or angry that he's the only one who does. I don't know how to feel, other than sick. I hunch my shoulders, hold my breath as the car dips and swerves along the wooded ridges.

The church, when we reach it, isn't much to look at. Just a squat brick building at the end of a long dirt road. If it weren't for the sign you'd never even know. It's a lot less impressive than the church Grandma Margaret took me to when I was younger, but that one has since shut down because the building was too expensive to keep up. Margaret drives to a church in Delphi now.

The pastor leads us inside. The room is carpeted. High-ceilinged, but plain. Instead of pews, there are rows of folding chairs. The stained-glass windows are just regular windows, painted. One shows a faceless Jesus with blobby hands. Another, a misshapen snowball in flight. Or maybe it's meant to be a dove.

The pastor carries a deflated plastic kiddie pool out from a room in the back and sets it up in the front corner. It's decorated with cartoon fish. Not the baptismal font I was expecting. Sheila and I take turns blowing it up while the pastor drags a hose through the entrance and fills the pool with about a foot of luke-warm water. We finish just as the first parishioner arrives, a thin old woman with a walker who I think I've seen at Minnie's before.

I pick a chair in the back of the room and sit, feeling dizzy from inflating the pool, and too hot. I want to roll up my sleeves, but I can't because someone might notice my wrist.

The pastor stands by the entrance, greeting everyone who comes in. Apart from Sheila and two families with kids, there's hardly anyone who looks younger than sixty. Most of the fold-ing chairs are still empty when it's time for the service to begin. I understand why Grandma Margaret looks down on this, though in a way there's less artifice here than there was at her church. No hiding behind fancy architecture. No cold and echoey stone, no statues staring you down, judging you through the centuries.

Not that I'm about to convert or anything. But the pastor is the only person in my entire life who believes me, so I guess I'm feeling charitable.

At the front of the little room, the pastor calls on the Lord to bring this country not only to its feet again but to its knees. I wish Savannah weren't mad at me so I could tell her that and we could both laugh.

The pastor pops a cassette tape into the little stereo on the chair beside him, presses Play. It's a recording of voices singing the hymns. At Margaret's old church there was an organ, a choir. I move my mouth without actually singing. The tune sounds vaguely familiar, but I don't remember the words. Two rows up from me an old lady warbles along a whole octave higher.

"Let us now exchange the sign of peace," says the pastor, when the song is done.

Everybody stands up. A tiny old woman with watery eyes behind thick peach-rimmed glasses staggers over to me and clutches at my arm as if she were falling.

"Bless you for coming, honey," she says. "So many kids these days have lost their way."

A cloud of perfume thick as a swarm of gnats envelops me, clogs up my nose and catches in my throat. It takes every ounce of willpower I have not to retch. As soon as the woman moves on, another takes her place. There's a whole procession of them, each one older than the next. And the older they are, the stronger their perfume. One of them grabs both my hands, sandwiches them between hers.

"Peace be with you," she says.

"Uh, thanks," I say.

There's a crash from behind us. Everyone freezes. I whip around. One of the painted windows is smashed, glass strewn across the carpet. A rock rolls to a stop inches from the inflatable pool in the corner. The little old lady next to me gasps, tightens her bony grip on my hands.

Another window shatters, this one closer to where we're standing. Shards of painted glass clang against the metal legs of the folding chairs. Several people scream. The pastor is telling everyone to stay calm, to get away from the windows.

I jerk my hands free and run for the door.

Glass crunches under my shoes. More shards glitter in the water in the inflatable baptism pool. One must have pierced the plastic because the pool is sagging to the side, the cartoon fishes slumping into one another, a wet spot darkening the carpet.

I push through the door, skid to a stop as it bangs shut behind me. There's a low mound of earth to the left of the building. And there, at the top, with a rock clutched in one fist: her.

She's here. In the daylight. Her blue dress the same color as the sky. She is perfectly still for a moment, watching.

The church door swings open behind me. My sister drops the rock and runs.

I start to follow but there's a hand on my arm.

"Where are you going?" the pastor demands.

"It was her," I say, trying to pull away. "My sister. She ran that way."

The pastor stares down at me, brow furrowed.

"It was her," I say again. "She was throwing rocks. She must have been the one who broke my window."

I can hardly believe it, but it seems clear now. She was here, in the daylight. She is breaking all her own rules. She is going to finish what she started. She is going to destroy my whole life. I try to jerk my arm away, but the pastor doesn't let go. He's just staring at me, like he doesn't believe me after all.

"I thought you were on my side," I say, and I intend it to sound angry, but instead my voice hitches like I'm going to cry.

A flicker of something crosses the pastor's face. And then he lets go of my arm—so suddenly I almost fall—and before I can react, he's off running, scrambling up the mound, disappearing beyond it.

"What's going on?" somebody asks from behind me. "Was it teenagers?"

I run.

On the other side of the mound there's a small gulley before the ground swells upward and the forest begins. The pastor has stopped just beyond the tree line. I slide down into the gulley, run up the other side.

"Did you see her?" I ask when I reach him.

"I saw someone," he says. He's scanning the trees, but there's no sign of her. The forest is still and quiet. I can hear the pastor's wheezing breaths. He's out of breath already from his short sprint.

"There," he whispers, and I look and she's stepping out from behind a thick oak. She meets my eyes. She was waiting. Waiting for me.

The pastor races toward her. She turns and runs. He'll never catch her. I overtake him easily, follow the flashes of blue.

I'm not used to doing this in the daytime. The sun knifes in at sharp angles, cutting stripes across the trees, shooting through the undergrowth. Everything is so bright it almost seems fake.

I circle around a huge fallen tree to cut my sister off, but she darts the other way, and I stumble over a jutting root. The pastor goes scrabbling past me, sending dead leaves flying in his wake. I try to follow, but the sun gets in my eyes and in a moment I lose sight of both of them.

Up ahead, the pastor shouts. A quick sharp cry of surprise. I push myself forward, muscles burning, small branches whipping against my chest, my face. My head pounds. My wrist throbs so hard I can practically hear it.

I skid to a stop just in time to avoid careering over the edge of a small drop-off, where the ground falls away suddenly before continuing about five feet lower.

The pastor is lying on his side down there, clutching his leg and groaning. My sister is standing a few feet from him. Not running away. Just standing there, watching him.

I crouch at the edge of the drop-off and jump down. Lee turns to face me. Her ribs heave, straining against the fabric of her dress. It looks worse in the daylight, ripped, stained, and faded. Everything looks worse. Her matted hair. Her dirty nails. Fresh scratches on her legs stand out bright red. She's left her plastic heart purse somewhere, stowed in a hollow tree or under a rock.

"What are you doing?" I shout at her. "This is crazy."

"Run away," she says.

"I think I broke my damn ankle," says the pastor.

"Get up," I tell him.

"No," says Lee. She crouches, digs around in the dead leaves. When she stands she's holding a fist-sized rock, jagged, with clods of dirt and dead grass still clinging to it.

"We just want to help you," gasps the pastor, his voice tight with pain as he struggles to stand. He's leaning against the rocky face of the drop-off, trying to pull himself up without putting any weight on the injured foot. He wobbles, puts his foot down to catch himself, grunts, drops back down to his knees.

My sister takes a step forward.

"Wait," I say. "Don't hurt him."

"You," she says. She's looking at me, not at the pastor. She's coming toward me. I back up a step, but the little cliff is at my back. She broke my window. Last night. Was she coming to break me out? Or to break me?

"Lee," I say, trying to sound calm, "just wait a second, let's talk, okay? Forget about him. Let's just talk. You and me."

"You and him," she says.

"No," I say. I take a few sideways steps, away from the pastor. "No. Just you and me."

"You and him!" she shouts, her voice cracking. I'm not sure whether she means the pastor or Henry.

She marches right up to me until we're face to face. The cut on her cheek has scabbed over. Her eyes are so much like mine, her nose, her mouth. And yet everything about her face is absolutely different. She is the most important person in my life and I have done everything for her. Protected her. Kept her secret. Why can't she see that?

"You and me," I say again, staring back. "I don't even care about him. I swear."

There's a shuffling sound. We both turn to look at the pastor. He's dragged himself away a little. He's got something in his hands, which are shaking. His phone.

My sister lunges at him with the rock.

"Wait!" I shout. The pastor throws an arm up to protect himself, hand blocking his face. My sister swings the rock, but she's not aiming for his head. The rock connects with his other hand, knocks the phone out of it. The pastor howls. The phone skitters away in the leaves. Lee scrambles after it, raises the rock in the air, and smashes it down right in the center of the screen. She bashes the phone again and again with the rock, shattering the glass.

The pastor crawls toward her in the dirt. My heart thuds along with the rock. This is happening too fast. I feel light-headed.

Lee doesn't notice the pastor until it's too late. He grabs her arm. She tries to pull away, but he's strong. He's a grown man. Next to him, my sister looks so small.

"Don't be scared," says the pastor. "I just want to help you."

She tries to kick him, but he just grabs her ankle with his free hand. She bucks and squirms. I can see her panic in the way she moves. Frantic. Uncoordinated. She's not thinking. She's flopping like a hooked fish. Her dress bunches up from the friction of her squirming, rides up over her ass, over her crotch.

"Jesus Christ," says the pastor. "Help me hold her, Jo."

I take a few steps forward, but I don't know what to do. My sister's panic is contagious. The sunlight is too bright. I'm not used to seeing her this way. Exposed. Weak.

I'm mad at her. I should be mad at her.

My sister tries to bite the pastor, but he pushes her back, twists her around so she's facing away from him. He wraps his arms around her chest, pinning her arms firmly at her sides. She kicks uselessly at the dirt and leaves in front of her. She shrieks. A flock of birds startle from the brush. The pastor kneels behind her, trying to keep her still.

"Jo," he says, "can you get her to calm down somehow?"

"Stop struggling," I hear myself say. My voice sounds far away, disconnected.

My sister just kicks harder.

"Stop kicking," I say. "It's not helping. He's stronger than you."

My sister stops kicking. She wriggles a few times, then goes still, lets her hands drop.

"I'm trying to help you," says the pastor. "Don't be scared. I'm a friend of Jolene's and I want to help both of you. Tell her, Jo."

"Don't be scared," I say. I'm frozen, just standing there uselessly. I should move. I should help one of them. But which one?

"What's your name?" the pastor asks. "What did you call her, Jo?"

My sister has gone limp. She's slumped in the pastor's arms, head dangling down toward her chest, legs in the dirt, and I'm worried he's hurt her, squeezed her too hard, forced the breath out of her or snapped a rib. She looks so much smaller than usual.

"Lee?" I say.

My sister's hands move, clutching at the dirt. She ducks her head down and in one swift move, snaps her arms up, sending two handfuls of dirt flying backward, right into the pastor's face. He yells, lets go, and clutches his face.

She wrenches free, jumps to her feet, but the pastor grabs blindly at her dress, manages to get a fistful of skirt. My sister lunges forward, but she's caught again. The pastor wipes his eyes, then grabs her skirt with his other hand. She strains to break away, pulling like an animal caught in a trap. The kind of frantic struggling that only gets them tangled.

"Don't be scared!" I shout.

My sister freezes in place. She puts her hands up in the air, like she's surrendering.

Then she falls, suddenly—just collapses to the ground like a dropped doll. There's the sound of ripping fabric and she's up again and running, butt-naked, the dress discarded in the dirt, the pastor grasping at nothing.

He stares down at the dress, head bowed. Touches it with one hand, as if to reassure himself. He looks up to where my sister has disappeared already over the crest of a small ridge. Finally, he turns back to me. He's breathing hard. His eyes are red and watery, his face streaked with dirt, collar askew.

"Jesus," he says. "Lord and savior. She's real. You weren't lying."

"No shit," I say. I wish it were Aggie or Savannah here with me. Wish, almost, that I could go back to before, when nobody believed me. It feels so strange now, to have the secret out in the open. Feels dangerous.

"Look what she did to my hand." He holds it out. I take another step forward. The jagged rock sliced the base of his thumb a little. There's a bit of blood smeared on his palm.

"At least she didn't bite you," I say. My wrist still throbs dully. A steady pain.

I crouch beside the torn remnants of my sister's blue dress, brush my fingers over the fabric. She's worn it for five years, stubborn as anything. The fabric's so thin, it's a small miracle it didn't fall apart before now. It had been a gift from Grandma Margaret for my tenth birthday. I don't even like dresses. But my sister's eyes lit up when I brought it to her that night. She tore off her old dress immediately and put it on, stroked the shiny fabric, admired the lace, spun in giddy circles.

The pastor pushes himself slowly to his feet, groaning, takes a few stumbling steps to the nearest tree, and leans against it

"You've got to help me," he says. "I think my ankle's just sprained, but it hurts to put weight on it. You help me back, then we'll put a search party together."

"Search party?" I straighten up. "No."

"God. I can't believe she's even alive."

"You can't tell the police," I say. Here it is. All my fears, all Lee's fears, coming true all at once. It's her fault this is happening, but it's mine too. I told the pastor and now I'll lose her. This is happening too fast. "They'll lock her up. Promise me you won't tell them."

"Jo," he says softly. "She's obviously . . . she needs help."

He tries to take a step toward me, winces.

"She's fine," I say. I stand up too quickly and my head spins. He doesn't know anything. Doesn't know her.

"Fine?" The pastor looks aghast. "Jesus, Jo. Did you see her? She's a mess. She's probably sick. I mean, what does she even eat? She's so skinny. She's got to be half starved."

"She's a good hunter."

"She's a child." He takes a lurching step over to a skinny tree, leans heavily against it. "I can't even imagine what it must have been like for her out here, all alone."

"She's wasn't alone." I take a step backward, away from him. "She had me."

"I'm sorry, Jo," he says, "I know this must be tough for you. But you did the right thing telling me about her."

I'm not sure if I did.

"The Lord brought me here for a reason," says the pastor. "Your mother . . . I couldn't save her. But now—" He gives me a lopsided smile, tears sparkling at the corners of his eyes. "Now I've got a second chance. It's why I came back, Jo."

"What?" I take another step backward.

"After I left Lester," says the pastor, still with that funny smile, "I never wanted to see it again. But when I heard Pastor Nelson had died, that they were looking for someone to take over his church, I knew it was a sign. I knew I had to come back for you."

For me? What the hell is he talking about?

"I can save you," he says. "I can save both of you."

Something boils up inside me. My sister's bare legs kicking at the dirt. That dark valley between them. The pastor's hands on her shoulders. The pastor's arms around her, holding her, pinning her, squeezing her. How small she looked.

He wants to trap her. Wants to make her that small forever.

"No," I say, backing up.

"Jo," says the pastor, holding out his hand, still leaning against that reedy little tree, still smiling with tears in his eyes. "Help me."

Help him or help her. It's one or the other.

I have been trying to have it both ways for so long. Keeping one foot in the normal world and one in the world of my sister. Splitting myself in half. But I can't anymore.

I take another step backward. The pastor's smile drops away. He lets go of the tree, tries to take a step forward, winces.

"Jo?" he says. He looks scared now, blue eyes wide, outstretched hand quivering in the air.

I turn and run.

"Jo!" shouts the pastor behind me. "Jo, wait. Come back. Jolene!"

I don't know where I'm going. I just run, sloppily, panting, half tripping on roots, sliding on leaves, letting branches whack against me. I don't make it very far before I have to stop, lean against a tree, catch my breath. My head is spinning.

I hear a stick crack and I whip around and it's her, bare as a winter branch. He's right. She *is* skinny. I can see her ribs. Her hip bones jutting like roots. Her chest is flatter than mine, her breasts barely swells.

Maybe he's right. Maybe she really isn't getting enough to eat. I don't know.

She steps closer, holds out a thin dirty hand.

I take it.

CHAPTER TEN

We run for a long time. I don't think. I open my chest, open my head, let the air stream through them as I run. In some places the trees are so thick that the sun doesn't reach us, caught in the web of leaves high above. In other places the sun whips across our faces, sets the weeds on fire.

I outrun my pain, outrun my thoughts, outrun my body. When I run long enough I forget that I even have a body. I forget who I am. I am only motion.

I am free.

My sister finally slows, drops down to a jog, and then stops. We must be a long way from Lester, deep into the national forest. Miles away from houses, miles away from anybody.

I lean against a tree and try to catch my breath. I feel like I'm still running, like the wind is still whipping through me. My stomach lurches. I buckle to my knees and dry heave.

"Don't be stupid," says Lee.

But I can't help it. Waves of nausea pulse through me, each one bigger and stronger than the last until it is too much and I puke, liquid splattering across the leaves. Afterward my throat burns with bile and my limbs feel shaky, weightless.

"Gross," says Lee. I laugh. My laugh feels hysterical, like it's spewing out of me too.

My sister pulls me to my feet. My wrist is throbbing. My head is throbbing. I've puked from running before, when I push myself too fast, too far. It's no big deal. I just need to sit down.

She leads me through some brambles to a shallow cave carved into the side of a rock overhang. Bare tree roots jut out above the entrance, which I have to stoop to walk through.

I sink down along the side of the cave and lean my head against the stone. I've seen some of her hideouts before, but never this one. I'm almost offended that she's never brought me here, but maybe it was just too far. At the back of the cave there's a big green trash bag propped against the wall and beside it another trash bag, this one folded up flat and held down with a pile of rocks. Lee squats beside it.

"You really need to put on some clothes," I tell her. Her spine pushes out from her back like a line of stepping-stones. There's a big yellow bruise on one hip. Scratches on her thighs. Bug bites dense as freckles. I've caught fleas from my sister a few dozen times, lice twice.

She removes the rocks carefully from the flattened trash bag and pulls a thick dirt-colored book from the folds. If I hadn't already lost my library card, this would do it for sure. I don't even remember checking this book out. How long overdue must it be?

Lee holds it out for me to take, grinning.

"I don't want to read right now," I say. "My head hurts." Everything hurts.

She pushes the book into my hands. The front cover is barely attached, worn at the corners and dappled with water stains. There's no Lester County Library sticker. The spine is black and cracked, pieces of it flaking away, but I can make out, faintly, the embossed words running along it: *Holy Bible.* I blink at it, confused. This copy doesn't even have pictures. Where did she get it? Maybe I brought it to her a long time ago and then forgot?

"Come on," says Lee. She scoots over to sit next to me, folds her bony knees up to her chest, still naked, unashamed. The book smells moldy. I open it to the first page and something falls out, flutters into my lap.

It's the picture of Mama. The one Lee stole, all those years ago, the school photo. Mama is beautiful. Prettier than me, I think. She's got a small nose, long eyelashes, black eyeliner. She looks sort of like if you crossed me and Savannah.

I squint, and sure enough, there's a thin silver chain around her neck—the pastor was telling the truth about the necklace. You can only see it at the sides, and then it disappears into her shirt.

Lee reaches for the picture, but I clutch it to my chest, cover it with both hands.

"This is mine," I tell her, calm but firm. "You stole this from me."

She frowns, but takes the book instead. I slide the picture into the pocket of my jeans, alongside Savannah's phone. My sister traces the letters on the spine of the Bible, opens it, flips through the first few pages. They're ruffled from water damage, some ripped.

"In the beginning," she says, "was nothing because nothing had been created yet. The world was empty and darkness was on the face of the deep."

The font in Bibles is always small and cramped, and Lee is not reading slow and halting like she usually does. I'm impressed, until I realize her eyes aren't following the words on the page at all. She's reciting from memory. Maybe I stole the Bible from Grandma Margaret when we were both little? Maybe I read it to her?

But I don't think so. I think I would remember that. This must be from before. The Cantrells.

"In the beginning was nobody," says Lee.

"Is it hot in here?" I ask. We're shaded from the sun, but my skin feels like it's burning.

Lee tilts her head at me, reaches out to touch my cheek. I put the back of my hand to my other cheek. It feels warm. My forehead too.

"I don't feel so good," I say. My arms and legs have begun to ache. Not the satisfied ache after a hard run, but a sharp ache like my bones have been replaced with knives.

My sister sets the book down and crawls over to the big trash bag at the back of the cave. She unties it, pulls out a brown blanket. She scoots back over to me and tucks the blanket around my shoulders. It's scratchy and smells worse than the book. I push it away. She should use it to cover her own nakedness. Not that it really matters this deep in the woods. No one to see. No one to make it into something wrong.

"Come on," Lee says. "Don't be stupid." She wads the blanket up and pushes it against the cave wall. She shoves my shoulder, trying to tilt me over. I laugh but indulge her, flop sideways onto the blanket.

This is all new for her. I've always been the one who takes care of her, not the other way around. When she had a particularly bad cut, I brought Band-Aids and antibiotic ointments. When she sprained her wrist, I made her a splint out of sticks. I brought her shampoo for the fleas once. Anti-itch ointment for the flea bites when the shampoo didn't work.

It was more than I could ever really handle, I guess. If she'd been able to come live with me and Aggie, she could have gone to a doctor, but of course she'd never let a stranger so much as get near her, let alone touch her, hold their fingers to her wrist, press a strange metal instrument to her chest.

Now, she scrabbles on all fours over to the cave entrance, leaps up, and moves out of sight.

"Lee?" I call, sitting up. The movement makes me dizzy. A moment later, she pops her head back around the side of the cave, backlit, the stringy hairs around her face dangling like vines. She waves a hand at me forcefully, indicating that I should lie back down.

"Where are you going?" I ask.

"Food," she says, and then she's gone again.

I picture her coming back with a bloody squirrel dangling from her mouth, and my stomach turns. My sister eats raw meat. She has for as long I've known her. I guess she's just used to it, has built up a tolerance. If I tried, I'm sure I'd be sick. Sicker than I already am.

I lie down, on my back this time, and stare up at the ceiling of the cave.

There's a crack down the middle of the stone, shooting up into darkness. The rock to either side of it is smooth and mottled with swirling patterns of white calcium deposits. In places the patterns look like faces. They remind me of the shadow girl on the wall on the high school. Well, here I am. I've crossed over into her world. When I stare at the faces they move. One opens its mouth as if to speak.

I squeeze my eyes shut. The waves are back, pulsing through me. The moldy smell of the blanket wraps around me. I breathe through my teeth, try to push the feeling down.

There's a rustling and I open my eyes and she's back. She's not holding a squirrel carcass, but a can of Campbell's soup.

"Where'd you get that?" I ask. It seems so out of place here. Did she pop into the local forest 7-Eleven, pay the deer cashier in pebbles?

She crawls into the cave, turns the can upside down, and starts scraping it against the rock floor. Most of the label has peeled off the can, but I can make out the letters C-R-E. Cream of mushroom? Cream of squirrel?

My sister scrapes the can back and forth. The muscles of her upper arms stand out, taut and ropy. She might be thinner than me, but she's way more muscular. Bare as she is now, I can see there's hardly a curve on her. All angles and bones, almost like a boy. That's another way we're different. I got my first period three years ago, when I was twelve. I figured she'd get hers around the same time, gave her an awkward explanation of tampons one night, brought her a few. But my sister has never bled.

"What are you even doing?" I ask her. There's a wet spot forming on the stone where she's scraping the can. She stops, turns it right side up, and pushes the lid with her fingers. There's a moment of resistance, then the lid pops inward with a splash.

Malnutrition can keep you from getting your period. I looked it up once. But the pastor is wrong. He's got to be. How can she be malnourished, when she's as resourceful as this? I didn't even bring her this soup, didn't teach her how to open cans. She must have scavenged it, figured it out on her own.

She scoots over and tries to tilt the can to my mouth. I notice how her wrist bones stick out. Her fingers, though bony as the rest of her, look tougher than mine, thick with callouses.

"Hey," I say, taking the can from her. She watches me

expectantly. She's not smiling, exactly, but her eyes are a little wider than usual. It makes her look younger. Softer.

I take a cautious sip of the soup.

It's cold and nasty and too thick. Feels like snot. Tastes like snot. I retch. Set the can down too quickly, spilling half of it.

I try to say, "I'm not hungry," but I barely get the *I* out before my stomach lurches. I scramble to the entrance of the cave and just make it before I vomit again.

There's not much left in my stomach, just a thin dribble of liquid and some bile. It burns my throat on the way out. I break out in a cold sweat. My limbs shake. The world is spinning.

When it's over I feel better. Scraped out. Heavy limbed. Exhausted. But better.

I crawl back over to my sister, who hasn't moved. She's looking at me differently now, eyes more guarded, posture wary. I slump over onto my side, rest my head on the wadded blanket.

Lee reaches out and brushes some hair off my forehead. I close my eyes. She rubs her palm slowly across my forehead, back and forth. It's weird but sort of soothing. Something about the rhythm of it. Makes me feel like a baby. "Where did you get that Bible?" I ask her. I open my eyes. She's got a scrunched expression, lips pursed, but she keeps stroking my forehead.

"Did someone give it to you?" I ask.

"It's mine," she says fiercely, as if I threatened to take it.

I can tell if I push I'll just make her angry. I close my eyes again. "Remember when you first came to see me?" I ask instead.

"Yes," she says, voice returned to neutral. This is a happy memory.

"How did you find me?"

"I saw you."

"Where?"

"The window."

I've asked her versions of this question many times, and she's given the same answer. It isn't a proper answer. It doesn't explain how she knew to come to Margaret's backyard. Who knows, maybe there's some truth to the things people say about twins.

I mean, I definitely can't tell where my sister is through magic. And even when I'm around her, I often have no idea what she's thinking. Especially now.

But it's true that I feel different around her than I do around anyone else. More comfortable. More myself. I don't have to pretend, don't have to keep secrets. I can just exist. "You must have been lonely," I say, "before you met me."

I find that, somehow, despite everything, despite the pain in my wrist, the little spark-sharp aches in my limbs, I'm beginning to relax. It's only midday, but I'm exhausted and sick. Rest is probably what I need.

My sister stops rubbing my forehead. Instead she traces one finger in a line from my hairline down to my nose. It gives me a little shiver, but it's kind of nice. Then she traces another line across my forehead the other way, like a plus sign. Or a cross. I wonder what it means as I drift off to sleep.

I wake in pain. All over. I try to sit up and pain shoots through my back. I groan. The ground is hard. My neck is stiff. My wrist throbs.

I pull myself up, pushing off the puffy gray coat that my sister must have draped over me while I slept. I'm alone in the cave now. There are long shadows stretching out along the stone floor. The sun is low, but not quite set, so I can't have slept for more than a few hours. It's still Sunday.

"Lee?" I try to crawl to the entrance, but I can't put any pressure on my left wrist, so I just kind of scoot, until the ceiling slopes high enough for me to stand.

"Lee?" I call again. There's no answer.

I have to pee, so I walk a little ways out into the forest, shimmy my jeans down to my knees, squat with my back against a tree.

I know it's kind of gross, but I've always felt that pissing in the woods is one of the most satisfying things in the world. It's best in winter, after it snows. Your body is hot, ninety-eight degrees, and so the pee comes out hot too and melts the snow, wisps of steam rising off it like little piss ghosts.

If I felt better this would be fun. An adventure. I've day-dreamed about it a thousand times. What it would be like to live in my sister's world. I've often wished we could spend longer than a few hours together at a time. Wished I could see more of her life, could share more of it. I'd contemplated schemes, in the past, to sneak off for a whole weekend. A fake away-meet for track? A pretend field trip? But I'd never gone through with it. Always settled for dreaming about the day when I was finally eighteen, finally out of high school, finally in charge of my own life.

So, yes, in a way this was something I always wanted. But I never wanted it to happen like this. Never wanted to be forced into it, with everyone against me and the secret of my sister out.

Has the pastor told everyone what he saw? Do they believe *him*?

I'm feeling light-headed, so I return to the cave and lie down again. I roll my left sleeve back, gently unwrap the bandage. Underneath, my wrist is so swollen that it's not even narrower than the rest of my arm anymore. I try resting a finger on it gently, and it feels like it's on fire. The pain is as strong as ever.

There a swoosh of leaves, and my sister's back. She's clothed again, wearing a dress I recognize as one I gave her about a year ago. I bought it myself, for two dollars at Goodwill.

It's a simple T-shirt dress, the fabric printed with fat red-orange flowers and neon-green leaves on a background of black. Across the chest in giant glittery gold letters it says SASSY. I'm not sure if Lee actually knows what that word means, but I knew she'd like the glitter.

She kneels beside me, eyes bright, body relaxed. She's got her plastic heart purse again. She unzips it, turns it upside down. Out fall a bunch of saltine cracker packets, the kind they give you at restaurants to go with soup. I used to sneak them into my pockets when I was younger and bring them to her. The crackers inside these packets are totally smashed, nothing but crumbs.

Lee holds one out for me to take but drops it when she catches sight of my wrist. I didn't rewrap it yet. She puts out her hand, touches the wound.

I scream. The pain is shocking, shooting up my arm. My sister scuttles backward.

"I think I need to go back," I say, when I catch my breath.

"No," says Lee, predictably.

My wrist is infected. That much is clear. I'd been trying not to think about it. But it's not getting any better.

"I need to go to a doctor," I say.

"No!" She's angry now, shoulders tensed.

"This is your fault, you know." She has no right to be angry. I'm the one who should be angry. "You bit me."

She reaches for my wrist again, but I yank it away.

"I need to go home," I say, and just the thought of that is enough to fill me with longing. Warm bed. Soft sheets. The plastic stars on my bedroom ceiling are nothing compared with the real ones, but they keep the rain out, keep the cold out.

It is starting to get cold.

"Home," my sister says, stabbing a finger at the floor of the cave.

"This is your fault," I say again, nearly shouting. "You're the one who went crazy."

But it wasn't completely crazy, was it? I finally ran away. She got exactly what she's always wanted.

Maybe that's what this was all about. Attacking Henry. Breaking my window. Coming to the church. Letting the pastor see her. She forced me into a corner. Forced me to choose one way or the other.

It was risky all right, but it worked.

She's won.

"I'll come back," I say, unsure if I really mean it. "Okay? I'll go and then come back. Run away for good. Like you wanted me to." I could do it right. Pack some clothes. Some food. It would be hard to get away. They'd be watching me. And the police . . .

But I can't think about that now.

"I just need to get some medicine," I say, "and then I swear I'll come back."

"Medicine?" Lee asks.

"Yes," I say, frustrated. "Otherwise my wrist will get worse and I'll get sicker and sicker and then I'll die." I don't even think that's a lie. People died of infections all the time in the old days. I'm feeling feverish again, hot and achy, and it scares me.

"Medicine," Lee repeats dully. Her body language now isn't threatening, isn't even angry. Just miserable. Folding down into herself.

"I don't know the way," I say. "You have to show me." She lets a little huff of air out of her nose and her shoulders sag. She droops her way over to the cave entrance, gestures for me to follow.

"I'll come back," I tell her as I drag myself after her, relieved. "I promise."

We've been trudging uphill for what feels like forever. The sun is gone now, the cloud-covered moon doing little more than outlining the darkness. We are going slowly, walking instead of running. I feel weak, exhausted. My lips are cracked from dehydration. My throat burns. My sister jogs ahead of me, circles back to tug on my right arm.

She makes me stop. I'm relieved, ready to sit and rest. She points out something in the dark, low to the ground. I can't tell what it is. A spiderweb? She steps over it. I do the same and then I see it. A string, thin as fishing line, looped between trees. One of her traps?

We keep going. I wish I'd grabbed the puffy coat. I'm shivering, although maybe that's more from the fever than the cold. I scan the trees, hoping with every step to see the lights of Lester up ahead. I can barely think of anything but the pain. It's all I can do to keep myself moving.

Up ahead, my sister pushes through some brambles. I stumble after her and find that we've come to a small clearing, maybe fifty feet across.

In the center of the clearing is a camper.

Or what used to be a camper, anyway. It seems to have sunk into the landscape. There's moss growing over the roof, weeds reaching up to the windows.

"Where are we?" I ask. Lee has paused a few feet from the camper. This isn't Lester, isn't home, isn't anywhere I recognize. If this is another hideout of hers, then she's really been holding out on me.

Even in the dark, I can see that the siding is stripped away in places, streaked blackish in others. The whole structure appears to have partially collapsed at one end and been rebuilt with plywood, logs, and tarp. I smell smoke. Something is on fire.

"Medicine," says Lee.

"What?"

In response, she picks up a rock and throws it at the camper. It hits with a clang, knocks a hunk of siding off.

"Stay here," says Lee, pointing at me. Then she turns and runs, full speed, into the darkness.

"Wait," I gasp, stumbling to follow. My limbs are heavy. My head spins. I lurch, fall to my knees.

The door of the camper swings open and warm light pours out like honey. There's someone standing there. They're backlit, so I can't see any details. Just a shadow in the shape of a man.

I freeze.

The man leans to the side, then straightens holding a lantern in one hand. The flickering light floods the clearing, throws his features into relief. He's got weird hair, hacked oddly around the ears. A long brown beard.

I've never seen him in the bar. Never seen him around town that I can remember. He's a stranger. He's squinting at me.

I push myself, shaking, to my feet.

"Jolene?" he asks.

I'm too startled to move, to speak, to run. All I can do is stare.

"Damn," he says, "you look just like her."

CHAPTER ELEVEN

I don't know much about the Cantrells. Logan was three years older than Mama, Brandon one year. They were raised by their grandparents, though by the time Mama went to live with them, their grandma was dead and their grandpa was in a nursing home with his mind gone. They were bad kids. Everybody says so.

Everybody has always said that Brandon left after Logan went to jail. They say he ran off in the night, abandoned their old trailer on the ridge. Left it for the pastor and his friends to burn to the ground. This is certainly no double-wide trailer. It's barely even a full camper.

But this is him. It must be. Why else would my sister bring me here?

Brandon watches me for a moment, silhouetted in the doorway of the camper. If he takes a step toward me, I decide, I will stagger away as fast as I can. Try to find Lee. But he doesn't. He simply turns around and goes back inside without another word, taking the light with him.

People say Brandon was quiet. They say he was strange. They

say, *We never trusted that boy, always knew there was something off about him.* I should be scared of him, this strange man in the woods, but my sister wouldn't have brought me here if he was dangerous, right?

A small black cat appears in the open doorway. It regards me warily for a moment, before hopping down and slinking toward the trees. There's no sign of Lee. I don't know if she's coming back.

I take a deep breath and walk across the clearing, step up onto the cinder block that serves as a front step. Inside the camper, the walls are paneled with dark wood, the floor covered with a threadbare Oriental rug in fallen-leaf colors. There's a brown couch slumped against the back wall, and beside it, on a heavy wooden cabinet, an aquarium.

I lean in. To the left there's a closed door. To the right, kitchen cabinets and glass mason jars with canned food stacked on top of them. In the center of the room there's a small old-fashioned-looking black stove with squat legs. I can feel the heat of it, even from the doorway. Against the front wall is a small table. Brandon is sitting at it, eating his dinner.

"Are you Brandon Cantrell?" I ask.

He looks up, briefly, nods once, looks back down at his food, keeps eating.

I step up into the camper. A little gray cat unfolds itself from the corner of the couch, jumps down, and pads over to rub against my legs. The warmth of the woodstove wraps around me.

"I thought you moved away," I say.

Brandon shifts one shoulder so slightly that I'm not sure if it's a shrug or just a coincidence. I'd never really thought of him as a real person. More like a character out of some ancient story, a myth. But here he is. He's wearing jeans, a long-sleeved gray

Henley. He's thin. The lantern, as old-fashioned as the stove, with a curved glass bulb and a burning wick, sits on the table beside him, though there's also faint light coming from the aquarium, which seems entirely out of place here.

"You hungry?" Brandon asks. His voice is low, gravelly. He's not looking at me, and so at first I think he's talking to the cat, but then he says it again. "You hungry?"

"I . . . I don't know."

Brandon gets up and opens a cabinet along the far wall, pulls out a plate. He bends over the woodstove, dishes food out from the cast iron pot on top of it.

Maybe he'll take me to town. He did it once before, didn't he? When I was only a baby. I cross the small room, barely more than six feet across, and sit on the couch. The aquarium beside me glows with a gentle greenish light. There's a cord snaking down from the lid. It ends not in a plug, but in two split ends, scraped of their plastic coating and attached to the contacts of a large battery. The plants inside the tank are growing like crazy, an underwater jungle. I feel like I'm dreaming.

Brandon approaches carrying a plate piled with a stew made of green beans and something that might be sausage. He sets the plate on the floor in front of me. I stare at it, baffled. He takes a seat back at the little table and stares out the window, though it's full dark out there. Nothing to see.

He's treating me like a cat, I realize. Or like my sister. Trying not to startle me. I grab the plate from the floor, moments before the gray cat pounces on it. I nibble at a green bean, take a tentative bite of sausage. It tastes good, salty and hot, but I'm worried I'll puke again, so I don't take more than a few bites.

I know I shouldn't, but I feel oddly safe. Maybe it's the cats.

Or the otherworldly glow of the fish tank. Tiny multicolored fish dart this way and that, fins flashing in the light. One looks like a sunset; another is an electric iridescent blue.

"They're so pretty," I say. "They look like candy."

Brandon snorts. "She ate them," he says.

"What?"

"Jolene. She ate them." He doesn't look at me when he speaks. It makes me feel like a ghost.

"I . . . What?"

"Fished them out with a net and ate them," he says. He smiles down at his hands. "At the old trailer."

Jolene. Mama. My stomach knots up, the room seeming to draw to a point suddenly. Brandon's hands twist against each other.

"She ate your fish?"

"Ate a lot of weird stuff," he says. "She had cravings."

I'm struck again with the reality of who is sitting a mere three feet from me. He knew Mama at the very end. He probably knows what happened to her. What his brother did. My stomach knots up. Mama ate his fish. She had cravings.

Pregnancy cravings.

"Do I really look like her?" I ask.

Brandon turns to me finally, gives me a long look. "A little."

"I thought you said I looked just like her."

"I meant the other one."

"The what?" I ask, but even as the words leave my mouth, I realize who he means. My sister. The other one.

I start laughing. It's all just too much. I'm laughing and it's coming out strange, too high, too much. Here's someone for the first time in my life who knows everything. He knows all of it.

The look on his face is confused, wary. He reminds me of

my sister in that moment and that only makes me laugh harder. I mean hell, the two of them are probably related, after all. He's probably our uncle.

I run out of breath from laughing. There's a stitch in my side. I gasp a few times, try to calm down.

"The other one," I say. I stick out my wrist, pull the sleeve up. "She bit me," I say. "It's infected, I think."

He leans forward to study the wound on my wrist.

I study him back. He's got a thin crooked nose. Dark eyes, with dark circles underneath. It looks like he probably cuts his hair himself. Hunks of it are radically different lengths. It's longer in the back, not quite a mullet, but close.

His beard is mostly brown, though there's a streak of gray on one side, hints of red throughout. It's thick around his chin, thins out to a scraggly point at the middle of his chest. The beard makes him look older, but I know he must be roughly the same age as the pastor. About thirty. Twice my age.

He certainly doesn't look anything like I thought he would. I tracked down a mug shot of Logan online in the school computer lab once. He was smirking, eyes bloodshot, head shaved, tattoos climbing up his neck. He had a defiant look to him, like he'd happily do it all again. I guess I figured his brother would be the same. Tough, brash, looking like the kind of trash Margaret is always complaining about. But instead he's this strange, quiet, sleepy-eyed mountain man who speaks and moves as softly as my sister when she doesn't want to be seen.

Brandon drifts through the door to the left, returns a moment later with a bottle of rubbing alcohol and a fishing tackle box.

He kneels in front of me, uncaps the alcohol.

"To disinfect," he says.

I hold out my wrist. He tilts the bottle.

It burns like a thousand fucking suns, hissing against my wrist. I yowl and yank my hand away.

"Fuck," I say, shaking my wrist, though that doesn't help any.

Brandon opens the tackle box. Instead of bait and hooks, it's full of little plastic bottles. Translucent. Orange. White labels, white lids.

Medicine.

My sister must have known about this. It must be why she brought me here. She's been lying to me. For years. Every time I asked her about the Cantrells. Every time she said nothing.

Brandon digs through the box, pulling out bottles, setting them on the carpet. The gray cat bats one of them over by my feet and I pick it up. Percocet. Prescribed for someone named Tammy Reed.

"Here," says Brandon, holding out a thin cardboard box, about the size of a wallet. "Antibiotics."

I take the box. Zithromax. Prescribed to Meredith Gross. There're five pills nestled in plastic punch-outs. The foil on the back is unpunctured, smooth and shiny. So they're safe, right?

"Water?" asks Brandon. He talks like my sister. Never two words if one will do.

Or maybe she talks like him. I was right, that the Cantrells raised her. I just never dreamed that one of them was still around.

"Who is Meredith Gross?" I ask instead.

"An old friend," he says.

"What about Tammy Reed?"

Brandon's mouth quirks up on one side and he tilts his head, bemused.

"Where did you get all these?" I ask.

"I guess you know about Logan," he says. "You want to know if I'm like him."

I want to know if he's dangerous. If I should trust him.

I mean, I shouldn't trust him. Obviously, I shouldn't.

"I just want to know whose medicine I'm taking," I say.

"Well," he says, "all right. Maybe you know some of this. Logan was part of a big thing. Pipeline down from Columbus. Had ties all the way out to Detroit. Police broke that up pretty good when they got him. But he had some backups, too. Just regular people. In other towns. With clean records. They'd get prescriptions the normal way. Sell to him. Not directly to him, though. He managed to hide that side of it pretty well. Cops didn't crack it, and anyway they were more interested in the big fish. After he got locked up I kept some of the backups going. Just a small thing. A little money here and there."

I blink at him. He's a drug dealer. A drug-dealing possible murderer hiding in the woods.

"Meredith actually was a friend, though," he says, with a slight smile.

"Was?" I ask.

"She's dead."

My heart thuds. I drop the pills.

He picks them up, holds them out to me.

"Died of a heart attack," he clarifies. "About a year ago. At the age of ninety-four. She'd been a friend of my grandmother's."

"So you took her stuff?" I point accusingly at the pills.

"Believe me or not, but I helped her out. Brought her groceries twice a month. Did her yardwork. She lived alone. Her son was Logan's friend. He's in jail now. Never cared for him, personally." He scowls. "Anyway, I'm the one who found her. I called the police, and before they came I took a few things. She didn't need them anymore. I've got her blood pressure pills in here somewhere." He digs around in the tackle box with his free hand. The pill bottles rattle.

"Why?"

He shrugs. "You never know." He gives up looking for the pills, pushes the pack of antibiotics toward me. I take it.

"Water?" he asks again.

"Okay," I say. He crosses to the kitchen, rummages through the cabinets, fills a speckled red camping mug from a tall silver cistern with a spigot sitting on one of the counters.

When he hands me the mug, I take a cautious sip. Tastes like water. Slightly tinny water.

I poke two of the Zithromax out of the foil, swallow them. The second pill sticks in my throat and I have to chug the rest of the water.

Brandon picks up the Percocet bottle. He opens it, shakes a little white pill out onto his palm. He holds it out.

"For the pain," he says.

I stare at the pill. Brandon's palm looks rough beneath it, cracked with lines. His fingers are long and thin, his nails dirty. You aren't supposed to take drugs from strangers. You aren't supposed to do any of the things I'm doing. But he's not exactly a stranger. We've met once before, though I don't remember it. He's held me in his arms.

After a moment, Brandon shrugs, tilts his head back, pops the pill in his mouth, swallows. He closes the bottle and sets it on the cabinet next to the fish tank.

"I'll leave it here," he says.

He gathers the other bottles, replaces them in the tackle box.

He hasn't asked me why I'm here. Hasn't asked any of the things a normal person would.

"My sister," I start, but I can hardly think of where to begin. "You know her?"

It's a dumb question. I know he does.

In reply, he rolls up his own sleeve, points to a spot about halfway up his right forearm. There's a scar there. Two shiny pink semicircles, like parentheses.

Well, shit. "What happened?"

"Snowstorm. Tried to get her to come inside."

"That big one two years ago?"

"Yeah."

It was January. The snow came up to my knees in drifts. My sister put on her tights, her puffy coat, her knit cap, and we heaved snowballs at each other, built a lopsided igloo in a clearing at the top of a ridge. I had tried to get her to come inside, too. Said I could hide her at Myron's house, bring her hot cocoa. She refused, predictably.

She was lying to me, back then.

"How long have you lived out here?" I ask.

He considers. "Just over ten years, I guess. Doesn't feel that long."

"Everybody always said you left town."

He nods, grave. "I keep away from Lester. Don't associate with anybody I can't trust to keep their mouth shut about me."

"Does my sister ever stay here?"

He shakes his head. "She never comes inside. Just stops by for food."

I'm oddly relieved by that. It would be unfair if she went inside for him, but not for me. "How often?"

He shrugs. "Every couple of days."

She's been lying to me for as long as I've known her.

While I was hiding her from everyone else in the world, she was hiding him from me. Why would she do that? Why would she protect him?

Unless she thought she was protecting me?

What I want to ask, what I need to ask, is what happened to Mama. Would he tell me? *Logan killed her,* he'd say. *I had nothing to do with it. There was nothing I could do to stop him. Such a tragedy. Such a crying shame.*

But I don't ask. I don't even know how I would form the question. *Why are you hiding out here? Did you kill her? Are you the monster everyone thinks you are?*

I'm starting to feel sick again, starting to feel scared.

Brandon picks up the box and the rubbing alcohol, walks to the door on the left. He's about to step through, but he stops, turns back to me, says, "I'm glad you're here. I've been waiting a long time."

And then he's gone and my heart is racing again. He's been waiting? What the hell does that mean? I push myself up from the couch. I feel dizzy.

I should go. There's no way this is safe.

I shouldn't have taken the pills. I shouldn't have drunk the water. He's probably going to wait until I'm unconscious and then do what men do and then kill me.

I get up and stumble toward the front door. I let myself be lulled, somehow, by how still he was, how quiet. But this man is, at absolute best, an accessory to murder. He wouldn't be hiding out here if he wasn't guilty of something.

My sister brought me here. She told me to stay here. But my

sister has been lying for so long. Not just forgetting. Not blocking things out. Straight-out lying. How many times have I asked her if she remembered Logan and Brandon? If she knew anything about them? My sister brought me here because Brandon had medicine, but that doesn't mean she trusts him. Lee doesn't trust anyone. She just wasn't willing to take me to town, to give up her victory.

I'm standing by the front door, hand on the knob, when Brandon comes back in with a pillow and a folded blanket.

"Where are you going?" he asks, frowning. He sets the pillow and blanket on the couch.

"I—I thought I heard my sister."

He moves toward me. I shrink against the wall. He reaches past me, though, pushes the door open, steps out. He stands there, perfectly still, blocking the doorway, for what feels like a long time. He is listening, squinting out at the trees.

"No," he says finally. He comes back in, shuts the door. Latches it. "It's cold. You can sleep on the couch."

He picks up the lantern from the table, puts it out. The room gets darker, but the aquarium light is still on. He crosses to that next, switches it off. I gasp a little, involuntarily, at the darkness.

"I guess I can leave it on for you," he says, switches it back on. He leans over the woodstove, adjusts something on the side. Then he walks past me, wordlessly, goes through the door on the left, into the darkness, out of sight.

I'm shivering again. I don't know if it's the rush of cold air from outside or the fever or something else. I feel very alone all of a sudden, and I pull Savannah's phone from my pocket.

I could call Aggie.

But what would I say? *Come pick up me please. Where, you ask?*

Oh, at Brandon Cantrell's secret camper in the middle of the woods. Yeah, you can't miss it.

The way things are going these days, Aggie would probably send the pastor to come get me. I can't act like a little kid who needs rescuing. Can't admit defeat. That's exactly what the pastor wants. To save me, whether I want him to or not.

On the phone, there's a long string of texts from Dakota's number.

fuc u bring me my phone
if u don't i will say u attacced henry
i will say i saw it
im the only witness
answer me u coward
jo
JO
jo?
dakota says u ran away
did u?
where r u?
r u okay?
y won't u answer me?
im worried about u

I've always told Savannah she should spell words out. But the *u* makes me smile now. Poor *u*, what a fool. Never can keep out of trouble. I miss Savannah terribly. I never even got a chance to show her the pictures. If I did, she'd believe me. She would have to, right?

I type a reply, saying I'm okay, but that's a lie, isn't it? I'm not okay at all. I'm sick and lost and everyone I know has betrayed me. Even Savannah. Especially Savannah. If I sent her the pictures now, she'd probably fire back with *Jack says that's just you* or *Jack says it's obviously shopped.* She can claim to be worried all she wants, but a few texts earlier she was threatening to turn me in. To frame me.

You don't give a shit about me, I type instead.

The phone buzzes almost immediately, a flood of replies.

where r u?

what happened?

did he hurt you?

For a second I think she means Brandon, but there's no way she knows about him. No one but my sister knows where I am now. Does she mean Jack? I start to type another reply, but her texts keep coming.

r u safe?

i checked myron's u weren't there

No shit.

jo please im really worried

I type: *I'm sure Jack will be happy to comfort you.* Hit Send.

There's a moment of nothing, then the phone buzzes like crazy. Incoming call. It startles me so much I drop the phone. Frantic, I snatch it back up, power it off, shove it in my pocket with the picture of Mama. I squint toward the dark doorway where Brandon disappeared, but I can't see a thing.

If I unlatch the front door, will Brandon hear it? Will he come after me? Maybe he'll get his gun. He must have a gun. Everybody who lives in the woods has a gun.

The room is swimming around me. The fever is definitely back. My mouth has gone dry. I stumble over to the kitchen area. My eyes are mostly adjusted to the gloom. I can make out a pulpy red mess of tomatoes in one of the many mason jars stacked on the counter, skinny green beans huddled together in another. One jar holds what looks like a dozen blind eyeballs. Onions, maybe.

There's a sink but when I turn the handle, nothing happens. Which makes sense. He's off the grid out here. That's why he's got the big jug of water sitting on the counter.

There's a large metal box with a latch on the floor against the front wall. It looks like a smaller version of the chest freezer we have at the bar, though it isn't hooked up to anything as far as I can see. I open it. Inside, a hunk of flesh sits on a slab of ice. Raw. Bloody. A jut of bone. My heart leaps, and I shut the freezer.

I take a few shaky breaths, open the freezer again.

It's just meat. Venison, I'd guess. Most of it wrapped in plastic. There are a few beers sitting beside it. I grab one, pop the tab. Take a swig.

It tastes perfect. Cold and sharp, with a warmth that follows, unfolding slowly through my body. I chug the rest, crumple the can, and shove it deep into the black trash bag hanging from a nail on the wall.

I could unlatch the door, dart out. Run, but not straight ahead like an idiot. Run around behind the camper. Disappear into the woods. Keep running until my legs fail.

And then what? I'd be cold and sick and alone. I don't know the way back to town. I'd have nothing. Worse, I'd be a coward. I'd be giving up my best chance to learn the truth. The real truth. Not just hearsay. Not just the gossip of old drunks, twisted by the years.

The little black cat appears and winds around my feet, mewing plaintively. I shush it, ease open drawers, most of them empty, until I find the knives.

In my mind they glitter like emeralds, catching the faint green light of the aquarium, but really they are dull, pitted and water stained. I grab the biggest of the bunch: a butcher knife with a smooth black handle.

I march back through the living room and through the door on the left. There's a tiny bathroom, no bigger than a closet, and then another door, which is slightly ajar.

The little black cat squeezes past my feet, swishes through. I follow.

This room is the half-collapsed one. Even in the gloom, I can see where the walls stop and the plywood and tarp begins. Dark shapes hunch in the corner. A cracked mirror leans against a beam.

Brandon is tangled up in a big quilt on a mattress, which takes up most of the room. One bare calf sticks out from the bottom of the tangle. One bare foot, the toes long and bony.

There's nothing threatening about him like this. He's practically tied up. I take a step into the room. I'm the threatening one now, awake in his house while he sleeps.

I take another step, startle when I catch movement out of the corner of my eye. But it's just the mirror, flashing myself back at me. My knife hand shakes. I don't know what I was thinking. I'm not my sister.

Brandon's face in the dark is like a painting. Broad brush-strokes. Cheekbones catching the light, eyes sunk in shadow. The more I stare at it, the less it even seems like a face. The whole room is like that. Not a room, really, but a collection of shadows.

I'm sure he's got a gun somewhere. I could find that, instead. Kill him before he even wakes.

Or I could hold the gun to his temple, the metal rim cold, pressing an *O* into his forehead. His eyes fluttering open, focusing slowly on me, on the gun.

You, I would say, *are going to tell me everything.*

And he would. He would be crying, tears catching in his beard. He would beg my forgiveness. He would tell me how they shot her. Or strangled her. Or beat her. How he stood by and watched his brother. Or how he did it himself. He would cry and cry, beg me to spare him. It would hurt, to hear how she died, but I would pull every little detail from him. I would force it out. I would stay strong. I would not cry. When I had wrung him dry I would say something about how Mama lives on in me and I would brace myself for the kickback and I would pull the trigger. Blow his face apart, blood blooming like a rose on the pillow. His jaw hanging loose. I'd walk out the door, camera tight on my face, a few flecks of blood on my cheek, a wry smile on my lips.

Brandon grunts and shifts on the mattress.

I stumble backward, heart pounding, and nearly trip over the little black cat. I gasp, slap a hand over my mouth.

Brandon sits up. His chest is bare. The light catches on his ribs, the darkness settling in the valleys between them, tangling in his beard.

He's staring at me. At least I think he is. His eyes are all shadow. I hide the knife behind my back.

"Jolene?" he says.

"No." My mouth has gone dry again.

"You can sleep in here," he says, "if the couch is too hard."

"I—"

"There's room."

"No thank you," I say.

"You do look like her," he says. "In the dark, you look just like her."

He stares at me a moment longer—I can't breathe—and then he lies back down, pulls the quilt over himself.

I scramble back to the door, through the bathroom, into the living room. I'm feeling bad again. Dizzy. Nauseous. My forehead is blazing.

The muted light from the aquarium makes the whole room seem like it's underwater. I sink onto the couch, unable to stand. With shaking hands, I slide the knife under the pillow. Then I slump over onto my side, tuck the blanket around me, shivering. I will rest, but I will not sleep. I slip one hand under the pillow, trace the smooth plastic of the knife handle with my thumb, think of the blade beneath my head, keeping me safe. Think of swinging it, letting it slide through flesh like butter.

CHAPTER TWELVE

I startle awake and sit bolt upright, scaring the shit out of the little black cat, which flings itself off the couch and dashes across the room. Sun peeks through the curtains and the door of the wood-stove is open, a cheery flickering light coming from its belly. Brandon has his back to me, doing something at the kitchen counter. I slide my hand under the pillow, reach for the knife.

Brandon turns around.

His hair looks even worse, which I wouldn't have guessed was possible. It's sticking up in the back, plastered this way and that.

"Coffee?" he asks. There's a tarnished silver pot with a black handle and a glass knob on top of the lid sitting on the woodstove.

"Okay," I say.

I let go of the knife, stand up carefully and stretch. I feel a lot better actually. My forehead isn't blazing. My wrist still hurts, but it looks like the swelling has gone down.

Last night doesn't feel real.

I fold the blanket, set it neatly on the couch. Savannah would absolutely lose her shit if I told her that I'd slept over at some guy's place. That he was offering me coffee now. It seems a very grown-up thing. To be offered coffee in the morning by a stranger.

I watch the little candy-colored fish dart through the plants in the aquarium, their iridescent scales catching the firelight from the stove. The tank light is off. I try to switch it on, but nothing happens.

"Battery must have run out," Brandon says. "I usually don't leave it on for long."

He sets two tin cups of dark liquid on the table. Everything seems less sinister in the daylight. I'll be strong. I'll ask him what happened to Mama. I'll ask him to tell me the things my sister never has, about her life before she met me. And then I'll ask him to take me back to town.

"Can I feed the fish?" I ask instead. There's no rush.

"Go ahead." He smiles. "Just don't eat them."

I open the lid of the tank, shake a few flakes in from the plastic jar. The fish swarm up, their tiny snouts, or whatever it is you call the front end of a fish, pushing at the surface of the water.

Something glints in the back of the tank, deep within the plants, in the shadow of the driftwood. Another fish? I squint at it through the glassy distortion of the water.

"Can I have some water?" I ask Brandon, who is sipping his coffee, watching me.

Wordlessly, he turns to fetch another cup.

I roll my right sleeve up as far as it will go and plunge my arm into the tank. The fish dart away from my hand, which looks bloated and pale in the water. Little bubbles cling to my skin. I fumble at the gravel until my fingers close around something thin and metallic.

"What are you doing?" asks Brandon from behind me.

I yank my arm back out of the water, flinging water across the couch, the carpet. I've got my fist clutched tight.

"Don't eat them," he repeats, a note of panic in his voice.

I open my fist.

The broken chain of a necklace lies curled in my palm. Hanging from the chain: a tiny silver cross.

Mama.

I look up at Brandon. He's standing by the curtain, cup of water in one hand.

"You killed her," I say.

"What?" he says, frowning.

I hold the necklace out, let the cross dangle in the air between us. He recognizes it, I can tell, though he looks more sad than surprised. I feel rage building up in my chest, hot as a fever.

"You fucking killed her," I say.

"Nobody killed her," he says. "It was just an accident."

I turn and push the pillow off the couch, grab the knife from beneath it. I hold it out in front of me, blade pointing at Brandon's belly.

He wasn't expecting that. Good. His eyes widen. He puts his hands up in the air, still holding the cup of water in one of them. He shakes his head.

"You and your fucking brother," I say. "You're monsters."

I move slowly toward the door, still holding the knife out, not taking my eyes off Brandon for a second. I will run, run until I find Lester or my sister or until someone finds me. I will tell everyone where Brandon lives. I'll tell them what I found. I'll tell the pastor. I'll tell Aggie. I'll tell Grandma Margaret. They'll come out with their shotguns, with their Bibles. We will set this fucking camper on fire. We will burn it to the ground with Brandon still in it. Mama the white-hot heart of the flames.

"I didn't kill her," says Brandon, hands still raised.

"Shut up," I tell him. I've sidled nearly to the door now.

"Nobody killed her," he says again. "I thought you knew that."

The little table is between us. The door is two steps away. I'm holding every muscle in my body tense, ready to run. The door is still locked. If I fiddle with the latch will that give him the opportunity to grab me? Tall as I am, he's even taller. He's thin, too, but I'm sure he's stronger than me. He's a full-grown man. If I run now, he'll chase me, I'm sure. He'll get his gun.

"You killed her," I say again, doing my best to make my voice hard. I try to dredge up the self I imagined last night, the dry-eyed one, the one with no mercy. "Or Logan did and you helped."

"No," Brandon says. He looks deeply sad, his face all knotted up. Remorse? His arms are still in the air like he's strung up by the wrists.

Maybe if I run now he won't chase me. Maybe he'll pack up his cats, his fish tank, his knowledge of what happened, and fuck off. Get away with it again.

"Where did you hide her body?" I demand. My heart hammers hard against my breastbone, but I move slowly around the little table, toward Brandon.

"I thought you knew," he says, which is stupid. If I knew I wouldn't be asking, would I?

"Where did you hide the body?" I ask again.

All those fake graves I made for Mama over the years, pulling flowers from the weeds around the edges of the cemetery, piling them at the base of some tree. Somewhere out there is her real grave. I could have run right by it a hundred times, run right over it even, without realizing. This man knows where it is.

There's barely two feet between us now.

"Where?" I demand, and I jab the knife toward him quickly, a feint. He drops the cup. It hits the floor, splashing water across his boots. The cup rolls away across the floor. If he moves toward me, I think, I will thrust this knife with all my strength into his stomach. I can do it. I will do it. I am strong. I'm as wild as her.

"Nobody killed her," Brandon says. He tries to take a step backward, but bumps against the wall. He reaches for the back of the chair to steady himself. "She wasn't dead."

"That's a lie." I'm tense, ready, every muscle in my body clenched like a fist.

Brandon is squinting at me. "You really don't know, do you? I thought you knew."

"You make no fucking sense," I say. He's as bad as my sister. Can't seem to spit out a sentence longer than four words. He's lying anyway, covering his ass, trying to talk me down. I'm holding a knife. I'm the one with the power here.

"She didn't die when you were a baby," he says. He lowers his arms.

He's lying. She is dead and he is lying.

If she were still alive she would have come back for me. I know that. I can't let him trick me, can't let myself hope.

"So, what," I say, "she's just in the next room, huh? She's going to jump out and shout surprise?"

"No," says Brandon, shaking his head. "Shit, I'm sorry. I thought you knew all this. She *is* dead. But she didn't die at fifteen. She was alive. She lived to twenty. Overdosed."

I don't understand why he's saying this. It's cruel. My knife hand is shaking slightly. I transfer the knife quickly to the other hand; hope Brandon didn't notice the shaking.

"I'm sorry," he says. "I thought she would have told you."

"Who?"

"Your sister."

"What are you talking about?" I hold the knife a little higher, pointing it at his heart. He doesn't seem afraid of me anymore. Maybe I should stab him, just a little. Show him I'm not fucking around here.

"Have you asked her about your mother?" he says.

"Of course I've asked her. She doesn't know anything."

He shakes his head again. "Jolene raised her," he says. "For the first five years, anyway. She really never told you?"

He's lying. Right? Mama died.

"No," I say.

And yet . . .

There was no body. I know that. Everybody knows that. The police never found a damn thing at the Cantrells' camper. No sign of a baby, for sure. But my sister survived somehow. I'd taken it for granted that the Cantrells kept her, raised her, at least for the first few years. It seemed like the only answer.

"I really thought you knew," Brandon says again.

He is lying. He must be. And yet . . .

I remember when my sister stole the picture of Mama. She snatched it out of my hands before I even told her who it was. I always thought she did it just to make me mad.

But what if she recognized Mama?

If she recognized her.

If she knew her.

"I'm sorry," says Brandon.

I squeeze Mama's necklace so hard that the points of the cross dig into my flesh. So hard that it hurts.

And I remember yesterday. My sister rubbing my forehead like a mother comforting a child, tracing a shape with her finger. The shape of a cross.

I lunge around the table, unlatch the door, push it open, stagger out into the light.

I try to run, but my left leg cramps up and I fall to my knees. The knife slips from my hands. I grab for it, scrabbling frantically at the leaves, heedless of the danger of the blade, until my fingers find cold, sharp metal.

I roll over. Brandon is standing in the doorway.

"I'm sorry," he says again. The sun is coming up, but the camper blots it out. I can't see his face.

I launch myself up and swing at him with the knife. He throws his hands out to stop me. We collide. One of his hands wraps around my wrist, the other pushes my shoulder, my head knocks against his chin, the knife drops out of my hand. I am crying.

It makes sense. I don't want it to, but it does. Mama raising my sister. Mama teaching her to hide.

I pull away from Brandon, stumble backward, and collapse. I am sucking in strained, snotty breaths, trying to shove down sobs the same way I kept the waves of nausea down before. My fingers are bleeding. Brandon is clutching one of his palms. He's bleeding too. I cut him. But he doesn't look angry.

"I'm sorry," he says again. He sounds like he means it, and I can't help it, I believe him.

I believe that he's sorry. I believe she was alive. I believe she raised my sister, hid her from all of us. I don't know how she did it. I don't know why.

But if it really is true, if Mama didn't die fifteen years ago, then there's another question.

What about me?

———

Brandon and I sit in the clearing. Me on the ground, legs splayed in the leaves, and him on the cinder block, pressing the hem of his shirt against the cut on his palm, staring off into the trees. The little black cat winds past him out the door. It sniffs the air, pads over to me. I wipe my nose on my sleeve. My lungs hurt. My fingers sting from where I grazed them on the knife blade. There are drops of blood scattered on the leaves around me, but the cuts aren't deep and they've already stopped bleeding.

Cold morning light filters through the trees. The ground beneath me is wet with dew, the grass sparkling. The trees are ghostly, ringed with mist. It's quiet, even the birdsong hushed, distant.

"Why do you have her necklace?" I ask, my voice still thick from crying. "Why was it in the fish tank?"

Brandon is silent for a moment. I pet the black cat, which has stretched itself out at my side. Its silken fur is a comfort, its rumbly purr.

"They were sitting on the couch," Brandon says finally, "Jolene and the baby. The baby was playing with the necklace."

The baby. "My sister?"

"Yes," he says. "She dropped the necklace in the tank. I was going to fish it out, but Jolene laughed, said leave it there."

"They lived with you here?"

"No, they didn't live with me."

He lapses back into silence. I'm trying to work it all out, what this means. Mama was here, at this very camper. She sat on the same couch where I slept. But after we were born. After everybody already thought she was dead. Was that before or after Logan went to jail? Before or after the double-wide trailer was burnt down? How old had my sister been? Was it before or after she met me? "She's here," Brandon says.

For one moment I think he means Mama, means she's buried here, that her body is here, beneath us even now, but then I hear rustling and I twist around.

The print of the new dress blends in with the leaves, but the sun sparkles off the SASSY and gives her away. She takes one step into the clearing and stops.

I push myself to my feet.

All three of us stare. I find myself searching for a family resemblance. We ought to look a little like Brandon. If his brother is our father. I don't think we do. But maybe that's just because we don't have beards. Nobody says a thing, except the wind.

Abruptly, Brandon stands up and goes inside the camper.

As soon as the door shuts behind him, I walk fast toward my sister. I stop just in front of her, pull the picture of Mama from my pocket, hold it out between us like I held the necklace out to Brandon. An accusation.

"You knew her," I say. "You fucking knew her."

My voice is too loud. It frightens a bird from a nearby tree. A sudden rush of wings and then silence. Lee reaches for the picture. I yank it away.

"You lied to me," I say. "You've been lying to me my whole life."

"No." She lurches back, muscles locking up, shoulders hunching.

"Yes. It's true, isn't it? Mama was alive." My voice falters, comes out hoarse. I think I'm going to cry again, but I choke it down. "Mama raised you."

My sister doesn't say anything, but she doesn't have to. Her eyes flick quick from the picture to my face and then back again. Her eyes are wet. Shining. She is trying to shrink down into herself, trying to hide in plain sight.

It's true. It's absolutely true. Brandon was a big enough thing to omit, but how could my sister keep this from me? I used to tell her everything I knew about Mama. Whatever measly details I could glean from other people's vague recollections. How could she have sat there and listened to me and said nothing?

I look into my sister's face, so similar to mine, and I feel like I am looking at a stranger.

"I'm not going to chase you if you run," I tell her.

Her shoulders are hunched, her rib cage heaving. She reaches out a branch-thin arm to touch my wrist. I jerk away from her touch.

"Why didn't you tell me?" I say.

Her eyes dart to something behind me. I twist just enough to see Brandon standing on the cinder block again. He's holding one of the plastic-wrapped hunks of meat from the fridge, watching us.

I turn back to her. "Because of him?"

She shakes her head no. A twig falls loose from her matted hair.

"Why didn't you tell me?" I ask again, my voice hard.

My sister's eyes are dark pools. She's still, but I can see her struggling, twisting around herself. Her voice, when she speaks, comes out as a whisper.

"Don't you ever tell a goddamn soul," she says.

"What?"

She reaches for the picture again, looking about as close to crying as I've ever seen her. I hold the photo tight but don't yank it away. She puts her palm flat against it, like she's trying to block it out.

"Don't you ever tell a goddamn soul," she says again, slowly, pronouncing each word carefully. "Every last one of them is the devil."

She looks up at me, face stricken, eyes wide, bulging, whites for days.

"You see someone," she says, "you run."

And she does.

She's off like a fucking shot and I keep my promise, I don't even try to follow her. I watch her go as long as I can, which isn't long, the earth sloping down and taking her out of sight.

She doesn't talk like that. She never talks like that, in complete sentences, unless she's copying me. Echoing my words back at me. And the way she said it, like reciting. Those weren't her words.

They must have been Mama's.

Reaching me, through the years, through death, even. Mama talking right to me.

Brandon is sitting on the cinder block, tossing the hunk of meat from hand to hand. I stride over through the dead leaves, feeling tall, feeling held up by some power not my own. Feeling like someone else entirely.

Mama's words.

Brandon looks up at me. "Guess she wasn't hungry," he says.

I am towering over him. I am blazing. My voice, when it comes out, is not a whisper, not a sob. It is hard and sure and carved from the bedrock of these hills, these almost-mountains.

"You," I say, "are going to tell me everything."

CHAPTER THIRTEEN

Brandon and I walk through the woods. He's telling me about what Mama ate.

"Baking soda," he says. "Toothpaste. My fish. Glass pebbles from the bottom of the tank. I had a nicer tank back then, in the old trailer. Coffee grounds. Strips of wallpaper. Dirt. That was her favorite."

He stops for a second, studies a tree, adjusts our course. There is no path. We crackle through the undergrowth, snapping sticks, picking up whole families of burrs. It's a gray morning, the flat disk of the sun barely visible through a veil of clouds.

"She said it was your fault," Brandon says.

"Me?"

"Well, the two of you I guess." He gives me a look that isn't quite a smile, but almost. I mean, his mouth doesn't actually move, but he's smiling somehow anyway. "Giving her cravings. She ate so much dirt I thought she might give birth to an earthworm."

At the crest of a hill ahead of us, there is something wrong with one of the trees. It bulges oddly in the middle, branches growing straight out to the sides, then curving up like a cage.

"Come to think of it," Brandon says, "she ate earthworms, too."

This is what Brandon tells me.

Mama came to live with them about five months into her pregnancy. That I already knew. She fought with Logan often. The fights got violent sometimes, both of them screaming and throwing things. Mama would call him the devil. He would call her a whore. Logan hit her, but she hit him back just as hard.

Logan and Brandon had dogs then. Hounds. Mama started taking them out with her for long walks along the ridges. Early in the morning. Late at night.

Sometimes the hounds would wander home without her. Sometimes she would be gone all day.

Logan thought she was off seeing other guys. That was one of the things they fought about. Logan, of course, was sometimes off seeing other girls. But Brandon always figured Mama just wanted to be alone. He felt the same way. Lots of people came by the trailer back then. Logan's friends. Logan's customers.

Once, Brandon followed her when she went out. Tracked her through the woods the way his grandfather had taught him to track deer. And she led him to this tree. She was big by then, lopsided, front-heavy, but that didn't stop her from climbing. There was a deer platform halfway up the tree, and around that she'd made an odd sort of nest, weaving vines and sticks through the branches.

Maybe a bird instead of a baby, he had thought. Maybe a big

speckled egg that she would keep warm with her body, until one morning: a thin branching crack in the shell.

We climb the tree. There are notches carved into the trunk, healed over now like old wounds, which act as a ladder. We have to squeeze between two thick horizontal branches to reach the wooden deer platform. It must have been here a long time, to have forced the branches to grow up around it the way they do.

I settle down cross-legged, run my hand along the wood. It's worn smooth, like the stone in my sister's cave. The branches arch up all around the platform, enclosing us, with patches of sky between them like windows.

The tree is at the crest of a hill and you can see other hills and valleys stretching far into the distance. A sea of leaves shifting in the wind.

"She did disappear," Brandon says. He's sitting with his bony knees scrunched up to his chest, his arms wrapped around them. He doesn't look at me. "Logan and me weren't lying about that when we told the police. They didn't believe us, but it was true. Neither of us knew a thing when they first showed up. She went for one of those walks and she never came back."

I stare down at the ground beside the tree. There are some little brown birds hopping around down there. As soon as they stop moving they disappear, indistinguishable from the fallen leaves.

"Logan thought she'd gone back home, but I knew she wouldn't do that. She hated everybody from town, hated her mother especially. So I searched the woods. Took the hounds out. Checked this tree, of course, though she wasn't here.

"It was a couple of days before I found her. When I did she'd already given birth. She did it in the woods. On the ground. Alone."

As I watch, one of the little brown birds beneath the tree takes flight, like a dead leaf that has decided to fall in reverse. Decided to return, suddenly, to life.

I try to picture what Brandon has told me, but I don't know how. I see Mama looking like the school photo, brown hair parted neatly in the middle, lips pink with gloss, blue shadow on her lids. I see her standing in a grove of trees, cradling a baby girl in each arm. I see her beatific, with a ray of light splitting the sky above her, bathing her in its soft warm glow.

Brandon says Mama made him promise. Made him swear he wouldn't tell a soul where she was. *Let them think I'm dead,* she told him, *then they'll be fucking sorry.*

Mama was fifteen. Brandon was sixteen. Couple of kids, he says. And that's all there was to it. Everybody thought she was dead. Brandon kept his promise; didn't tell them they were wrong.

"No," I say. "Wait, hold on. You're leaving everything out."

He shrugs. "That's what happened."

"You took me into town, though. You took me to Grandma Margaret's."

"I did."

"Why?"

"She told me to."

I try to picture that, too: Mama holding me out, tiny, naked, fragile as a baby bird. Her hands shaking, saying—saying what? *Take her, please. It's too late for me, but save her. Let her have a normal life.*

"What about my sister?" I ask.

"What about her?"

"Why didn't you take her?"

"Jolene didn't want me to."

My heart drops. "Why not?"

Brandon shrugs.

"You must know," I say.

"I just did what she told me to do. That's all I ever did."

"No," I say. That's not good enough. He must be leaving something out.

"She was stubborn," he says. But I already knew that. We all are, the women in my family. "She had her own reasons for doing things. I didn't always understand them. Sometimes I felt helpless.

"Hell, even I didn't see her for weeks after that first time. I was scared she really was dead. But I brought her food and clothes. My grandma's old things, because no one would miss them. I left them in trash bags, hidden up here or under piles of leaves. I had to be careful. The police were watching. When I came back to check, days later, the bags were gone." I picture Mama climbing down from a tree, my baby sister lashed to her back with strips of torn black plastic. See her wearing a dead woman's cardigans, a dead woman's pearls, ripping open a trash bag, ravenous. In my mind her face becomes my sister's face. Her hair my sister's hair. She is my sister. And Brandon is me, keeping her a secret, sneaking out at night to meet her.

"It was a difficult time," he says. "Everyone hated us."

"They thought you were murderers," I point out. "They had good reason."

"Maybe. Maybe they didn't need much reason at all."

"You could have just told them she was alive."

He shook his head. "I promised her I wouldn't."

I want to know this, need to know this, but it's hard to take in.

Hard to reconcile with the image of Mama I've built up over the years. So much of what I'd believed about her was wrong. She's not the tragic figure I thought she was. Not a bright spark extinguished too soon. She was something stranger and more complicated. I don't know what to think now. Was she a victim or a villain? Crazy or brave?

"They tried to kill us, you know," says Brandon.

"Who?" I ask, not following.

"Group of men from town. Drunk, I'd say. A few months after she left."

I think about what the pastor told me at the bar. How he could have killed Logan. How he went out once to try.

"They had guns," Brandon says. "I saw the headlights coming through the trees, so I ran and hid in the forest behind the trailer. Logan wasn't even home. They shot into the trees. Shot some of the hounds."

I flinch involuntarily. It was fifteen years ago. And my sister kills animals all the time, so why should I be bothered by this? But they weren't killing those dogs for food. It seems brutal, senseless.

The way Mama's murder would have been, if it had happened.

The pastor was probably one of those men. I wonder if he had a gun. I know he helped burn the trailer down. When he'd told me that, I'd been firmly on his side. Seemed like the least he could do.

And now?

Now I don't know.

"How did no one find them?" I ask Brandon. "Mama and Lee, I mean."

Brandon gestures around us. "Miles and miles of trees," he says, as if it's as simple as that.

I glare at him. His mouth quirks up slightly on one side. "That's not a real answer," I say. He relents.

It had been spring when Mama went missing. That worked in her favor, Brandon tells me. Rainstorms obscured her tracks. The foliage was dense. Besides, the searchers, whether they admitted it or not, were looking for a body, not a girl. And none of them were looking for a baby, either. Nobody knew she'd had twins.

Both Mama's parents had been hunters, had taken her out with them when she was young. She knew how to stay hidden, how to stay still. She roved deep into the national forest, moved between caves and hollows, treetops, old deer blinds.

In summer, Brandon says, he found this old camper that someone had abandoned. It was overgrown, vines through the windows, no door, leaves and dirt coating the floor, half collapsed. He started fixing it up, cleaning it, rebuilding. He installed the woodstove. Mama and Lee spent their first winter living there.

Brandon would visit when he could, when he could get away without Logan noticing. He was always afraid Logan would follow him. He took long, circuitous routes to reach the camper, never the same way twice. Mama was more afraid than he was. She made trip wires by stringing fishing line between the trees, ankle-height, connecting it to empty cans that would alert her if anyone jostled the line (I remember the nearly invisible string Lee had shown me the other night). More than once, Brandon came and found the camper deserted, Mama and Lee scared off, in all likelihood, by a hapless deer. At Mama's insistence, he dug underground hideouts for them.

Brandon says Mama made him promise over and over that he wouldn't tell a soul about her. She told him she was never going back, that they couldn't make her. He wasn't always sure who she meant by *they*. Her family. The police. The whole town. The whole world.

Brandon wanted to get away for good. He made plans to fake his own death. Pin it on Logan, maybe, a neat trick.

Then Logan got arrested. They questioned Brandon, too, but they didn't have any evidence. Logan had never trusted him with more than minor errands. As soon as Logan was charged, Brandon took his chance. He packed up everything he could from the double-wide. Sold his fish tank. Dropped a casual mention here and there around town that he was headed to Columbus.

Instead, he came to the camper. Cut himself off from all society, all contact. Men from town burnt down the trailer less than a week after he left, he says, though he didn't hear about it himself for months.

"So the two of them did live with you there," I say. "You lied to me about that."

"No." He shakes his head sadly. "They didn't live with me."

"They didn't? Why not?"

"She got worse." He's looking out at the trees, not at me.

"Worse?"

"More afraid," he says, pauses. "Paranoid, I guess. She didn't even trust me, sometimes."

He might as well be describing Lee, not Mama.

"She would make me prove," he says, "every time I came, that I was who I said I was. Prove I hadn't been switched or something. She stopped living in the camper. She wouldn't tell me where she went. I think she moved around. Sometimes caves, sometimes places like this." He puts a hand on the platform, traces the burnished head of a nail with one finger. "She'd stop by, but always at different times of day. I still gave her food and other things."

"A Bible," I say, thinking of the book Lee had in the cave. "She had a Bible?"

Brandon tilts his head at me, bemused. "Of course."

"Grandma Margaret always said she'd turned her back on God."

He snorts. "That woman would know about turning her back. No, Jolene talked about God all the time. She said the forest was the best church there is. Said out here you could actually be quiet for once and listen. Hear what he was really saying."

The wind rustles the sea of leaves, a wave passing down the valley with a shushing sound. Brandon and I are both silent for a while, watching. Listening.

Mama was right about that, I think. I mean, despite all Margaret's best attempts, Aggie raised me skeptical, so I might not have the same words for it. But there's something truly magical out here. Something holy.

"But she died," I say quietly. "How?"

Brandon stares out across the sea of leaves, doesn't answer. He's hunched over now, hugging his knees even tighter. I think of last night, the confession I was going to pull from him. I don't have a gun, so I just kind of nudge him in the back with my shoe. He shoots me a quick glance.

"She liked to float," he says, reluctantly.

"Float?"

"Yeah," he says. "Benzos. Xanax. That kind of thing. They calmed her down when nothing else would. She needed them."

"Oh."

I knew that Mama drank and smoked, did all the things she wasn't supposed to, but this still surprises me. This doesn't sound like partying or rebellion. It sounds like she was an addict.

I've always figured addicts were weak. That they just let themselves slide. But Mama wasn't weak. She can't have been weak.

"I found her here." Brandon says it quietly. Won't look at me.

"Right here?"

"Yes."

I run my hand over the smooth wood of the platform again. There's a lump in my throat, which is stupid. I've always known Mama was gone.

I wonder if she felt the same way I do sometimes. Like I'm burning up from the inside out. Like I will explode. The only thing that helps me is running. Being with my sister. Mama didn't have that. Aggie loved her, I know, but she couldn't understand her. And Grandma Margaret didn't even try.

"You found her?" I ask, trying to keep my voice even.

"Yes."

"And she was dead?"

"Yes."

"Because of the pills."

Brandon shoots me another glance. "She got them from me," he says. "I know you're thinking that. And you're right. I gave them to her. I would have given her anything she asked for."

Brandon says there was nothing he could do. He says it was too late. It must have been a day or two already because the flies—he doesn't finish that thought.

He says he buried Mama's body. Under this tree. Where the brown birds are. He says my sister watched him. Says she didn't cry.

She was five. Brandon thought he would take care of her. Thought it was the least he could do. When he talked to her, she didn't answer, though she'd always talked before. She'd been a skittish child, sure, but she'd babbled on about nonsense like any kid. When he tried to put a hand on her shoulder to comfort her, she ran.

"It felt like history over again," he says. "I searched for her. Left food in all the likely places. I thought she must be dead."

"Why didn't you call the police?" I ask, honestly shocked. I mean, okay, sure, neither had I, but I was only five myself when I first learned about my sister. He would have been twenty-one, then. A grown-up, more or less. "Or child protective services or something."

He frowns at me, looking almost as baffled as I feel. "I gave my word."

People in town are right. Brandon is strange. Maybe he always was. Maybe he's gotten stranger after all these years of living alone.

Though maybe he had a good reason not to trust anyone. I remember suddenly what the pastor said to me about Logan. How he put his own little brother in the hospital more than once. Nobody called CPS then. Or if they did, nothing happened. No one helped Brandon.

"But," says Brandon, "when I finally did see her again, I told her about you. I told her you were sisters, twins, two sides of the same coin. I led her to the edge of Margaret's yard. Told her that was where you lived."

That night comes flooding back. The window glass against my palm. My sister's pale face. Fireflies in the dark. My life turned upside down. I didn't know, didn't think to look for another figure farther back in the woods. Brandon, from the beginning, shaping the course of my life from the shadows.

"I'm not heartless," he says. "Jolene made me swear a thousand times I wouldn't tell a soul about her or her child. I wouldn't break that promise. I couldn't." He gives me a look, like he wants me to understand, wants me to say it's okay. I give a small nod, uncertain. He goes on. "But I thought if she saw you, she might choose to go live with you. Margaret might be a monster, but this was only a kid and I was worried she wouldn't survive in the woods."

He shrugs. "I was wrong."

I know now where my sister got her winter coat. I know how she survived all these years. I know how much she's been lying to me, how much she's been hiding.

"She talked to me again eventually," he says. "Came to me for food. She was like a wild animal. I had to earn her trust. Maybe I did the wrong thing. I don't know."

Neither do I.

"I grew this beard," he says. "Started going back to Needle, some other towns now and then, making the rounds of Logan's old backups. Never Lester. Never stores or anywhere public. I'd get the same people I bought the pills off to pick up groceries and things. Things I needed and things she needed. I helped her as much she would let me. I did the best I could."

This last he says with an air of finality, as if that settles it. The tale is told.

Everything.

But I feel unsatisfied. Feel like he's leaving things out, still. Even after all of that. Why did Mama do the things she did? He tried to explain, I guess. Sort of. Maybe there are things only my sister can tell me. "My sister," I say as a bizarre thought hits me. "Did Mama give her a name?"

"I don't know."

"You don't know?"

"We always just called her 'the baby.'"

I intend to laugh but it comes out weird.

"I know you call her Lee," he says. He smiles over at me. "She told me."

In the distance, above the trees, a firework goes off. It flashes, still rising, sparks red, stubs itself out against the sky.

We both stare at it. The ghost of it. A faint trace of smoke.

"What the hell was that?" I ask.

"A flare," says Brandon. "Must be for you."

"Me?"

"They must be searching for you."

The thought gives me a chill. It shouldn't, really. Of course Aggie would wonder where I've gone, want to find me. But it feels sinister, somehow. To be pursued. "I haven't been gone that long," I protest.

Savannah's older brother ran off once when he was still in high school and they just waited a few days and he came back. I think he went to go stay with his girlfriend in Needle or something. They're married now, three kids in.

"We'd better go dark for a while," says Brandon.

"What?"

"Hide, I mean."

"Isn't that what you're doing already?"

He laughs. Which startles me, actually. I think it's the first time I've heard him laugh. It starts quietly and then builds before cutting off abruptly, the sound bright and quick as the flare.

"I'm not taking any chances," says Brandon. "They'll kill me if they find me."

I wonder if that's true. It's been a long time. But people still talk about what happened to Mama. They haven't forgotten.

Brandon doesn't ask me if I want to go back. Doesn't ask me why I ran in the first place. Maybe he doesn't care. Or maybe he just understands without needing to ask.

I pull Savannah's phone out of my pocket, power it on.

"What are you doing?" Brandon says. The force of his voice startles me. His whole body has gone tense.

"I was just checking it," I say. "I thought my friend might text if people were out looking for me."

"Does she know where you are?" He speaks quickly, urgently.

"No."

"Does she know about me?"

"No. I haven't told her anything."

Brandon frowns, but he relaxes ever so slightly. There are four texts from Savannah.

jo come on pick up

jo im sorry

just talk 2 me

im sorry

"She didn't say anything about a search," I tell Brandon. "Maybe it's just hunters."

He shakes his head. "We should go."

He scoots to the edge of the platform, grabs a branch, swings himself down, drops to the ground. Before I put Savannah's phone away I send her a quick text.

Call me

I linger a few moments longer before climbing down. I stare up through the branches of the tree. Watch a tiny ant weave through the maze of the bark. Watch the leaves shimmer like sequins in the breeze.

Maybe this is what Mama saw before she died.

Savannah calls me back just as we're reaching the camper. I stop in the middle of the clearing, answer the phone.

"Hello."

"Jo?"

"Yeah, it's me."

Brandon has stopped with one foot on the cinder block. He's watching me the way my sister watches, wary, waiting.

"Oh my God, I've been so worried," Savannah says. She's whispering.

"Where are you?" I ask.

"Weird bathroom," she says. I know the one. Tucked down a dark hallway in the basement of the high school, filled with a perpetual cloud of pot smoke. I'd forgotten that it was Monday, a school day. School feels like another century ago.

"Where are *you*?" she asks.

"I'm fine," I say. I talk loudly, clearly, so Brandon can hear. He's still just standing there, watching me so hard it makes my skin crawl.

"Where did you go? Everyone is talking about you. Half the town is out looking for you."

"Looking for me?" So Brandon was right, about the flare. I'm officially a fugitive. I catch myself glancing nervously at the trees.

"They think the pastor hurt you," Savannah says.

"What?" I wasn't expecting that.

"He chased you into the woods and then came back alone with his hand all bloody. He was saying you attacked him or something."

I should be relieved, that he didn't send the police after Lee.

But instead I feel rage, flaring quick. I'm not going to be blamed again for my sister's crimes. "That's not what happened at all."

Brandon steps down from the cinder block. I move backward, hold up my hand to mean *wait, please, just give me a second.*

"Well, he didn't say it was you, exactly." Savannah pauses for a long moment. "He said it was a girl who looked just like you."

I breathe out loudly. Relief. "I fucking told you."

"Jo," says Brandon. "Hang up."

"Look," says Savannah. "Nobody believes the pastor either. They don't believe him that there are two of you. They think he's crazy or covering for you or that he killed you or something. Everybody at school thinks you attacked Henry, though. They think you've gone insane."

I can feel the eyes on me already, hear the whispers. If I came back now. If they caught me. It would be worse than before.

I ran, didn't I? That will make me look guilty in their eyes. Judge jury executioner in a glance.

"I'm hanging up," I say loudly.

"Wait, Jo, don't!" Savannah has stopped whispering. "I believe you, okay? I believe you." I'm glad to hear her say it even if it is too little, too late.

"Hang up," Brandon says again. I turn away from him, cup my hand over the phone.

"Who was that?" asks Savannah. "Are you with someone?"

"Is Aggie out looking for me?" I ask instead of answering. I hope she's sorry that she hit me, sorry that she yelled. I wonder if she believes me, too.

"I don't know."

"Have you seen Henry?"

"No, he's still out of school, but I hear he's okay." I'm glad to hear that, though I haven't thought much about Henry. He's just some boy, it turns out. Not like my daydreams at all. He's real.

"What about Jack?" I ask.

"What about him?"

"Are you—"

Before I can finish the sentence, Brandon yanks the phone roughly out of my hand. He fumbles with it for a moment before stabbing the End Call button.

"You shouldn't talk to anyone," he says, quiet but angry.

"I didn't tell her anything."

He shakes the phone at me, lecturing like the pastor, though he has even less right. "They could track you."

"Who could?"

"Them," he says. "All of them. You need to get rid of this."

"I can't." I grab for the phone, but he pulls it away, and I feel a surge of anger. Who does he think he is? "Give it back."

"This is dangerous," he says, holding it far away from himself as if it will burn him. There's a flash of something in his eyes. Just for a second and then it's gone. Real fear.

I think of what he told me, about the men coming with guns, shooting the hounds. Brandon's been hiding out here for a long time. He's just like my sister. She's just like him.

A few hours ago, I'd still been thinking about going home. Now that it's day, maybe I could find my way. And then what? Pack a bag and run away for real? Go back to the way things used to be?

I can never go back to the life I had before. The pastor knows about my sister. So does Savannah. And I know about Mama. I know that everyone was wrong.

She wasn't murdered, wasn't abducted. She left. It was her choice. She chose to run.

"It's my friend's phone, okay?" I say. I'm not ready to go back, but I'm not willing to give up my only connection to the other world. "Nobody knows I have it except her and she won't tell anybody. I swear. I'll keep it turned off."

I hold my hand out, do my best to look plaintive and harmless. Brandon looks uncertain.

"You can trust me," I say.

"Just keep it off," he says.

I snatch it quickly when he holds it out. I put it on silent and power it off, show him the black screen, shove it into my pocket. When he turns to go back inside, I slip my hand into my pocket, turn the phone back on.

Inside, Brandon prepares to go dark. He drapes a blue tarp over the fish tank, positions a ragged two-by-four gently across the tank as if it had fallen there. He grabs a handful of leaves from outside, scatters them across the sofa, the floor.

"So it looks abandoned," he says.

I help him carry armfuls of mason jars out from the kitchen. A few feet from the camper, hidden beneath the leaves, is a wooden trapdoor. It opens into a hole, about four feet deep, the sides and bottom lined with soggy-looking boards.

"Is this . . . ," I start, but trail off.

"Yes," he says, understanding.

One of Mama's hideouts. It seems a miserable place to crouch in the dark, waiting, with a small child. I don't understand. What was she so afraid of? I ask Brandon, but he just says *Everything.*

We stack the mason jars in the hole. Brandon wraps his dishware in the blanket from the couch, shoves the bundle into a heavy-duty trash bag. The beers go into another trash bag. The bags go into the hole.

We bag up the bedroom. It turns out I was wrong, before. Brandon doesn't have a gun, but a crossbow. A mean-looking one, with taut black wires and a scope on the barrel. He strips the quilt from the bed, wraps the bow and some bolts in it, shoves it all in a bag.

We fill the first hole, and a second one behind the camper. Brandon has planned for this. He's been ready.

"Where will you go?" I ask.

"Friend's place."

"What about the cats?" I ask.

"They can take care of themselves," he says. "They're good hunters."

We load the meat from the fridge into a large grubby cooler to take with us. He's got a backpack already loaded with necessities. The last thing he grabs is the tackle box full of pills.

The little black cat follows us through the woods for a while. I try to pick it up, but it wriggles in my arms and jumps free, shoots away through the trees. I could do the same, but I don't want to be out there alone right now, with half the town looking for me. I don't want to be found. Not yet. Maybe not ever. The sun breaks out from behind the clouds finally, stabs down like a searchlight.

We're almost right on top of the truck before I see it. It's camouflaged by a brown tarp weighted at the corners with stone, and strewn with leaves and branches.

"How often do you use this?" I ask. It seems like a lot of work to uncover.

"Been about a month, I think, since I last went out."

I wonder what his life must be like, in that little camper deep in the woods. Lonely, I would think. No phone. No neighbors. He doesn't even have a television.

He has Lee, I guess, though she's not much for conversation.

I help him uncover the truck, and we push it a few feet through the brush to a little dirt road, not unlike the one I went down with Henry and Savannah and Jack the other night. Friday night. Only three days ago. Might as well be a lifetime.

The truck smells shut up, damp and earthy. Brandon revs us over a little embankment, and then we rattle down the hill. It's steep, full of bumps. We don't go far before Brandon has to stop again to undo a chain stretched across the road and hooked around two posts with a sign that says No Entry.

The dirt road lets out eventually to a normal ridge road, though even that is rough and pitted with holes, barely wide enough for two cars to pass. The trees lean in toward each other, blocking the sun. We pass a thin gravel drive that I know well—it leads to Grandma Margaret's house. But her house is far back, hidden by trees, and we don't see any other cars. I stare out the window, thinking of my sister.

If she sees any searchers, hears them calling me, she'll hide. She'll cower in some dark hole or cling to the top of the tallest tree.

If there's one thing she's good at, it's hiding. She's been hiding her whole life.

Even from me.

Once, I think I see her out the window, through the trees. I twist in my seat, craning my neck to see as we rattle on. But it's only a scrap of fabric tied around a tree. Fluttering in the wind.

CHAPTER FOURTEEN

We emerge from a steep stretch of wooded road into a small valley dotted with houses. We're in Needle, a town that's only a ten-
minute walk from Lester, maybe three driving. You just go past
the high school, down the street a quarter mile, and there it is.
The two towns should probably be one. Lester has the middle
school and the high school for both of them. Needle has the
Kroger. There's no proper grocery store in Lester. Anyone who
doesn't have a car and can't walk that far has to do their shopping
at the Dollar General.

I could get home from here easily, if I wanted to, if I thought
I could face everyone, face the stares and questions and accusa-
tions. Face the pastor, what he must be telling everyone. Can
what Savannah said be true? That nobody believes him? I hope
so. They didn't believe me when I told them about my sister, but
he's an adult, a man. If I went back now and said he was lying,
that there is no girl in the woods, that they shouldn't look for
her, would they believe *me*?

We're nearing the main drive, the one that leads to Lester,

when Brandon pulls into the driveway of a squat one-story house. There's a porch with a white railing, but someone has nailed sheets of plywood behind the railing, all the way around the porch, closing it off.

We climb out of the truck, and I shoot nervous glances at the street, gripping the tackle box. I don't want anyone to spot me. Don't want the cops coming to rescue me or something, thinking I'm just some poor little girl who got mixed up with the wrong man. Around here that would cling to me forever. I'd never live it down. I've got enough to live down as it is. If I go back, I'll do it on my own terms.

"You wait here a minute," Brandon tells me.

I lean against the far side of the truck, partially obscured. Brandon walks to a door on the side of the house and knocks. A woman answers. For one dreadful moment I think it's Sheila from Bible study. They've got the same bleached hair, the color of buttercream icing, but this woman is a little heavier. She has sharp bangs that hang down over her forehead like the spokes of a rake. A cigarette hanging from her mouth. She's wearing a man's undershirt and no bra.

Savannah once said she thought women should be required by law to wear a bra at all times. I laughed so hard at her she went red in the face. *Well, okay,* she said, *maybe not by law. But still.*

My own breasts are just big enough to be annoying when I run, so I mostly stick to sports bras. Savannah wears neon lacy ones.

I wish she were here.

"What you got for me, honey?" the woman asks in a gravelly smoker's voice. I peer around the side of the truck. The woman puffs on her cigarette, leaning in the doorway. Her breasts are extremely large. I shouldn't stare.

"Something different," Brandon says. He's got one arm on the doorframe, one leg up on the step.

The woman laughs, says something I can't hear as a car rumbles past behind me.

"I need you to do something for me," Brandon says.

"Anything for you, honey."

Brandon turns toward the truck. My first instinct is to duck and hide, but he's waving me over. I trudge toward the doorway. The woman's eyes snap from him to me and back, her expression hardening.

"Aw no, honey," she says as I come up next to Brandon. "You ain't bringing your little jailbait piece here to fuck on my couch."

I feel a flush of shame, even though it isn't true. I look away, afraid to face the judgment in her eyes, the same kind of judgment I'm trying to avoid by staying away from town.

"She's my niece," Brandon says coldly. I wonder if he knows that for sure. I hadn't thought to ask. There'd been too much else to take in.

"Oh," says the woman, taken aback.

"She ran away," says Brandon. He grabs my left arm so quick I don't even have time to be surprised. He yanks my arm out straight, pushes my sleeve up a little, twists my wrist to show the woman the bite wound, which is starting to scab. His grip is firm. Painful where his fingers dig in.

"Bad stuff at home," Brandon says. "I was going to let her hang out with me until she figures out what to do, but the camper's no good for guests."

"Aw shit," says the woman, squinting at my wrist. "Sorry, honey."

I wonder if she thinks I did it to myself. You can't tell it's a bite anymore, the half-moon shape blurred by the scabs. It doesn't hurt as intensely as it used to, but it still aches. It's worse if I move it too much. I took another antibiotic pill while we were packing up the camper, so hopefully the worst of the infection is over. Brandon drops my arm and I hug it to my chest, wrist throbbing from the motion. The woman looks me over again. My clothes are probably a mess. My hair almost as snarled as my sister's.

"Well, guess you'd better come on in," says the woman.

I follow Brandon into the house. It's dark inside and it smells strange. An unpleasant smell I can't quite place. The windows are all covered in thick curtains. Something moves in the shadows, and with a start I realize there's a parrot perched on the back of the couch. A big blue-green one with a yellow belly and a clownish white face.

It squawks and then launches itself right toward me in a storm of feathers. I drop the tackle box, throw my hands up to cover my face.

"Shut that door," snaps the woman. Brandon reaches around me to push the door shut. The parrot adjusts course and swings up, coming close enough that I can feel the wind of its wings on my face. It alights on a tall shelf beside the door and starts preening itself with an air, I think, of embarrassment.

The woman disappears through a doorway toward the back of the house, and Brandon picks up the fallen tackle box. He follows the woman, closes the door behind him.

I sit on the couch, which creaks in complaint, and wait. The parrot watches me from its perch on the bookshelf, head tilted. Surveillance camera. It's as big as a hawk, and the black beak looks wicked sharp. I'm worried if I move too much it will fly at me again. There are faint squawks coming from somewhere else in the house. More birds. I can't hear anything from the room Brandon and the women are in.

I check the phone, find another long stream of texts from Dakota's number.

jack says he is sry
i told him i knew it wasnt you
i told him he was wrong
he is sry he yelled at u
hes not a bad guy
i havent told any1 u texted me
not even dakota
not jack
unless u want me 2 it is secret
u can trust me
im sorry okay u can trust
me

I want to believe Savannah, want to trust her, but she's still seeing Jack. She's still talking to him. She's defending him, even.

There's a flutter of wings again and I look up in time to see the parrot swoop across the room and land on the television. I notice, for the first time, faint streaks of white on the furniture, the floor. Gross. I wrinkle my nose, turn back to the phone.

lisa says they r sweeping the woods

I imagine everyone in town armed with a broom, brushing away the leaves, the dirt. Searching the bare stones, the packed earth, the twist of tree roots, looking for clues. Looking for me.

The door to the other room opens and Brandon comes back in. I quickly shove the phone into my pocket, but he doesn't look at me, just strides straight to the front door. I jump up from the couch.

"Where are you going?" I ask.

"Getting the stuff out of the truck," he says.

"Can I help?"

"Sure."

I follow him out. I didn't want to be left alone in that dark bird-shit house, with that woman who called me jailbait. But now, out in the sunlight, I'm worried again about being seen, caught. I don't want to be dragged back, a broken-legged lamb. I pull my hood up, stare down at the gravel.

Brandon hands me the grubby cooler full of meat. I hustle it to the side door and he follows with the backpack.

Inside, he leads me through the living room into the kitchen. I set the cooler down in front of the fridge. There's another door off the kitchen, a white metal door with glass panes. The squawks I heard earlier are louder here. I try to peer through the glass, but there's newsprint on the other side covering the panes.

"She's crazy about birds," Brandon says as he unloads the venison. "You can look if you want."

I turn the handle and the door opens with a wheeze. The squawks crescendo as I step through into the boarded-up porch. The smell out here is overwhelming. I breathe through my mouth, try not to gag.

Cages line the plywood walls. Cages full of birds. There's a pale-blue one with zebra-striped wings. A pair of small sunset-colored ones with scarlet beaks. A butter-yellow one with a spiky headdress and a pink spot on its cheek like an old woman's rouge. It snaps at the bars of the cage with its beak, making a rhythmic clacking. The blue one pushes a small bell with its foot. There's a gray-and-white one off to the side that sits motionless in its cage. It looks like it has plucked half its feathers out. They line the bottom of its cage. One slips out, drifts to the floor.

The plywood goes all the way around the porch. It reminds me of my room after Aggie nailed the window shut, the sun trying to shimmy through the cracks.

The sunset-colored birds shriek like shoes skidding on a gymnasium floor. The blue bird rings the bell faster and faster.

All I can see is my sister. My sister sitting in a dark little room like this with bars on the windows. No trees, no sky.

The bell rings and rings. The yellow bird bites the bars of its cage. The gray-and-white bird gives a small strange cough that sounds almost human.

I can see everyone I've ever known, hands outstretched, walking slowly through the woods, relentless, calling my name. And the wind carrying just a sliver of the sound, carrying it to my sister, so she is sure that they are calling for her.

If they find me I'll be branded, forever, a crazy bitch. A monster. I will be whispered about and looked at sideways in hallways and on the street. I'll be sentenced to three years of strict parenting, locked windows, and mandatory Bible study.

I'll have to face all that eventually. There's no way around it.

But if they find Lee, her life is over.

Everything she's ever known—endless trees, the night sky, freedom—will be ripped away. She'll be caught and held and touched and stared at and inspected and checked over by doctors and washed and subdued and fed by a tube and stuck with needles and *seen* by so many people. Photographed, maybe. Put on the evening news. Feral child found in forest; worst case of neglect seen in years.

Does she deserve that?

She lied to me and she tricked me and she attacked Henry and I want very badly to hate her, to leave her to own fate for once. But I'm her sister. I'm all she has.

Mama would want us to watch out for each other, no matter what. I know she would.

I pull Savannah's phone out of my pocket and punch in the only number in this world I know by heart.

Jessi answers. "Joe's Bar and Grill."

"Is Aggie there?" I ask.

Jessi doesn't say a thing, but there's a faint crackle and then Aggie is on the line.

"Where are you?" she says, not angry so much as frantic. "Are you okay? Whose phone is this? Where are you? I can come get you."

"Don't scare her off," I hear from the background. Grandma Margaret's voice. Aggie must really be desperate if she asked her mother for help. Maybe she had no choice.

"Jo," Aggie says, "please, baby, say something." She never calls me baby.

"I'm okay," I say.

"Did he hurt you?"

For a moment I think she means Brandon, like I thought with Savannah, but Aggie doesn't know about him either. She means the pastor.

I could lie. She would believe me, I think. She would leave him. Worse than leave him. Turn against him. Drive him out of town. Set Grandma Margaret on him, maybe.

At least I hope she would, hope that she would choose me.

"No," I say. "I'm fine. You don't need to search the woods."

"Where are you? What's that sound?"

The bell rings. The birds shriek. The gray one is looking at me sideways with one white-irised eye. "It's the TV. I'm staying with a friend. You can stop looking for me."

"I need to know where you are. You've been gone a day and a half, Jo."

"I'm in Needle. You can call off the search. I'm fine. You can call it off."

"I can't call off the search," says Aggie.

"You can. I'll come home."

"Jo," she says, "they aren't just looking for you."

"I'll come home," I say again, and then her words sink in.

"There's another girl," says Aggie.

"No." The shrieking of the birds drops away. No sound but the thrumming of my own blood in my ears. I didn't hear her right. I can't have heard her right.

"You were right," says Aggie. "The pastor was right. I still didn't believe it, but some of them saw her. When they were out looking for you. They thought it was you at first. But it wasn't you."

"No." I squeeze my eyes shut. I'm all she has. I can't let them catch her. "It *was* me. They saw me. Running in the woods. I remember."

"I'm sorry," says Aggie, ignoring my lie. "I should have believed you. I just can't—I don't understand how—but it's going to be all right. They've got the state troopers in now. Going to get some kind of heat sensor thing."

"No," I croak. My mouth has gone dry.

I should be happy. Aggie believes me now. Aggie is sorry. It's exactly what I wanted, what I hoped for. Everyone will be sorry now. Everyone will know it wasn't me.

But everyone will know.

How could I have ever wanted this? How could I have been so selfish?

There's a clink behind me, and I turn to see Brandon leaning in the doorway to the kitchen. He's got a beer in each hand. Green glass bottles. He's watching me. Wary, waiting.

"I have to go," I say quickly. Aggie is starting to say something else, but I hang up. Power the phone off, hands trembling, so she can't call back. Adrenaline buzzes through me. Electric wires. I want to run and keep running until it isn't true.

"Who was that?" asks Brandon. His expression and tone are neutral.

"My aunt Aggie. Sorry, I just—"

"You told her you were in Needle." It isn't a question.

Brandon is still, statue still. But there's something under that stillness. Something threatening. It crackles through the space between us like the air before a thunderstorm. The birds must sense it, too. They've all suddenly gone quiet.

"I—"

"Why would you tell her that?"

Before I can answer, the woman shouts for us from the other room. The birds all start up again, louder than before. Brandon turns abruptly and walks away. I follow, closing the door to the porch behind me, shutting out the shrieks.

The woman is standing by the door holding a big leather purse. She's got a sleepy, contented look, like a cat in the sun. I recognize that look. Aggie's pointed it out to me on the faces of people we pass on the street. She's high.

"Heading to Mickey D's," she says. "You want anything?"

"Fries," says Brandon.

"What about you?" she asks me.

"That's okay, thanks."

"You sure, honey? Not even a milkshake?"

"I don't have any money."

The woman laughs. "I'll get you a milkshake, honey. Don't you worry about it. I been where you been." She comes over and squeezes my shoulder. I hold very still, uncertain. She smiles at me, her foundation cracking around her eyes. "Sometimes you got no choice left but to run. Chocolate or vanilla?"

"Uh, thanks. Chocolate."

She sweeps away in a jangle of keys. The door shuts. Brandon turns on me.

"I'm sorry," I say quickly. "I was trying to convince her to call off the search."

"Why would you tell her you were in Needle?"

"I just thought—"

"You weren't thinking," he says. That stillness is back. That dead-air eye-of-the-hurricane feeling. He's angry, I think, furious, but he keeps it hidden, just under the surface.

"It doesn't matter, anyway," I say. "They're not just searching for me. They're searching for my sister, too."

That breaks through his brick wall. He wrinkles his brow. "Your sister?"

I nod, miserable.

"You told them about her?" He sounds more incredulous than anything, as if this was unthinkable.

"No," I say. "Of course not. I would never do that."

But I did. I told Savannah, told Henry, told Aggie, told the goddamn pastor of all people. I did it selfishly. To protect myself. I threw away every promise I'd ever made to my sister just so people wouldn't think I was a monster.

"She attacked a boy from town," I tell him. "He was out in the woods. He saw her."

"When?"

"Two nights ago. That's why I ran away."

Brandon slumps down on the couch, puts his feet up on the coffee table, takes a slug of beer. I can't tell if he's still angry. I can't read him as well as I can read my sister.

"Aggie says they've got some kind of heat search thing," I say.

"Heat search thing?"

"I don't know. She says the state troopers are in on it."

"Did the kid die or something?"

"No. He's fine."

Brandon shrugs, returns his attention to his beer. "They'll give up. She'll hide. They won't find her."

I would have thought the same thing, but Aggie said they saw her. I should have asked more. Who was it? When? Where? How many people? How close did they get?

Close enough to realize she wasn't me.

They won't give up.

"I've got to go back," I say.

Brandon looks up sharply.

"To Lester," I say. "To my aunt."

"She's got the truck," he says, waving vaguely at the door.

"It's okay, I can walk from here."

"No," he says bluntly.

"No?" I recoil, scowling at him. I thought he'd be upset, but he has no right to order me around. He has no authority over me.

"You don't want to go back," he says.

"I do."

I'm not sure if that's true, but I know that I need to go back. I need to undo this. I can tell them it was all a hoax. Convince them that I made the whole thing up. I had a wig, or something. It was me who the searchers spotted in the woods. It was me who attacked Henry. I can tell them that. Tell them I was lying, doing it for attention. They'll believe it, won't they? It's what they believed all along.

Brandon shakes his head slowly. "You can't go back."

I'm getting angrier by the moment. He's as bad as the rest of them. As bad as the pastor. He doesn't really see me, just sees what he wants to see. Sees the role he's written for me. I'm tired of it. Tired of everyone else trying to make choices for me.

"Well, *sorry*," I say. "And thanks for helping me, I guess. But I'm going back."

I turn away, hear the couch springs groan as he stands. The big blue parrot is off in another room or something, so the door is unguarded. I take a step toward it and Brandon's hand closes around my arm, his thumb pressing too hard. I slap at his hand, anger rising. How dare he?

"You can't go back there," he says. "You don't belong there."

"You're the one who took me there in the first place," I point out, furious now. Everyone's always telling me where I can and can't go. Telling me who I'm supposed to be. I try to pull my arm away again. He tightens his grip.

"I shouldn't have," he says. He isn't shouting at me like Jack or Aggie, but that quiet anger, that electric air, is almost worse, and suddenly I'm afraid of him again. "It's a bad place. Full of bad people. I should never have taken you there. I should never have separated you two."

"You're hurting me," I say, doing my best not to let any hint of fear into my voice. "Let go." I wish the parrot were here, wish it would fly at his face.

"No," he says quietly. "I finally got you back. I can't let you go."

It isn't fair. It's like the pastor and Lee. Or Jack looming over me outside Minnie's. Brandon is older and taller and stronger and so he thinks he has all the power. Thinks he can tell me what to do, possess me. And it's true, I don't have much power in this world. I can't even keep my sister safe. Can't keep myself safe, either. But I'm sick of them, all of them, and their unearned authority.

So I kick him in the shin. Hard as I can.

Brandon stumbles back so fast that he loses his footing and falls onto his ass with a grunt. He's swearing and cradling his shin and I'm backing up toward the door, and he's all folded up, hunched over, eyes closed, teeth gritted against the pain, and I'm reaching out behind me for the doorknob, afraid to turn my back on him, but then suddenly he's laughing.

He's laughing, the sound of it soaring up to the ceiling, beating against the window like wings.

"You want me to tell you everything?" Brandon says. He looks up at me, defeated, all that swagger and intimidation melted away. "Well, you stay and I'll tell you."

My hand slips off the doorknob.

"Everything?" I ask. I knew he was leaving things out. Knew there was more to the story. Like the pastor before him, he's found my true weakness.

And just like that, I'm caught.

———

Brandon sits on the floor with his back against the couch and a slab of chilled venison held against his shin. There are two empty beer bottles and two full sitting on the floor beside him and he's guzzling another.

"I found her because of the blood," he says.

I'm sitting on a stuffed chair across from him. The blue parrot has returned and taken up a station on the bookcase by the door, staring down at us like a prison guard.

"The blood?" I ask.

Brandon swigs more beer, closes his eyes.

"I was out with one of the hounds a few days after she went missing. The cops had already been around, asking questions. I saw the blood on the ground and I was afraid. Afraid she was dead. And there was this smell. But then the hound was nosing at something at the base of a tree and you started crying."

I'm digging my fingernails into my palms. My heart is beating fast as if I'm scared or something. But I'm not scared. I don't know what I am. This is my story. This is me.

"You were covered in leaves," he goes on. "A little mound of them. Piled on top of you. I pulled you out of the leaves. All slimy. And crying. Screaming. There was this thing on your stomach and that scared me. I thought it was your insides coming out."

I know how this story ends, but I'm holding my breath. I know how it ends, but not how it begins.

"Turns out it's supposed to be there," Brandon says. "Umbilical cord. I didn't know that. Nobody ever told me. I didn't know anything. But I picked you up. And you were disgusting."

I laugh. He looks at me, startled, as if he forgot I was there.

"Sorry," I say, "keep going."

He closes his eyes again.

"You were bawling and I was even more sure then, that she was dead. The hound had gone off on a new scent and I followed it and once it stopped to sniff at a leaf and I looked and there was blood on that too. And you were bawling and I was holding on to you but I didn't know what to do."

Was Mama hurt? Unconscious? I know she wasn't dead, not yet. I'm scared for her anyway. I know how this ends, but I'm scared.

"And then the hound stopped at a cave," says Brandon. "Little cave. And she was inside. She was in there. She was bent over something with her back to me. I yelled at the hound to stay back and I set you down on the ground. Just down in the dirt. I don't know why I did that. I wasn't thinking."

He pauses.

"It's okay," I say. "I'm fine."

He takes a long drink, keeps going.

"So she's there and she's sitting, bent over a little, and she's not moving really or reacting and I don't know what to think and I have to get on my knees because I can't stand in the cave and I go to her and I am saying her name, I am saying are you okay, I am saying that it's just me and I get close enough to put my hand on her shoulder and then she looks at me and she says—"

He stops, like he's listening, like he's hearing the words again. I'm afraid to speak, afraid to break the spell.

There's nothing else. No birds. No house. Just the two of us.

"She says none of them fuckers are getting their hands on her. And there was another baby. But you know that. She was holding it. It was so still lying there and its face was kind of gray and I knew it was dead. I was sure of it. My heart broke. For Jolene. For me, too, maybe, because I didn't know what to do.

"But then the baby moved its hands. Wiggled its fingers, small as maggots."

Brandon tilts the beer bottle up to his mouth, his eyes still closed, but it's empty. I push myself up from the chair, close the distance between us, my legs seeming to move of their own accord, and I pick up one of the full bottles and I twist it open and I push it into his hand. He drinks.

"The baby didn't cry," he says. "She didn't cry. Didn't make a sound. She was so quiet. And I realized then that you weren't crying, either. You'd stopped. I ran back out of the cave. The hound was licking you all over and I thought it was eating you or something and I shouted at it and pushed it away, but that made you cry again and you were fine, just cleaner than you had been."

I'm standing over him, looking down. I'm frozen. I was there, I think. In that same cave. Just yesterday. I didn't know.

"I tried to hand you to her," he says. "I pushed you at her but she wouldn't even turn her head to look. And you were crying and I said something dumb, something like, *Here, you dropped this,* and she said, *That's not mine.*"

I draw in a sharp breath. It is loud in the small room, but if Brandon notices he doesn't show it, just keeps talking.

"And I said of course it was hers. Said I found it. And I think I hadn't noticed you were a girl before that, but I noticed and said, *Here, take her, she needs you.*

"But she said, *No, that one is his.*"

I let out my breath in a rush. Like I've been hit in the stomach.

"No," I say. It comes out hoarse, barely a whisper.

221

The bird rustles its wings. I think I hear a car door. "You were so different," Brandon says, "the two of you. You crying and pink all over. And the other one so quiet.

"I tried to put you her in arms and she jerked away and clutched the other one to her chest and she screamed at me so loud, she said, *Don't you touch her, don't you fucking come near us, all of you goddamn devils just leave us alone.*"

He is talking very fast now, the words just pouring out.

"And I did. I left her. I ran back through the woods. I took my jacket off to wrap you up, tried to hold you so you wouldn't bounce too much, and I ran straight back to the trailer and all I wanted was to get rid of you."

He shoots me a look again. I don't say it's okay. Don't say anything. Don't think I could even if I'd wanted to.

"I wasn't thinking of anything but that, and Logan was gone with the good car, so I took the old truck, and I put you on the passenger seat, but you slid around and almost slid off as I was flooring it toward town, so I had to drive with one hand on the wheel and one reached over, holding you still, and I drove to Jolene's mama's house in town and I wasn't thinking about how it would look yet. I wasn't thinking about that. I thought about just leaving you on the porch, but when I carried you out of the truck, you hooked a little fist into my shirt and I thought something bad might happen if I just left you so I knocked and Jolene's mama opened the door and I held you out and she took you and I was so relieved that I just turned and ran to the truck before she could change her mind and give you back.

"When Logan got back it was dark and I had taken a shower and drank all the beer we had and he asked me what the fuck happened and I just told him I found a baby in the woods and that's all I told him, and that's all I told the police, too, because I knew she wouldn't want me to tell them, to tell anybody, and Logan swore and kicked over the table and then went out to find Jolene, but it stormed that night and the rain washed the blood off the leaves and he didn't find her as far as I know and neither did the police and the next day he beat the shit out of me for taking the baby into town and he broke my rib, I think, or maybe that was later, after the police came again, and they said we killed her, but they were wrong and then those men from town tried to kill us because they thought we had taken her away from them, but she had taken herself away, she didn't want anything to do with them, because they had driven her away, driven her crazy. She saw the devil in their hearts. Their secret faces. They wouldn't help her when she needed it. They didn't give a shit about her, not a one of them. Not until they thought she was dead."

The woman comes back and fills the house with the salt-fat smell of french fries. She drops the truck keys and the paper bags, already translucent with oil, on the table in front of the couch.

We watch *The Price Is Right,* with Brandon still slumped on the floor, and the woman sitting on the couch, playing with his hair, running her fingers through it. She gets up every now and then to get them both more beers. I suck up the sweet metallic milkshake, let it melt down the back of my throat, numbing it. The parrot sits on the television set. Brandon drinks his beers mechanically, eyes glassy. When *The Price Is Right* ends, the woman flips channels and we watch ten minutes of this and ten minutes of that, lingering just long enough to catch a single thread of plot before the whole thing is ripped away. The shows blur into one another and I can't follow them.

That's not mine, she said. *That one is his.*

She was wrong. She was wrong. It isn't fair. She was crazy. Did she see the devil in my heart? Did I look more like Logan? Is that even who she meant? *His.*

I was only a baby. So what did I do wrong? From the very first, I did something wrong. I cried while my sister was silent, and so Mama didn't want me. Is that it?

But what if she had kept me? What if I'd grown up like Lee? Hiding in holes beneath the ground. Trusting no one. Lean and tough and scared, always scared. What if it were the two of us out there now, terrified, pursued, afraid of everyone?

I can see it. All of them out there tracking my sister. With dogs maybe. Chasing her. Snapping at her heels. One of them leaping onto her back, jaws open wide.

Or not with dogs, but with some mysterious device, a radar screen showing the woods blotchy and dark, and in the middle of it a tiny blaze of red. Beating heart of the forest. Can their machine tell a girl from a deer? A girl from a wolf? They circle around her, closing in, closer and closer, locking their hands together in a ring, a chain, a cage.

Until finally they are upon her, pulling her out of whatever dark hole she is cowering in. She's fighting, kicking and scratching and biting, but there are too many of them, the devil in their hearts, and they hold her tight and she goes limp, tries to drop to the ground. But it won't work this time. They'll carry her back and she'll play dead and some of them will think that she is.

And then, where? To the hospital probably. They'll push a needle into her arm. Sedate her. Strap her to the bed. Shave her head.

I will come to see her, sit in a chair in the corner. The smell of medicine. Of bleach. A doctor talking to Aggie about vitamin deficiencies. My sister's bare head lolling on the pillow. Her eyes shut. Floating.

Outside, the sun sets. I don't know what time it is, but I don't dare turn my phone back on. Brandon nods off slumped back against the couch. The woman leaves the TV on, but she turns the volume down. She shows me a small room in the back of the house with a twin bed. It's covered in piles of clothes, but she says I can push them onto the floor. Says, *You can stay here long as you need to, honey.* She leaves me there, goes off to her own room, the television still flickering through the open door.

I sit for a few minutes amid the clothes. I could stay here. Keep hiding. I don't think the woman would tell anyone about me, even if she is a junkie. She's kept Brandon a secret, hasn't she? I could leave my sister out there. Leave her in the dark the same way she left me for so many years. This is her fault, not mine. I owe her nothing. *That one's not mine.*

I stand up instead, walk into the living room. The door to the woman's bedroom is shut. Brandon's eyes are shut.

The truck keys are where the woman left them, buried under crumpled burger wrappers. I extract them slowly, trying not to crinkle the wrappers. They still smell of oil and salt, globs of melted cheese clinging to them like scabs.

I walk toward the door. I can't leave my sister to her fate. I've got to prove that Mama was wrong. I stop with my hand on the doorknob. The parrot is perched on top of the bookshelf again, watching me with one beady black eye. It cocks its head, questioning.

I turn around and walk through the dark kitchen. Ease the door to the porch open. The birds rustle on their perches. I unlatch their cages one by one, whisper at them to be quiet, please. They are sleepy, blinking unsteadily at their freedom.

"Come on," I whisper to the ragged-feathered gray one.

When it doesn't move I reach in and coax it onto my uninjured wrist. It shuffles on, nodding its head, sharp little talon feet digging into my flesh. I carry it back through the house.

I stroke its half-plucked back as we walk past Brandon toward the door. He moans in his sleep and I lose my nerve, hustle back into the little bedroom.

There's a window behind the bed. Kneeling amid the clothes, I push the thick curtain aside with one hand. I open the window, kick the screen free. It falls onto the tall grass below. I hold my arm out into the cool night.

"Go on," I tell the bird. When it doesn't move, I give it a gentle nudge with one finger. It unfolds its wings, flaps a few feet into the air, perches on the gutter. I climb out the window and circle around to where Brandon's truck waits in the driveway.

I fumble with the keys, my hands shaking, until I find the right one. The door swings open and I climb inside, shut the door again. I stare at the dashboard. I've never driven a car. Dakota has been teaching Savannah, letting her tool around empty parking lots, and Savannah tells me it's easy. I turn the key in the ignition. The truck grumbles to life, shaking beneath me. I grab the steering wheel, bite my lip. Brake on the left, gas on the right. Right?

I press on the gas pedal gently with my foot. Nothing happens. I swear. Parking brake? I grapple with the lever by my side. The car lurches forward a few inches. I slam my foot on the brake.

There's a tap on the window.

I jump in the seat, turn to see Brandon blinking at me through the glass.

In a perfect world I would slam on the gas, make a daring getaway, but I haven't even figured out how to go backward yet and before I can do anything, Brandon's got the door open. I should have locked it. I wasn't thinking.

"You trying to steal my truck?" he asks.

"Yes," I say.

That makes him laugh.

"You're something all right," he says.

"I'm not going back to town, okay? I'm going to the woods. I'm going to find her before they do."

He stares at me for a moment. I reach out for the knobby thing, the gear shift, sticking up next to the parking brake, which I have finally remembered is how you go backward. I'll push him away from the door, maybe. Book it.

"Okay," he says. "Shove over. I'll drive."

CHAPTER FIFTEEN

We rattle up the hill, away from Needle, away from Lester. My plan is to go back to the camper. Maybe my sister will be there, waiting for me. If she isn't, I'll check the cave. I'll check every place I can think of until I find her. Will people still be out searching now that it's dark? I have to get to her before they do. I should never have left her alone out there. She was only doing what she was told. What Mama told her to do.

Never tell a goddamn soul.

Not even me.

We pass the narrow gravel drive that leads through the woods to Grandma Margaret's house. I wish we could drive with the headlights off, but there are no streetlights up here along the ridges and the moon is hidden by clouds, and in the darkness we'd probably just hit a deer or something and then where would we be?

"Is that the turn up there?" I ask. The sooner we're off the public roads, the better. "Did we pass it?"

"No, it's a little farther."

There's a light up ahead and I think it's someone with a flashlight and my stomach clenches, but it's too bright for that, I realize. Up over the crest of the hill ahead of us, another truck appears, headlights blazing.

These roads are narrow, so Brandon steers to the right shoulder, slows a little, but the other truck doesn't go rumbling past us. It veers suddenly, swings sideways, and stops, blocking the road.

"Shit," I say, sliding down in my seat. Brandon slams on the brakes.

The driver's side door of the other truck opens and a woman steps out with hair like a gray thundercloud. Face hard and thin as Aggie's face. Mouth pulled down at the corners.

Grandma Margaret. She turns and reaches into the bed of the truck for something. I slide down farther, crouch below the dash. Did she see me?

"Who's that?" I hear her shout.

"She's got a rifle," Brandon whispers. Shit shit shit.

"Girl went missing round here," Margaret shouts, her voice muffled only slightly. "We got to stop everyone."

Brandon cranks his window down a few inches.

"I haven't seen anybody!" he shouts back.

"Well, all the same," Margaret says. I can tell from her voice that she's walking closer. "I'm just going to have to—"

She stops speaking. My leg is starting to cramp from the awkward way I'm crouched. I wish I could see what's happening.

"Brandon," she says.

He flinches.

I sit up.

Margaret's eyes dart to me, but she doesn't move. She's standing about five feet in front of our truck with the rifle braced against her shoulder. Pointed right at the windshield. Right at Brandon. An easy shot.

"Jolene, baby," she says, "get out of that truck."

She's wearing a camouflage jacket printed with false trees. She is out here hunting me. Brandon and I don't move a muscle. My heartbeat ticks in my ears, loud as a hammer.

The headlights from the two trucks stare each other down, the beams dissolving into one another. Dust swirls in the light. I focus on that dust, the little dancing motes.

Margaret tilts the rifle up and fires into the sky, a crack like a falling tree. Brandon sucks in his breath. If anyone is searching nearby they would have heard that. I glance at the trees, half expecting to see the whole population of Lester come streaming out of the dark.

I wonder if Margaret is thinking about Mama, if she's picturing that day fifteen years ago when Brandon showed up on her front porch before the sun was up.

Behind her, the passenger door of the truck opens. A moment later, hobbling around the side of the truck, comes none other than the goddamn pastor, his ankle in a brace.

"Come on out, Jolene!" he shouts. "It's okay."

He's talking to me, but both he and Margaret are staring at Brandon. They must think they know the situation. He is a murderer. A monster. They must think he's kidnapped me or something. Must think that this evil man has got ahold of their innocent little Jolene. Lured her away from the flock. Little lost lamb. Big bad wolf.

They are writing their own stories. They think they know me, but they don't. They think they are going to save me, but they can't. I don't need saving.

I want them to understand that I chose this, that I made Brandon come here, not the other way around. I'm the one in charge here, the one with the power.

I want to hurt them. To show them how little I care what they think. So I do the only thing I can think of in the moment. I click my seat belt free and let it slither back across my chest into its holster. I turn and I grab Brandon's jacket in one hand and with the other I yank his face toward me, and I lean forward and in full, perfect, view of Grandma Margaret and the goddamn pastor I press my lips against his. The most wrong thing I can think of. It's not much of a kiss. Dry and too hard, his beard scraping my face, but it only matters how it looks to those two.

Their worst nightmares come true. Mama all over again. Wild girl. What I would give to see them now. What I would give to see their faces.

A gunshot cracks into the silence. Brandon jolts away from me. I think for a second I am dead. I think we're both dead. Maybe I went too far. I slide down quick, off the seat, crouch again beneath the dashboard. There's a hole punched clean through the windshield, little silvery cracks spiderwebbing out from it. There's no pain in my body, though. No wound. Brandon's folded up beside me. His breathing is fast, loud. I can feel it against the side of my face. My hands are shaking, heart going way too fast for sitting still.

"Oh Jesus Lord!" I hear the pastor shouting. "You could have hit her. Did you hit her? You didn't hit her, did you?"

"You just stay back." Grandma Margaret's voice. "You've done enough."

"Are you hit?" I whisper to Brandon. I can't see his face, can't see anything but the underside of the dashboard. I'm already regretting the kiss. That wasn't like me at all. Savannah's the one who would do something like that.

"No," Brandon whispers back. Should I explain to him why I did it? I don't want him to get the wrong idea.

I won't pretend it wasn't a little thrilling, to do something so wrong. But I don't like him that way. He's probably my uncle, after all. There's another shot, then, and a sort of pop, and the truck slumps a little to the left. It's even more terrifying than when I was a kid and Margaret shot out the window at the trees. She's insane.

"Brandon Cantrell," shouts Grandma Margaret, "you get the hell out of that truck with your hands up."

"We should do what she says," Brandon whispers.

"They're monsters," I say. "You were right. They're the monsters."

Brandon gives something between a cough and a laugh.

"You really are just like her," he says.

And this time I know he doesn't mean my sister. He means Mama. I know he does.

I grin, in the dark, despite myself. I would almost kiss him again, though maybe on the cheek this time, just for saying that. It's the best gift anyone could give me. "By God if you don't get out of the truck I will come in there and get you!" Grandma Margaret shouts. "Don't think I won't. You all know me."

Brandon shifts beside me. I think of him cowering in the forest as the men with guns came to kill him and his brother. How scared he must have been. He was only sixteen.

Well, I'm only fifteen, but I'm not scared.

I'm just like her.

I sit up.

"Grandma," I say, one hand on the door. My hand is still shaking slightly but that's just adrenaline, not fear. I'm not scared. I refuse to be scared. "Don't shoot him. I'm not moving until you promise."

"Little girl," she says, "you don't know what you're playing at."

I think of saying please, of begging, crying even, pretending to be frightened or sad. But I'm not going to give anybody here the satisfaction. They think they know me, but they don't.

"If you shoot him I'm telling the police you did it in cold blood."

We stare each other down through the tiny cracks in the windshield. Brandon is still crouched under the dash, powerless. I'm thinking of all those daydreams I used to have in school. Henry and I fugitives, persecuted, living in the woods. It's like those dreams are coming true, but twisted.

"Fine," says Margaret. She swings the rifle up to rest on her shoulder, threatening only the stars.

I slide out of the car.

My feet hit the gravel at the side of the road. The trees are so close. The dark of the trees. Leaning toward me, welcoming. I could just run into their arms, run and run and never stop.

But I won't. I'm not scared. I refuse to be scared. I'm going to stare them down. I'm going to face them. I take a few steps forward. I feel like I felt back at the camper. I am strong, electric.

Mama was wrong. She was wrong.

I'm hers.

I'm more hers than my sister could ever be.

"Come on over here, baby," Margaret says, her eyes on the truck. The left front wheel is flat, slumping down in a black puddle.

The pastor is limping toward me, a funny lopsided almost-run, going faster than you'd think a person with an ankle in a brace could go. Margaret shouts at him to hold still, but he doesn't listen. The pastor barrels into me and I'm so confused. Is he trying to knock me down, is the truck rigged to blow and he's going to shield me from the blast?

But he's hugging me, squeezing me so hard I can barely breathe.

"Fucking hellfire," says Margaret. I try to twist to see what Brandon is doing. He should run, I suppose. Get away into the woods. Hide. Like he's so good at. Like he's been doing all his life. Like Mama. Like my sister.

I will not hide.

"The devil got you," the pastor whispers into my hair. He sounds like he's crying, voice thick and clotted with snot. "I won't let it happen. Not again."

I can see Brandon out of the corner of my eye. He's sliding over to my side of the truck. He's climbing out. Is he going to run?

"My baby," the pastor says.

"I'm not your baby." I try to push him away, but he holds tight. Like he held my sister. Everybody always trying to tell me who I am. Who I should be. Trying to hold me back.

"Let go of her," says Brandon, beside us now. His voice is steady as still water.

The pastor ignores him.

"You might be," he says to me.

"What?"

"I'm sorry, Jo." The pastor leans back just far enough to look me in the eyes. There are tears in his. "I should have told you sooner."

And it hits me, hard. I understand.

Everyone always said Mama was friendly, too friendly. I knew what that meant. Everyone always said Logan was probably my father, but not for sure.

You might be.

"I said let go of her." Brandon grabs the pastor by the shoulders and yanks him away from me. I'm stunned, thankful. Brandon isn't gentle. The pastor stumbles, then pivots and throws a punch, which Brandon dodges.

"You should have stayed the fuck away," the pastor says. He throws himself at Brandon, knocking him against the side of the truck.

I might be. Might be his baby.

The pastor lands a punch in Brandon's side. Brandon hits him back hard, right in the jaw. The pastor stumbles back, nearly falls. Grandma Margaret swings her gun down from her shoulder, aims at the two men.

The pastor must have had sex with her. With Mama. I don't want to think about it. Don't want to think about what that means. Did Aggie know?

With a chill I remember the things he was saying in the woods. *The Lord brought me here for a reason. I've got a second chance. I knew I had to come back for you.*

"Jolene," says Grandma Margaret, "you get your ass over here."

I move toward the front of the truck instead, getting between Brandon and the gun. I don't know if he's my uncle or not anymore, but he as good as raised my sister and I'm not letting Margaret shoot him. The pastor is hissing swear words under his breath. I've got my back to him and Brandon, but I can hear them grapple, hear someone slamming against the truck again, a grunt of pain.

"Do you even know what you've gotten yourself into?" Margaret shouts at me. "Do you know who that man is? That's one of the rotten pieces of shit who murdered your mama."

"No, he—"

She cuts me off. "I warned her, but she didn't listen. I'm warning you, too."

"He didn't kill her," I shout. "You did."

"That what he told you? Little girl, you ain't that dumb."

"You didn't even care about her," I shout. "She was alive. After she had me. She hid in the forest. She didn't want you to—"

Before I can finish, someone slams into me from behind, knocking me to the ground. My face hits the gravel. Things start happening very fast. Out of the corner of my eye, a swinging fist. A crunching sound. A shout. Grandma Margaret standing over me. Light glinting off the barrel of her gun.

I try to push myself up. Brandon is kneeling over the pastor, who is down on the ground, on his back like Henry. Brandon's got his hands around the pastor's throat, the muscles of his arms straining, twisting like snakes under his skin. He is stronger than my sister. There is blood on the pastor's face. *You might be.* I don't want him to die. Not really. I don't want either of them to die. This is too much.

Grandma Margaret is aiming.

"Lord Jesus, give me strength," she whispers.

I throw myself forward, knock into her legs. She pulls the trigger. Her shot goes wide. She shouts at me. "Idiot girl!" The pastor rolls out of Brandon's grip. His nose is bleeding, broken-looking. His eyes meet mine for a moment, a split second. Bright blue. Pleading. I scramble to my feet.

"Run!" I shout at Brandon, and I am doing just that.

I am running headlong into the dark. It's hard to see, but I just blow ahead, don't give a shit when branches whip my face, my arms. When I stumble, when I fall, I just get right back up and keep going. There are gunshots, but they are hardly louder than the sound of sticks snapping beneath my feet. I can hear Brandon running behind me.

Flashlight beams come swinging at us through the trees, but all they do is light our way. The pastor and Grandma Margaret can't keep up. We know the forest better than they do. We belong out here, me and Brandon. We are cut from the same night sky.

We run and the darkness opens up to receive us. This is home, as much as the bar ever was. The trees are silent old men, gently drunk, swaying in the wind. They watch us go with sad eyes, thinking of their own sons, their own daughters. The wind picks up and for a moment they are all dancing, waving their thin arms out of rhythm, moving to some song only they can hear.

"Stop," Brandon gasps from behind me. I skid to a halt.

I don't know where we are. The top of some hill in the national forest. There is moonlight pouring down on us, brushing the ground, the wildflowers, frosting the little bundles of dead leaves that hang from a shrub beside me. That's the work of the cicadas, I know, from the heart of summer, when they drilled holes in the tips of the branches to hide their eggs.

Brandon is leaning back against the trunk of a white tree, hand to his side.

When those eggs in the branches hatch, the baby cicadas drop to the ground, their first act in life a long fall with no one to catch them. The instant they hit the dirt they start digging, don't come back up again for years.

Brandon's eyes are shut, his face is pale. I think he has a stitch from running, but then I see it, beneath his hands—a shadow, a patch of darkness.

The darkness is spreading and for a moment I think it's the night sky, leaking out.

But it's blood. Grandma Margaret hit him. When we ran, she shot into the dark, and she hit him.

"You're okay, right?" I say. "You're going to be okay."

"It burns," he says, between clenched teeth.

She can't have hit anything important. He was running. He's still standing. In movies people just drop like a sack of potatoes. I move closer to him, push his hand out of the way. The blood is coming, I think, from a spot above his hip. Nowhere near the heart. He's fine. He's still standing.

I pull off my hoodie. I'm hot from running, sweat cooling against my skin. I wad the hoodie up and push it against his side. He grunts in pain.

"You've got to put pressure on it," I say.

"I know," he says, "I know." His eyes look wild in the dark. But he's fine. He's standing.

We work together, peel his jacket off, one whole half of it wet with blood. We use that to bind the folded hoodie against his side, tying the sleeves of the jacket together, pulling it tight, tighter, tight as it will go, while he gasps, sweat beading on his forehead, eyes squeezed shut. I knot the sleeves, wipe my bloody hands on some leaves.

Brandon leans back against the tree.

"What do we do now?" I ask.

He doesn't answer right away. I'm scared he will pass out and leave me here alone. I don't know what I'd do. I get this feeling in the pit of my stomach, like falling and falling through endless darkness. But I'm standing still.

I reach out and shake Brandon by the shoulders. His eyes flutter open.

"Fuck," he says.

"Should I call 911?" I ask.

"What? No." He presses his hands harder over the hoodie, grimacing. "They'd kill me."

Of course we can't call 911. We're on the run. We're fugitives now. My daydreams coming true, but twisted.

I think of kissing Brandon in the truck. I think of what the pastor said. *You might be.* A horrible thought occurs to me.

"Did you sleep with her?" I ask.

"Hmm?"

"Mama," I say. "Did you sleep with Mama?"

He doesn't answer.

"Jesus," I say, reeling, "are you my father too?"

"I'm not," he says.

"You might be."

"No," he says firmly. "You were already— It was *after*."

"Oh."

Were you in love with her? I want to ask. But I think I know the answer. He's told me as much already. *I'd give her anything,* he said. *Anything she wanted I'd give it to her.*

"Is Logan my father?" I ask instead. I always assumed he was. Always assumed he was a murderer, too. But even innocent of that crime, he sounds like an awful guy.

Maybe it would be better, to know that I'm not half monster.

Brandon shakes his head. "I honestly don't know."

Any scrap of certainty I once had in my life is gone. I don't know anything anymore. Don't know who I am. Don't know what to do.

The plan was to find my sister. To get her somewhere safe. I'll stick to the plan.

"Cover your ears," I tell Brandon. He blinks at me, confused, but puts his one free hand over his left ear. Good enough.

I take a deep breath, lean back my head, and howl.

I do it loud and long, do it until my throat aches and my lungs burn. The air here is cold. I take a deeper breath, howl again.

If there are searchers nearby, let them hear it. Let them be afraid. They won't think it's the sort of sound that could come from a girl. Must be some kind of animal, they'll think. Some kind of monster.

The sound dies away. I gasp for breath. Brandon pulls his hand away from his ear, presses it back against his side.

The adrenaline has worn off and I feel shaky and weak. Feel like my limbs might float away. I squint at the dark trees around us. I see no shapes detaching themselves from the shadows. No searchers, but no sister either.

Brandon coughs, his body bent in pain. I want him to tell me what to do. I want someone, anyone, to tell me what to do. I've always wanted the opposite of that. To be free. To do exactly as I please. To need no one.

But right now I need help. With trembling hands, I pull the phone from my pocket, power it on, ignoring the missed calls from the bar, and dial Dakota's number.

Pick up pick up pick up.

"Oh my God, Jo. I'm so glad you called," Savannah says before

I even get a hello out. Her voice seems like something out of another world. A world I'm leaving farther and farther behind. "Are you okay?"

"I'm fine," I say automatically, though I've never been less fine in my whole life.

"Where are you?"

"The woods."

"I still haven't told anyone about talking to you," she says. "Not a single soul. I swear."

"Thanks," I say, searching for the right words. Should I tell her everything?

"But look," she rambles on, oddly cheerful under the circumstances, "I've got to tell you something. You won't believe it."

Brandon is leaning his head back against the tree, eyes squeezed shut. He's pressing both his hands into his side. His breathing is heavy, loud.

"Savannah," I start. I'm going to need a lot of help. Margaret and the pastor must have raised the alarm by now. "Can you—"

"I had sex," she blurts out.

"What?"

"I had sex. Like one hundred percent all the way."

"What?" I can't help myself. It should be nothing compared to the things I've learned today, but I'm still shocked. "With who?"

"I just had to tell someone," she says, "or I thought I'd explode."

I just got shot at, I should tell her. Savannah's news doesn't matter at all. But I can't help confirming an awful suspicion.

"Was it Jack?" I ask. She doesn't answer, so I know it must be true.

Jack. I can see him leaning over me, shouting. The veins in his neck. The scraggly hairs on his chin.

"I haven't told anyone else about it," Savannah says. "Not even Dakota."

"How could—" I say, but I stop myself. How could you, Savannah? How could you let him touch you, let him do that to you? I want to hate her for it. Why Jack? Of all people? I want to be disgusted. It makes me uncomfortable, the thought of letting yourself be so vulnerable with another person. What pleasure I've had is a secret, a private thing, something I do alone. Something I'm a little ashamed of, if I'm being honest.

But Mama had sex when she was our age. A lot of it, if what people say is true. With Logan. With the goddamn pastor. Grandma Margaret threw her out of the house because of it. Pastor Nelson turned her away at the door. They thought she should be ashamed. They wanted to make her ashamed. I'm better than them. I can be better than that.

"Look, Savannah," I say, urgent, "I need your help right now. If you care about me at all—"

"Jesus, Jo," she cuts me off. "Of course I care about you. You're the only one I wanted to tell."

"Well, then please just do this one thing for me."

"Yeah, of course. Anything." She has no idea. If she did she wouldn't sound so eager.

"You've got to get a car," I say.

"What?"

"A car. From Dakota or from—I don't know. Just, I need to borrow a car. I need you to take it to Myron's house. I need you to meet me there. Alone."

I'm expecting Savannah to protest, to say that's impossible, that's too much to ask, how the hell is she supposed to get a car, that's crazy. It is.

"I think I can do that," she says.

"Oh my God," I say, overwhelmed with relief. "Thank you. I'll meet you there. As soon as you can get it."

"What's going on?" Her tone is more subdued now. She gets it. This is serious.

"I'll explain everything when I see you, okay? I've got to get moving."

"Okay," she says, "okay."

"Thank you, Savannah. I owe you." I could kiss you.

I hang up.

"Can you walk?" I ask Brandon.

"Yeah," he says. He tries to push himself up with one hand, keeping the other pressed to his side. I rush to help him and he leans on me. I can smell his stale beer breath and his sweat and something else, a smell that reminds me of the rusty fire escape outside my old window.

The two of us stagger along, our progress awkward, Brandon leaning heavily on my shoulder. I don't even know which direction to go. I can't tell one tree from another, can't tell north from south. Every darkness looks equally deep. The trees are too thick here to see the stars.

We move forward and with every step, the voice in my mind grows louder. The one saying, *I am lost, I am lost.* How did I get here? How did everything go wrong so quickly?

There is another world where everything went differently. Another world unfurling behind me like a white flag. I could have gone home. I could have made it so Brandon got away unscathed. I could have stood like a shield while he escaped.

I could have stayed. That instant before I ran, when I met the pastor's eyes and they looked sad and scared and kind. There was a whole world in there.

I take a step and then another step and then I stop. I think I'm going to cry. I think I'm going to collapse. Just curl up in the dirt and wail until someone finds me. They're looking for me, aren't they? They're out here trying to find me. I could just let them.

"What is it?" asks Brandon.

"I don't know," I say. "I'm lost."

He shifts his weight, grunts in pain. I turn to look behind us. Maybe we should just try to find our way back to the road. I open my mouth to say so.

And then she is here.

From the darkness beside me she appears, stepping forward as silent as a ghost. She stretches a thin hand out to touch my arm.

She has put on a pair of black tights, though they are so criss-crossed with runs and tears that they can't be much warmer than no tights at all. It's cold tonight, getting colder. She has on the big puffy coat, too, and the brown knit cap, and her shoes, a pair of sneakers I got from the thrift store double discount bin. They were white when I got them, but are now unrecognizable, gray-black with caked mud.

"Lee," I say. "I'm sorry." For what, I'm not entirely sure. She should apologize to me, too, but I won't hold my breath.

"There are too many people," she says, quietly, and I know what she means. The once-empty forest, infested.

"I know."

"They want us." She looks very afraid, very tired. She sleeps during the day, usually, but she wouldn't have been able to with people nearby.

244

"It's okay," I say. "We'll run away. They won't find us."

She glances over at Brandon. Neither of them says a thing, but something unspoken seems to pass between them. This is what they wanted. What they both wanted.

"Take us to the tree," I say. "Our meeting tree by the cemetery. Please." She's the only one of us who could find the way in the dark. She knows these woods so well.

Her little plastic heart purse is strung by its rope strap across her chest. It's like she knew somehow. Got all dressed up, all packed up, ready to go. Maybe she and Brandon had been planning this for years. A way to lure me away from town, to paint me into a corner so tight I had no choice except to run. Just another story that isn't mine.

But I could still go back, could still give up. It isn't too late. I am choosing this. Choosing the same way Mama did.

I take my sister's hand, reach my other hand out for Brandon. I pull him forward and he stumbles along after us.

Once, in the distance, I hear people shouting my name. But we keep going, moving through the dark like we are part of it. Nothing but shadows. Nothing but ghosts.

CHAPTER SIXTEEN

We walk in a line, holding hands like children on a field trip. My sister in front, me in the middle, Brandon at the back.

Lee tried to run, but Brandon couldn't keep up. We had to go back for him, had to help him to his feet. Maybe he's just drunk, I thought. All those beers back in the other world. You'd think being shot would sober you up.

But we move as fast as we can. My sister leads the way. Out here, she is a better guide than any star. I follow behind her, try to focus on nothing but her. The back of her head, her snarled hair, her torn tights. Try not to think about how hopeless this is. Even if Savannah somehow manages to drive Dakota or her mother's car away, surely they'll notice before she gets very far. I try not to think about that. I follow my sister. In the darkness, the flowers on her new dress are all different shades of black. Everything in the forest at night is black and silver, like a silent movie. Savannah and I watched one on her phone once. A man stood perfectly still and silent while a house fell around him. While the whole world fell apart around him.

We are going downhill now and my feet keep sliding on the fallen leaves. I recognize an uprooted tree that I know isn't far from Queen of Heaven.

"We're nearly there," I whisper.

Brandon's hand slips out of mine.

I stop, jerking my sister to a halt. Behind me, Brandon's dropped to his knees. His head bobs forward like he's falling asleep in class.

"Brandon?"

His breathing is ragged and shallow, his eyes are shut. I kneel too, grab his shoulders and shake him gently. "Come on," I say. "We're nearly there."

He doesn't answer and I can see, in the filtered moonlight, that our makeshift bandage didn't keep the darkness from spreading.

There's too much. Too much of it outside his body. Panicked, I press my hands against his side. My gray hoodie has gone black. It's soaking wet. There's blood all down the leg of Brandon's jeans. I think, wildly, of trying to gather the blood up somehow, pour it back inside him.

I shake him by the shoulders again. He slumps forward, his head falling against my shoulder. I wrap my arms around him to keep him steady.

"It's okay," I say, because I think that is the sort of thing you are supposed to say in these situations. What do I do, what do I do? "You're going to be okay."

I can feel his chest rise and fall. This is my fault. We need to go to the hospital. His head is heavy as a stone on my shoulder.

His breath rasps out, barely audible. His chest rises and falls. Rises and falls.

Doesn't rise again.

"Brandon?" I say. I push him away from me, hold him out at arm's length. He's gone heavy, motionless. He is drunk on the night, I think. He has passed out. Right?

That must be all. He just needs to sleep it off. Tomorrow, he'll be fine. He has to be fine.

I shake him by the shoulders. His head flops around, chin banging against his collarbone. I press my ear against his chest, try to hear a heartbeat, feel the rise and fall. It must still be there, but too quiet, too slight. I must just be missing it. I press my fingers against his wrist, searching. I shake him again. I keep saying his name. Over and over.

He isn't gone. He can't be. He was just here.

When I look up, Lee's standing behind him. She's leaning down, prying my fingers from his shoulders. She pulls him away from me. I'm frozen, kneeling in the dirt. Not sure I could move even if I wanted to.

Lee drags him backward, lays him down, stretched out on the ground. Surprisingly gentle. She kneels and presses her ear against his chest. Her eyes closed, she rests there for a long time, listening.

My sister the wild one. The witch. She's going to save him, I think.

I watch, afraid to speak, hardly daring to breathe,

She is still, so still, listening.

Suddenly she sits up, scrabbles at the ground beside her, gathering a big handful of dirt and dead leaves. She holds her hands straight out in front of her and drops the leaves on Brandon's chest. She stands up.

I stare at him. He's okay. He's going to be okay. Right? He has to be.

Lee is behind me now, hands under my armpits, pulling me to

my feet. I won't take my eyes off Brandon. Any moment now, he'll move. He'll wiggle his fingers, clasp and unclasp his rough hands. He'll open his eyes. He has to.

He was just here. Just moments ago. He was breathing. It can't happen that quickly.

I'm shivering, though it hasn't gotten any colder.

Lee's taken off her puffy jacket. She's tugging my right arm into the sleeve. When she grabs my left wrist it hardly even hurts anymore. She gets the jacket on, though I give her no help. My body feels distant, numb. I don't want to go. Don't want to leave him here alone.

She has to pull me away. Has to drag me, my heels scratching long, thin scars in the dirt.

I move like I'm in a dream. My limbs not quite attached. They are somewhere far from me, working on their own.

I can't stop. He didn't want them to find me, didn't want them to catch me, to keep me.

It's my fault. My fault that he ran when I told him to. My fault he was in the truck. My fault that he had to leave his camper in the first place.

It can't be for nothing.

He wanted to fix the mistake he made all those years ago, taking me into town. He would want me to keep going. Would want me to run and never look back. I tell myself this, over and over. It's the only way to keep moving.

Maybe if we'd let ourselves be caught, they could have saved him. Maybe if I'd realized sooner, I could have called 911. Could have gotten an ambulance.

But he didn't want that. I've got to keep going.

When we reach the edge of the cemetery, Lee tries to head toward our meeting tree, but I hold her back, pull her wordlessly up the hill toward Myron's house. I've shown her the house before, though I could never convince her to go inside. We circle around, still shielded by the forest. My heart pounds with how close we must be to people. What if they're scouring Queen of Heaven? What if they're waiting for us at Myron's? Savannah could have told them. Betrayed me again.

The house, from what I can see through the trees, looks how it always looks. Dark. Empty.

"Wait here," I tell my sister.

I search her eyes, her posture. She looks calmer than she should, when I feel like I might shatter at any moment. I haven't forgotten what I thought back at the camper. That she was a stranger. That I don't know her at all, not really.

"Why?" she asks.

"Savannah's here." I hope to God that's true. My sister stiffens. "I asked her to come," I say. "She's on our side, okay? And you can't hurt her."

Lee's shoulders are hunching, she is closing herself up.

"We're running away," I say, trying to sound hard and sure. There is no room for argument now. "Like you wanted. She's going to help."

Lee seems about to protest when we both hear voices, shouts. I whip around, peer through the trees toward Myron's house. I don't see anything. The shouting comes again. It is distant, difficult to make out words, but it could have been *Jolene*, could have been my name.

"Stay here," I whisper. "Don't move. I'll whistle if it's safe for you to come out."

I don't give her time to object. There is no time. I sprint out of the trees to the side of the house and move carefully along it, crouching low.

I peer around the edge of the porch, expecting nothing. Or maybe Margaret. Maybe Aggie. Maybe the pastor. Maybe an angry mob.

There's a car in the driveway.

I squint at it. The moon is brighter here, pouring down unobstructed into the clearing, and I realize I know this car: a low-slung little sedan, nothing special, scratched gray paint, dent in the hood.

This car belongs to Jack.

No. He can't be here. Did Savannah send him? Did he follow her somehow?

I back up around the house, heart hammering, reaching for the phone in my pocket, when a voice, small, scared, says, "Jo?"

I whip my head around, unsure at first what direction the voice came from, and then I see Savannah, poking her head out the kitchen window, cigarette in hand, tiny cherry flare in the darkness.

"Savannah," I say, almost too happy to speak. I run to the window.

Savannah is wearing her plaid jacket with the fake-fur-lined hood, zipped only halfway, so the top of her tank still shows and, bent over as she is now, the top of her breasts too.

"Is he here?" I whisper.

"Who. Jack? No."

I sag against the side of the house, relieved. Savannah swings her legs over the sill, jumps down. She's got her Tupperware of cigarettes from the Naked Lady Room tucked under one arm.

"How'd you get his car?" I ask.

She shrugs. "It makes him go to sleep."

"What does?"

"You know."

It takes me a second to understand, then it hits me. It shouldn't matter. Not now, after everything. But I still feel a sick lurch in my stomach and my face must betray my disgust, because Savannah frowns at me.

"You did it again?" I ask

I told myself I wouldn't judge her. That I would be better than that. But it's hard, when he's the worst possible person. How could she let him touch her like that? He's gross and she's perfect. He shouldn't even be allowed to look at her.

"Why?" I ask.

"I don't know," she says, stubbing out her cigarette on the side of the house. "I didn't really mean to, the first time. It just kind of happened."

Which makes no sense. How can that just *happen*? It's not like you just trip or something and then suddenly you're doing the one thing that pretty much everyone your whole life has told you not to do. That everyone in your whole life will judge you for.

I know everyone judged Mama. They judged her right out of town. Judged her to death.

I won't be like them.

"I guess it doesn't matter," I say, and it doesn't. It really doesn't. Nothing matters. Brandon is back there in the forest. He looks like he's only sleeping, but he won't ever wake up. I know that, but

I can't think about it. I don't have time to think about anything. They are looking for us. Hunting us. It can't have been for nothing.

"You brought me a car," I say. "You're amazing,"

Savannah smiles at me and I'm hit with this rush of feeling. The end to a longing I didn't even realize the strength of until this moment. Savannah is back. She's on my side. Her eyeliner's smudged a little, and I love that. I missed that. It's only been what, two days since I saw her? And yet I missed her. I didn't even realize exactly how much. I can't help it; I throw my arms out and hug her tight. She hugs me back.

I could cry. I could kiss her.

When we finally let go, I turn back toward the trees. My sister's out of sight. I whistle, whistle again.

Nothing happens.

"What are you doing?" asks Savannah.

"Goddammit, Lee," I say under my breath, ignoring her. "Come on."

I can still remember what it felt like, all those nights when I'd make Savannah wait with me in Grandma Margaret's backyard. That desperation, that yearning. The woods like a magic eye picture—if I only stared long enough maybe the picture would change, reveal the figure of a thin girl in a too-small dress. But it never did.

The next night, when I was alone again, she'd show up and I'd demand to know why she didn't appear. *You know why,* she'd say, or she'd just scowl at me and ignore the question. *Please,* I'd beg her. *Savannah is really cool. You'd like her.* It made no difference.

But everything is different now. She attacked Henry. She broke my window. She fought the pastor. And I know that she was never as reclusive as I had always believed.

"Lee!" I shout, risking it.

"Who is—" Savannah starts, but then something shifts in the distance and suddenly there's a girl standing by the tree, slight as a moth. Savannah sucks in her breath sharply.

"No fucking way," she whispers.

"I told you."

I gesture for Lee to come toward us, but she doesn't move.

"Maybe you should leave," I whisper to Savannah. She doesn't answer and when I glance over at her, she's staring, eyes wide, at the tree line, at my sister.

She lifts a hand, waves.

My sister takes a step forward, out of the trees, and then another, and then she's running, closing the short distance between us.

I shift sideways, blocking Savannah, thinking of the bridge. Henry. Lee stops abruptly a few feet away, whole body tense as a guitar string.

I turn back to Savannah. She looks terrified.

"Savannah," I say, "this is my sister, Lee. Lee, this is Savannah."

It's so strange. This is exactly what I always wanted, all those years ago. It hardly seems real now. It's the sun shining at midnight, all the stars coming out at noon.

"It's okay," I say, to them both. "She won't hurt you."

Lee shuffles closer and grabs my arm with both hands, gripping it tight. She peers over my shoulder at Savannah.

"I can't believe it," whispers Savannah. "She looks like you." She reaches a hand toward my sister, as if she needs to touch her, to prove she's no ghost. Lee hisses in a breath between her teeth, digs her nails into my arm.

I grab Savannah's hand quickly to stop her. Her short nails are painted. The glittery polish sparks in the moonlight.

"Thank you," I say to Savannah. "So much. I owe you forever."

My sister is making a rumbling noise in her throat, nearly a growl. She's holding her muscles so tight they are shaking.

"We've got to go now," I say.

Savannah tears her gaze from my sister, finally. Smiles at me. "Where are we going?" she asks.

"You can't come with us," I say.

"No." She yanks her hand out of my grasp, face falling. "No, fuck you."

Lee tightens her grip on my arm. I think I hear the shouts again, far away.

"We're leaving," I say. "We're not coming back. We're going on the run." Going dark.

"So?" she says, defiant. "I'm coming with you."

"You don't want to come with us," I say. I'm sorry to leave Savannah, but she has no reason to run. They aren't chasing her. And she always fit in better than me, anyway. She belongs in the real world.

"Yes I do," she says.

I shake my head. She must think this is a game. An adventure. "It's not—"

Savannah cuts me off. "No," she says. "Listen. I stole a goddamn car for you, okay? I can't stay here. Even if I don't get arrested somehow, Jack will tell everyone what happened. He'll be mad and he'll tell everyone and they'll all know. They'll know what I did."

She isn't talking about the car anymore, I know. She's talking about the other thing. The thing that even her best friend in the whole world wanted to condemn her for. I know how the girls at our school talk, how everyone in the whole town talks. How they talked about Mama.

"But your family," I say. "Your mom."

"Whatever. You know her. She'll probably be over the moon that there's one less mouth to feed."

I shake my head again.

"You need me," Savannah says. "You don't even know how to drive."

Which is true. I guess I'd assumed that Brandon would—

But he can't.

Savannah pulls something out of her coat pocket, shakes it at me. The keys. She marches over to Jack's car. I twist to look at Lee, who is staring after her.

"You can't hurt her," I whisper. My sister meets my eyes.

She isn't a stranger. Liar or not, I know her. I'm a liar, too. And I can see she's as desperate and scared as I am.

I'm all she has.

Savannah isn't entirely a stranger, either. My sister has been hearing about her for years. She's seen her, too. Only from a distance, of course. From the dark cover of the forest. The other little girl standing next to me in Margaret's backyard. The one she used to be scared of. Too scared to get close.

But she's older now, braver. We all are.

"Okay," I say. "Okay. Let's go."

Savannah clutches the steering wheel so hard her knuckles go white. Her shoulders are hunched forward, rigid. In the backseat, I squeeze my sister's hand.

We reverse out of the driveway, fast, gravel crunching under the tires. Out the back window I can see the lights of the processing plant down the hill. I made Savannah turn the headlights off before we started.

Savannah turns sharply, heads up the narrow ridge road into the forest. Behind and below us, I can see the lights of cars moving on the busier roads through town. I can see all of Lester. So small. And then it's gone, swallowed by the trees.

"Go faster," I say.

"I can't even see the road," Savannah says. Lee is bent over beside me, kneeling on the seat, head pressed into my shoulder, breathing heavily. She smells like forest floor, like wet leaves and spicy bark and like death, like something rotting. That's probably her breath. I'm pretty sure my sister has never brushed her teeth in all her life. She chews on bones, instead. Gnaws them to get at the marrow.

As far as I know, she's never ridden in a car before, either.

It was a struggle getting her inside. I had to tell her that people were going to catch us for sure if she didn't get in. Had to tell her I was sure they were close. Nearly upon us. That wasn't a lie, really. We'd both heard the shouts. When she still resisted, I had to whisper in her ear, *Mama would have wanted you to.* Had to practically shove her in anyway, even after all that.

My stomach jumps as we crest a hill going too fast. My sister gasps. There are headlights coming toward us suddenly, flashing along the trees that line the road.

"Don't stop!" I shout to Savannah in the front seat. "No matter what. Go around if you have to."

The other car lays on the horn. Savannah swerves. The other car swerves. My sister howls and topples off the seat. I hadn't even tried to make her put on a seat belt. The two vehicles zoom past each other so close that our whole car shakes.

I whip around to look out the back window. Before the other car disappears over the crest of the hill I glimpse a hand, sticking out the driver's-side window, giving us the middle finger.

"Shit," says Savannah in a shaky voice.

I drag my sister back onto the seat. She hunches down, arms clamped over her head. She's breathing fast and loud, like she's running or drowning.

"Is she okay?" asks Savannah.

"Yes," I say. No. But there's nothing to do about it.

We come down the other side of the hill, go up another one, down, and then we're out of the trees and into the open and Savannah's merging onto the state highway, turning the headlights back on. I haven't heard sirens yet, haven't seen any cars I recognize following us, but I can't stop looking out the back window.

We are well beyond Lester, beyond Needle, rushing through the tiny towns scattered along the highway.

They whip past us, these little towns, many of them small as Lester. Towns I've never heard of, never thought of. Are they all the same? Full of the same kinds of people? Full of girls like us, straining at the thin bars of their cages, eyeing the plywood walls with hearts full of sky.

"Where to now?" asks Savannah, her tone a forced casual.

I have no idea. I have no plan at all. But I can't tell her that.

"West Virginia," I say. When we left Myron's, Savannah just turned away from Lester and drove. I said we needed to get away fast. But we're headed south, so if we keep going, West Virginia is the first state we'll hit. From what I hear it's mostly mountains, Appalachian foothills covered in trees. Seems as good a place as any to hide.

Savannah snorts. "Lester wasn't hick enough for you? We should go to New York City."

"What the hell would we do in New York City?" I say. I can't see Savannah's expression from the backseat. Is she kidding? Probably not, it's Savannah after all.

"Or at least Cincinnati or something. We can go to my cousin's." She twists around in the seat for a moment. Frowns at my sister.

"Watch the road," I say. "We can't go to a city. We've got to hide."

"So? Can't we hide in a city?"

I try to imagine the three of us descending on some poor unsuspecting city cousin, crowding into her tiny city apartment. My sister can't even handle a town. How in the world would she survive a city? So many people, so many lights. Savannah doesn't understand.

"No," I say firmly, "we're going to hide in the woods,"

"The woods?" asks Savannah.

A semitruck barrels past us with a roar. My sister lifts her head to look and then scrambles into the far corner of the backseat, pressing herself as flat as she can against the door, eyes wide.

"Yes," I say to Savannah. I try to tug my sister back to the middle. She's breathing fast again.

"You were just in the woods," says Savannah.

"Look," I snap, "I told you not to come." I don't even have a plan. They'll catch us. And now we'll all go to jail for being in a stolen car. Maybe we should have stayed in the national forest. Found the most remote cave. Hunkered down. Dug deeper into the earth.

"No," Savannah says. "That's fine. The woods. Sure. Whatever. West Virginia."

"Just keep going south," I say again, rubbing my eyes. I'm so tired.

My sister knocks her head against the car window.

"Be careful," I say, pulling on the sleeve of her dress.

But she does it again. Her skull makes a hollow *thwack* as she headbutts the glass. I pull harder on her sleeve. She bangs her fist against the window.

I undo my seat belt with one hand, the other still holding on to my sister's sleeve. She bangs her fist against the window again, scratches at the glass.

"What's she doing?" asks Savannah. I meet her frightened eyes in the rearview mirror for a moment, but then my sister gets ahold of the door handle, and she yanks it down and pushes the door open a crack. The wind rushes in, the roar of the tires on the asphalt.

"Shit." I lunge sideways, grab Lee by the shoulders, hold her down. "We need to stop."

"Do I just pull over?" Savannah's voice is panicked, rising in pitch. The car door bounces open and shut.

"I don't know." I've got Lee pinned under me, one arm hooked around her chest. With the other arm I grope forward, trying to catch the door handle.

The car swerves suddenly. The door bangs open. I can see the road rushing past beneath us like an angry river.

The car swerves the other way. The door bangs shut. We jerk to a stop and I tumble off the seat. My sister is up and out the door before I can unwedge myself.

"Shit," I say. "Shit, shit, shit."

Savannah appears at the door a moment later and reaches in to help me up.

"Where did she go?" I ask as I stumble out of the car. We're stopped in the parking lot of a bank. It's closed, dark and empty, though there's a glowing row of ATMs holding vigil outside. Savannah gestures vaguely to the far end of the parking lot, to the line of trees.

It's no forest. Just an unshaved strip of wilderness no one cared about enough to remove. I can see through the trees to another parking lot beyond. I run over, shout my sister's name.

"There she is," says Savannah from behind me. I turn and follow the line of her pointing finger.

My sister's already halfway up a tall pine, arms and legs wrapped around the trunk. She's mostly obscured by the needles, but her pale skin gives her away.

"Lee!" I shout. "Come down!"

She shimmies up a few more feet, the branches shaking wildly as she pushes against them.

"What the hell is she doing?" asks Savannah.

"Climbing," I say, though I know that's not what she's really asking.

It's so strange being around Savannah and my sister at the same time. I'm not sure which version of myself to be. The nighttime or the daytime. I feel like I've had to smash together two halves that don't fit, that don't quite add up to a whole.

"What's wrong with her?" Savannah asks as we hurry over to the trees.

"She's not used to cars."

"Is she like mentally challenged or something?"

"No. Jesus." I turn on Savannah, clenching my hands into fists.

She doesn't know my sister. Two days ago she didn't even believe in her.

"Sorry." Savannah shrugs. "I mean, she's not *normal*."

"She's fine," I say, as much to myself as to her. "She just got scared."

It's stupid, because Lee is acting foolish, putting us all at risk, but I feel defensive about her with Savanah. It's like the pastor saying she was too skinny, saying she couldn't survive all alone. He and Savannah don't know her. They have no right to judge her.

I don't like being forced to see Lee through their eyes. I take it for granted sometimes, how wild she is. When it's just me and her alone I get a little wild, too. Piss in the dirt and howl, narrow the gap between us. Maybe I've never eaten an animal raw, but I've touched their dead bodies after my sister kills them. I've touched their still-warm hearts. Used the blood, once or twice when we were children, for finger paintings on the sides of trees.

Savannah and I both crane our necks up at the pine. Lee is so high up I can hardly even see her anymore. The tree sways in the wind. I look back toward the road. Cars zip past in the dark, headlights flashing through the trees. We're in shadow here, but the stolen car parked in the middle of an empty lot is not exactly subtle. We've got to get out of here. We can't get caught now. We just can't.

"Can she talk?" asks Savannah.

"Of course she can talk." I hadn't really noticed until this moment, but it's true Lee hasn't said a word in front of Savannah yet. It's like when she first met me, all those years ago.

"I don't understand," says Savannah. "Where did she come from?"

"The forest." I circle the pine tree, searching for a good foothold. I don't want to explain this all to Savannah right now. I don't think she'd understand.

It could be worse. Henry called *me* weird, so God only knows what he made of Lee. What would Maisie say? Or Nicole? Or Lisa? They'd understand even less. Probably wouldn't even give her a chance.

"So she just lived out there?" Savannah asks.

"Yes."

"All alone?"

I don't want to talk about Mama or Brandon. Not now, not yet. Maybe not ever. I don't even know where I'd start. "Mostly," I say.

"How did she survive?"

"She's smart." Which isn't strictly true, I guess. My sister has a very narrow field of knowledge. "Here," I say, "help me up."

Savannah pushes on my butt as I reach for the lowest branches of the pine tree. She's not very helpful, but I manage to pull myself up anyway. The branches aren't thick enough to hold my weight, so I have to climb the trunk, gripping it with my legs and hauling myself up bit by bit, pushing off the flimsy pine boughs, twisting my shoulders up through them like a maze.

"What should I do?" shouts Savannah.

"Just wait," I call down.

Lee has shimmied even higher up, so high the whole pine sways with her weight. By the time I reach her, my hands are gummy with sap and my thighs burn. I stretch one arm up and grab her ankle, give it a little tug.

"Lee," I say. "Get down. You can't stay here."

"No." Her voice sounds small, far away.

"We're going to a new forest, okay? A better forest. You just need to stick it out a tiny bit longer. Just a little more time in the car and then you can climb all the trees you want. Come down."

She peers down at me.

"We'll have the forest to ourselves," I tell her. I pull on her ankle, harder. I wonder if I could pull hard enough to knock her right out of the tree. She'd probably just take me down with her. "And I'll be there with you all the time. Not just at night. I promise, okay?"

"You and me?" she asks.

"Yes," I say. "Just you and me."

Her gaze shifts beyond me, to the ground.

"And her," she says.

I twist around. Though the needles I can just make out the small figure of Savannah, pacing back and forth at the bottom of the pine.

"Well, yes," I admit, "and her. But she's helping us."

Lee makes a low noise of discontent.

"For fuck's sake," I say. "You can trust her."

The tree sways. I feel queasy. I see Savannah pacing and pacing. So what if she had sex with Jack? People act like that one little thing changes you forever, ruins you, but it's nothing, it's stupid. Savannah stole a whole car for me. That's something.

It's me and her. Like old times. Me and her against everyone.

"She's just like Mama," I say to Lee, and pull on her ankle so hard that she slips and tumbles down far enough to kick me sharply in the side, before she gets her footing again. . . .

When we finally make it down, Savannah is waiting for us, looking absolutely miserable. She's got her arms tucked in tight against her body, and her shoulders are hunched.

I slide to the ground. Lee leaps past me, landing in a crouch.

Savannah jumps back, still terrified. My sister stares. She's study-ing her, I think, this strange monster, with her eyeliner and her push-up bra peeking out under her tank top. I always thought that in the pictures I'd seen Mama looked like a cross between me and Savannah. Maybe even more like Savannah than me. Mama wore makeup. Mama was beautiful.

Did she still wear blue eye shadow when she lived in the woods? I don't know. I'll have to ask Lee, later.

"We better go," Savannah says, backing away.

"Start the car," I say. "I'll be there in a second."

I yank on the lowest branch of the pine tree, brace myself with one foot against the trunk, jerk the branch back and forth. Finally it cracks and tears free in ragged splinters like a broken bone. I carry it back to the car.

"It's a portable forest," I tell my sister, who has trailed along behind me. "Just for you."

Savannah laughs. A nervous laugh, which skitters away into the dark.

I shove Lee and the branch into the backseat and climb in after. I attempt to buckle her seat belt, but after she slaps my hands away enough times I give up. She holds on to the pine branch, rubbing her fingers against the bark, occasionally whacking me in the face with it. By accident, I think. Pine needles shake loose and fall onto the floor of the car, steady as rain.

My sister is silent, but Savannah can't stop talking.

As she pulls out of the parking lot and back onto the highway, she rattles off the plot of every television show or movie she's ever seen that features people on the run. She says maybe we should all three of us dye our hair. Or at least cut it. Or maybe we could all shave our heads and dress in men's clothing. *You could probably get away with that, Jo, she says, since you're so tall and flat-chested. Heck, you even have a boy's name. I guess nobody would believe that I was a boy. Not with these puppies. Anyway, we should get fake IDs. We should fake our own deaths. We should jump a train, ride it to the end of the line.*

"We need gas," Savannah says. She's lit a cigarette, is smoking it fast, ravenous, tapping the ash into the cupholder. My sister's humming to herself, head bent down to her chest, eyes closed.

"We can't stop," I say.

"The little needle says it's low."

"I don't have any money," I say, realizing it for the first time as I say it. I think, with regret, of the fifty dollars socked away beneath my mattress. My sad little life's savings.

This whole thing is impossible. Where are we going to go? What are we going to do? I didn't think this through. I didn't think.

"I do," says Savannah. "I have money."

"You?" I've never known her to save a penny. Every cent she gets she spends on makeup or cigarettes. Something pretty or something deadly.

"I don't think he was actually in love with me," she says. She catches my eye in the rearview mirror. "I mean, he said he was, but then, afterward, I don't know. He acted different."

"You took his money?"

She laughs and I recognize that laugh. That note of hysterical underneath it, that note of terrified. We are totally off script now. No idea what we're supposed to do. Nobody writing this story but us.

"The garage pays him cash under the table," she says. "So he had a lot."

"Well, goddamn," I say. "You're my hero."

If I could, I would throw my arms around her again. I would kiss her for real. I'm so shocked, so delighted. This is the Savannah I used to know. The wild one, who didn't need anybody, who never did what she was told. I am so happy to have her back.

"I really think we're going to run out," Savannah says.

"Okay," I tell her, "we can stop."

I've got to pee, anyway. Should have done it back in the woods. Wasn't thinking.

Savannah jerks us into the turn lane too quickly. Somebody honks. My sister snaps her eyes open, clutches at my sleeve. We swing into the parking lot of a Sunoco.

Light spills into the car. Savannah pulls in behind a pickup truck. It doesn't even look like Grandma Margaret's truck— wrong color, wrong size—but my heart seizes up for a second anyway.

My sister presses her head against my shoulder. She's scared. Her whole body practically quivers with it. It makes me want to forgive her for everything. I can't stay mad at her when she's like this. I want to protect her, instead. She seems so helpless, so harmless, a frightened baby animal. I don't think this is what she wanted, after all. Not exactly.

"Come on," I say. "Just hold on to my hand."

I've followed her through the forest so many times. But now we're in my world. Now she's got to follow me. I coax her out of the car while Savannah pumps the gas. I wouldn't even have known what kind to use.

Lee flares her nostrils at the scent of the gasoline, flinches every time a car whips past on the road behind us. I start to take off the puffy gray coat she gave me, thinking I'll make her put it back on, less for the cold than to cover up the scratches on her arms. But there's blood on my shirt underneath. Dried brown now, the color of earth. I zip the coat back up quick.

I wrap my arms around my sister and hold her while she shivers, trying not to think. Trying not to remember holding Brandon. Trying not to remember whose blood is on my shirt.

When Savannah's done, we head into the store. Lee has a death grip on my hand. I feel sure that when she finally lets go there'll be an imprint of her hand on mine, bruised purple, indelible. She's been in town before, between the houses, been in Brandon's camper as a kid, I guess. But it must have been years since she's walked inside a building. She tries to pull me away several times before we get to the door, but I pull her back, trudge forward.

Coming out of the darkness into the store is like an explosion. My sister's eyes are huge in the bright lights, pupils tiny pinpricks. A bell chimes. The colors shout at us.

Lee freezes as the door swings shut behind us. She is perfectly still except for her eyes, which dart wildly this way and that.

"Come on," I say, trying to pull her toward the bathroom, which Savannah has already disappeared into, but I might as well not be there. She's looking at everything except me.

She reaches out to the nearest shelf, runs a hand across a bag of chips, spicy barbecue, the shiny foil crackling like dead leaves.

Whatever spell she was under breaks, and suddenly she's touching everything. She's picking up a can of Pringles, shaking it, prying off the lid. When I grab the can from her, she just picks up another one.

I have to drag her by the wrist to the bathroom. She's still try-ing to reach for the refrigerator case—all those rainbow bottles sealed behind glass—as the bathroom door bangs shut.

I go to the handicap stall, drag her in with me.

"You're going to get us caught," I say. She blinks rapidly, eyes still wide.

She watches me as I pee. She had better manners back in the woods, when we'd piss on trees. She's seen toilets before, at the junkyard and at the camper, I guess, but I don't know that she's ever used one. I ask her if she has to go, feeling like someone's mom, but she just stares. I shrug and go to wash my hands.

Savannah is standing by the sinks, twisting a paper towel. She side-eyes my sister, who has discovered the automatic dryer.

"What if the cashier is calling the police right now?" Savannah asks.

"They won't have heard about us this far out." I don't know if that's true or not, but I say it like I'm sure of it. Some small part of me has been listening for sirens this whole time.

Lee crouches down and sticks her face under the dryer, lets the hot air blow back the few loose tendrils of dirty hair around her forehead. When the dryer shut offs, she blinks up at it, dis-appointed.

"What if there's like an ABP or something?" asks Savannah.

"ABP?"

"Or whatever it's called."

"Just act normal," I tell her. I comb my hair out a little with my fingers. My sister goes over to the sink, starts playing with the motion sensor, darting her hands in and out of the water. Savan-nah edges away nervously. She's still thinking about Henry, I bet, that night on the bridge. Remembering what this weird dirty girl is capable of.

There's not much I can do about Lee's hair without a pair of scissors. She's got on the brown knit cap, but that doesn't hide much.

I wet the edge of a paper towel and try to scrub some of the dirt off her face. She yelps, flails her arms, manages to whack me in the face twice before I give up. She looks a little better, I guess. It's a relief at least that she's wearing the leaf-print dress instead of her old blue one. With her torn tights and hair that devolves essentially into one giant dreadlock, she could pass, I hope, for some kind of punk rocker. I pick a small leaf from where it's caught behind her ear.

"This is so crazy," whispers Savannah.

My sister looks up, takes a step toward her. Savannah shrinks back against the paper towel dispenser.

"Lee," I say, "what are you doing?"

My sister reaches toward Savannah's face. Savannah squeezes her eyes shut. I move forward. Before I can stop her, Lee swipes a quick finger across Savannah's eyelid. Gently, though. She looks down at the smudge of glittery black eye shadow on her fingertip, draws a line with it on her own arm.

"That was very rude," I say, putting my arm around Savannah's shoulder. "You scared her."

"I wasn't scared," mutters Savannah, under her breath.

Lee appears unrepentant, though she's looking at Savannah differently than she used to. Not with hate or fear. I see something else there. Curiosity, maybe. Admiration.

———

The cashier isn't paying any attention to us when we come out. She's playing a game on her phone, the incessant bleeps and bloops audible even beneath the tinny song on the store speakers.

Savannah walks ahead of us down the aisle, toward the counter, but stops abruptly between the slushie dispenser and the coffee machines.

"I can't do it," she says, turning back to me, wide-eyed, caught between swirling neon and gleaming metal.

"Give me the money," I say. "I'll handle it. Just act normal."

She pulls a scuffed black leather wallet out of her jacket pocket. Her hand is shaking, so I sandwich it between my hands, like the little old ladies at church, and I look her in the eyes, or try to anyway. She keeps darting glances toward the front counter. She's worse than my sister. If the cashier isn't suspicious of us yet, she will be the moment she lays eyes on Savannah.

If I was Jack she'd feel safe. I know she would. If I was any boy. If I had broad shoulders and smelled like cigarettes and motor oil and Axe body spray in Tropical Testosterone or whatever. I know she'd feel safe, then, would trust me to hell and back, at least until I cheated on her.

Boys are strong. Boys are solid. Savannah wants to lean against them, shelter beneath them in a strong wind. I want to judge her for that, but I won't.

Even though it's stupid. How many families do we know in Lester where it's the woman who pays the bills? Who works double shifts at the McDonald's in Needle, or the graveyard at the Walmart three towns over? That's how it works in her own family, for God's sake.

But Savannah still believes it. Like the tooth fairy, or the Easter Bunny. She believes in boys.

I wish I could turn the clock back on her heart, wish I could convince her to see boys the way we both did when we were younger. As nothing special. As not so different from us.

Boys aren't magic. They can't save you. The Cantrells didn't save Mama. The pastor didn't save her. She had to save herself. Even Grandpa Joe, as kind and wonderful as everyone says he was, just went ahead and drank himself to death and left everything behind for Grandma Margaret to deal with.

You can't rely on anyone else. You've only got yourself. I wish Savannah saw it that way, but I know she doesn't.

So I put on my Uncle Myron voice, the one I used to tease her with when we cut class. When we talked and laughed in the Naked Lady Room. A world away now. Back when the two halves of my life still knew their place.

"Cheer up, sweet cheeks," I say. "Give your poor old uncle a smile, put a little sunshine in his life."

It works. Savannah smiles, stifles a laugh.

"Aw, yeah, that's the sugar in my tea," I say, and I lean forward and I kiss her.

She's still laughing as I do it, her smile going wider, and my bottom lip knocks against her teeth, but she kisses me back. Her lips are soft, her whole mouth is soft, and warm, and for a moment that's all there is.

Everything else falls away.

My sister yanks on my hand and I pull back, suddenly embarrassed. Savannah laughs again.

It was just a joke, for her.

At least Lee didn't try to rip her throat out. My self-appointed chaperone. Maybe she really did think Henry was hurting me, back on the bridge. Maybe she didn't quite understand. That was a different kind of kiss. Not as soft. Not nearly so soft.

"I'm getting a coffee," I say, suddenly deciding. It's a grown-up thing to do, buying coffee. I think of Brandon setting two cups on the table back in the camper.

I try not to think about that.

I grab a cup and go straight for the black coffee, dark roast, night sky. Savannah follows my lead, though she goes for mocha vanilla caramel instead. Lee stands at my shoulder, watching the dark liquid piss out of the little machine. She puts out a hand to touch the stream, but I pull my finger off the button.

"It's hot," I say.

She scowls, mad at being treated like a baby, I guess. I grab a handful of little flavored creamers, stuff them in my pocket. My sister catches on quickly, loses no time shoving some into her purse. She takes sugar packets too. Napkins. She grabs a package of tiny chocolate muffins from a rack beside the coffee, but I snatch her wrist before she can put those in her purse as well.

The cashier gives us a tired look when we come to the counter. She's not that much older than us. Dakota's age, maybe. I smile at her and stand in front of Lee, blocking both of them from each other's view as much as I can. Savannah wasn't lying about the cash. When I open the wallet, I see fifties. An actual hundred. I'm thinking maybe Jack was lying about his real source of income, but who knows. I dig out some twenties, pay for the coffees and the package of chocolate muffins and gas on pump four.

Savannah walks too fast to the door, pushes it open, gives me a look like *Hurry the fuck up,* but I take my time. I stride, acting casual, leading my sister by the hand.

Before we even get to the truck, Lee tears the muffin package open with her teeth and pops three of the muffins into her mouth at once. Savannah laughs and then slaps a hand over her mouth.

But my sister doesn't pay any attention. She licks the top of the fourth muffin, nibbles a chocolate chip off, then pauses. Reluctantly, slowly, she holds it out to me, offering to share.

"That's okay," I say, pushing her hand back. She hesitates, considering.

And then my sister, miracle of miracles, extends her arm toward Savannah, shoulders hunched, muffin offered up on an open palm. Savannah gives me a stricken look. I shrug.

"Uh, no thank you," Savannah says, overenunciating the words. It's the first time, I think, Savannah has spoken directly to Lee. It's progress.

My sister relaxes, pops the final muffin in her mouth. Chews with her eyes shut, content.

A few miles on we hit a stretch of road with trees rising up on both sides. We're rushing through the forest, going so much faster than we've ever gone before. Lee squeezes my hand hard again, as if she means to crush all the small bones. I let her, despite the pain. It feels like the least I can do.

We are farther from Lester now than Grandpa Joe ever dared go his entire life. Farther than Aggie has ever gone, farther than Mama.

The picture of Mama is still in my pocket. I can feel it, light as it is, bending slightly against my thigh as I shift in the seat.

Somewhere back there, deep in the woods, Brandon is opening his eyes. He's climbing to his feet. I know he is.

And Mama is standing there. She's holding out her hand. She's forgiving him, maybe, or thanking him, or just offering him a little comfort. Offering to lead him through the forest she knows so well.

I hope he's telling her about me. I hope she's listening, hope she's realizing that she was wrong, all those years ago. I hope that she's sorry. But also, just maybe, a little proud.

I'm hers.

CHAPTER SEVENTEEN

In the dark, in the cold, in the backseat of a stolen car, with the scent of pine and smoke, with the lights of little cities whipping by like islands in an ocean of darkness, with my sister humming something tuneless, more like the drone of an insect than a song, with Savannah stubbing cigarette after cigarette into the cupholder, with whatever little scrap of calm and reason I have left, I do my best to make a plan.

We have two hundred eighty-four dollars and sixty cents. I counted. We have a Tupperware of cigarettes, though that's emptying out quick. We have the clothes we're wearing and this car and whatever is in my sister's little plastic heart purse and that's it.

Which isn't so bad. We have a car. We have two hundred eighty-four dollars and sixty cents. That's more money than I've ever had in my whole life.

We hit the river, which marks the end of Ohio, sooner than I expected. I've only been this far south once in my life, for a track meet in seventh grade. All the towns along the river are broken, split down the middle by the water, with one half in Ohio and the other half in West Virginia.

We pass through the Ohio half of one of these towns, and cross the first bridge we come to. Directly ahead of us, across the river, is a Walmart Supercenter, filling our view like the squat white end of the world.

"Pull in there," I tell Savannah.

In the Walmart parking lot, my sister and Savannah are both nervous wrecks. Lee clings to my sleeve, twisting the rope strap of her plastic heart purse with one hand, shrinking away from the cars. The parking lot is less than a fourth full, but it's so big, an ocean of asphalt, that even this is more cars than I would have hoped. At the gas station, we were the only customers. Savannah pulls the hood of her jacket up, hunches her shoulders, scowls.

"Come on," I tell Savannah as we head toward the store entrance. "This will be fun. A shopping spree. We can pick out new clothes."

"I don't know," says Savannah. She's looking sideways at Lee.

"Just think of it as a weird forest," I tell my sister. An apocalyptic forest, maybe, the trees petrified white, the sun gone cold. She managed better than I could have hoped at the gas station, but this place is at least ten times the size of that. It's one of those enormous Walmarts that has swallowed a grocery store. There will be so many colors and lights and sounds and, worst of all, people. I'm thinking maybe we should just leave her in the car, risky as that feels.

A car door slams several rows over and Lee drops to the ground, nearly dragging me down with her. She's crouched, looking ready to run. There's no way she'll agree to stay in the car. Savannah is burrowed so deep in her hooded jacket I can barely see her face, but the set of her shoulders says enough.

"Okay," I say to Lee, "okay. How about we play a game? Close your eyes. Keep them closed."

I coax her back to her feet and, after some more convincing, get her to close her eyes. I wish I could tie something over them. Maybe give her earplugs, too, but we'll probably look weird enough as it is.

"This seems like a bad idea," says Savannah, and part of me agrees, but I can't let on.

"Nonsense," I say, striding toward the entrance. "This is going to be fine."

My sister startles as the automatic doors whoosh open ahead of us, flickers her eyes open and then shut again, but she's keeping it together. Before we left the car, I allowed her to stuff both her pockets full of pine needles.

Once we're inside, I grab two red baskets, shove one into Savannah's hands.

"Okay," I say, "food first." Lee has opened her eyes. She's staring at the ceiling. There's a small bird up there, perched on one of the metal rafters.

"Close your eyes," I say. She ignores me.

The doors whoosh open again behind us. Lee whips around. An elderly couple is shuffling in. She tries to run. I grip her hand tight with both of mine and drag her away. She reaches for the plastic tubs of candy stacked near the entrance as we pass them, manages to knock one over. Savannah replaces it, casting paranoid glances around as she does. Great. Really keeping a low profile here.

My sister is straining toward the bright mounds of fruit in the produce section, but I want to get farther from the doors and the registers, though it seems like only two are open at this late hour. I pull her by the wrist toward the back of the store. She reaches for every bright new thing she sees, eyes darting rapidly like at the gas station. Savannah shuffles along behind us.

"What should we get?" she asks.

"I don't know. Bread. Peanut butter. Stuff that won't go bad."

With a sudden burst of strength, my sister yanks her wrist out of my grip and darts down the breakfast aisle. She goes not for the cartoon-mascot-adorned cereal boxes, but for one of the big discount bags of knockoff stuff down near the floor. Fruity Gems. Before I can reach her, she's grabbed a bag, ripped it open. In her excitement, she rips too forcefully. Cereal scatters, a rainbow cascade. Lee drops to her knees, scrabbling frantically after the little colored balls, snatching up handfuls, shoving them in her mouth.

Savannah is laughing her head off.

"It's not funny," I say, exasperated.

I crouch and try to brush the cereal back into the torn bag. At least the store is mostly empty this time of night. No one saw, I hope. Lee is chasing a few pieces that rolled down the aisle. Savannah fishes some out from where they went beneath a shelf.

"Hey," she says, "here."

It takes me a second to understand that she's not talking to me. She's talking to my sister.

To my disgust, she holds out the dust-covered pieces to Lee, who, after only a moment's hesitation, takes them and pops them into her mouth. Savannah laughs again.

From somewhere nearby, maybe the next aisle over, comes the high-pitched squeal of a squeaky cart wheel. Lee flinches.

"Stop it," I say. "Both of you. We're going to get kicked out or caught."

"Sorry," says Savannah. She stands, dusts some cereal flakes off her jeans.

My sister is reaching for another bag of cereal. Nutty Chocolate Spheres. I knock her arm away, grab her by both shoulders, shake her.

"You can't touch anything," I tell her, but she won't even look at me. Her eyes are fixed on the shelves behind me, flitting restlessly from item to item.

There's someone else in the aisle, I realize. A man. He's reading the ingredients on a box of instant oats. I hadn't noticed him before. He must have just arrived. I hope he just arrived. Did he see Lee spill the cereal? Did he see her acting crazy?

He isn't looking at us, and I don't want to give him a reason to. He's just some guy, in jeans and a long-sleeved T-shirt, but he makes me uneasy.

"Okay," I say to Savannah, quietly, urgently. "You get the food, I'll get some clothes, and you can meet us in camping stuff."

Savannah looks miserable, but I give her a big confident smile. This is fine, this will be fine. I put my arm around Lee's shoulders and steer her forcefully down the aisle, away from the man, away from the food. We weave through the clothing section. Lee trails her free hand along the racks of shirts, stops short in front of a sweater display.

I grab a purple sweater to appease her, and pull on her hand, but she won't move.

"Come on. What's wrong with you?"

She picks up a sky-blue sweater, rubs the fabric against her cheek, eyes closed again. She's acting too weird. People will notice. I spot another shopper a few racks over. A man. No, *the* man. Same one as before. A coincidence? He's looking at some jeans. My sister hasn't noticed him, I don't think.

I have to imagine this from her perspective. She doesn't understand stores or money. All her life Brandon and I have just given her things. She's spoiled.

But she must be overwhelmed, too. The lights and colors. The noise. An onslaught on all fronts. She should have just listened to me and kept her damn eyes closed.

I drop my voice. "There are hunters in this forest," I say, "so we have to be quick, okay?"

I yank the blue sweater out of her hands and shove it in the basket. Lee drags her feet, but allows me to pull her away, through the workout section and into the little kids' section, her free hand still trailing out, touching everything.

We get about five feet before she jerks away from me and makes straight for a rack of sequined skirts.

"Goddammit." I run after her.

She yanks a skirt off the hanger

"Stop it, Lee. You can't just grab things."

My sister shakes the skirt so it sparkles in the light. I catch movement out of the corner of my eye and turn to see the same man from before. He's a few feet away, sorting through a stack of kitten T-shirts. I almost point him out to her, but stop myself. What if she attacked him? Or even just started running wildly?

"Put it back," I tell my sister. "That won't even keep you warm."

Lee ignores me, pulls the skirt on over her dress, does a little shimmy to make the sequins flash. The man has moved slightly closer to us, is now thumbing through a rack of flouncy dresses. He's a stranger. I've never seen him before in my life, I'm sure of it. And yet there's something about him, maybe just the way he holds himself, that reminds me of the pastor. Does he recognize us? Is he looking for us?

"Listen," I say, desperate. I grab my sister's head, turn it so she won't see the man, so she has no choice but to look me in the eye. "This is an evil forest. Some of this stuff is poison."

She narrows her eyes at me, frowning. She isn't a baby. She isn't dumb. But she *is* different. She thinks differently.

"Some of it is safe, but you can't tell just by looking at it. I've been here before so I can tell, okay? That"—I point at the skirt she's wearing—"is poison."

I make sure to keep my expression dead serious, though I'm already certain this won't work, certain that walking into Walmart was the worst decision I've ever made. Any moment now she's going to freak out, start climbing shelves, throwing things. Store security will be on us in a second.

"Poison?" Lee whispers, eyes still narrowed.

"Yes," I say, thinking fast. I can't lie to my sister, but maybe I can stretch the truth. "They treat some things with dangerous chemicals." That's true, in a way. God knows what they use to manufacture this junk. Lee knows about chemicals, knows not to drink from Monday Creek because of them. "It's so people don't try to steal stuff. If they steal, they die."

And that's true enough. If we stole, security would catch us. If my sister keeps messing with stuff, they will catch us and I will lose her forever.

I'm afraid. Genuinely afraid, and she must be able to feel the truth of that, at least, because she gasps and struggles to pull off the skirt. I help her, replace it on the hanger.

"We'll be okay," I tell her. She's shivering a little. A few stray

pine needles shake loose from her pocket and fall to the floor. "Just don't touch anything else."

My sister nods gravely and lets me lead her away. She keeps her eyes down now. Savannah catches up to us by athletic equipment. Lee seems happy to see her. She doesn't say anything, just shifts a little so she's standing closer to Savannah as we walk.

"Did you have any trouble?" I ask Savannah.

"No," she says, though she sounds as nervous as I feel. "You?"

"Let's just hurry," I say. It takes all my willpower not to run.

My heart is racing by the time we reach the camping aisle. I hand Lee my basket, tell her not to move a muscle, not to touch a thing. Savannah and I scan the tents until we find the cheapest one.

I grab a lantern. A sleeping bag. Savannah gets a frying pan with a folding handle. Both our red plastic baskets are already overflowing. I snag a couple of cheap disposable rain ponchos.

My sister has gone very still. She is staring toward the end of the aisle.

The man is there. The same one as before. Pretending to look at the fishing gear. He glances over at us. I meet his eyes for a moment before he looks away.

Shit. I grab Savannah's arm, whisper into her ear. "Don't look, but there's a guy following us. Store security, I think."

She turns to look. "That guy?"

"Dammit, Savannah, I said don't look." I force myself not to turn around. It's not a coincidence. Four times is way too many. "We've got to go now."

My sister is reaching for a hunting knife in a plastic package, but she stops herself, fingers hovering at the edge of the shelf.

"That's poison," I tell her. She drops her hand, shoulders

sagging. I should have left her in the car. Locked her in. Let her scratch her fingers bloody trying to get out.

"You need to take her outside," I tell Savannah.

Her eyes go wide. "I can't do that."

"You've got to."

"What about you?"

"I'm going to buy this stuff. I'll meet you."

I grab the basket of food from Savannah, grab the basket of camping stuff from my sister.

"Lee," I whisper to her. "Follow Savannah outside. You can trust her, okay? As soon as you're out the doors, run."

I carry the baskets to one of the two open checkouts. It takes all my strength to keep my hands from shaking as I pile the items on the conveyor belt. I smile at the cashier.

"Going camping?" she asks as she scans the tent.

"Ha, yeah," I say. "Astronomy club field trip."

"Oh yeah? You must know all the constellations."

I shrug.

Somebody gets into line behind me and I know who it is. Even before I look, I know, but I look anyway. The man grabs a single pack of sugar-free gum, puts it on the conveyor.

"You here by yourself?" the cashier asks.

"My dad's in the car," I say, loud enough for the man to hear. "He didn't want to come in."

The total comes to just over a hundred dollars. I pay with the hundred and one of the fifties.

The cashier hands me the plastic bags containing my purchases. The tent already came in an oblong canvas bag with a zip-

per and a strap. She asks if I want that in a plastic bag, too, and I shake my head, wishing she'd hurry up. She hands it over, finally, and I sling it over my shoulder.

"Have a nice day," she says. "Hope you see lots of stars," and I can't stop myself. I run, skidding across the shiny linoleum, pumping my legs full-out to the doors.

I whoosh through, burst out into the freedom of the cold night air, and keep running toward the car, bags banging against my legs.

I'm halfway across the parking lot before I realize: the car is gone.

I stop short, scanning desperately. I know exactly where it was parked: third row from the left, two spots down from a cart return. That space is empty. And the cars around it are not Jack's car. An SUV, a pickup, but no beat-up gray Nissan-or-something with a big dent in the hood.

I spot a gray car at the far end of the parking lot. My heart leaps and I run toward it, but I don't get far before I see: there's a bike rack on the back. Jack's car did not have a bike rack.

Jack's car is gone.

It's really and truly gone. I stop again, spinning one way and then the other, panic growing.

I glance back toward the store. The man is standing in front of the automatic doors, watching me. Watching like the pastor used to watch. Like Brandon even, back at the house of birds. The man is suspicious, the man knows I am up to no good. He is talking into a phone. Calling the police. Calling reinforcements. Calling it in.

I can't think. I don't have time to think. I just run.

CHAPTER EIGHTEEN

I huddle with my back to a brick building, breathing hard. It's dark here. I'm shielded from the road by a bank of shrubbery and from the Walmart by the solid hulking mass of the building behind me. An empty parking lot stretches out in front of me. Any second now it will probably fill up with cop cars, lights screaming. It will fill up with searchers, hunters, flashlights, spotlights, guns. Every one of them pointed right at me.

I try to slow my breathing and collect my thoughts. But instead I start crying. I squeeze my eyes shut, rub the heels of my hands against them until I see fireworks, flares in the dark.

I couldn't bear to drop any of the Walmart bags, even though they slowed me down. They're all I have now.

Savannah is gone. The car is gone. My sister is gone.

They just left. They left me behind. I grind my hands harder into my eyes. Did Lee freak out and hurt Savannah? Did Savannah decide to turn us in? Did she just give up and turn back toward home?

Hopefully the man from Walmart didn't know who we were. Hopefully he wasn't on the phone to Lester PD. Hopefully he just thought we were shoplifting. It would make sense. Three teenage girls, alone at this hour. I don't actually know what hour it is, but it must be late. My sister's time.

But even if that man didn't know who we were, even if he wasn't calling it in, they will still be looking for us. They must be alerting every station in the state. They won't stop until they find us. We stole a damn car. You don't just get away with that. We need to run faster. We need to run farther. We need to go somewhere nobody can find us.

Well, no, not we. It's just me now.

There are trees. To my left, across the wide parking lot. If I run I'll be visible from the road. But maybe I could make it to the trees. Maybe the police aren't here yet. Maybe they aren't even coming.

I push myself up into a lunge. Take a few deep breaths. Adjust the Walmart bags and the tent bag.

One two three.

I run. The bags swing wildly, knocking against my legs, slowing me down. Out of the corner of my eye I can see the street, headlights whizzing by. The trees seem so far away. A bag bangs into my knee, and the plastic twists up, tightening around my arm. I stumble. The tent bag whacks me in the back.

My leg starts buzzing and I cry out and tumble forward. I drop some of the bags, bang my knee on a cement parking curb. The buzzing feeling continues. A pinched nerve? Some kind of stroke? What the fuck?

I writhe on the ground for a moment before I realize.

Savannah's phone.

I push myself up, feeling like an absolute idiot, and pull the phone from my pocket. The caller ID says Dakota.

"Savannah?" I whisper into the phone.

"Where did you go?" her voice crackles back.

"Where did *you* go?"

"We're in the car. Are you still at the Walmart? I circled back, but I didn't see you."

"I had to run. I'm by some building." I scan the parking lot, feeling exposed. There's a sign at the far end, by the road. I squint, make out the words *Wahama Senior High*. That's some irony, all right. I ran away and ended up at a high school. I tell Savannah to come and get me. I gather up the bags as best I can, ashamed of my panic, but angry, too.

Moments later, headlights swing into the parking lot. I run to meet the car. Savannah brakes hard when she sees me.

I open the door. My sister's sitting rather primly in the middle of the backseat, holding the pine branch against one shoulder like an ersatz seat belt. She doesn't appear to be hysterical, or even particularly upset, which I don't understand. Less than an hour ago she was beating her head against the window.

"What the hell were you thinking?" I say to Savannah. I slide in beside Lee, dump my bags on the floor.

"You said a guy was following us."

"So? You should have waited for me."

"Sorry," says Savannah, though she doesn't sound like she means it. She circles around the school parking lot and merges onto the main road. "Anyway, she was really freaked out. She kept repeating *run* over and over again and wouldn't calm down until I said we could drive away and then come back for you."

"Jesus," I say, surprised that my sister spoke to Savannah at all. "What if she'd jumped out of the car and run into traffic or something? Did you even think of that?"

What if she'd attacked you? Tried to tear out your throat like she did with Henry?

"Well, she didn't. She's fine." Savannah turns around for a moment and smiles at my sister. "You're doing fine back there," she says, "right?" and her voice changes as she says it, becomes the kind of voice people use to talk to little children.

I clench my fists, glance at my sister. I'm mortified on her behalf. Savannah shouldn't talk to her like that, like she's an idiot or an infant, but Lee doesn't even seem to care. She's looking at the back of Savannah's head with the sort of warmth she usually reserves for candy bars.

"Should I keep going south?" Savannah asks.

Maybe Savannah really does remind my sister of someone else. Someone with black eyeliner, a small nose. Someone she knew a long time ago.

It isn't fair. I wanted them to get along. I wanted Lee to like Savannah. I always told her she would. But I didn't want her to like Savannah *better*.

"You abandoned me," I say. Now I'm the one who sounds like a baby. I know I do. Savannah has no idea, though, how it felt back there, alone in that parking lot.

"We didn't," says Savannah. She sounds annoyed now, too. "We came back for you."

"Yeah, well. You should have waited."

Savannah scowls at me in the rearview. I look away.

"Let's just get away from the river," I say.

Savannah pulls into the turn lane, makes a left down a side street.

My sister drops the pine branch to rustle through the plastic Walmart bags. She digs around in one, comes up with the box of

Pop-Tarts. I try half-heartedly to take it from her, but she jerks away from me, hugging the box close to her chest.

"I still can't believe you stole a car," I say to Savannah. I mean it as a peace offering. I shouldn't be mad at her. She was only trying to help.

"Me neither," she says with a small laugh.

"Did you steal Dakota's phone, too?"

"Nah, she gave it to me. She wanted a new one."

My sister sniffs the Pop-Tart box, scratches at the picture on the front with her fingernails.

"We should get rid of the phones," I say.

"What? Why?" Savannah sounds horrified.

"They can probably track us." It's what Brandon said, back at the camper. I thought it was stupid at the time, but who knows. Maybe they can. Phones have GPS. They've got all kinds of things. People say Facebook listens to your calls so they know what ads to show you.

"I'll just turn it off," says Savannah.

My sister gnaws on the corner of the Pop-Tart box, spits out a wad of damp cardboard.

"No," I say, and I'm not thinking of GPS, not really. I'm thinking of Aggie. That other world. How easy it would be to pick up the phone, to say, *No, I've changed my mind, I want to come home.* "We need to get rid of them."

I pull Savannah's old phone from my pocket, roll down the window, and throw it out into the dark.

"What the fuck?" shouts Savannah, hitting the brakes, twisting in her seat to glare at me.

"Keep going," I say calmly. I'll get rid of Dakota's phone, too, when I get a chance. Savannah's even more likely than me to have a moment of weakness. "We can't stop."

"You're as crazy as she is," says Savannah, but she presses on the gas.

"She isn't crazy." I glance at my sister. She's still gnawing on the box, tearing up the cardboard with her teeth. Well, whatever. She isn't crazy. She's just who she is.

I twist around and look through the back window. This road is dark. No streetlights. Just the occasional house or building whipping past between long stretches of trees. There are no police cars racing after us. No cars at all in fact. Not yet.

"We need to get rid of the car, too," I say.

"That's stupid," says Savannah. "We can't get rid of the car."

"Jack will probably report it as stolen, right? They'll know to look for it."

"So? We need it."

She still doesn't get it. I'm only just getting it myself, really getting it. We've got to be like Mama. Leave society behind for good. There's no place for us there. I put a hand over her picture in my pocket.

I can't do this halfway. I've got to prove she was wrong about me.

"We don't need a car in the forest," I say.

"We'll still need it to go places, though, won't we? Like the store and stuff?"

"We aren't going to go places."

"What about for food?"

My sister has successfully bitten through the Pop-Tart box, but she's having trouble with the foil envelopes inside. She twists one, tries to tear it with her teeth.

"You don't understand," I say. "You haven't understood from the beginning."

"Well, you didn't tell me anything." Her voice rises to a whine. "How am I supposed to understand? Jesus, Jo."

"I told you not to come."

"Oh, don't even start with that. I'm here, okay?"

"This is for real, Savannah."

"I know."

I grab the foil package from my sister. She yelps. I rip the package open. The Pop-Tarts inside are broken and crumbly. I pull out a large sticky piece and hand it over.

"This isn't just some fun little getaway," I say. "This isn't a vacation."

Savannah whips around in her seat to look at me. "You don't trust me at all, do you?"

"Watch the road!"

Savannah huffs, but she turns around.

My sister tries to snatch the Pop-Tart box from me. I shove it back into one of the plastic bags, guard it with my feet. Savannah messes with the radio, switching from static to static to slightly different static.

My sister returns to her pine branch, amuses herself by plucking off the needles one by one and throwing them at me.

I stare out the window, into the dark.

I don't know what I'm looking for until I see it. And even then we're about five minutes down the road before it really hits me.

"Turn around," I say.

"What?"

"Turn around. Just do a U-turn. The road is clear."

Savannah keeps driving straight ahead. She gives no indication that she even heard me.

"I'm sorry I yelled at you," I say. "I'm just stressed out, okay?"

No reply.

"I really am sorry," I say. "And I shouldn't have told you not to come." That's a lie. "I'm glad you came. I don't know what I'd do without you." That's not.

Savannah still doesn't say anything, but a moment later she makes a right turn onto a tiny side road. She stops, backs out, returns the way we came.

"There," I say, pointing, "turn there."

We pull into a small junkyard. Or at least I think it's a junkyard. Maybe it's just where rusty old cars instinctively go to die. Whatever the case is, there's a lot of them, pointing this way and that, weeds growing up around them. Weeds growing through them in some places, branches poking out through broken windshields. Piles of twisted scrap metal here and there between the cars.

There's a small wooden structure at the far end with a light above the door. But there's no light coming from inside the building. The junkyard itself doesn't look nearly cared-for enough to warrant an overnight security guard. There's not even a fence.

I direct Savannah through the maze of vehicles, as far from the road as we can get. She pulls in between an ancient-looking pickup and an upside-down tractor, bumping over stones and branches. I dig around in the plastic bags at my feet until I find the lantern.

Savannah puts on the parking brake, kills the engine. We all tumble out of the car and I divvy up the bags.

I switch on the lantern and start off toward the trees.

"Where are we going?" asks Savannah from behind me.

"Somewhere nobody can find us."

The lantern casts a weak light. It's solar powered and I guess sitting in the harsh artificial light of the store was only enough to charge it a little. Still, I'm thankful that I thought to grab one at all. My sister and I are used to walking through the woods in the dark, but Savannah would probably be hopeless without the light. Even with it, she walks much slower than I do. And she makes an ungodly racket, shuffling through the leaves, her feet apparently intent on finding and snapping every dry twig and stick.

Lee darts ahead of us and then doubles back. She runs in a circle around me and Savannah. She's happy, back in her element, her steps bouncing. She waves the pine branch like a flag.

"It's cold," says Savannah beside me. I think it must be well past midnight now, the deepest part of the night. The temperature has dipped, though it's still only October. If we're going to live out here, we'll need to make provisions for the true cold. For winter.

My sister runs up to us. She tries to start a game of tag, tapping each of us on the arm and darting away, but we ignore her. She tries to hand me the pine branch. I bat it away, too exhausted for games. Lee shoves it at me, yanks the lantern out of my hands, and runs off.

"What the fuck?" says Savannah, stopping short.

"She's just playing," I say. "She'll bring it back."

The light of the lantern goes bobbing away through the trees.

"Rude," says Savannah.

I laugh. I really do feel bad for yelling at Savannah in the car. She didn't ask for this. She wouldn't even be here if I hadn't asked her for the impossible. We'd be lost if she hadn't brought us a car. She saved us.

"Come on," I say. I reach out for her hand. She takes it and I pull her gently forward. She stumbles a little, but follows.

After a minute or two, we see the lantern light bobbing back toward us, and then my sister bursts through the trees at a run, face shining.

Savannah jumps back, startled. One of the bags she's carrying catches on a branch and rips. The contents scatter.

Savannah drops to her knees, frantically trying to gather up all the spilled items. My sister, chastened, sets the lantern on the ground. Savannah is swearing. But I feel calm for the first time in hours. We made it. We're alone out here, far from Lester, from Ohio, from Walmart. Far from everything. We're safe.

"I'm tired," says Savannah, for what seems like the fiftieth time. "My feet hurt."

"I just want to get a little farther from the road," I say.

"We must be miles away already. We've been walking for hours."

"Come on, there's no way it's been longer than twenty minutes."

"Let's just stop for now," says Savannah. She drops the bags she's been carrying and sits right down on the ground. "We can go farther tomorrow."

"Okay, fine." We've been going uphill for a while, and I have to admit my legs are getting tired too. "But not here."

I turn to Lee. After her initial burst of enthusiasm about being back in the woods, she settled down and has mostly been walking alongside us. "We need to find a place that's flat," I tell her. "For the tent."

I'm not entirely sure if my sister knows what a tent is. I can't remember ever seeing one when I was with her, but maybe she's spotted one from afar. Or maybe she and Mama had a tent. I don't know. I should have asked Brandon. There's so much I should have asked him. I thought there'd be time. I thought—

I didn't think.

In any case, Lee seems to understand her mission. She runs ahead of us. Savannah begrudgingly gets back up and we do our best to follow my sister, though the path she takes is erratic. She'll run for a few feet, stop, inspect her surroundings, then shoot off in a different direction.

"She is crazy, though," says Savannah, so quiet I almost don't hear.

"What?" I ask.

"Never mind," she says. "My feet hurt."

I decide to let it go.

Maybe she's right, anyway. I don't know. Maybe I'm crazy, too. The ground, to my relief, starts to level off and I think we've reached the crest of this particular ridge. Ahead, Lee stops again. She's staring up at a tree.

Trees in the deep forest tend to be packed together so tightly that they're forced to grow straight up for fifty feet or more before they have room to branch out. This tree, though, like the one with the deer platform, is set apart from the trees around it. It had plenty of space to stretch its limbs, to reap the rewards of being alone.

By the time we reach my sister, she's already kicked off her shoes, dropped her plastic bags at the base of the tree, and heaved herself up into it, swinging onto the lowest branch and up to where the trunk splits in several directions.

"There she goes again," says Savannah.

"This is a good spot, though," I say. There's a wide swath of ground around the tree that is relatively flat. I hang the lantern on a nearby thornbush and start uprooting everything I can.

Within minutes my hands are cold and scratched and my left wrist is sore, but the effort of clearing the ground warms the rest of me more than walking did. I'm even sweating slightly by the time we're done.

With Savannah's help, I stretch the limp body of the tent out on the ground. It is half surrender-flag white and half sunset orange, terrible for camouflage. The bag it came in was deep green, which seems misleading. I wish I could go back, spend more time in that Walmart aisle, pick more carefully.

The ground here is hard, so we have to stomp on the stakes to get them into the dirt. Lee watches from her tree as we snap together the telescoping tent poles and poke them through some tabs. When we bend them, the tent springs to life, jumping up like a startled creature.

The rain fly keeps flapping away in the wind, and when I finally get it staked and tied, it's lopsided, covering more of one side of the tent than the other, but I'm too tired to fix it.

The tent has two big mesh panels on either side, with no way to seal them. A summer tent, I guess, though it said no such thing on the package. I hope the rain fly will do something to keep the chilly wind out as well.

Savannah is already crawling into the tent.

"Take your shoes off!" I shout at her. "Put them in a corner or something."

"Fine, Mom!" she shouts back.

I feel unreasonably proud of this dumb, lumpy-looking tent. A home I built myself. I remember the camper with its plywood bedroom. I try to image Brandon building it, all those years ago. I hope the searchers in the forest find it. I hope they feed the fish.

I will build a home out here in the forest, too. Like I planned to do when I was older. The timeline has shifted, that's all. I can do this. I can be strong.

Savannah pokes her head out of the tent.

"We should probably bring all those bags in here," she says.

"You're not supposed to keep food in a tent," I say. "Or else bears and raccoons and stuff will try to come in."

"Shit, are there bears here?"

"I don't know. Probably raccoons, though."

"If we leave the food outside, then raccoons will definitely get it."

"Yeah, I guess." I gather the bags, hand them to Savannah.

"Is she coming in?" Savannah asks. My sister is still sitting in the tree.

I shrug. "Are you coming in?" Savannah shouts up at her. "It's nicer in here."

In reply, Lee unzips her plastic heart purse and pulls out a big loop of dirty nylon rope. She ties one end of the rope around a branch. My sister has always been good at knots. I used to wonder where she learned that, because it certainly wasn't from me. I tried to bring her a book on wilderness survival once when we were nine, but she had zero interest. I ended up reading it myself, dreaming of the day I could leave school behind and live in the woods full time like her. Well, here I am.

I guess I know now where Lee learned all her skills. Mama or Brandon. Mother or father. Not our real father, of course. But he was there for her. Not Logan. Not the pastor. Our half-hearted, fair-weather fathers. They didn't even know about her. Brandon was the only one.

"Is she going to sleep up there?" Savannah asks. She's kneeling at the entrance of the tent, watching my sister work.

"She is." She always has. *Isn't it wonderful?* I almost say.

My sister loops the rope around another branch and then around one of the trunks, weaving a funny little hammock like the one back at the Queen of Heaven sycamore.

I fetch the lantern from the bush and climb into the tent. I pull off my shoes, set them beside Savannah's.

"She can't just sleep in a tree," Savannah says, frowning. "Is that even safe?"

"Sure." I'm unreasonably pleased to be back to the normal state of things. Savannah baffled by my sister. Me unruffled. "Zip that up, it's cold."

Savannah reluctantly zips the tent shut, watching my sister until the last possible moment.

"I still don't get it," she says, turning back around, settling cross-legged on the floor of the tent.

"Get what?" I line the Walmart bags up against the far wall of the tent. The lantern is getting noticeably dimmer, barely brighter than a firefly. I think it'll go out soon.

"I don't know. Everything. How did nobody know about her?"

"Your family has secrets, too." Myron's dealing was a secret before he got caught. Another of Savannah's uncles is raising a kid who everyone but him knows isn't really his.

"Not like this," says Savannah.

She's right. Not like this. Nobody has a secret like this.

It's not even a secret, not anymore. Everyone must know, back in Lester. Everyone's probably talking about me, about us. Maybe I've got my picture in the paper, as famous as Mama.

I wonder if they've found Brandon yet.

"I'm beat," I say, avoiding her eyes, pulling out the sleeping bag.

Savannah nods. "Me too. Are you sure she's okay out there by herself?"

"She's fine." More comfortable than us, probably.

Savannah unzips the tent partway, sticks her head out. "Good night," she calls up to Lee.

I unroll the sleeping bag. It's blue on the outside, gray inside. Has a faint chemical smell.

"You only grabbed one?" Savannah asks.

I shrug and pull the two sweaters out to use as pillows.

We try unzipping the sleeping bag and draping it across the two of us like a blanket, but even through the tarp floor of the tent, through my jeans, through the puffy coat, the bitter cold of the ground seeps into my skin. I feel as cold as a corpse on a metal table.

"Cold as a witch's tit," Savannah says, and I laugh at her because that's the kind of thing I would expect to hear from the old drunks at Joe's Bar.

We flip the sleeping bag around and lie on top of it, which is better, but still cold. The wind whooshes right in the mesh on one side of the tent and out the other, the rain fly doing nothing to stop it.

So we zip the sleeping bag back up and squeeze in together, sardined.

Savannah shivers against me.

"I'm cold," she says.

"Are you a witch?" I ask.

"What?"

"Are your tits cold?"

Savannah laughs.

I put on my Uncle Myron voice. "Come 'ere, my little glass of sweet tea, let me warm those up for you."

I maneuver one hand up between us and onto her breast, which is, in fact, very warm.

"Quit it," she says, batting my hand away, but laughing.

I used to imagine it, in history class. Running away, living in the woods. My daydreams came true, but different. Not Henry. Not even Brandon.

Savannah.

I reach out, switch off the lantern. The tent goes dark. So dark I can't see my hand, can't see the walls of the tent, can't see Savannah. So dark it's like we were suddenly erased from the world. I try to express this thought to Savannah.

"You're weird," she says.

The wind shakes the tent. I can't see it, but I can hear the fabric rippling above us.

"This is kind of scary," whispers Savannah. Her mouth is inches from my ear, her voice so close it could almost be inside my own skull.

"Don't you worry your pretty little head," I say, in my Myron voice again. "I won't let nobody, not even a bear, get their paws on you."

The truth is I'm scared too, but not for the same reasons as her. I don't mind the night, the sounds of the forest, distant hooting and scrabbling, the orchestrations of insects.

I'm scared because we did it. We got away. We're absolutely free.

Now what?

CHAPTER NINETEEN

I wake before the break of dawn, open my eyes to a darkness barely distinguishable from the inside of my eyelids. My throat feels raw from the cold air. My nose is stuffed up. My neck is cricked. Savannah is warm beside me, though her elbow is sticking into my side

As I lie there, the tent begins, slowly, to glow. It's a weak glow at first, just enough to give shape to the darkness. I shift cautiously, trying not to wake Savannah, and stare up at the cathedral arch of the tent. I watch insects climbing on the underside of the rain fly, watch some kind of moth flutter against the mesh, trying to get in.

Beyond the glowing skin of the tent, birds shout at each other in the treetops. They caw and hoot and trill and one makes a sound like an old smoker coughing. The glow of the tent grows brighter. I don't think the air is getting any warmer, not yet, but the sunlight through the nylon takes away the sting, turns the air crisp and light as the inside of an apple.

Slowly and with much wriggling, I extract myself from the sleeping bag and crawl over to the door. I unzip it cautiously.

"Where are you going?"

I turn. Savannah has pushed herself up onto one elbow. She blinks at me groggily.

"Time to get up for school," I say, grinning. Savannah snorts. I feel oddly ecstatic. Here we are, in another world. "Nah, I just have to pee, I'll be right back."

I step out, rezip the tent, and approach the tree my sister made her nest in. The loops of rope are still there, but she's gone.

"Lee?" I call, but only the birds answer.

I wander a little way from the campsite, relieve myself behind a tree.

I seem to have sweated profusely in the night, despite the cold. My shirt feels clammy against my skin. I take off the puffy coat, drape it across a bush. Looking down at my shirt, I'm hit hard with a memory of last night. Of the wet darkness, spreading. Brandon's body gone heavy. I pull my shirt off, feeling sick.

The dried blood covering the front could just be dirt, just be rust.

With my top half bare apart from a sports bra, chill morning air prickling my skin, I dig into the hard ground with a stick, heaving up clods of earth. I only manage a shallow hole, but I fold the shirt carefully and place it in the center, then shove the displaced dirt back. I drag a heavy rock over and lower it gently onto the turned earth.

"I'm sorry," I whisper, though I know he can't hear it. "It won't have been for nothing. I promise."

When I return to the tent, puffy coat clutched at my side, Savannah is still snugged into the sleeping bag. She frowns up at me. I pull on the purple sweater I'd been using as a pillow all night.

"This is awful," says Savannah. "I'm hungry and my back hurts."

"I'm starving," I say, trying to sound cheerful. "Let's see what's on the menu this fine morning."

I scoot over to the pile of plastic bags in the corner, which survived the night unmolested by either bears or raccoons. I dump them out, sort the contents into separate piles of food and supplies. Savannah gets up and crawls over to help.

"What the hell happened to the Pop-Tarts?" she asks, holding up the half-gnawed box. "Did an animal get in here?"

"That was my sister," I say.

"Oh." She looks horrified for a moment, and then laughs. "I guess that's better."

Savannah unwraps a Pop-Tart for herself, offers one to me, which I gladly take.

The piles, when I am finished sorting, are disappointing. Savannah got a loaf of bread and a jar of peanut butter like I said to. She also got one bunch of bananas, a jar of strawberry jelly, the aforementioned box of chocolate Pop-Tarts, one tube of Flaky Layers Butter Tastin' Biscuits, and a jug of orange juice.

It's not a great selection, but in fairness I didn't do much better. And I am infinitely thankful that she thought of the orange juice. I twist the cap off and take a glug. Savannah wrinkles her nose at me.

"What?" I say. "We don't have any cups."

We'll need water. That is highest priority. When this jug is empty we can use it to collect rainwater, though a bucket would have been better. A purifier.

I should have made a list before we went into the Walmart. Warm clothes. Better food. The rain ponchos I grabbed are probably of limited use. They were one dollar each and are made of thin see-through plastic. Maybe they can be repurposed for water collection. The frying pan was a good choice, seeing as our food supply is so woeful. We'll need to supplement our diet with things we can scavenge. Things my sister can catch.

"Shit," says Savannah. "I left my cigarettes in the car."

"I thought you smoked them all." She was going like a chimney practically the whole way here. Anyway, it doesn't matter now.

"No, there were some left."

"What about your lighter?"

Savannah digs in her pocket, retrieves a little orange Zippo.

"Well, thank God for that," I say.

"What's the point of a lighter without cigarettes?"

"For a campfire, dummy."

Something scratches at the side of the tent. Savannah screams.

I laugh and unzip the door. My sister is squatting right outside, holding the limp body of a gray squirrel in one hand.

"Good morning," I say.

Lee holds the squirrel out, tentative, offering. It flops across her hands, belly up. Tiny eyelids shut. There's no blood, so she must have broken its neck.

"Oh God," says Savannah, "don't let her bring that inside."

"Thanks, Lee," I say, ignoring Savannah. She'll have to get over her squeamishness sooner or later. I think she's exaggerating out of habit. Still playing to the imaginary crowd. "This looks delicious."

I take the body of the squirrel. It's still warm. I stroke the soft fur for a moment, pushing away memories of last night, of that other forest, that other world. Then I hold the body upright so that its little legs dangle in the air. I swoop it toward Savannah.

"Dead squirrel loves you," I shout over her furious shrieks. "Dead squirrel wants to spoon."

She scrambles out of the tent. I chase her. My sister joins in, trying to get the squirrel back from me. I tuck it under my arm like a football, dodge and weave.

"Go long!" I shout to Savannah, and hurl the squirrel at her. It flops to the ground, barely a few feet from me. Savannah laughs then, disgust momentarily forgotten.

We abandon the squirrel and just chase each other, playing tag like Lee wanted to last night. Savannah was a sprinter back when we did middle school track together, but she's out of practice and slowed down considerably by the need to hold one arm across her chest to keep her breasts from bouncing. Still, Lee lets herself be caught more than once. I do too, for that matter.

I'm blissfully happy. It's like old days. Like when we were kids. No burdens, no rules. We can just be.

The sun is up all the way now, streaming down into our little clearing. We all three run in circles until we're worn out and we flop to the ground like dead girls, limbs flung out, heads lolling. We catch our breath, stare up at the sky, the little veins of blue running through the skin of green above us.

Savannah goes off to find rocks, while my sister skins the squirrel with the folding knife from her purse. I gather sticks, arrange them in a tepee shape, feeling capable and resourceful. I'm an adventurer, an explorer. We are pioneers of old. A history class daydream come true.

Lee cuts a slit at the base of the squirrel's tail and then, holding the tail down with her foot, yanks on the squirrel's legs. The skin peels away easy as pulling off a sweater.

"Where did you learn to do that?" I ask her, impressed. I've never seen her do this in the daylight before.

She doesn't answer, absorbed in her task. She saws off the head, the feet. The squirrel's naked body is pastel pink. It looks like a very skinny chicken.

"Did Brandon teach you?' I ask. "Or Mama?"

Lee flinches at the last word. I've talked to her about Mama before, mused about what she was like, about how much I wished she were still around, but it's different now. The secret is out. My sister knew her.

"Did Mama teach you how to hunt?" I ask. I can see that it's upsetting her, but she can't keep it all to herself. She's been selfish far too long. She's got to share.

Lee makes a small noise, which could mean yes or could mean no. I can't tell. She slits the belly open gently. The smell hits me and I have to turn away for a moment. Even at night, Lee usually did this sort of thing out of sight for my sake. But I want to see. I need to know all her secrets now. I need to be like her.

When I turn back, she's pulling out the glistening, jewel-colored organs and piling them in a small mound of pink and blue and purple and red. She pops a tiny maroon blob into her mouth and chews. Heart? Liver? I don't know, but I want to. Next time, maybe, I will make her share that part with me. I can almost imagine it, my teeth piercing the raw flesh. Lee's hands are lightly stained, as if she's been crushing berries.

"Do you remember Mama at all?" I ask. "Do you remember what she was like?"

My sister shoots me a look so sad that I nearly stop. Her face is twisted as if in pain. But I need to know.

"Please, Lee," I say, softly. "She was my mama too. I never got to know her. What was she like?"

"Pretty," she says, very quietly. She lifts one hand to her face, traces a finger along her eyelid, leaving a faint trace of red. Eye shadow. "Like her."

"Oh my God, that is fucking disgusting." Savannah appears

beside us, drops an armful of rocks onto the ground. "There is no way I'm eating that."

"We're going to cook it," I say. My sister would happily eat the whole thing raw, I'm sure, but there's no need for Savannah and me to go that far. Lee's built up some kind of tolerance, I suppose, over the years. I think of what the pastor said, about my sister getting enough to eat, think of all the food I used to bring her. Candy bars and sugar packets. Little tubs of jam stolen from Minnie's restaurant. A jar of cherries from the bar. Not the most nutritious, I guess. I was just a kid. I'm sure the food she got from Brandon was better.

"It's still disgusting," says Savannah.

"Suit yourself. More for us."

My sister licks her hands clean. I pile the rocks around the tepee, stuff some dry leaves into the cracks, set the whole thing ablaze with Savannah's lighter.

We roast the squirrel in the frying pan. Savannah retreats to the tent in dismay, occasionally poking her head out to scowl and tell us how gross we are. It smells good as it cooks, and I'm plenty hungry. I've eaten squirrel before, though not like this. Margaret used to make stew out of them sometimes, well simmered and seasoned.

Lee and I share the meat. It's a little overdone, maybe, since I erred on the side of caution, and a bit tough, but it's hot and the taste is light, almost sweet. I can honestly kind of see why my sister likes them so much. Savannah makes herself a sandwich, using her fingers to scoop the peanut butter and jelly from their jars, spread them on the bread.

My list of things I wish I'd bought at Walmart grows longer by the hour: knives, forks, plates, cups, bottled water, pillows, a second sleeping bag. The label on the tent bag claims that the tent fits one queen-sized air mattress and I can't say I'd be opposed to one of those, either. My back and neck are stiff from just one night of sleeping on the ground.

My sister, of course, misses none of these things. When we finish our meal, she drinks one of the flavored creamers she took from the gas station, and then she takes my hand and shows me the traps she's rigged up near our campsite. Each one is basically just a branch leaning against a tree, with small loops of wire set up down its length. If a squirrel runs down the branch and through one of the loops, the wire will pull shut like a noose.

My sister's little plastic purse, it turns out, is stuffed to the gills with rope and wire. Still, I add that to my wish list: more rope, more wire. I didn't even think to ask my sister, back at the Walmart, what sort of things she might need.

So we got off to a bad start, yes, but the traps make me feel good about our prospects. Last night I had planned to go deeper into the woods, but today I think that can wait. It seems a shame to uproot our campsite now, given the work we've put into it.

Eventually, I think, we can make a more permanent shelter. Maybe we'll be able to find a cave like my sister had back in the old woods. Maybe we'll build something, like Brandon did. We could make night runs to the junkyard where we left the car, scavenge scrap metal.

We will have to scout the woods nearby to find a suitable spot. Maybe somewhere near running water.

"Hey," I say to Lee, "you know how to find clean water, right?"

She glances up from the trap she's adjusting, gives a curt nod. The next moment, she is up and running through the trees, kicking up leaves, gathering speed.

"Hey!" I shout, but she's out of sight already, over the crest of a ridge. I could try to chase her, but I'd never catch up. Well, fine. If she finds a good spot, I can make her show me later.

For now, though, we should secure this site. Maybe build up a little fence perimeter. I check the tent stakes, make an attempt at fixing the crooked rain fly.

I'm thirsty, and tired already, though it's barely past noon, judging roughly from the position of the sun.

Inside the tent, Savannah's on her phone.

"What the hell are you doing?" I ask.

"Chill out," she says. "There's not even a signal. I'm playing a game. See."

She turns the screen in my direction to show a grid of candy-colored gems. I think of pointing out to her that there's no way to charge the battery out here, but she's probably figured that out already. I'll wait until it dies, I think, to get rid of the phone. Maybe I'll lie and say Lee stole it. I don't want Savannah to be mad at me. Without her, we never would have made it this far, but she's also the least suited to this new life. I'll need to ease her into it.

"Squirrel's not so bad," I tell her. "Honest."

She sticks out her tongue.

"You've never had any? Some of your uncles hunt."

She shrugs. "I've had venison."

I don't think that Lee could take down a deer. Although now that there are three of us, who knows.

"Well," I say, locating the orange juice jug, taking a swig. "You'll get used to it."

"We forgot to buy toilet paper."

"Toilet paper?"

Savannah looks at me like I'm an idiot. "Yes."

"Oh," I say. "Right. Well, there are these things called leaves."

Her expression changes to one of such abject horror that I can't help myself. I crack up laughing.

"You'll get used to that too," I say.

Savannah shakes her head, returns glumly to her game.

Maybe in a week or two, we can risk another trip to a store. It would have to be a different one. Maybe there's an all-night gas station near the border of the forest somewhere. I could go alone, on foot, use the last of the cash on supplies. It would be risky, but I can compromise a little, for Savannah.

I want to tell her about my plans, maybe make plans together. I know she's always dreamed about having a house of her own. And sure, maybe a rustic deep-woods cabin made out of scrap metal isn't exactly her dream, but still. We can make it nice. Line it with moss and wildflowers.

She'll stay, right?

She said she wanted to come. She didn't have to. But she wanted to get away. Wanted to be with her best friend. With me.

"I'm glad you're here," I say.

She smiles at me before returning to her game and I feel warm and calm and like everything is going to work out fine.

I should probably be doing something useful right now, camouflaging the tent with leaves, collecting more firewood, but I slept terribly and I feel every bit as tired as I would on a normal Tuesday, nodding off in math class.

Well, I'm free now, aren't I? I can sleep whenever I want.

I unroll the sleeping bag again, crawl in. It's much roomier with just me in it and I relax, let my eyelids go heavy. The walls are closer and brighter and they have no pictures, but if I ignore that, we might just as well be back in Myron's bedroom. We might be the way we always were.

The tent is warm when I wake, the sun hitting it full on, giving the red-orange part of the walls a ruby glow. It reminds me of Minnie's Home Cooking, the red plastic cups they always serve their root beer in, and I'm hit with a sharp pang of thirst.

"Savannah?" I ask, but she's not here. I crawl out of the sleeping bag, find the orange juice jug, take a sip. I'd love to chug it, but I don't want to burn through it too quickly until we've got something to replace it.

I grab a handful of the empty Walmart bags, carry them outside.

"Savannah?" I call again. She's not in the little clearing, not over by the firepit. Probably she's off peeing or something. No doubt discovering on her own the many delights of leaves as TP.

I go over to a bush and try hanging one of the plastic bags across the top of it, handles twisted around the spindly branches, body of the bag carefully stretched down between them. It looks ridiculous, like an infant ghost. My idea was to string the bags up so they'd collect rain and dew, but I'm already doubtful.

I've spent a lot of time in the woods, but never for more than a few hours at a time. I always had the normal world to go back to afterward. A soft bed and warm food. I've never even gone camping. Grandpa Joe took Aggie and Mama out when they were kids, I know, but nobody ever took me. I wish I could remember more of that wilderness survival book.

My sister drops down out of her tree with a thump, startling me. I hadn't even realized she was up there. She must have been extremely still.

"Lee," I say, "have you seen Savannah?"

She shakes her head. I walk in a wide circle around our campsite, calling Savannah's name, but there's no response. I'm getting worried now.

She could be lost, could be hurt. If anything happened to her, it would be my fault. She'd still be home if I hadn't called her. She'd be safe in her bedroom, texting Jack, no doubt.

But there's another possibility, even more likely, almost as terrible. Maybe she isn't lost, isn't hurt.

Maybe she went back for the car. Maybe she intends to abandon us. To go home. To confess everything.

Lee has been trailing along behind me. I turn and tell her we need to go back to the junkyard.

"Do you remember the way?" I ask.

I hadn't thought to mark the path last night, hadn't even tried to look for landmarks. My sister, however, just nods and sets off running.

We really aren't that deep in the woods. It only takes us about fifteen minutes at a run to reach an embankment that overlooks the junkyard. As soon as I get my first glimpse of the road through the foliage, I wave at my sister to stop.

I creep forward slowly, my view of the junkyard limited to shifting peep-show slits between the trees.

I spot Jack's car first, sitting where we left it, nestled in among its battered fellows. I feel a pang of relief. Savannah is not gone. But then I shift a little, peering through the branches, and my relief vanishes. Because there's Savannah, smoking a cigarette, leaning against the hood of the car.

Talking to a man.

CHAPTER TWENTY

I am paralyzed up there on the embankment, watching Savannah flick her cigarette and play with her hair. I can't hear her or the man. Can't see the man's face. He's standing with his back to me. I think of Jack. The pastor. The man from Walmart.

Lee watches beside me, though I can feel her growing restless.

"What the hell is she doing?" I ask. "She should get out of there."

"Run," agrees my sister, tugging on the back of my shirt.

I inch forward, trying to get a better look at the man. He laughs at something, throwing his head back. It's not the pastor. Not Jack. I don't recognize him at all. A cop, maybe? Plainclothes? He's wearing jeans and a white tee.

Lee tugs on my shirt again.

"Stop it," I say.

"Man," says my sister, as if it were the worst curse word. She grabs my arm, tries to pull me backward.

"Quit it. We can't just leave Savannah. You like her better than me now anyway, don't you?"

She pulls harder.

"This is all your fault," I snap, pushing her away. "You know that, right? If it weren't for you, we wouldn't be here. We'd all be back in Ohio and safe and nobody would be chasing us and Brandon wouldn't be dead."

She lets go of my sleeve, deflated. I turn back to the junkyard, but Savannah and the guy are gone. Alarmed, I creep closer, eyes straining for movement.

There's a shuffle of leaves behind me and I turn to see my sister running. Not back toward camp, though, but off to the right, down the slope of the embankment toward the junkyard. Shit. Just what I need. Is she going to attack this guy? We need to stay hidden.

I run, too, trying to overtake her, though I know I probably can't. I'm nearly down to where the ground levels out when I see Savannah up ahead, trudging back into the forest. Alone, thank God.

Lee skids to a stop about twenty feet in front of her. Savannah looks up, startled. She's clutching her Tupperware of cigarettes and she nearly drops it. "Hey," she says uncertainly, stepping backward. Lee snatches a pebble from the ground, throws it at Savannah's head. Savannah tries to duck, but the pebble hits her in the arm.

"Ow," she says. "What the fuck?"

"Knock it off, Lee," I say as I push past her, though I'm not even sorry, really. What the hell does Savannah think she's doing?

"What the hell do you think you're doing?" I shout, marching up to Savannah. I meant to say it nicer.

"I was getting these." Savannah frowns and shakes the Tupperware at me.

"You just disappeared."

"Chill out." She tries to move past me, but I block her. She sighs and marches off to the left instead. I hurry after her. I see Lee, out of the corner of my eye, running back in the direction of our camp.

"You could have gotten us all caught," I insist to Savannah. "You should have waited until dark."

"It was fine, Jo. I just snuck in and got the cigarettes."

Now who's the liar?

"Who was that?" I demand.

"What?" Savannah turns to me, startled. She didn't realize we'd seen her.

"You were talking to a man."

"Yeah," she says, reluctant. "Briefly."

"What did you tell him?"

"Nothing." She waves a dismissive hand at me. "He asked about the car and I said I was camping with my family. Said my parents were trying to avoid parking fees or whatever."

She turns away and keeps walking, circling around to head back toward camp. I should be impressed, I guess, that she managed to find her way to the junkyard on her own. Although I suppose she just sniffed the air, homed in on the scent of testosterone.

I kneel and prop a stick at an angle against the base of a tree. A sign, for next time. Just in case.

"You shouldn't talk to anyone," I say, when I catch up with Savannah. She needs to understand. She can't do that again.

"He saw me digging around in the car. I had to say something." She pulls a cigarette out of the Tupperware, pops it between her lips.

"You should have just run."

"Come on, it was fine." She lights the cigarette with her plastic lighter, takes a thoughtful puff. "He doesn't even work there or anything. His uncle owns it. He just likes tinkering with the cars. Making broken things whole again."

That seems awfully personal. And there's something about the way she says it. A buoyancy in her tone. The way she waves one hand through the air, fingernail polish catching the morning sun. My guard goes up.

"So you know his whole family history now?" I say, trying to keep my tone light, teasing. "Had a nice long chat?"

"Oh, shut up," she says. But I can see the hint of a smile on her lips and I know: she's been caught already, fat little squirrel, fur gleaming. She ran right up to that loop of wire, thrust her neck through with glee.

It's Jack all over again. Are Savannah's loyalties so flimsy that all it takes is a man smiling at her and all bets are off?

"How old was he anyway?" I ask. I don't bother to sound teasing this time. I'm angry.

She shrugs. Older than us, I'm sure. Probably too old.

"What if he reports the car or something?"

"He said it was fine if we left it there for a few days. Said his uncle probably wouldn't care."

"We aren't leaving it there for a few days, Savannah. We're ditching it." Does she really not get it? This is it. This is our life now. "We can't keep driving a stolen car."

Savannah shrugs again. "I still think we should go to New York. Ditch it there."

I open my mouth and then shut it. *You aren't taking this seriously,* I want to shout. *You put us all in danger. You shouldn't be here.*

But I want her here. That's the problem. This idiot would-be mechanic is a danger to me and Lee, but he's a far bigger danger to Savannah. I don't want her to leave. I don't want her to hate me.

I still need her on my side.

Lee is far ahead of us, crouched down to inspect something on the ground. I run from Savannah, catch up to my sister, and help her pick oyster mushrooms off a rotting log until I'm calm enough to think.

When we get back to our camp, I build another fire. Savannah helps me, her spirits notably lifted after her visit to the junkyard. She lights her cigarette on the fire, laughs at my clumsy attempts to whittle a fallen branch to a point with my sister's folding knife.

The fire crackles and spits. Savannah's face glows in the light of it. Lee experiments with dropping different items into it. A pine cone, some leaves, one of the mushrooms. She watches them burn, little flames dancing in her eyes.

I try to put the incident at the junkyard out of my mind and focus instead on plans for the short-term future. Next time my sister catches a squirrel, I will make her skin it somewhere that Savannah can't see. We will cook it out of her sight too. It really doesn't taste so different from other meat. Perhaps, presented with the final product, but ignorant of the process, Savannah will be willing to try it.

We can find more mushrooms. Savannah refused to eat those too, claiming they were probably poisonous. But she'll come around. We can cook the mushrooms. Maybe we can find some dandelion greens or berries. I'm not sure if it's too late in the season for those or not. Maybe walnuts. I think the wilderness book said that if you soak acorns in water for a while you can eat those, too.

My sister knows things about the forest, knows which leaves won't make you sick, which mushrooms, which berries. She'll gather resting grasshoppers from leaves in the morning, crunch them up like chips. I've seen her shimmy up a tree to pluck bird eggs from a nest. She pokes a hole in one end with her knife, sucks the yolk out raw. I suppose some of it she learned from experience, some from Brandon, maybe some from Mama. I know Grandpa Joe would take his daughters hunting with him when he was still alive. Aggie used to say it was a pity he wasn't around to take me. Margaret hunts, too, but she never took me with her. I wish she had now.

I honestly think Margaret hated me, still hates me. I was painful to her, a reminder. Of the daughter she lost. The daughter she failed.

I pop open the can of biscuits from Walmart and shove a ball of sticky dough onto one end of the pointed branch. I hold it over the fire, turn it slowly.

Despite my best efforts, the dough catches and burns black as coal. But when I pull the little biscuit cinder from the branch and take a bite, I find that it is delicious. Warm and soft and buttery in the middle, the burnt skin only enhancing the delicacy of the inside.

There's no use rationing them, since we can't very well store the raw dough, so we run through the whole can of biscuits. Savannah finds her own stick and manages, through extreme patience, to cook the dough without burning it. Lee, on the other hand, delights in setting the balls of dough on fire and then running around in a circle, waving her stick, blowing the small flames out like birthday candles.

When the biscuits are done we pass the orange juice jug around. Lee watches Savannah and me carefully and when it's her turn she copies us, taking a delicate sip, licking her lips, checking the jug to see how much is left. She's been a bit cool toward Savannah since the junkyard incident. Not that she's said anything, but she hasn't been looking at her as much.

I shake the jug. It's nearly empty. "Tomorrow, first thing, we need to find some fresh water."

"We could just drive to a gas station," Savannah says. I glare at her. She rolls her eyes. "Fine, whatever, no car."

"Water," says Lee.

"Right," says Savannah encouragingly, turning to her with an exaggerated smile, "very good."

"She's not an idiot," I snap.

Savannah shrugs.

"Use full sentences," I tell Lee. "Stop being lazy."

She scowls at me. "Water," she says. "To drink."

"That's not—" I protest, but before I can finish, she snatches the juice jug out of my hands and bolts.

"Wait!" I shout after her. "Where are you going?"

But she's already gone. I can't even see her in the gathering dusk. I guess she found water earlier. I guess that's good. But I'm tired of still being caught in the middle here, halfway between Savannah and Lee.

"She's so weird," says Savannah. She shoots me an apologetic glance. "Sorry, I mean—"

"No, it's okay," I say. "You're right. She's weird." No use pretending.

I let the fire burnish my cheeks and warm my hands. Savannah smokes another cigarette. We sit in silence, listening to the crackle of the branches, the hum of the heated air, the distant calls of birds, the rustles and grunts of squirrels.

"I guess it's kind of nice out here," says Savannah.

"Yeah," I say, heartened to hear her say something positive for once. She'll learn to love the forest, surely, the way that Lee and I do.

Savannah turns to look at me. "I was so miserable those times you made me wait out in the yard."

I'm surprised to hear her say that. I try to remember if Savannah seemed unhappy those nights, back at Grandma Margaret's. I remember how reluctant I was to give up and go inside, sure that any moment my sister would appear. Maybe I never much noticed, or cared, how Savannah felt. I will have to try to do better now.

"I just wanted you to meet her," I say, lamely.

"I thought you were the biggest liar."

"Well," I say a little more sharply than I intend, "now you know I'm not."

Savannah turns back toward the fire, her eyes glittering in the light. "It was so scary. Waiting out there."

I snort. "You weren't scared."

"I was. I tried not to let on, but I was terrified. The woods were so dark. And I was scared that your grandmother would come out of the house and catch us. She always seemed mean."

"She was," I say quietly. *You have no idea.* I almost tell her about Brandon then, but it's like saying it out loud will make it too real. If I don't talk about, don't think about it, I can pretend it never happened. "She still is."

I close my eyes. I can see the headlights again, from the two trucks. See the dust drifting slowly through the beams, swirling in lazy eddies. I can hear the gunshots.

"Did she know?" asks Savannah.

"About my sister? No."

321

"What about Aggie?"

"No. Nobody knew."

"Someone had to know, though."

Someone did, yes. He's gone now.

"You did," I say instead, teasing. "I told you. You just didn't believe me."

"Yeah, but I mean how—like when she was a baby—who took care of her?"

The fire is burning low, coals pulsing with a deep orange glow. I could just say it. *Brandon Cantrell. And Mama.*

"Wolves," I say instead.

Savannah laughs. "Goddammit, Jo. You really are the biggest liar in the whole world."

"I doubt that," I say.

I should tell her everything, I guess. She deserves it. But I can't make myself. I can't even open my mouth to start. Mama, Brandon. Even the words are like broken glass. I'm afraid my tongue would bleed.

I change the subject instead. We talk about school, about all the things we don't miss. About the teachers who thought we were stupid. About the boys Savannah didn't love. About the girls who made fun of us, who called Savannah a slut for the way she dressed, who called me a prude or a dyke for the way I did.

"Fuck everybody," says Savannah. "I'm glad we got out."

The sun drops lower. Lee isn't back yet, which makes me a little nervous. But that's stupid. I used to see her for only a few hours out of the day. Less than that even, most of the time.

Savannah says she's getting cold and retreats to the tent. I get up and kick dirt onto the fire until it seems like it's out, then I hear the sound of the tent unzipping behind me. I turn to see Savannah reemerging. She shoves her hands in her jacket pockets and walks away.

"Where you going?" I ask, thinking I'll tease her about forgetting her roll of two-ply quilted leaves.

"I'll be back in a bit," she says, and there's something about the way she says it. Like she's trying too hard to sound casual. My stomach sinks.

I run over and catch hold of her arm so she's forced to stop, forced to meet my eyes.

"Where are you going?" I ask, trying to keep my voice neutral.

She wrenches her arm away. "You're not in charge of me, you know."

"Where the hell are you going, Savannah?" I give up trying to sound calm. My anger is rising. I think I know where she's going, think on some level I've known it all along, though I still hope I'm wrong.

"It's none of your business." She turns away, scuffs the toe of her sneaker against some moss.

"It *is* my business," I insist. "You're putting us at risk."

Savannah snorts.

"It's not the same for you," I say, moving around so I'm in front of her, so she has no choice but to look at me. "You can go back. If you get caught, it doesn't matter."

"That's not true." She looks hurt. "I stole a car."

"You could blame me for the car. Everyone thinks I'm an insane criminal anyway. I wouldn't mind." The corner of her mouth quirks up in a smile when I say that. Encouraged, I go on. Maybe she really doesn't understand. Maybe I just need to make her see. "You could go back to your life. But if we're caught we can't go back to our lives. If they get ahold of Lee, they'll lock her up. Study her. Try to force her to act normal."

"Maybe that would be a good thing."

Savannah barely gets the last word out before I slap her.

I regret it immediately.

"I'm sorry, Savannah," I say, rubbing my palm, which stings. "I'm so sorry."

Savannah has her hand to her cheek. There are tears in the corners of her eyes, the moonlight catching on them. I think of Aggie. How she looked after she hit me.

I guess it's true what they say, about becoming your parents. No matter how hard Aggie tried not to become like Margaret, ultimately there was no avoiding it.

But Aggie isn't really my mother.

Mama.

Is that who I'll become? She pushed everyone away. They called her wild because she didn't act the way she was supposed to, but she was more than wild. She was crazy, I think. And if she really was crazy, then they should have helped her, but nobody did, except Brandon, and he couldn't give her the kind of help she needed.

Maybe there's no help for me, either.

"You don't give a shit about me," Savannah says. "You didn't even want me to come. You just needed a car."

"That's not true."

"Of course it's true. You said it yourself."

"No." I reach for her arm, but she flinches, shoves her hands deep in her pockets, walks away fast.

It's true and it's not true. I hadn't planned to bring her with us, and she's putting us at risk, but the thought of her leaving now makes me want to cry. I need her. Need somebody to talk to, somebody who understands how much I've left behind. Without Savannah, I'd fall apart. In a way, I'd be alone. Even with my sister here, I'd be alone.

Mama had Brandon, after all. Savannah can be my Brandon. I run to catch up.

"I'm glad you're here," I say, breathless, as I speed walk alongside her. "I really am. I'm sorry I told you not to come. I was just worried you wouldn't be able to handle it."

Savannah stops, shoots me a disgusted look. "What's that supposed to mean?"

"No, shit, I'm sorry," I sputter. "That came out wrong. I just meant that it was a lot to ask of you." I stop, trying to pick the right words. Savannah's watching me, face set, daring me to say the wrong thing. "I knew it wouldn't be fun. We've got to stay hidden."

"So?" she says. "I know that. I don't want to go back, either."

"You—" I start, and then stop myself. "My sister," I say instead. "I have to take care of her. I'm all she has. She's weird, like you say. But it would kill her if the state took her or they sent her to a mental hospital or something. I know it would. You've got to understand. I can't let that happen to her."

Savannah wipes her eyes with a sleeve. Her expression has softened. She understands, I think.

"Clayton and I agreed to meet up again around ten," she says.

"Clayton," I say dully.

"The guy you saw. At the junkyard."

"You're going to see him?" I know the answer. I just want to hear her say it.

"Yes."

"Why?"

She shrugs, as if it's not a big deal at all.

I can't help myself. The anger comes washing back over me. "Are you going to fuck him or something?"

Savannah wheels around, marches away through the woods.

"Wait." I chase after her, fear washing in just as quickly as the anger did. If she hates me she might not come back. "I'm sorry I said that. Just be careful, okay?"

"He's really nice," she says, stopping short. "You'd agree if you met him. He's going to bring me a Big Mac."

I snort. "How romantic."

"Shut up," she says. She's smiling, though, and I think she doesn't hate me after all. Maybe this will be okay. Maybe it isn't a total disaster. Clayton isn't Jack. Clayton is . . . well, it doesn't matter who he is. He doesn't matter. She'll get tired of him. Right? She'll get this out of her system. One final goodbye to her old life. I can't stop her or I'll be no better than all the people I ran from.

"Don't tell him about us," I say. "Please, promise me, not a word."

"I promise."

"You'll come back?" I almost add *to me* at the end of the question, but I stop myself.

"Yeah," she says. "Of course."

She reaches out, gives my hand a squeeze, and then she turns and walks away into the dark.

I lie awake in the tent for a long time, straining to decipher every little sound outside. Being alone makes everything sound threatening. It makes the ground harder, the air colder. I become aware of how badly I smell, like sweat and dirt, find myself longing for a hot shower, a real bed. I suddenly miss Aggie, her sporadic cooking. I imagine her tapping on the flap of the tent. *Time to wake up, Jo. Get your ass out of bed. Time for school.* I imagine this so hard that I can almost smell the pancakes cooking in the kitchen. How long ago was that? A week? A year? Forever?

I was wrong. This is impossible, hopeless. It's cold out and only going to get colder. We don't know what we're doing. Even my sister has never lived like this, not really. I used to think of her as nearly invincible, strong and independent. Almost magic. Seeing her at the gas station and Walmart showed me how, out in the real world, she can barely function. We might be twins, but she's younger than me in a lot of ways.

Even back in the old woods, it turns out, she was never quite as independent as I thought she was. Brandon gave her food. The puffy coat, the brown knit cap. I thought she'd stolen them or found them, but she didn't. He gave them to her. He took care of her. There's no one to take care of us now. No one to turn to. Just us, all alone.

That other world. The one I left behind. I can see into it, a bright little window in the dark. If I hadn't run. If Brandon hadn't run. Maybe I could have saved him. Maybe I could have saved everyone.

There is rustling outside and I leap up, unzip the tent. There's a girl-shaped shadow moving through the trees.

"Lee!" I call. "Did you find water?" I run toward her, equal parts relieved that she's back and disappointed that she isn't Savannah. I have to keep myself from hugging her. She doesn't like that. It makes her feel trapped or something. I wonder if Mama ever hugged her.

Lee holds out the jug, which is nearly full.

"Where?" I ask.

She waves a hand vaguely at the woods behind her. "In some rocks."

The water doesn't look clean exactly. There are bits of dirt swirling around and a thin layer of sediment gathering at the bottom, but I decide I don't care. I take a sip and it's cold and refreshing, even if it does taste somewhat earthy.

Tomorrow, I'll get her to lead me to where she found the water. Maybe I can even figure out how to filter it. It will be fine. We can live like this. We will figure it out.

We've got to.

I make Lee come sit in the tent with me for a while, which she does, but it's clear she doesn't like it. She startles at noises from outside that normally wouldn't faze her, appears preoccupied with the faint spidery shadows cast by the moonlight onto the rain fly.

We share a banana from one of the Walmart bags and the water from the jug. I read her the big white warning tag sewn into the side of the tent. *Do not smoke in tent. Do not cook in tent. Do not light candles in tent.* Basically, don't set the tent on fire. Lee plays with the zipper on the flap. She's shredded her tights even more. Her toes and heels stick out completely. I add that to my regretful Walmart wish list: more tights.

"Please, Lee, will you tell me about her?" I don't say the word. Don't say Mama. I don't want to upset her more than strictly necessary.

My sister zips the tent flap all the way open, zips it all the way closed.

"She wore eye shadow," I suggest, to get her started.

"Sometimes."

"She looked like her picture?"

My sister shrugs. She won't look at me. I wrap the sleeping bag around my shoulders. It's turning into a chilly night.

"Did she tell you about me?" I ask.

"No."

My heart sinks. I know I shouldn't ask, but I can't help it. "Did she ever mention me at all?"

"No."

So my sister didn't know about me, the same way I didn't know about her, until we were five. Until after Mama was dead.

Did Mama think about me? Had she forgotten me? She can't have forgotten. Right? She was wrong about me. When she said, *That one isn't mine.* She was wrong.

I try to forgive her. She was crazy. She was scared. She needed help.

But it still hurts.

"What about Brandon?" I ask. There's a lump in my throat. "He told you about me, right?"

"Yes."

"What did he say?" I press.

She stops playing with the zipper for a moment and closes her eyes, the same way Brandon did when he told me about finding Mama, as if calling the memory up from a long way off.

"Your sister," Lee says, finally. "She's lost."

For some reason, that's what does it. The tears come flooding in. I look away so my sister won't see.

"Why didn't you tell me about him?" I choke out.

"Don't you ever tell," she says, playing with the zipper again.

"Yeah, but it was me. You could have told me." I put a hand on her ankle. She flinches and turns. "You could have trusted me. Why didn't you?"

"I was scared," she says slowly.

"Why?" I say.

She hesitates a long time, working out the sentence maybe, staring straight at me the whole time, an intense gaze. I try to blink back the tears.

"I didn't want him to die," she says finally.

I let go of her ankle. For a moment I don't understand, but then with dawning horror I see how it must have looked to her. She told me about Brandon, despite years of secrecy drilled into her by Mama. She brought me to him because he had medicine and it was the only way to keep me away from Lester, which in her mind she had finally saved me from.

A day later, Brandon was dead. Because she told.

"I'm sorry," I say, and I mean it. Because in a twisted way she's right. It's my fault he's dead. "I'm so, so sorry."

We sit in near silence for a while. I sniff, wipe roughly at my face. There's more I want to ask her, but I think if I speak again I will start sobbing. Eventually, I tell Lee she can go back to her tree if she wants. She hesitates, puts her hand out, and brushes it across my arm a few times, like I'm a cat and she's petting me. It's funny, I guess, but soothing too.

"Thanks," I say. She brushes my arm once more and then she scrambles out of the tent and I'm alone again.

I zip myself into the sleeping bag and close my eyes.

I try not to think about Mama or Brandon or Aggie or the pastor or any of the things I left behind. Instead, I think about Savannah.

What she is or isn't doing right now. Who she is or isn't doing it with.

———

When I wake, the sun is up and Savannah's still gone. I'm hit with a stab of panic and, nearly as strong, an overwhelming thirst. My lips are cracked and my tongue feels like a dryer sheet. I chug the gritty dregs of the water and then scramble out into the morning.

Lee is crouched by the makeshift firepit, bending little loops of wire.

"Have you seen Savannah?" I ask, trying not to completely lose it. "Did she come back last night?"

"No," Lee says flatly.

"Shit," I say, heart racing. "I'll be right back. Don't leave."

I jog off in the direction of the junkyard, build up speed until I'm running.

I follow the signs I made for myself last time we walked back from the junkyard. I tried to be subtle: a stick propped at an odd angle, a half-broken branch. Things only I would recognize.

I'm not sure what I'll do when I reach the junkyard. Not sure if I'll even find anyone there. Savannah could have left with that guy. They could be anywhere. I have no plan. I've never had a plan.

If I wasn't running I would cry. If I wasn't running I would scream.

But then, about halfway to the junkyard, I spot Savannah shuffling through the leaves ahead of me, hands in her jacket pockets, head down, looking at her feet. Alone again. I nearly collapse with relief.

"Hey," I say when I reach her, forcing myself to sound like it's no big deal, voice slightly hoarse from exertion. "There you are."

"Here I am," Savannah says, holding her palms out upright, with a shrug.

"I was worried," I say, though I try not to make it sound like an accusation. Is that why she stayed away so long? To punish me for the things I said last night?

"I saved you some fries." She pulls an oil-soaked paper bag from one pocket, holds it out. I remember the woman back in Needle. The milkshake she brought me. What I would give for a milkshake now. I feel sorry, for a moment, about letting her birds out.

I'm sure she loved them in her way, even if she wouldn't let them be free. The same as Aggie loved me. Loves me still, I hope.

That other world. The one that's safe and warm and bright. There it is, the window open just a crack, just enough to let in a sliver of light.

I fall into line beside Savannah and we walk together, sharing the soggy fries. I can't tell if it's the salt or my relief at having Savannah back and safe that makes them taste like the nectar of the gods, but they are gone too soon. I lick my fingers, tear open the bag, and lick the inside of that, too. I'm too hungry to save any for Lee.

Savannah's quiet, doesn't even laugh at me for licking the bag. She walks slowly, kicking at the leaves. Is she upset or just tired? I can't tell.

"What happened?" I ask. I would have thought she'd be in a better mood, after a night with a boy she likes. Usually she can't wait to tell me what went down. Is she still mad?

"Nothing," she says.

"I was scared when you didn't come back." I hear myself getting close to recrimination. It's like I need her to say sorry. Or to scream at me and say I deserved it. I need her to say *something*, not just act like nothing happened.

"I'm coming back now," she says, without looking at me.

"Well, yeah. I was worried, though."

"Sorry," she says, with another half shrug, a kick aimed at a mossy stone. It seems clear she isn't sorry at all.

"I mean, what did you—" I stop myself. I don't want to fight. I just want her to talk to me. Her reticence is freaking me out. Did it go badly? Did something happen? "How was it?"

"Fine," she says, but she sounds even less convincing than when she said she was sorry. She walks faster, gets ahead of me. I catch up, but I'm afraid that if I ask more she'll think I'm gloating, saying I told you so. I'm afraid that I'll drive her away so soon after getting her back.

When we reach the campsite, Savannah sits beside the empty firepit, smokes cigarette after cigarette. She has a pack now. Marlboros. Clayton must have given them to her along with the food. What did she give him?

"You want the last Pop-Tart?" I ask her. She just shakes her head, pokes at the remnants of the fire with a stick. I don't think she's punishing me for last night. I think she's upset about something else. She seems distant, lost in thought.

I eat half the Pop-Tart while I mull it over, give the other half to Lee.

"What's wrong?" I ask Savannah, sitting down beside her.

"Nothing." Little gray plumes puff into the air as she swirls her stick through the ash.

"Are you upset? You're so quiet."

"I'm just thinking."

"About what?" Leaving?

"Stuff. Just thinking stuff over."

This is nearly as bad as a conversation with my sister. Something is definitely wrong. Savannah is always chatty. She can't help herself.

"What happened?" I ask again. She's different this morning. Even last night, when she was furious at me, she wasn't nearly so tight-lipped as this. Something must have happened.

"We just hung out and talked and stuff." Savannah jams her stick into the ground, sends up a thundercloud of ash.

"What did you talk about?" Did she tell him about us? Did he force her to? I can hear the frustration in my voice, the suspicion, though I'm trying to keep it from erupting into anger.

"I didn't tell him anything okay?" Savannah stands up and stalks toward the tent.

"Okay," I say, standing up too. "Sorry."

"I made stuff up," she snaps. "I lied. Like you."

Savannah crawls into the tent and zips it shut, forcefully. The closest we can get to a door slam out here. I stare after her for a while, trying to decide what to do. All my plans to survive feel like sand rushing through my fingers, slipping away faster than I can catch them. What do we eat, what do we drink, how do we stay warm and safe? How do I keep Savannah from leaving?

Lee comes over and pokes me in the arm with the half-burnt stick Savannah had been using to stir the ashes.

"You go talk to her, then," I say, entirely kidding, but to my surprise Lee drops the stick, lopes over to the tent.

She scratches at the door.

"Go away, Jo," comes the muffled voice of Savannah.

Being neither Jo nor particularly obedient at the best of times, Lee ignores her and unzips the tent, sticks her head in.

"Oh," says Savannah, and then something I can't hear. My sister crawls the rest of the way into the tent, tracking dirt, no doubt.

I hear Savannah's voice again, but I can't make out the words. I creep closer. Lee says something, then. Probably *no,* knowing her, but I can't hear it.

It's bizarre. I don't know if I'm worried or jealous, but I don't like it. I can hear Savannah talking again, just low enough that the words are unintelligible. What the hell is she saying?

I'm trying to decide if I need to barge in there, protect one or both of them from the other, when the tent unzips again and Lee clambers out, clutching the empty water jug.

Right. If we want to survive out here, that's still the most important thing. Don't die of dehydration.

Lee strides over to me. Savannah zips the tent shut behind her. Maybe the best thing I can do right now is give her some space.

"How far away was that water you found?" I ask my sister.

Lee shrugs. "Not far."

"You want to come get water with us?" I shout at the tent.

"No," Savannah, unseen, shouts back. "I had a soda."

So my sister and I head off alone.

"What did you talk about in there?" I ask as soon as we reach the edge of our little clearing. Lee doesn't answer.

"Oh, for fuck's sake," I say, "is nobody going to tell me anything?"

She shoots me a condescending look. I swear it. My sister. Condescending.

"The city," she says.

"Oh." Is that all? "You'd hate the city."

My sister pauses at a rotting log, orients herself, and sets off running. I run, too, and for ten minutes, maybe twenty, all worries are carried away on the wind and it is just this, just me and her and the dirt and the trees and freedom.

The water source, when we reach it, turns out to be a tiny water-fall. Although maybe waterfall is an exaggeration. More of a trickle, really, spluttering between some rocks. There's no flat ground right next to it, no caves that I can see. Still, maybe we can move the campsite closer. It would be worth it for water.

I press the empty orange juice bottle against one of the rocks. It fills so slowly that my arms grow tired from holding it. I try propping it but can't get the right angle. My sister has been amus-ing herself by turning over rocks, snatching up bugs she finds be-neath them, popping them in her mouth. I make her stop and take over for me.

I spend a while trying out different questions in my head. Maybe I could ease into the conversation somehow, get the infor-mation I want without upsetting her. But then again, why should I protect her feelings? I've done enough. I've done everything to protect her.

"Did Mama talk about anyone else?" I ask.

My sister stiffens, nearly lets the jug slip out of her fingers. I shout and she catches it just in time.

"I know you said she didn't mention me." I pause for a mo-ment, hoping, irrationally, that she'll remember something, say, *Oh, wait, never mind, foolish me, she talked about you all the time.* "But what about her mother? Or her sister?"

"Sister?" she asks, puzzled now.

"Yeah," I say. "She had a sister. Has a sister. You know that. Aunt Aggie."

"Oh." She's frowning. I've talked about Aggie plenty, referred to her as my aunt. As *your aunt too.* Mentioned, I'm sure, things Aggie had said about Mama. But maybe on some level my sister never quite put it together. Sisters. Like us.

"Well, did Mama mention Aggie? Or Margaret?"

"I don't remember." She's still stiff, every muscle in her body contracted, her arm muscles quivering as she holds the jug, hands clenched into unnatural-looking claws. She is so uncomfortable, but she owes me this. This and more.

"Do you remember when you two lived in the camper?" I ask. "You would have been pretty little, but maybe you remember something."

She shakes her head, so slightly it might be nothing. Brandon didn't give me an exact timeline. I don't know how old my sister would have been when they lived in the camper. Two? Three? As old as four? I have some vague memories from around three years old. Just little flashes. The time I fell down the stairs, for instance. Wearing a lacy Easter dress and hunting plastic eggs, but finding an actual robin's egg instead. That unreal blue.

"You hid," I prompt, remembering the caches I helped Brandon stock. "Under the ground. In a hole."

"Yes," Lee says. She is shaking now; the water jug is shaking. "We ate dirt."

"Oh." That shuts me up, for a moment. So she does remember, but she doesn't want to. Could eating dirt have been a game? Or did they spend so long down in those holes that they got hungry? Got desperate? There seems to be an almost infinite darkness hidden in those three words. I feel sorry for her, despite myself. "It must have been scary in the dark."

"Monsters," she says. She's talking so quietly I have to lean in close to hear her.

"What?"

"I was scared of monsters." She's staring straight ahead, at the stream of water, the rocks.

"What monsters?"

"People. Evil people."

"Is that what Mama said?" I'm talking louder now, too loud. I'm excited. I can't help myself. Finally, *something*.

"Evil gets inside them," she says, her tone gone flat like when she's reciting. This is what I want. This is what I went out into the church of the wilderness, the quiet, to hear. Mama's words. Mama speaking to me, through her. "It sneaks in under their fingernails. If you look at their eyes you can see it. If they touch you it will go inside you. If you see someone you run."

I recognize the last part. Lee said it before, back at Brandon's clearing. I think maybe she'll run again, like she did that time. I'm bracing myself to catch the water jug. But she doesn't. I've broken through to something. She's gone very still, stopped shaking.

"If they ever catch you," she says, and now I'm the one nearly shaking. This is what I wanted. "If they ever get you. If they ever try to touch you." She turns to look at me, stricken, her eyes darting back and forth between mine. She looks terrified. "Kill them."

She does drop the water jug, then, and runs. I dive for the jug, manage to grab it before too much spills. I let the sediment settle for a moment, let my racing heart settle, take a sip.

It's what I wanted. Mama's words. But I'm not sure I'm happy. I feel sort of sick. *Evil gets inside them.*

I think Mama was really messed up. And she messed up Lee, too. I don't know.

Here I am, trying to be Mama. Trying to follow in her footsteps.

But maybe Mama was wrong about more than just me. The people in town were wrong to judge her, it's true, but she pushed everyone away. Even Brandon, in the end. Even her own daughters. Both of them.

You can't live totally alone. You need somebody. Not everybody is evil. That was just her fears talking. Right?

I walk off in the direction Lee ran, calling her name. I'd howl, but my throat is scratchy from breathing the cold night air and crying so much over the last couple of days.

I'm worried maybe she's run off so far that we won't be able to find each other. I'm not sure I'll be able to find my way back to camp without her. And I don't know how she'd manage alone out here. These aren't her woods. She doesn't have all her traps, all her hideouts, all her little stores. She doesn't have Brandon.

She finds me, though, after a while, runs up. She doesn't say anything about what happened. I offer her the water jug and she chugs about half of it.

"I guess we can go get more later," I say. I take the jug from her, twist the cap back on. I hesitate. "Mama was wrong," I say softly. "You know that, right?"

In answer, Lee picks up a small handful of leaves. She tosses them at me and darts off. She's trying to get me to chase her, to play, but I don't feel like running.

"We should go back to the camp," I shout at her. She trudges back toward me, sweeps past, clearly disappointed. I follow her.

I don't want to leave Savannah on her own for too long. I'm

worried about her, too. I'm worried she wants to leave, worried she'll sneak away again when I'm not watching and never come back. Maybe it was wrong of me to bring us into the woods. Maybe we should find a motel or something. The money wouldn't last long, maybe a night or two, but at least Savannah would be happy.

Maybe we just need to go to another Walmart, stock up more thoroughly. Get that air mattress, that portable charger. Ease into this lifestyle. Do it right.

It takes me longer than it should to realize that my sister isn't leading me back to camp. Or if she is, she's taking a strange and circuitous route. We pass by a rocky outcropping that I swear I don't recognize, down into a small valley that rings no bells either.

She's following a sort of path, I realize suddenly. Not a wide path, not a human path. But a narrow and inconsistent line of tamped earth and crushed weeds. A deer trail.

I grab Lee's arm.

"We can track deer later," I tell her. "We need to get back to camp, okay? We need to get back to Savannah."

She frowns, but makes a sharp turn, away from the deer trail. I curse myself for not paying more attention on the way to the water source, not paying more attention now.

Ahead of me, Lee suddenly freezes. She turns her head one way and then the other. She sniffs the air like a damn dog or something and I laugh.

She waves a frantic hand at me, telling me to shut up.

"What?" I whisper. I don't hear anything or see anything.

In response, she grabs my hand firmly in hers, turns us around in the opposite direction. She walks quickly, half dragging me behind her.

"What's going on?" I say, panicking a little.

We seem to be backtracking. I see the rocky outcropping up ahead. Lee hesitates and then pulls me around the other side of it, hugging the rock.

We round the outcropping, and there, about ten feet ahead, facing us, is a man.

We freeze.

So does he.

He's older than us, older than Jack, I think, but not too old, maybe mid-twenties, his cheeks covered in stubble. His jeans are streaked with rust, the sleeves of his brown jacket stained with what I assume is grease. He looks every bit as shocked to see us as we are to see him.

"Hey," he says, after a moment. "You girls know Savannah?"

"No," I say, and I realize this is Clayton. It must be. The man I saw through the trees. He's coming to find Savannah. He's going to take her away. He's going to steal her away from me.

"Maybe you've seen her?" He holds a hand out in front of his chest, indicating height. "Kind of short. Brown hair. Seventeen."

"No," I say again. *Seventeen?*

"She's camping with her family." Clayton frowns, eyes darting back and forth between us. "You two out here all alone?"

"No," I say. My sister squeezes my hand.

"Okay," he says, still frowning. His eyes linger on my sister, taking in the torn tights, the matted hair, the scratched legs. I take a half step sideways, trying to shield her from his view. Maybe he'll tell his uncle about the strange girls he saw. Maybe his uncle will have heard something already. News bulletin. Amber Alert.

Maybe Clayton will force the truth out of Savannah next time he sees her. Maybe he'll look at her like she's the only girl in the world and she won't be able to resist.

"Well," says Clayton, "if you do see her, tell her I'm looking for her. Tell her I meant what I said."

He turns off the path, takes a few steps, planning to go around us, I guess, to keep looking. What did he say to her? *You're the only girl in the world. Run away with me.*

I can't let that happen.

"She doesn't want to talk to you," I say.

Clayton stops. Turns. "What?"

"She never wants to see you again."

"I thought you didn't know her."

"She hates you," I say. *I* hate you, I should say. You're trying to steal her. You've barely known her for a full day, but I've known her nearly all my life. She's mine. You're ruining everything.

He scowls. "Who *are* you?"

My sister squeezes my hand harder. I squeeze back.

"And she's only fifteen," I say, thinking of Jack. Thinking of what he and Savannah did. There's no way nothing happened last night. "So you're probably going straight to jail."

Clayton's expression darkens. He takes a step toward me.

My sister's hand slips out of mine.

She lunges forward, closes the short distance between us.

Clayton barely has time to react. My sister barrels into him with all her strength. She knocks him to the ground. Knocks him right over. My sister. Doing what I'd love to do, but would never dare. My perfect sister.

The man is on his back and she is pinning him down, straddling him, her dress bunching up around her hips, and I have seen this before, except her dress was blue then and now it's green and black, like the night sky seen through the leaves.

Her hands are on the man's neck. He didn't hit his head,

though. He's moving. He's flailing his arms, kicking his legs. He's making a fist. No no no.

The man punches my sister in the shoulder and she screams, but she doesn't let go. Her hands are twisted into his shirt. He is twice her size, but she's holding on tight. He slams a fist into her side. I'm paralyzed, afraid to move, watching.

My sister's face is down by the man's neck. His hands are closing around her throat.

I have seen this before.

I drop the water jug and run forward. The same way I did on Crybaby Bridge. I throw myself down, just fall really, let the weight of my body drop heavy on the man's right arm, ripping it away from my sister, pinning it to the ground with my hip. A bruising pain. The man struggles, shouts, and I reach out to grab his left arm with both of mine, tug it toward me with every ounce of strength I have.

He's shouting something, but I can't hear it. There's blood rushing in my ears. A river. There's blood.

My sister's face is against the man's neck, nuzzling like a lover. His right arm writhes beneath me like a snake. His other arm wrenches free of my grasp. It flails wildly, hits my sister.

She yanks her head up and back, hard.

More blood.

There's something in my sister's mouth, held between her teeth. A scrap of skin. She spits it out and bites the man again, her teeth scraping his neck, catching a roll of flesh, snapping shut, hard.

The man bucks suddenly, screaming with rage, and manages to throw us both off. I roll. He's up and he's running. There are drops of blood shaking off him like rain.

There is a river in my ears. A far-off ache somewhere in my body. I push myself up.

He stumbles, drops to his knees. Both his hands are around his own neck. Trying to hold himself together.

My sister's cheek is swelling already, one eye squished shut. Her lips and chin are dripping and bright, her teeth bared, in grimace or grin I can't say. Her teeth are oil-slicked red. She's breathing hard, her ribs pumping like wings. She's making a huffing, grunting sound. There are fresh scratches across her clavicles, the insides of her elbows. She holds one arm away from her, bent gently, suspended carefully in the air.

She coughs, spits blood.

I open my mouth to ask if she's okay, but no sound comes out.

The man has fallen down. I don't know if I should help him or if we should run. I crawl toward him with no plan, stop a few feet away.

There is blood pooling around him, spreading slowly through the dirt like an egg cracked into flour for pancakes.

"Clayton?" I ask.

I reach out and nudge his shoulder. A rivulet of blood reaches my knee and soaks into my jeans.

I pull Clayton's right arm toward me, press my shaking fingers against his wrist, searching for a pulse. I press harder. Harder. Press hard enough that it would hurt him if he was in any position to be hurt.

But he is not.

CHAPTER TWENTY-ONE

My sister's right arm might be broken, though I hope it's only sprained. Either way, it hurts badly enough that she won't use it. She pulls with her left arm only. I pull with both arms, but my sister's arms are probably stronger than mine anyway, so maybe it evens out.

"We saw a deer," I tell her, thinking of what Savannah said yesterday. *Goddammit, Jo, you really are the biggest liar in the whole world.*

The body is heavy. I've got ahold of one wrist, my sister the other. I try not to look at it, the way the legs slither through the dirt, how the head nods up and down, bumping over rocks and swollen roots.

"We were chasing the deer," I say, "or you were chasing it, I guess, and I was chasing you, and we fell. We tumbled over the cliff, like the pastor did, remember?"

My sister makes a small keening noise. The wrist she's holding slips out of her grip, flops to the ground. I stop and glance back. We're leaving a trail. Faint red streaks here and there on the leaves. My sister gets a grip on the wrist again and we keep pulling.

"That cliff back there," I say. "We fell off that cliff. You fell on your arm, smashed your face on a rock. Okay?"

"Okay," my sister says.

"We won't tell Savannah. We can't."

"Don't you ever tell a soul," says my sister.

I stop, suddenly. I thought I heard something. A voice. Far away. Calling my name.

"Did you hear that?" I ask my sister, but a moment later I hear it again and I'm sure. It's Savannah. Calling for me.

"Get down," I say. I crouch and quickly lower myself until I'm down on my belly, flat as the body. My sister lowers herself too, but slower, her movements awkward, hampered by her arm.

Jo?

I hold very still, hardly daring to breathe. I remember hearing my name in the forest two nights ago, remember fearing that sound, hiding in the darkness as strangers hunted me. But now it's Savannah I'm hiding from. Even she's a danger to us now. A threat. Everyone is. One by one they have all become strangers, monsters, unfamiliar shapes in the dark.

Jo?

My cheek is pressed into the dirt. Her voice sounds like it's moving farther away. I could get up. I could run after her, I could keep running, right back into that other world. That bright world, so warm and so light and so easy.

I lift my head and for a moment I think I see her, far off, moving through the trees. But then she's gone. The window to that other world is shut. Latched. I can never go back.

"Let's hurry," I say to my sister. I help her up from the ground, get a grip on the body again, keep moving.

We've barely gone another hundred feet when my sister whines, tries to stop. I ignore her and keep dragging. The body's jacket catches on a fallen branch. I tug until it rips loose.

"Stop," my sister pleads, and when I ignore her: "Can we stop?"

"No," I tell her. When we started I had no plan beyond moving the body farther from our camp, farther from Savannah, but it wasn't long before I realized that we need to do better. We need to hide it.

We can't bury it. We don't have a shovel. The ground here is hard. We can't burn it. The smoke, the smell. A lake? If we had one of those I'd be happy for lots of reasons.

I make my sister keep walking. Let her suffer. The sun moves across the sky, disappears behind clouds. The body is no longer bleeding. It is pale, bloodless. I'm not sorry. Evil gets in under the fingernails. We did what we had to do.

It isn't fair. Why should we have to hide it? He upset Savannah. Something must have happened between them. Maybe he hurt her. And he hit my sister too hard. He deserved to die. Right?

That gives me an idea.

I let my sister rest a few times, but never for long. She makes no attempt to abandon me. She knows we are in this together. We've been playing a game, I think, all three of us. Pretending that we were just friends on an adventure, just three normal girls. Pretending we were all the same.

Or maybe I was the only one pretending. Pretending that I didn't have to leave the other world all the way behind. Pretending I could still have it both ways, both worlds. My sister and Savannah. Night and day.

I can't have both. I have to choose.

Savannah isn't cut out for this. She never was. Maybe when we were kids, we could all have gotten along, but she's too different now. She's too much a part of the other world.

I'll let her go. She can take the car, say I was the one who stole it. I'll tell her, when we get back. When we've washed the blood off. *Go,* I'll tell her. Maybe she'll argue, but I know, deep down, that she wants to leave. She probably misses her mother, her sisters. Misses all the boys back in town, those lottery tickets she keeps scratching, week after week, sure each time that this is the one, this is the winner—and when there is no jackpot, no payout, well, the next one, she's sure. That'll be the one.

I will let her go.

No, I will *make* her go. Drive her away if that's what I have to do. I've made my choice. I know where I belong, what world I belong to.

Wrong or not, Mama is in my blood.

I have no real sense of direction to guide me. Even my sister doesn't know these woods, so it's no use asking her. But finally, up ahead, I see a break in the trees.

The road.

My sister and I crouch side by side, staring down the hillside at the empty road below us. Behind us in the dirt is the body of a man we never met before today. My back and arms ache from dragging him here. My sister's right eye is swollen shut.

The sun is hiding from what it's seen. The air feels tight, like maybe it will rain soon. It would be a blessing if it did. That trail we left on the leaves. I hope it rains hard.

My sister makes her small keening noise again.

"Just wait," I tell her.

We'll move our camp. Move deeper into the woods, farther from the road. Maybe we'll build ourselves a shelter high up in the trees, with floors and walls woven from branches and leaves. Deep in the woods. So deep no one will ever find us.

And it will be just the two of us. Alone, but together, in the dark.

There's a rumble in the distance, so faint I barely hear it. So faint it could be far-off thunder. But then, through the trees, I see it. What I've been waiting for.

A car is coming. A truck, actually. In the lane closest to us. A big one. Eighteen-wheeler. Perfect. Better than I could have hoped.

"Okay," I tell my sister, "just like I told you. On the count of three."

We position ourselves behind the body. I put a hand on the hip, a hand on the shoulder, my sister reaches one hand out to the knee.

"One," I whisper. "Two."

The truck is rushing toward us. It's bearing down. My sister sucks in her breath.

"Three."

Together we heave, as hard as we can, my sister using only her left arm, and the body goes tumbling off the cliff. I watch him falling, see a flash of headlights. I squeeze my eyes shut, turn away.

Behind me, the hiss of air brakes, the squeal of tires.

I reach out, grasp my sister's hand. There's no going back now. We can never go back. I open my eyes.

"One," I say. "Two. Three."

And we run.

CHAPTER TWENTY-TWO

The rain comes before we make it back. It comes sudden. A moment of stillness, an intake of breath. And all at once it is falling. The sound of a thousand voices hushing us as it rushes through the leaves.

The sun is gone now, hidden by clouds. It's as dark as the hour before dawn.

The rain grows stronger, louder, working itself up into a storm and I gulp huge mouthfuls of the cold wet air and it tastes electric and I am electric, too. Ecstatic.

I run. Water pours down through gaps between the leaves. Magnificent. Thin trunks of trees dance in the wind.

We are both drenched within minutes. My sister is running slowly. For once it's me who runs ahead and has to wait for her to catch up. She clutches her right arm against her chest with her left, trails me like a shadow.

A strong wind blows the water sideways, washes the blood from our hands, our faces. I run in circles, whooping. Screaming into the wind. The rain beats against my skin, every impact a reminder that I am alive. Alive. Alive. Thunder cracks in the distance. The sky flashes.

Who needs houses, who needs walls and windows, roofs and doors, when there is this.

In the small clearing where we made our campsite, without trees to interrupt it, the rain is coming down in actual sheets. The wind one moment steals my breath, the next rushes into me to replace it. Alive. Alive.

The windbreak on the tent is barely holding, flapping wildly. My sister goes right over to it. She's soaked through, her hair looks heavy and sodden. Her dress sticks to her legs and rain cascades down her arms, drips off the ledge of her nose. She hovers at the side of the tent, holding her wounded arm to her chest, waiting for me.

I stand at the edge of the clearing, just beyond the break in the trees.

I don't want to go in. Don't want to shut myself up. I'm soaked too, and the wind is stinging, but I want to run. I want to scream into the storm. I want to keep moving and never stop.

My sister crouches, huddled, by the side of the tent. She's miserable-looking, shoulders bowed as if they can keep the rain off the rest of her.

I take a step backward, deeper into the cover of the trees. She'd do the same to me. She has done the same to me, left me on the bridge, left me at Brandon's. Left and left and left. I take another step back and I feel like the wind is filling me up, like I'll blow away on it.

My sister cries out. Not with words, just a wounded, frightened gasp. She reaches toward me so desperately that she topples forward, has to catch herself awkwardly with her good hand.

She has seen, of course. She has seen that I am going to run.

The tent whips open and Savannah sticks her head out, wild-eyed. My sister shrinks back.

"Jo!" Savannah shouts as soon as she sees me. She shouts something else, too, but the wind carries it away.

She turns toward my sister. She's saying something to her, but I can't hear it. Lee has curled into a ball, wrapped protectively around her hurt arm. She's put her head on her knees. She's begun to wail. I can just make it out under the storm, a thin high keening that could almost be part of the wind.

Savannah leans farther out of the tent. The wind is whipping the rain right through the open door.

I see that Savannah is going to grab my sister's arm. She's reaching for her. I see, too, quite clearly, how my sister will react to that, in this state.

If they ever catch you. If they ever try to touch you.

I rush forward.

Reach her just in time.

"I was fucking terrified," says Savannah. She still has to shout to be heard over the storm. "I didn't know where you went."

Inside the tent is no quieter than outside. There's a steady patter of raindrops on the taut fabric, and the windbreak whips and snaps above us. Water spritzes in through the mesh top. The thunder, when it comes, is right on top of us, so loud I can feel it in my bones.

We're all crowded in, even my sister, who stopped wailing

once I approached. She crawled inside the tent after me with hardly any prompting. Savannah threw her arms around me in a hug as soon as I finished zipping up the tent, despite how wet I was.

"I thought you were dead," she shouts. "I looked for you and called you."

See how you like it. When the roles are reversed.

"Lee fell," I shout back.

My sister and I are both dripping massive puddles onto the floor of the tent. Now that I've stopped moving, the cold has caught up to me. I yank off the wet sweater, pull off my muddy sneakers, and, with some difficulty, peel off my jeans. Shove the whole sodden bundle by the door. I put on the other sweater, the sky-blue one, the last piece of dry clothing we have. There are no extra pants, so I sit there in my underwear. Which is also slightly wet. And the same pair I've been wearing for days. Add that to the wish list.

My sister hasn't moved. She isn't wailing, but she's still huddled, hunched, head on her knees.

"Come on," I say to her, and reach for her dress. She flinches away. "Fine," I say. "Die of hypothermia. Suit yourself."

She pulls her dress up herself, over her head, awkward with one arm, eases it ever so gently from her hurt arm.

"Jesus," Savannah says. I don't know if she's reacting to Lee's complete nakedness or her skinniness or her wounds. There are some bruises already coming up over her ribs. And then there are her ribs, of course, which you can count. I remember the pastor. The goddamn pastor. She's not getting enough to eat, he said. None of us are now.

Well, fine, we'll starve. Me and her together.

"Can you move that?" I ask her, gesturing to her arm. "Is it broken?" If it is I'll have to figure out how to splint it.

Lee makes a nearly infinitesimal gesture, grimacing, flexing wrist and elbow. Probably just sprained, then, which is a relief. Maybe I can rig up a sling. I unzip the sleeping bag and wrap it around her, soft side in. She huddles into it, draws it tighter, tucks her head in.

The next thunder crack sounds less directly overhead. The one after that practically distant. The rain slackens. Rivers still run down the side of the tent. But we can hear each other without shouting.

"What happened to your arm?" Savannah asks. She isn't asking me, she's asking Lee.

My sister looks up from her sleeping bag cave. She glances over at me, at Savannah, back at me.

"Deer," she mutters.

"What? Jo, what is she talking about? What happened?"

"She fell," I say, not meeting Savannah's eyes.

"You're hurt, too," Savannah points out.

"Yeah." I look down at my arms, my bare legs. I see bruises, scratches. I could be my sister. There are so many pains in my body it's hard to distinguish them as they compete for my attention.

"You have to fucking tell me what happened," says Savannah, a note of barely contained fury in her voice that I recognize. That I know all too well. "Tell me the truth."

"Man," says my sister quietly.

"What?" Savannah whips around to look at her. It takes all my self-control not to yell at Lee to shut up.

"Somebody saw us," I say quickly. "Some guy. We tried to stay out of sight at first, but he shouted at us."

Savannah is still looking at my sister, staring at her. Lee has huddled back down into the sleeping bag.

"He was hunting deer," I say. To explain my sister's first lie. The correct lie, the one we'd agreed on. "Or hunting something anyway. He had on an orange high-visibility vest and that's why he was shouting at us. Because we didn't. He was saying he nearly shot us and we'd better be more careful. He was yelling and coming toward us. He was super old," I add. "With a gray beard."

Not at all like Clayton.

Savannah glances over at me, frowning. "So?"

"So she flipped out." Close enough to the truth. Could I say she attacked this man? No, I already said she fell. "She ran so fast I almost didn't see which way she went." I gesture at my sister. "I went after her, but we got into this section of forest that was all cliffs and things. And she ran too close to the edge and some of the dirt came loose." The whole world shifting under our feet. "And we both fell about ten feet down a cliff and got banged up and I think she broke her arm and then we couldn't find our way back and then the rain. . . ." I trail off. Shrug.

"This is awful," Savannah says, sitting back. "We can't keep going like this."

I don't have the heart to argue. She's right.

Something occurs to me. I grab my wet jeans, reach into the pocket. The picture of Mama is so wet it's nearly disintegrating. When I try to pull it out, it rips.

The rain is only a steady drizzle now, the thunder barely a distant rumble. I unzip the tent, peer out. The storm has knocked all the loose leaves off the trees, left everything wet and gleaming and smelling of earth.

"We need to move the camp," I say.

"Why?" Savannah asks behind me.

"That hunter guy might find us." I start moving the Walmart bags outside.

"We should go back for the car instead," Savannah says. "Maybe we could go to Cincinnati. I've been telling Lee all about it. Right, haven't I been telling you?" This last is directed, singsong, at my sister. To my pleasure, Lee doesn't respond. Just stays slumped. "Lots of pretty dresses in the city."

Oh great, just what I need. Savannah trying to bribe my sister. I shove the wet clothes into a Walmart bag, set it outside. I pull my sneakers on, though they are still wet, and crawl out of the tent. Pantsless, but it hardly matters out here. No one to see. Not anymore.

"Come on," I say, beckoning to Lee, "let's go."

Slowly, reluctantly, she follows me out, still clutching the sleeping bag around her shoulders. We squelch with every step, our feet sinking into the mud, the earth trying to drag us down. I crouch and yank up one of the tent stakes.

"Jo," Savannah says, crawling out of the tent after us. "What's gotten into you?"

I heave another stake free from the soggy earth. "The hunter might say he saw some weird-looking girls in the woods and people might realize who we are and come find us."

I move to pull out a third stake. Savannah positions herself between me and the sagging tent, hands on her hips.

"All the more reason to go get the car," she says.

I hesitate. I shouldn't say it. I mustn't. I do anyway.

"What about Clayton?" I ask.

Out of the corner of my eye, I see my sister stiffen.

"What about him?" Savannah's tone is guarded.

"He might be there. At the junkyard."

He won't be. I know for a fact he won't. But she doesn't.

Savannah shrugs, face betraying nothing.

"Something happened the other night," I say. I duck around Savannah, yank up the third tent stake. "Between you two."

"Ugh. Why are you so obsessed with him? You jealous?"

"He did something," I insist, ignoring her. Was I jealous? Yes. I was. But that's not why he's dead.

I stomp over and pull up the final stake. The tent slumps to the side. Lee shuffles backward, toward her tree. I push wet hair out of my eyes, snatch the windbreak before it flies away. I shake the excess water from it, splashing Savannah.

I was protecting her. Protecting all of us. Doing what I had to do.

He deserved to die.

Right?

"You came back all upset," I say. "He did something bad to you."

Savannah frowns. "No."

He looked like he was twenty at least. Maybe older. Afterward, I tried not to look. Face pale, neck dark around the ragged tear. Her teeth went deep. Got the artery.

"He must have done something." I'm nearly shouting as I struggle with the tent poles, trying to pull them free. If he did something that means he deserved to die. Lee has backed all the way up to her tree. "Or forced you to do something. Something you didn't want."

"You mean sex," Savannah says flatly.

I turn to face her. Is she admitting it? I make myself speak quietly, gently. "Yes. Did he force you to—"

"Why?" she snaps, cutting me off. "Why is it so unthinkable to you that I would want to do it? Maybe I like it."

"Do you?" I ask, genuinely uncertain. I know Savannah thrives on attention, on feeling special. But Aggie and Margaret's lectures always made sex seem like something girls got talked into. Not something we'd pursue on our own.

I'm realizing, though, more and more, that I shouldn't trust their version of the world. I've got to figure it out my own.

Savannah shrugs. "I don't know. Kind of. It doesn't matter. We didn't even do that. Just other stuff."

I stare at her. "You're lying."

"I'm not, Jo. *You're* the liar." She pushes me away from the tent, extracts the tent pole herself with an easy, fluid motion. She throws it on the ground. It clatters like bones.

There's no way that nothing bad happened. Something must have happened. Savannah is folding up the windbreak, shoving it into the tent bag.

"What did he say to you?" I ask. It's one of the things he said to us. Some of his last words. *If you do see her, tell her I'm looking for her. Tell her I meant what I said.*

"What?"

"Did he say something to upset you? Savannah, you have to tell me."

I have to know if it was justified. If he deserved to die.

I have to know if I'm a monster.

Savannah heaves an exaggerated sigh. She wheels on me, face full of disgust. "He doesn't matter, okay? I was only using him, really. I told him a pack of lies. I was fed up with you. You were treating me like shit. But I didn't tell him about you, okay? Is that what you're so damn worried about? I said my parents were abusive. Said my dad hit me. I lied. Like you do. He said he could help me get away. He said I could come live with him. Said he could get me away from it all."

"No," I say quietly. I believe her, but I don't want to. "That can't be all."

"The truth is I fucking considered it, okay? That's all."

Was I really thinking of Savannah? Really trying to protect her?

Maybe I am a monster.

"We're going back to the goddamn car," says Savannah. I don't know if I've ever seen her quite this angry. She whips the other tent poles out of their sheaths. "You don't get to call all the shots, Jo. I know you need to protect your sister, but I know her now too, okay? I've talked to her. She likes me. Right, you like me?"

Lee is wide-eyed, back against the tree. She'd climb it if she could, I bet. But she can't now. She says nothing.

Does she feel guilty? Is that even an emotion she's capable of? She's the one who killed him, really. Right? It wasn't my fault. I didn't. I couldn't.

"Well, whatever," Savannah continues, undiscouraged. She kicks the puddled tent fabric into a pile. "We're going to go get the car."

"We can't," I say. There is truly no going back now. I'm a murderer, a monster. If they catch me they will lock me up forever and maybe I deserve it.

"We can."

"We can't. The police."

"The police probably don't care about us. We're just teenage runaways. Nobody cares about us."

I think of what Brandon said about Mama. *They wouldn't help her when she needed it. They didn't give a shit about her, not a one of them. Not until they thought she was dead.*

Am I like her? Or am I worse?

"I stole the car," Savannah says. "The car is mine. I took the money, so the money is mine. This is all mine. I can do whatever I want with it. If you don't fucking trust me, then fine, I'll leave you here and you can see how well you get on without me."

It's what I thought I wanted: for Savannah to leave, to go back to her old life without knowing the truth. I would let her go, make her go. Drive her away.

But I don't want to.

"Clayton is dead," I say. I don't plan to say it. I am surprised myself, to hear the words leaving my lips. *We won't tell Savannah. We can't.*

"What?" she looks exasperated, not shocked. She thinks I'm lying.

"There wasn't a hunter. It was him. He saw us. He was looking for you. He scared Lee. She knocked him down."

My sister lets out a moan. Savannah turns to look at her. When she turns back to me, her expression has changed.

"I thought he was going to kill her," I say. It doesn't feel freeing to tell the truth. It doesn't feel good. Savannah's going to leave anyway and now she's going to hate me. "He was hitting her and hitting her," I say. That's the truth, but I'm telling it to make myself look like less of a monster. I want to believe that I am not a monster. My sister moans again, covers her ears. "I thought he had hurt you, too," I say. Did I really think that? Or did I only think it afterward, when it was too late to change what I'd done?

Savannah has gone pale. It looks like there are tears hovering right at the edges of her eyes.

"No," she says.

"We killed him," I say. "He's dead."

I've killed two men. It doesn't matter if Margaret pulled the trigger. If my sister tore through the skin with her teeth. It was my fault both times. I'm a monster. Evil gets into everything I touch.

Mama was right. She was right.

"Is this true?" Savannah says, her voice quavering. She's not asking me, not looking at me. She's asking Lee.

Lee, miserable, nods. Savannah's turning back to me, but I don't want to see the horror in her eyes. Don't want to hear what she has to say.

So like my sister has done a hundred times before, when she doesn't want to face me, doesn't want to deal with the consequences, I turn and run.

I run mad, run scared, run the rage and terror out of my bones, run until my bones ache, keep running.

The ground is slick with mud. Dead leaves. I can feel muck splattering up onto the back of my legs. I slide down the first big incline I reach, fall into a puddle at the bottom. Get up, keep running. Uphill now, and then flat. Down, up, like flying, like sailing, skimming over the surface of the earth, the wind rushing through my hair, slapping my wet skin.

I hit another incline and my foot goes skidding out from under me. The world is spinning, too quick, and I roll and tumble off rocks and hit with a crunch and a snap of breaking sticks.

The lie I told made true.

The side of my face is pressed into the dirt. Into the mud. There's mud in my nose, some in my mouth. I can smell the wet-earth scent.

I spit, cough. I can't see, can't breathe. I flop over onto my back. At least I didn't break my neck.

The horizon is tilted. From down here the landscape is different. The trees could be mountains, each mound of dead leaves a hill.

I ache all over, but my right leg is worse than the rest of it put together. Sharp pain from the knee down. I deserve this.

I don't even try to get up. My feet are higher than my head. But you're supposed to elevate an injured leg, right? So it works out.

That makes me laugh. A laugh that catches. Turns strange, hysterical. Turns into sobbing.

I cry until it hurts, until I can't breathe. I gasp and sputter and spit.

I stare up at the sky. Think of Mama, floating.

What did she think about before she died?

Did she think of me? She must have, sometimes. Right? Even if she thought that evil had gotten me. It wasn't her fault she was insane. But it wasn't fair to my sister, I think. To raise her that way.

I guess I'm the lucky one.

I don't want to be like Mama. Not Jolene, but Jo. I don't want to be like the pastor, either, or Logan. Or the devil. Whoever my daddy was. No monster, no shadow. I want to be myself. I want to be something new.

Rising up out of the dirt like a twisted flower.

I probably won't get the chance now.

It was dark to begin with, after the storm, and it only gets darker. I don't know how long it took my sister and me to get water. How long it took to drag the body to the road. How long it took to get back. But it must have been a long time. The sun is going down. My legs are growing colder. At least that numbs the pain.

I don't know how far I ran from camp. Don't know if the others will be able to find me. If they would even want to.

I close my eyes. Maybe I'll freeze to death. I hear that's peaceful. You get warm and then you just sleep. When I open my eyes, I'm crying again.

Mama didn't want me. Mama was crazy. Maybe I'm crazy, too. It doesn't matter.

I'll die in my underwear in the dirt in the dark.

I laugh aloud into the nothingness. I cry. I try to move. A spasm of pain in my leg. I howl. Shove my hands over my ears, squeeze my eyes shut. I don't want to face this, don't want to face anything ever again.

I want it to be over.

I pretend I'm floating. On a dark and empty ocean. My head feels weird anyway. I can hear the orchestra of the forest at night starting up. Insects thrumming. Something hooting. Squirrels rustling the leaves.

Louder rustling. Very close.

A bright light shines on my face, the black behind my eyelids blazing red.

I blink my eyes open. My sister is standing over me. She's holding Savannah's phone, shining it in my face.

Since when does Lee use a light?

"Jo," she whispers, "you dead?"

She's got on Savannah's jacket, but unzipped, with nothing

underneath it. The hood is pulled up, though, and the fur lining makes it look like a bear is eating her head. She turns and flashes the light at the trees, waving it back and forth.

I close my eyes.

"Jo," she says again, shaking me.

Leave me alone, I try to say, but my voice is too hoarse from all the crying and laughing, so nothing comes out but a croak.

I open my eyes. Lee is staring down at me. I try to speak again, but I can't.

"Sisters," Lee says. "Sisters should help."

She stands up. Messes with the phone. The light of the screen hitting her face from below gives her a nightmarish look. It was smart of her, I realize, to steal the phone from Savannah. Otherwise Savannah might have called the police. Turned us in.

Savannah.

I left the two of them alone.

Is Savannah okay? Did Lee hurt her?

I can forgive Lee what she tried to do to Henry. I might have forgiven her even if he died. That probably makes me a bad person, but it's true. My sister is almost a part of me. She is in my blood, part of my heart.

But not Savannah. I couldn't forgive that. If she hurt Savannah. Or did more than that. If she—I couldn't. It would kill me, I think.

Savannah is part of my heart, too.

I try to move, but all my limbs are stiff from lying in the dirt for so long. My legs have both gone to sleep. Pins and needles add to the pain, a vicious cramp stabs through my side. My head spins.

Lee steps away from me. I manage a slight strangled cry, roll over enough that I can watch her.

She stops a few feet away. Holds the phone up in the air, looks at it. Pokes at the screen.

And then I see the strangest thing. So strange I'm sure I must be crazy. Sure I must be dying. My sister, my wild sister, holds the phone to her ear.

"Hello," she says into it, pauses as if listening. "Hello. Yes. Please help."

CHAPTER TWENTY-THREE

Savannah reaches us not long after, alive and well, carrying some of the plastic bags. My relief is too tangled with confusion, with a new fear. I feel like I'm swimming through the dark.

Savannah looks down at me, meets my eyes for a moment, but doesn't say anything. She takes the phone from my sister, who has been holding it this whole time, not saying much other than *yes* and *no* and *okay*. Savannah takes the phone and speaks into it.

"Sorry," she says, and "Are you going to tell anyone?" and "West Virginia," and "a junkyard."

"No," I manage to croak. They will lock us up and they will kill us.

"Okay, I know this part is going to sound insane," I hear Savannah say, "but can you stop at a Walmart real quick first?"

Lee kneels beside me.

"Don't die," she says, "please." And I can't hear what Savannah is saying into the phone. Something about Cincinnati?

I push myself up, try to nod, but it makes stars explode in front of my eyes and I lie back down in the mud.

"Thank you," says Savannah. "We'll be there."

And then she's kneeling beside me.

"Did you hit your head?" she asks. She shines the phone light in my eyes. I blink away from it. I feel dizzy, but I don't remember hitting my head. I think maybe all the blood just rushed to it.

She and Lee help me up to a sitting position. My head spins and spins.

"Can you walk?" asks Savannah.

She shines the light down at my right leg. There's a long gash from the knee to the ankle. The blood's dried and crusted. There's some gravel embedded in my knee. No wonder it hurt. But the cut isn't deep. And nothing looks swollen.

The two of them drag me to my feet. I notice that Lee is using both her arms, though she still favors the right. Both of us are pretty banged up, but surviving. My legs feel shaky and weak. Putting weight on my right leg sends pain shooting up my shin because of the cut, but I'm not a broken-legged lamb, at least. Not entirely. I don't think my ankle is even sprained.

"Come on," Savannah says. She puts one arm around my back so I can lean some of my weight on her. My sister mirrors her on my other side. We hobble forward, an awkward three-headed beast.

I thought I would die. Thought I'd never see either of them again. Thought they wouldn't want to see me.

"Don't you hate me?" I whisper. I would hate me. I do hate me.

"No," says Savannah.

I stumble, grit my teeth against the pain in my leg. The cut has reopened. I can feel fresh blood trickling down my shin.

"Where are we going?" I ask.

"The junkyard," says Savannah. I'm too tired to protest. I am ready to give up. To sleep, even if it's in a cell. "The tent?"

"I've got it," says Savannah, shaking the Walmart bags slung over her other arm.

"Who were you—"

"Don't worry about it," says Savannah, cutting me off, "it will be okay."

"Okay," echoes my sister.

It was the police, though, right? She called the police. Or whoever she called will call them. They'll be waiting for us. For me.

I understand. I deserve it. I'm thankful, even. For a way out. Even with all my planning, this was never going to work. We were never going to make it out here. I see that now.

I'm ready to face the other world, face whatever is coming to me.

I just don't understand why Lee is going along with it. At the last moment, maybe, she'll push me forward and run. I wouldn't blame her.

We stumble along, the three of us. I keep thinking I'll fall, but they catch me. My head feels thick and heavy, my limbs shaky. I don't think I could run if I tried, but I don't want to.

I'm not my sister. Not Mama. Just myself.

The moon peeks out from behind the lingering clouds. I recognize one of my signs, a stick propped against a tree. I hadn't meant to run in the direction of the junkyard, but I guess I did, unconsciously. Came much nearer to it than I realized.

I try to pull away, frightened despite myself, but Savannah tightens her grip on my arm to stop me.

"Come on, Jo," she says softly, "we need help."

We're circling down, drawing closer. I can see glints of rusted metal through the trees.

There are no sirens. No flashing lights. Not yet.

We pause at the edge of the tree line. There's a rusted blue car parked halfway into the underbrush, a sapling twisting up through the empty place where the front windshield used to be.

"Let's wait here," says Savannah. She helps me onto the hood of the car, jumps up to sit beside me. Lee sits on my other side. Savannah puts her arm around my shoulders. Maybe it's just so I won't try to get away, but I'm comforted by it nonetheless. I lean against her.

The junkyard looks dark, abandoned. I can see Jack's car where we left it. I don't see movement. Don't see anyone.

Headlights come sweeping down the road and I brace myself, but the car drives past. Now that we've stopped moving I'm cold again. I rub my bare legs to bring the feeling back. The fresh blood on my shin has dried again.

I don't know what we're waiting for. Don't know who. I'm afraid to ask. I hurt all over. The minutes stretch. Savannah pulls out her phone, looks at it, angling the screen so I can't see. Lee picks flakes of rust off the hood of the car, arranges them on her knee like fish scales.

Headlights again. They swerve this time, bump up over the edge of the road. A pickup truck. Pulling in to the junkyard.

"Don't be mad," says Savannah quickly. "She called me."

I shiver, suddenly afraid.

Margaret. The last person I want to see right now. Who else could it be?

"She called," Savannah goes on. "When I was with . . . when I was away. There's service closer to the road. She left a message. Said she knew I was probably with you. Said to tell you she was sorry and that she was coming to look for you, alone. Said to please call her back. I'm sorry I didn't tell you. You were so angry already."

The truck stops in the middle of the junkyard. The driver door opens, and someone gets out. I crane my neck, but the truck is between us.

"Sister," says Lee.

And the person walks around the truck and I see.

Not Margaret. Aggie.

With all that's happened, something as small as this shouldn't shock me. But it does. All her life, Aggie has never once gone more than twenty minutes outside of Lester. Never once driven me to an away track meet, or to the Target in Delphi. But here she is.

She's wearing one of her plaid shirts. Jeans. She's looking around. She can't see us yet. We're too far away, shadowed by the trees.

"I knew we needed help," says Savannah, her tone urgent. "I told Lee, told her how Aggie would help us. Said we needed to call her. Don't be mad."

I meet Savannah's eyes. She doesn't hate me. She really doesn't. This time is different. This time I told her the truth. This time she's on my side.

I should speak, tell her I'm not mad. Tell her that I'm so thankful, that I love her and I always will.

"Do you forgive me?" asks Savannah.

All I can do is nod. Any more and I'll start crying. I lean forward, wrap my arms around her, hiding my eyes against her shoulder. Savannah hugs me back, tight.

"I called," says Lee, from behind me. I can't read her tone, but when I turn to look at her she hops off the hood of the car, standing straight and tall. I think maybe she's proud. She steps forward, out of the trees, into the open.

Savannah takes my hand and we follow. Aggie still doesn't see us. She's turned away, squinting at the woods in the other direction. The three of us make our way quietly through the rows of cars.

We're only about twenty feet away, nothing but empty space between us, when a twig snaps under Savannah's foot and Aggie spins around. Lee freezes. Aggie's face lights up the moment she sees us. I don't see anger, just relief. Exhaustion. She doesn't run toward us. Doesn't move at all.

"Hello," says Aggie quietly, looking at my sister with a soft, sad expression. "I'm Aggie."

"Yes," says Lee. I reach for her hand, squeeze it gently.

"Jo," Aggie says, turning to me. "I'm so sorry."

"You've come to take us back," I say.

"No." Aggie shakes her head. "I'm leaving. For good." There are tears in her eyes. "I already left. I was heading this way. I'd heard someone might have seen you near the state border. So I packed everything up and left to come find you. I'm so glad I did. I was only about forty minutes away when I got your call."

That she would come this far to get me was already a small miracle. But it blows my mind all over again that she chose to leave Lester even before she knew where to find me. She said she packed everything up. Left for good. There's no way.

"What about the bar?" I say. "And Margaret? And the pastor?"

A flicker of anger crosses her face. "The way he lied about—" But then she stops, shakes her head, takes a deep breath. "A lot happened while you were gone. There were some things that were the last straw. Maybe I'd let too many straws go by already.

Anyway, there's nothing left for me back there. Nothing I wouldn't rather leave behind." She shrugs. "I'm sorry for not believing you. I really am, Jo. Will you give me a second chance?"

I nod, because it feels, once again, like I couldn't speak without crying. I don't know if I deserve this. "Oh, wait," says Aggie, suddenly brightening. She turns and opens the door of her truck. Pulls something out. Holds it in front her.

A dress.

A truly ridiculous dress. Rose pink. Sequined bodice, big poufy chiffon skirt. An attached sash with a fabric flower. It's clearly not meant for anybody older than twelve or so.

"Is this okay?" Aggie asks Savannah.

Savannah laughs beside me. "I think so."

My sister has already let go of my hand to reach for it, despite herself, eyes sparkling.

"It's for you," Aggie says to her.

Lee looks over at Savannah, uncertain, then at me.

"It's okay, Lee," I say. "She won't hurt you."

I think that's probably true.

Lee runs forward and snatches the dress with her good arm, a little rudely. Aggie doesn't even jump. Years of bar fights have given her nerves of steel. Lee scuttles back to a safe distance, admiring the sequins. She shucks off Savannah's jacket, pulls on the new dress. She's so skinny that it fits her fine, though she doesn't bother to zip it up. She spins happily, watching the skirt float up around her.

"I have all your clothes and things," Aggie says to me, eyeing my bare legs, the gash on my shin. She's holding back a little, I think, trying to play it cool. "I'll have to move the suitcases into the back. It'll be a little crowded up front with the four of us but we can squeeze in."

"Where are we going?" I ask.

"I'm not going back," Aggie says, shaking her head. "I can drop Savannah off with her cousin in the city. And then we can go anywhere. Somewhere new."

She smiles at me. A small smile, tight, that doesn't reach her eyes. Her eyes are full of tears again and she looks, I think, afraid.

I can't run, not with my leg all messed up. But Lee still could. I look over at her. She meets my eye. We aren't psychic. We are so different, the two of us. But in this moment, I'm pretty sure we're both thinking the same thing. She glances toward the trees. Glances back at me. At my leg.

She turns and walks toward the truck. Back straight, resolute, though her hands are shaking, I see. Branches in a storm. She walks toward the cab. Stops. Savannah and Aggie are watching her too.

Lee changes course abruptly, goes to the bed of the truck instead. Lifts one bare foot onto the runner rails. Hauls herself up using her good arm. Tumbles over the side. Easy as climbing a tree.

She sits up, pink sequins sparkling, and reaches her good arm over the side of the truck. Holds a hand out to me.

We sit side by side in the dark. The road racing by beneath us so fast. With the wind in our hair it's almost like running.

My legs are stretched out in front of me. I dug out some clean jeans and socks and pulled them on before we got going. The suitcases and plastic tubs that hold everything Aggie and I own bump and rattle around us. The plastic Walmart bags Savannah rescued flutter loudly.

Our hands are clasped. We're both scared. Not of the same things.

I don't know what will happen next. If Lee will be able to adjust. If what we did will catch up to us. But first a motel, a bath, a bed. Maybe Lee can sleep on the floor, under the bed. Or in the bathtub. We can bring in handfuls of dead leaves, make a nest for her.

One good thing is that Aggie needs to stay under the radar for her own sake as well as ours. I still belong to Margaret by law. So Aggie is kidnapping me, technically.

My sister belongs to nobody.

Savannah knocks on the glass of the cab to get my attention. She mimes taking a bite of something and a chill goes through me. I think of Clayton. My sister's teeth, tearing flesh. But then I see, up ahead, the neon yellow arches glowing against the night sky.

Savannah motions for Lee and me to lie down flat so nobody will see us. I smile at her. She smiles back.

Lee and I lie down flat. The truck slows, turns. My mouth waters as I listen to Aggie order over the tinny speaker. My sister squeezes my hand. I squeeze back. In the glow of the drive-through lights I can see that her eyes are shut.

Aggie pulls around, gets the food, parks. Her door opens and then she's peering over the truck bed.

"You sure you two are all right back there?" she asks as she hands me a heavy paper bag, two large cups.

"Yes," I say.

She glances over at my sister, who still has her eyes shut. Aggie shakes her head a little, disbelieving. Aggie, who is not my mother or my father. Who doesn't own me, but who loves me, which is all that truly counts.

"Thanks," I tell her.

She smiles at me, relieved, returns to the cab, starts the truck, pulls back onto the road.

The cups are chocolate milkshakes. It's too cold for them, really, but the sweetness feels like a blessing anyway, a pardon. We get going, speeding through the night.

Lee tears into the bag with gusto when I hand it over. She's skeptical of the burgers, but she gnaws gleefully on the chicken nuggets. Regards one, confused, finding no bone. Adjusts quickly, shoves the rest of them in her mouth, wipes the grease on her skirts.

"That dress looks nice," I shout over the rush of the wind.

"Yes!" she shouts back. I hand her the second milkshake. She slurps its, scowls at the brain freeze.

I bite into my burger. I was so much hungrier than I'd realized. How long has it been since I last ate? I was foolish, to think we could make it alone. It's stronger, maybe, to ask for help. It must have taken a lot of courage for my sister to make that call.

I pick up a fry, drop it, hit with sudden guilt, remembering the fries that Savannah saved for me. The man who is dead.

And then I think about Brandon, think about Mama. How can I have any hope, when my life was built on sorrow from the very beginning? And my sister, here in her new pink dress, glittering and wild and so afraid of the world. How will she ever survive?

"This is going to be hard," I say, leaning in close to Lee, huddling so she can hear me.

She nods, biting tentatively into a burger, chewing. "I'm sorry," I hear.

"What?" I ask. I think I must not have heard her right. No way my sister just apologized. That might be even stranger than the phone. Stranger than her trusting Savannah, trusting Aggie.

Maybe there is hope, if people can change. Lee made that call. And Aggie was able to leave Lester, to leave Margaret, to leave her past behind.

Maybe I can change, too.

Lee turns, speaking right into my ear.

"Mama was wrong," she says.

"Yeah," I say, overwhelmed.

"Please," Lee says, leaning back to stare at me with an intense look, serious and focused, ruined only slightly by the smear of sauce on her check, "don't float away."

My heart twists. I see my sister, five years old, sitting on the deer platform next to Mama who took too much, who floated away, too high and far to follow. As sad as it is, I wish I could have been there. Wish I could have helped them both.

"I'll only ever run," I say, and squeeze Lee's hand.

The trees whip past, the wind snatches at our hair. Lee turns her face into the onrushing air and opens her mouth wide and howls. A joyous wild sound. I join her.

We are lambs who refuse to learn, I think. We will wander until the end of our days, not afraid of wolves.

But together. Always together. Me and her, the two of us. Like it was meant to be from the beginning. Like it was, once, fifteen years ago, at the very start.

ACKNOWLEDGMENTS

Thanks to Axel, for the biscuits and brainstorming, and Toni, best former roommate. Thanks to my friends and classmates from SIU, especially Meg, Jen, and K. Thanks to my teachers, especially Pinckney for advising, Dave because Governor's School for the Arts saved my life (tell the state of Pennsylvania to re-fund it), and Mrs. Schultz, my third-grade teacher, because she was cool.

Huge thanks and a can of Diet Coke for my agent, Jim McCarthy. You make the business side of writing feel easy! Major thanks also to editor Krista Marino, who whipped this book into its final shape.

Thanks to the whole team over at Delacorte, including but not limited to Beverly Horowitz, Barbara Marcus, Judith Haut, Alison Impey, Jen Heuer, Colleen Fellingham, Kelly McGauley, Elizabeth Ward, Kate Keating, and Felicia Frazier.

Thanks to Mother and Father for, like, all the food and stuff. Thanks to Gamma Ray, even though she can't read.

ABOUT THE AUTHOR

Maria Romasco-Moore is the author of *Ghostographs,* a collection of short stories paired with vintage photographs. She is an instructor at Columbus College of Art and Design. *Some Kind of Animal* is her first novel. To learn more about Maria and her novel, go to mariaromascomoore.com or follow @BettaSplenda on Twitter.